Peyo

the SMURFS™ ANTHOLOGY

VOL. 2

PAPERCUTZ™

NEW YORK

Peyo GRAPHIC NOVELS AVAILABLE FROM PAPERCUTZ™

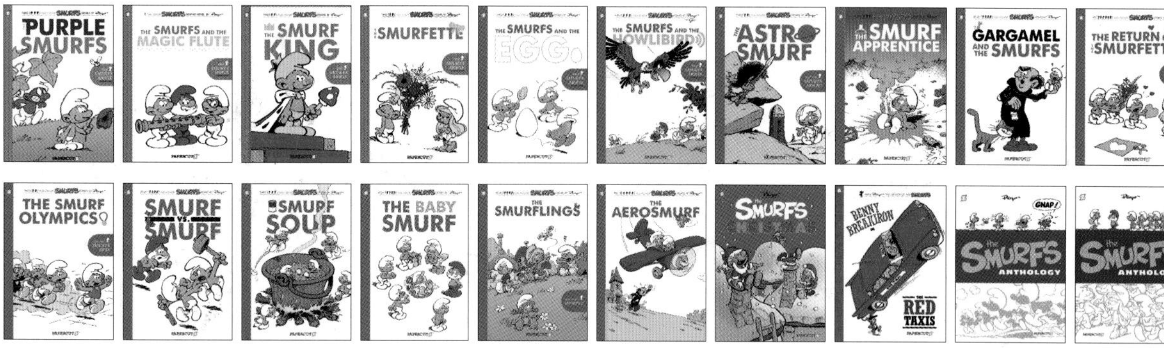

THE SMURFS

1. THE PURPLE SMURFS
2. THE SMURFS AND THE MAGIC FLUTE
3. THE SMURF KING
4. THE SMURFETTE
5. THE SMURFS AND THE EGG
6. THE SMURFS AND THE HOWLIBIRD
7. THE ASTROSMURF
8. THE SMURF APPRENTICE
9. GARGAMEL AND THE SMURFS
10. THE RETURN OF THE SMURFETTE
11. THE SMURF OLYMPICS
12. SMURF VS. SMURF
13. SMURF SOUP
14. THE BABY SMURF
15. THE SMURFLINGS
15. THE AEROSMURF

THE SMURFS CHRISTMAS

BENNY BREAKIRON

1. THE RED TAXIS

THE SMURFS ANTHOLOGY

– VOLUME ONE
– VOLUME TWO

THE SMURFS and THE SMURFS CHRISTMAS graphic novels are available in paperback for $5.99 each and in hardcover for $10.99 each; BENNY BREAKIRON graphic novels are available in hardcover only for $11.99 each; and THE SMURFS ANTHOLOGY is available in hardcover only for $19.99 each at booksellers everywhere. Order online at www.papercutz.com. Or call 1-800-886-1223, Monday through Friday, 9–5 EST. MC, Visa, and AmEx accepted. To order by mail, please add $4.00 for postage and handling for first book ordered, $1.00 for each additional book and make check payable to NBM Publishing. Send to: Papercutz, 160 Broadway, Suite 700, East Wing, New York, NY 10038.

THE SMURFS and BENNY BREAKIRON graphic novels are also available digitally wherever e-books are sold.

WWW.PAPERCUTZ.COM

THE SMURFS ANTHOLOGY

"The Smurfette"
BY YVAN DELPORTE AND PEYO

"The Hungry Smurfs"
BY YVAN DELPORTE AND PEYO

"The Smurfs and the Egg"
BY YVAN DELPORTE AND PEYO

"The Fake Smurf"
BY YVAN DELPORTE AND PEYO

"The Hundreth Smurf"
BY YVAN DELPORTE AND PEYO

"The War of the 7 Springs"
BY YVAN DELPORTE AND PEYO

Joe Johnson, SMURFLATIONS
Adam Grano, SMURFIC DESIGN
Janice Chiang, LETTERING SMURFETTE
Matt. Murray, SMURF CONSULTANT
Beth Scorzato, SMURF COORDINATION
Michael Petranek, ASSOCIATE SMURF
Jim Salicrup, SMURF-IN-CHIEF

ISBN: 978-1-59707-445-2

PRINTED IN CHINA
DECEMBER 2013 BY SHENZHEN CAIMEI PRINTING CO., LTD.
CAIMEI PRINTING BUILDING,
GUANGYAYUAN, BANTIAN, LONGGANG,
SHENZHEN, 518 129

Papercutz books may be purchased for business or promotional use. For information on bulk purchases please contact Macmillan Corporate and Premium Sales Department at (800) 221-7945 x5442.

DISTRIBUTED BY MACMILLAN
SECOND PAPERCUTZ PRINTING

This volume of THE SMURFS ANTHOLOGY
is respectfully dedicated to the memory of
Kim Thompson
1956 – 2013

THE SMURFETTE QUESTION

BY MATT. MURRAY, SMURFOLOGIST

As a Smurfologist, the question that I get the most is: How was it that Smurfette came to be the only girl in the Smurf Village?

My answer: she wasn't. She was one of three. (Extra credit in Smurfology to whoever can name the other two.)*

It's a cheat, of course, because for the first two decades of her existence, she *was* the only female Smurf. It wasn't until later seasons of *The Smurfs* animated series that the other ladies would rear their pretty, little, blue heads – and they were conceived in the Los Angeles offices of Hanna-Barbera during the 1980s, not Peyo's Belgian studio circa the mid-1960s; and by examining the latter part of that statement one can explain not only the "how" of the Smurfette, but the "why," although it does make the Smurfette question somewhat questionable to the modern reader.

Picture it, Smurfologists: it's Belgium circa 1966 and you are there...

Pierre Culliford, better known as Peyo, and his writing partner, Yvan Delporte, have brought back the Smurfs' nemesis, Gargamel, who is intent on exacting his vengeance upon the Smurf Village and disrupting their way of life. His plan, as they concoct it, is to let loose a destructive golem... a man-made monster constructed out of hatred... anger... and silk, pearls, and sapphires?

As you'll see in the following pages, if you didn't know already, the Smurfette didn't occur naturally in the species but was created by Gargamel in an effort to wreak havoc on the Smurfs. The spell he uses to fashion the little fashionista (she has in recent years launched her own clothing line on the runways of New York's Fashion Week, and has modeled in *Bazaar*) invokes the kind of mischief he's looking to let loose on the all-male population, and can be considered incredibly sexist in light of the language and materials used.

While describing "feminine nature" as flirtatious, sneaky, reckless, proud, greedy, foolish, cunning, and volatile (among other things), Gargamel adds ingredients such as a bird's brain, a viper's tongue (powdered), and a candle burned at both ends to his Smurfette stew. In fact, when *"La Schtroumpfette"* was first translated into English by award-winning linguist Anthea Bell in the late 1970s,

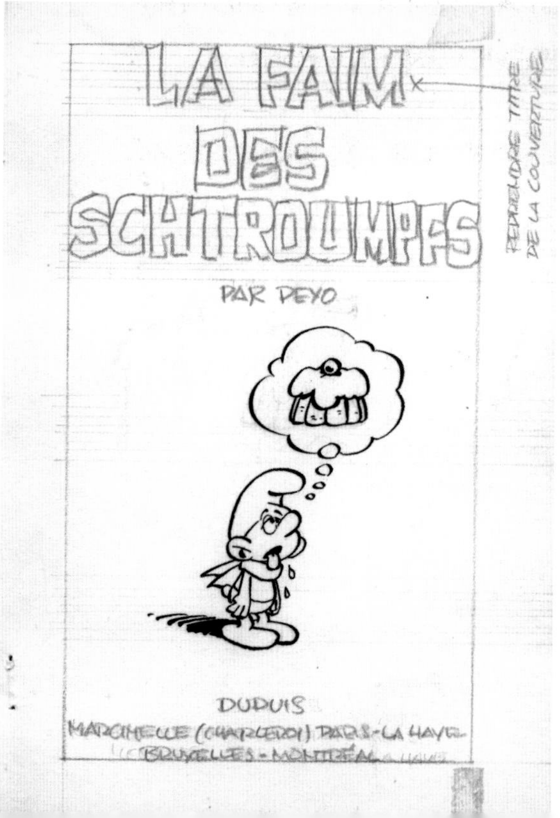
LA FAIM
DES
SCHTROUMPFS
PAR PEYO
DE LA COUVERTURE
DUPUIS
MARCINELLE (CHARLEROI) PARIS-LA HAYE
BRUXELLES-MONTRÉAL

* ANSWER: SASSETTE AND NANNY

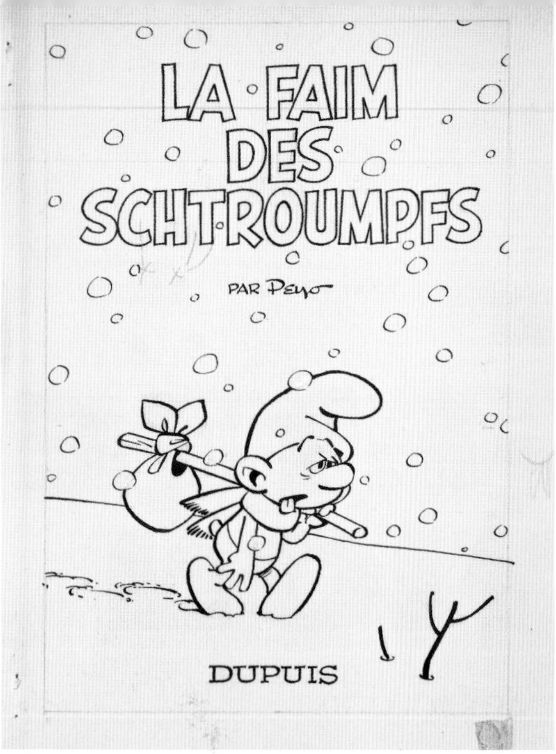
LA FAIM
DES
SCHTROUMPFS
PAR PEYO
DUPUIS

she acknowledged the misogyny by translating Peyo's lighthearted in-text footnote: "*Ce texte engage la seule responsabilité de l'auteur du grimoire 'Magicae Formulae', Editions Belzebuth*" as "The authors will not be held responsible for this formula which is the sole property of MCPW INC (Male Chauvinist Pig Wizards est. 1066)."

Even though Bell's interpretation is "politically correct" and adds another opportunity to chuckle not found in Peyo and Delporte's original script, it also subverts the original text. By changing the words completely, Bell ignores their original context which has roots in the "*chansons*" of French saloon singers such as Jacques Brel (like Peyo and Delporte, a Belgian), that celebrated the melancholy and sometimes absurd aspects of love through ironic, dryly humorous, and mostly offensive lyrics. One need only look at the lyrics of Brel's "Amsterdam" (1964) or "Mathilde" (released in 1966, as was "La Schtroumpfette") to understand the milieu these men were trying to work in.

Where in cases such as "The Purple Smurfs" (featured in THE SMURFS ANTHOLOGY Vol. 1) Papercutz has opted to change certain aspects of Peyo's original comics (the "zombies" were re-colored from black to violet) to steer clear of unnecessary controversy, it's interesting to note that the translation of the Smurfette spell and its footnote presented here is literal, allowing for and provoking scholarly conversation about the work and the environment it was created in. Let's face it though, no matter the country, the mid 1960s *weren't* exactly the best of times in terms of gender equality, and all irony and "cultural differences" aside, "*The Smurfette*" IS a document of that environment.

But before you go dismissing the entire story, or even the character, read the comic first. You may be surprised by some of the twists and turns the Smurfette takes along the way, and ultimately by a choice she makes in the final pages of the story which may come as a bit of a shock to those only familiar with the "blue girl in town" from the television show.

You may find yourself with some new questions worthy of some Smurfological studies of your own. •

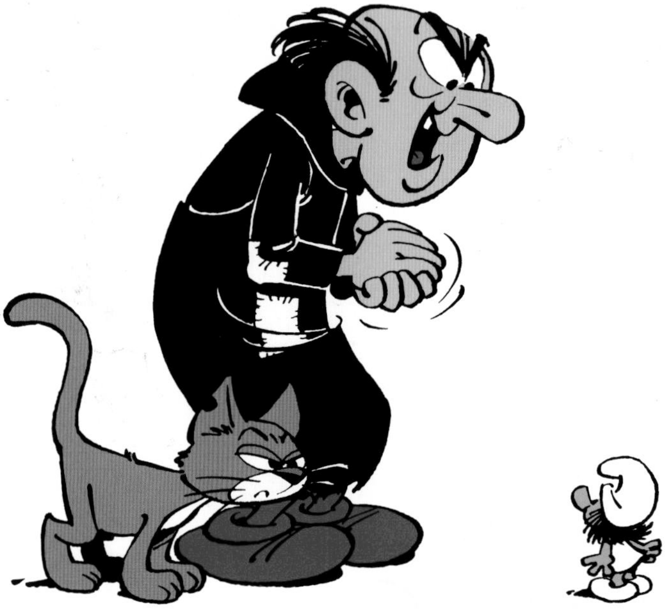

3ᵉ SERIE

2 Histoires de Schtroumpfs **par** *Peyo*

La Schtroumpfette

et
LA FAIM
DES SCHTROUMPFS

THE SMURFETTE

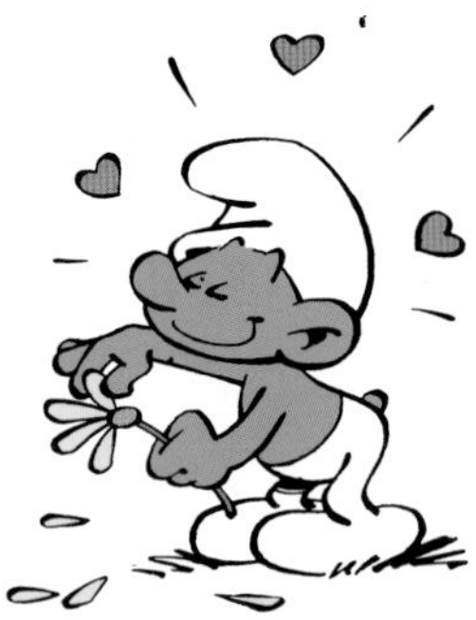

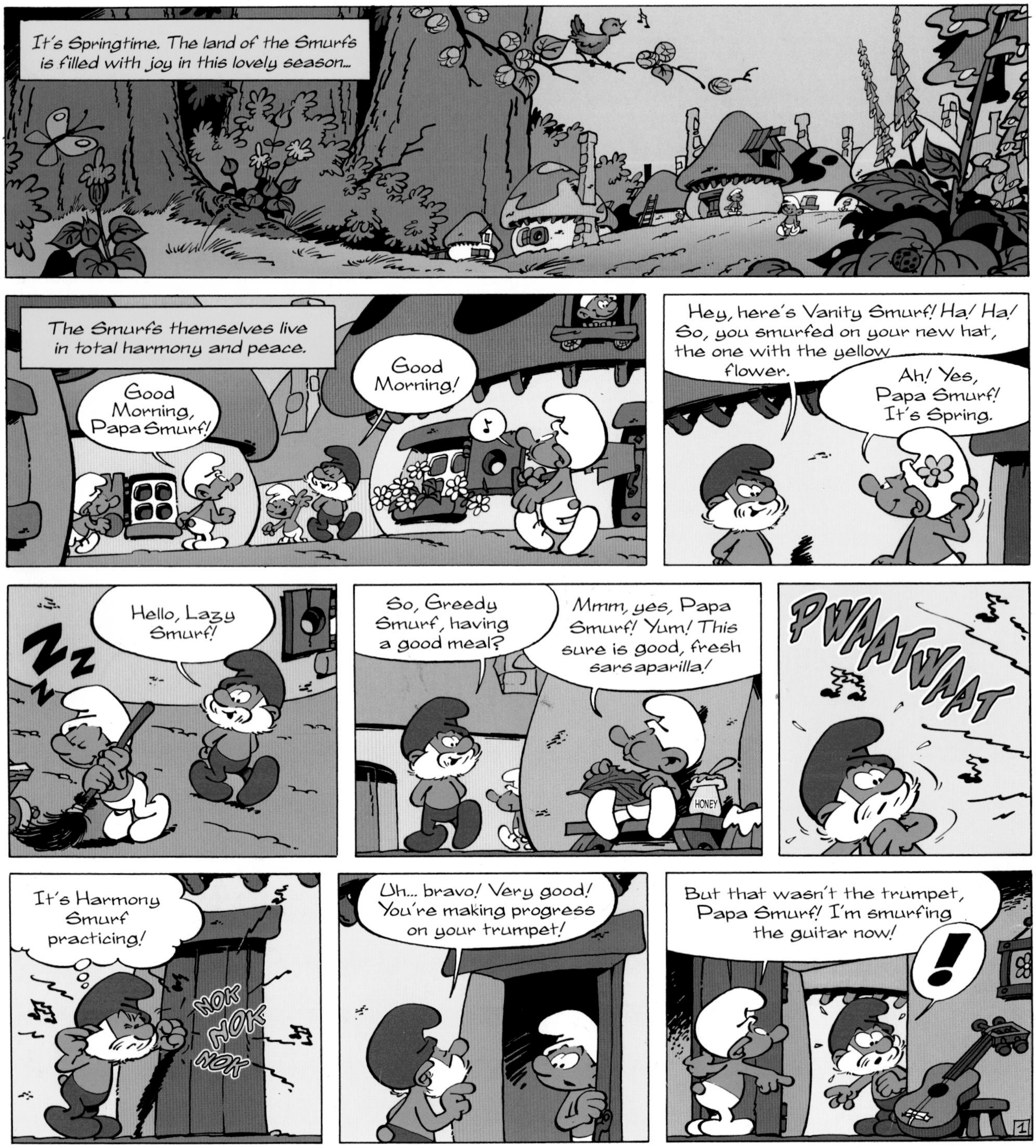
It's Springtime. The land of the Smurfs is filled with joy in this lovely season...
The Smurfs themselves live in total harmony and peace.
Good Morning, Papa Smurf!
Good Morning!
Hey, here's Vanity Smurf! Ha! Ha! So, you smurfed on your new hat, the one with the yellow flower.
Ah! Yes, Papa Smurf! It's Spring.
Hello, Lazy Smurf!
So, Greedy Smurf, having a good meal?
Mmm, yes, Papa Smurf! Yum! This sure is good, fresh sarsaparilla!
HONEY
PWAATWAAT
It's Harmony Smurf practicing!
NOK NOK NOK
Uh... bravo! Very good! You're making progress on your trumpet!
But that wasn't the trumpet, Papa Smurf! I'm smurfing the guitar now!
!
1

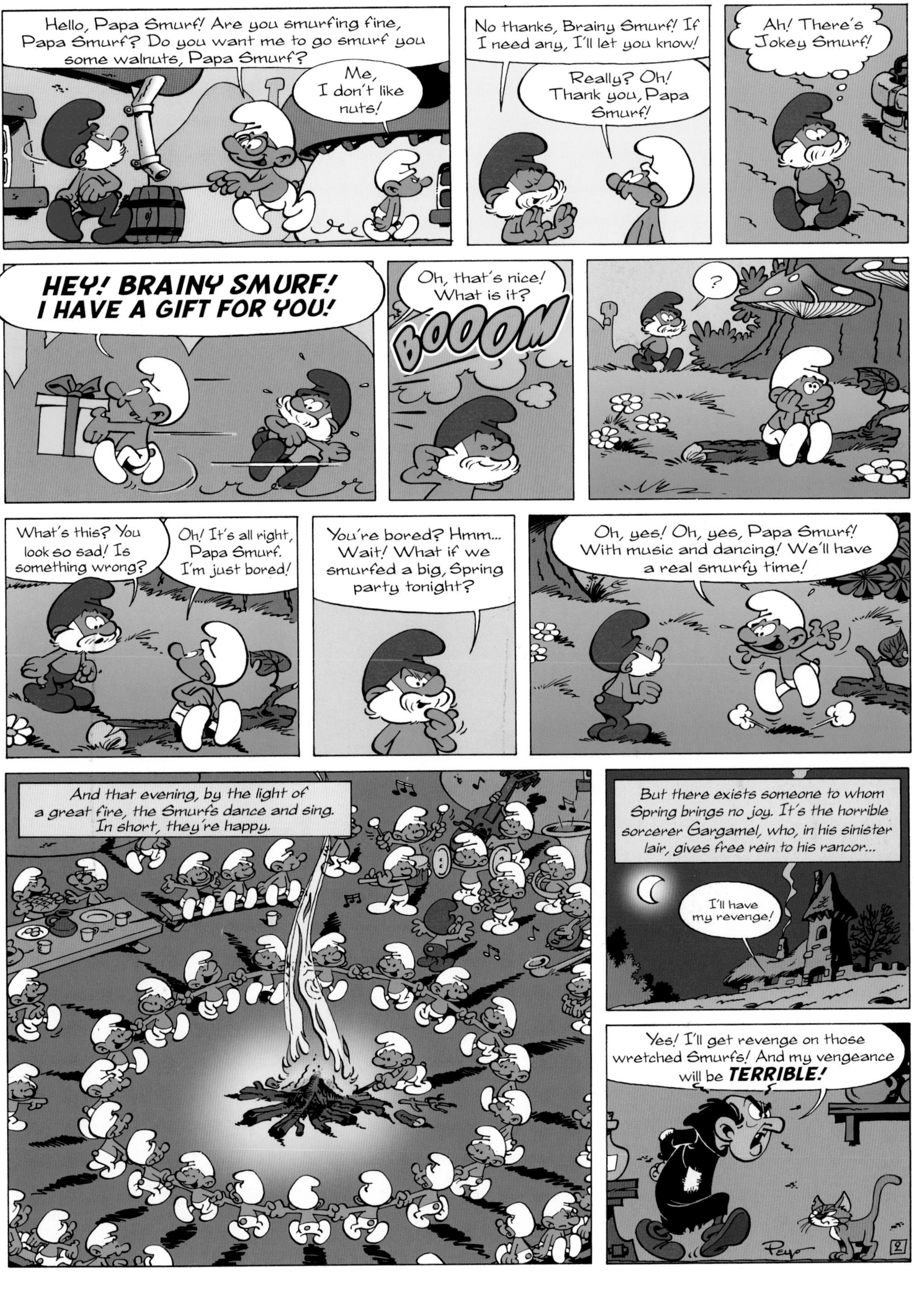

Hello, Papa Smurf! Are you smurfing fine, Papa Smurf? Do you want me to go smurf you some walnuts, Papa Smurf?
Me, I don't like nuts!
No thanks, Brainy Smurf! If I need any, I'll let you know!
Really? Oh! Thank you, Papa Smurf!
Ah! There's Jokey Smurf!
HEY! BRAINY SMURF! I HAVE A GIFT FOR YOU!
Oh, that's nice! What is it?
BOOOM
?
What's this? You look so sad! Is something wrong?
Oh! It's all right, Papa Smurf. I'm just bored!
You're bored? Hmm... Wait! What if we smurfed a big, Spring party tonight?
Oh, yes! Oh, yes, Papa Smurf! With music and dancing! We'll have a real smurfy time!
And that evening, by the light of a great fire, the Smurfs dance and sing. In short, they're happy.
But there exists someone to whom Spring brings no joy. It's the horrible sorcerer Gargamel, who, in his sinister lair, gives free rein to his rancor...
I'll have my revenge!
Yes! I'll get revenge on those wretched Smurfs! And my vengeance will be TERRIBLE!
Peyo
2

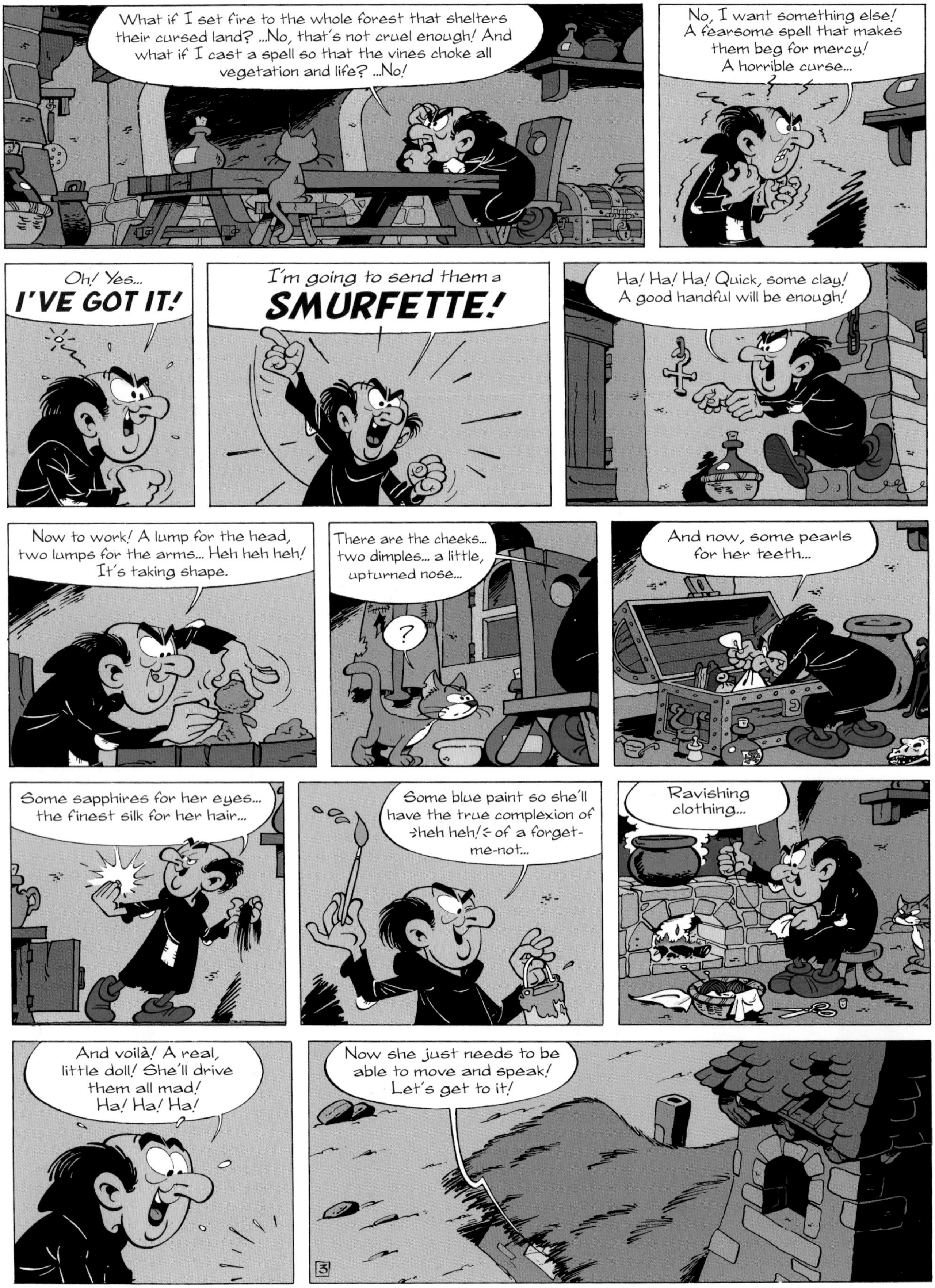
What if I set fire to the whole forest that shelters their cursed land? ...No, that's not cruel enough! And what if I cast a spell so that the vines choke all vegetation and life? ...No!
No, I want something else! A fearsome spell that makes them beg for mercy! A horrible curse...
Oh! Yes... I'VE GOT IT!
I'm going to send them a SMURFETTE!
Ha! Ha! Ha! Quick, some clay! A good handful will be enough!
Now to work! A lump for the head, two lumps for the arms... Heh heh heh! It's taking shape.
There are the cheeks... two dimples... a little, upturned nose...
?
And now, some pearls for her teeth...
Some sapphires for her eyes... the finest silk for her hair...
Some blue paint so she'll have the true complexion of -heh heh!- of a forget-me-not...
Ravishing clothing...
And voilà! A real, little doll! She'll drive them all mad! Ha! Ha! Ha!
Now she just needs to be able to move and speak! Let's get to it!
3

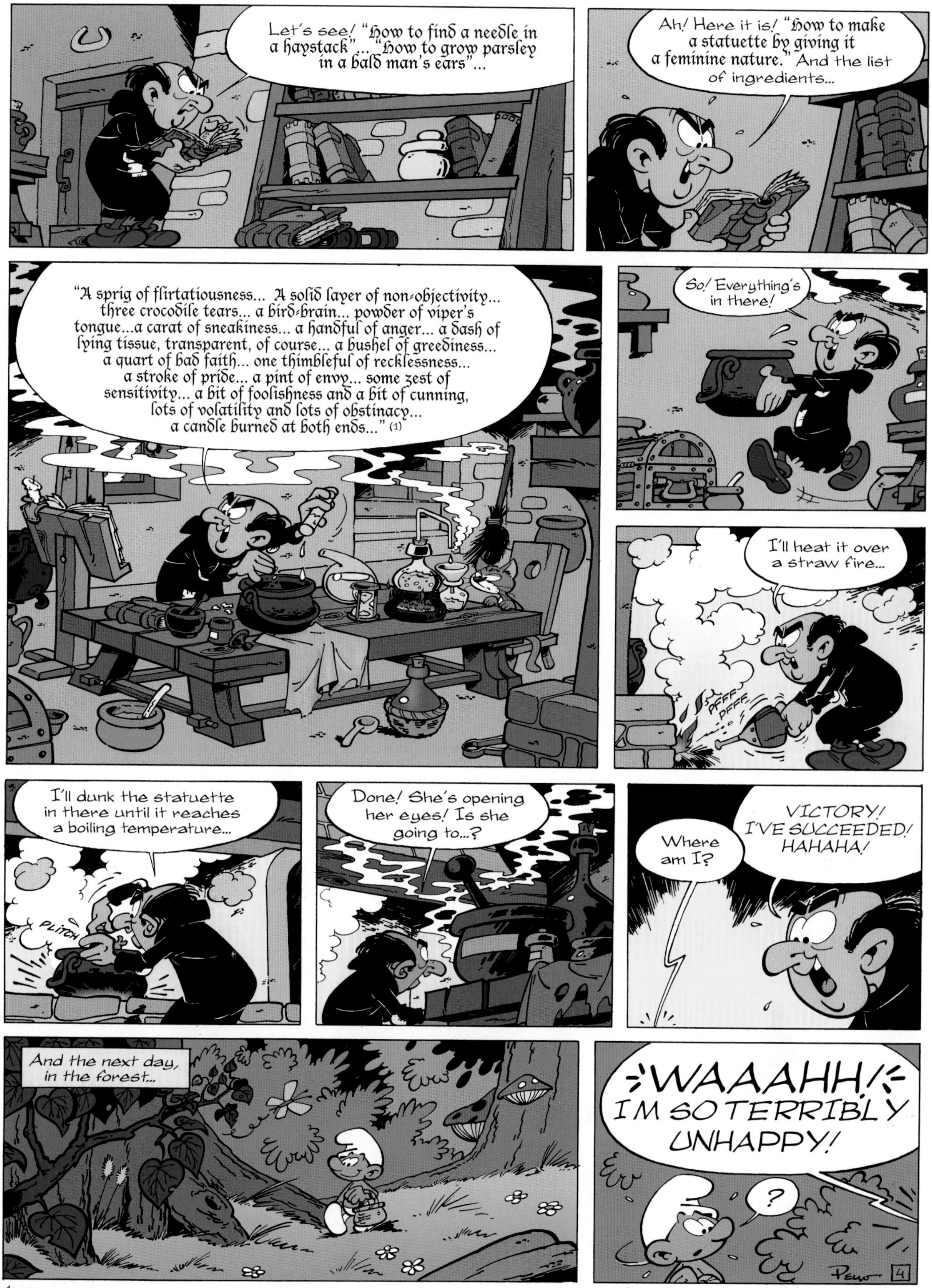
Let's see! "How to find a needle in a haystack"... "How to grow parsley in a bald man's ears"...
Ah! Here it is! "How to make a statuette by giving it a feminine nature." And the list of ingredients...
"A sprig of flirtatiousness... A solid layer of non-objectivity... three crocodile tears... a bird-brain... powder of viper's tongue...a carat of sneakiness... a handful of anger... a dash of lying tissue, transparent, of course... a bushel of greediness... a quart of bad faith... one thimbleful of recklessness... a stroke of pride... a pint of envy... some zest of sensitivity... a bit of foolishness and a bit of cunning, lots of volatility and lots of obstinacy... a candle burned at both ends..." (1)
So! Everything's in there!
I'll heat it over a straw fire...
PFFF PFFF
I'll dunk the statuette in there until it reaches a boiling temperature...
PLITCH
Done! She's opening her eyes! Is she going to...?
Where am I?
VICTORY! I'VE SUCCEEDED! HAHAHA!
And the next day, in the forest...
WAAAHH! I'M SO TERRIBLY UNHAPPY!
?
4

(1) This text is the sole responsibility of the author of the spell-book "Magicae Formulae," Beelzebub Editions.

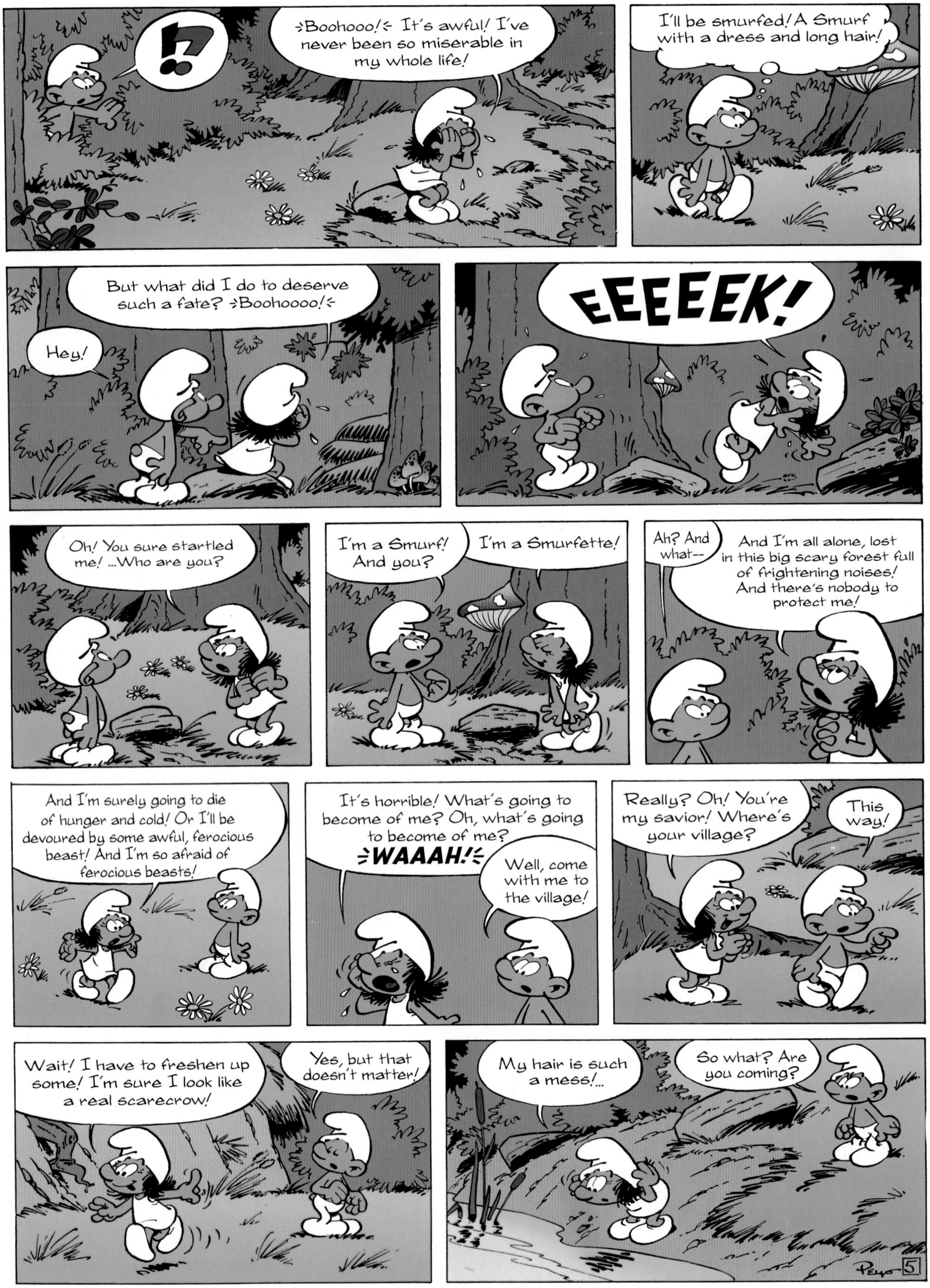

-Boohooo!- It's awful! I've never been so miserable in my whole life!
I'll be smurfed! A Smurf with a dress and long hair!
But what did I do to deserve such a fate? -Boohoooo!-
Hey!
EEEEEK!
Oh! You sure startled me! ...Who are you?
I'm a Smurf! And you?
I'm a Smurfette!
Ah? And what--
And I'm all alone, lost in this big scary forest full of frightening noises! And there's nobody to protect me!
And I'm surely going to die of hunger and cold! Or I'll be devoured by some awful, ferocious beast! And I'm so afraid of ferocious beasts!
It's horrible! What's going to become of me? Oh, what's going to become of me? -WAAAH!-
Well, come with me to the village!
Really? Oh! You're my savior! Where's your village?
This way!
Wait! I have to freshen up some! I'm sure I look like a real scarecrow!
Yes, but that doesn't matter!
My hair is such a mess!...
So what? Are you coming?
Peyo
5

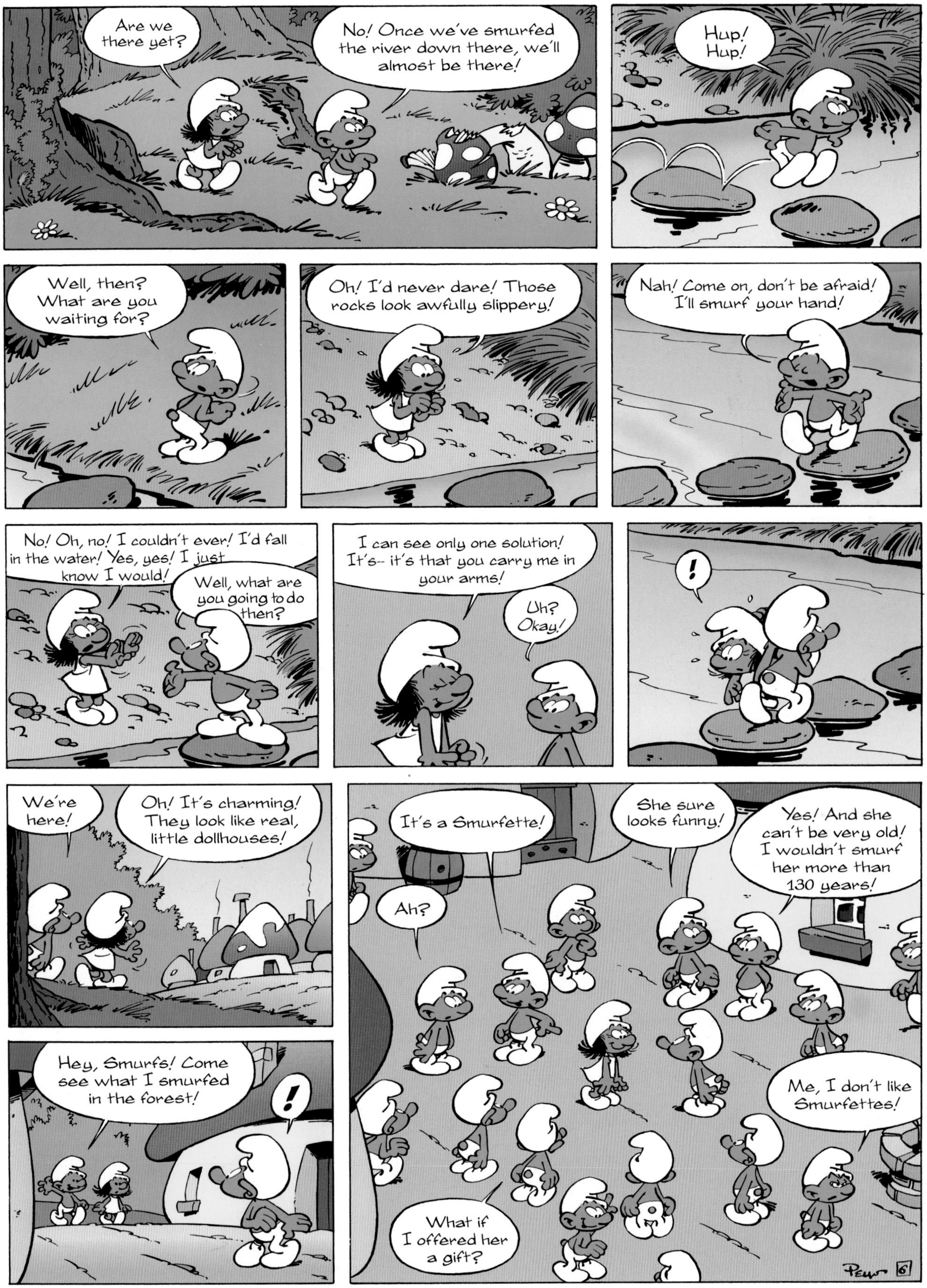
Are we there yet?
No! Once we've smurfed the river down there, we'll almost be there!
Hup! Hup!
Well, then? What are you waiting for?
Oh! I'd never dare! Those rocks look awfully slippery!
Nah! Come on, don't be afraid! I'll smurf your hand!
No! Oh, no! I couldn't ever! I'd fall in the water! Yes, yes! I just know I would!
Well, what are you going to do then?
I can see only one solution! It's-- it's that you carry me in your arms!
Uh? Okay!
!
We're here!
Oh! It's charming! They look like real, little dollhouses!
Hey, Smurfs! Come see what I smurfed in the forest!
!
It's a Smurfette!
She sure looks funny!
Yes! And she can't be very old! I wouldn't smurf her more than 130 years!
Ah?
Me, I don't like Smurfettes!
What if I offered her a gift?
Peyo
6

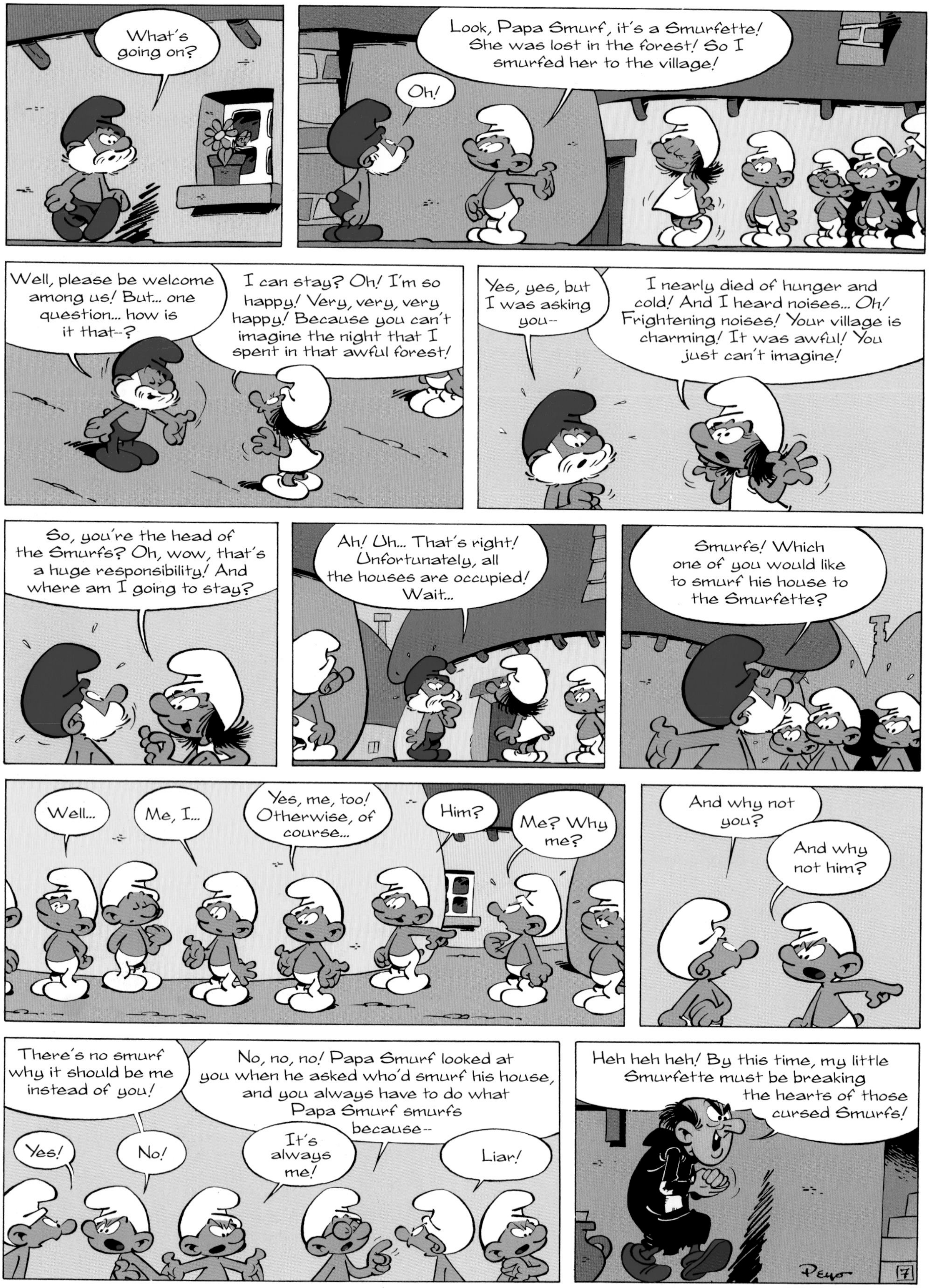
What's going on?
Look, Papa Smurf, it's a Smurfette! She was lost in the forest! So I smurfed her to the village!
Oh!
Well, please be welcome among us! But... one question... how is it that--?
I can stay? Oh! I'm so happy! Very, very, very happy! Because you can't imagine the night that I spent in that awful forest!
Yes, yes, but I was asking you--
I nearly died of hunger and cold! And I heard noises... Oh! Frightening noises! Your village is charming! It was awful! You just can't imagine!
So, you're the head of the Smurfs? Oh, wow, that's a huge responsibility! And where am I going to stay?
Ah! Uh... That's right! Unfortunately, all the houses are occupied! Wait...
Smurfs! Which one of you would like to smurf his house to the Smurfette?
Well...
Me, I...
Yes, me, too! Otherwise, of course...
Him?
Me? Why me?
And why not you?
And why not him?
There's no smurf why it should be me instead of you!
No, no, no! Papa Smurf looked at you when he asked who'd smurf his house, and you always have to do what Papa Smurf smurfs because--
Yes!
No!
It's always me!
Liar!
Heh heh heh! By this time, my little Smurfette must be breaking the hearts of those cursed Smurfs!
Peyo
7

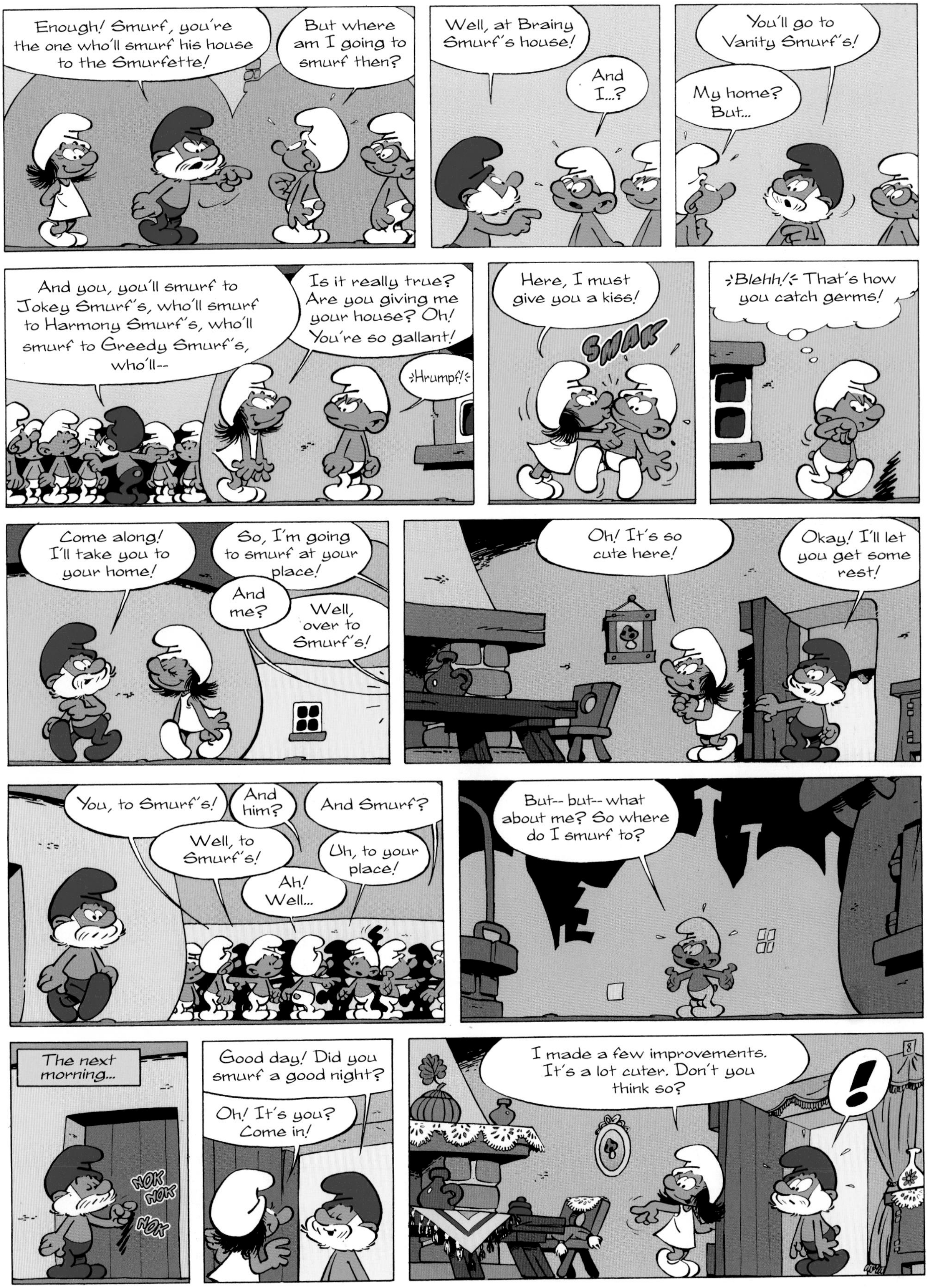
Enough! Smurf, you're the one who'll smurf his house to the Smurfette!
But where am I going to smurf then?
Well, at Brainy Smurf's house!
And I...?
You'll go to Vanity Smurf's!
My home? But...
And you, you'll smurf to Jokey Smurf's, who'll smurf to Harmony Smurf's, who'll smurf to Greedy Smurf's, who'll--
Is it really true? Are you giving me your house? Oh! You're so gallant!
Hrumpf!
Here, I must give you a kiss!
SMAK
Blehh! That's how you catch germs!
Come along! I'll take you to your home!
So, I'm going to smurf at your place!
And me?
Well, over to Smurf's!
Oh! It's so cute here!
Okay! I'll let you get some rest!
You, to Smurf's!
And him?
And Smurf?
Well, to Smurf's!
Uh, to your place!
Ah! Well...
But-- but-- what about me? So where do I smurf to?
The next morning...
NOK NOK
NOK
Good day! Did you smurf a good night?
Oh! It's you? Come in!
I made a few improvements. It's a lot cuter. Don't you think so?
!

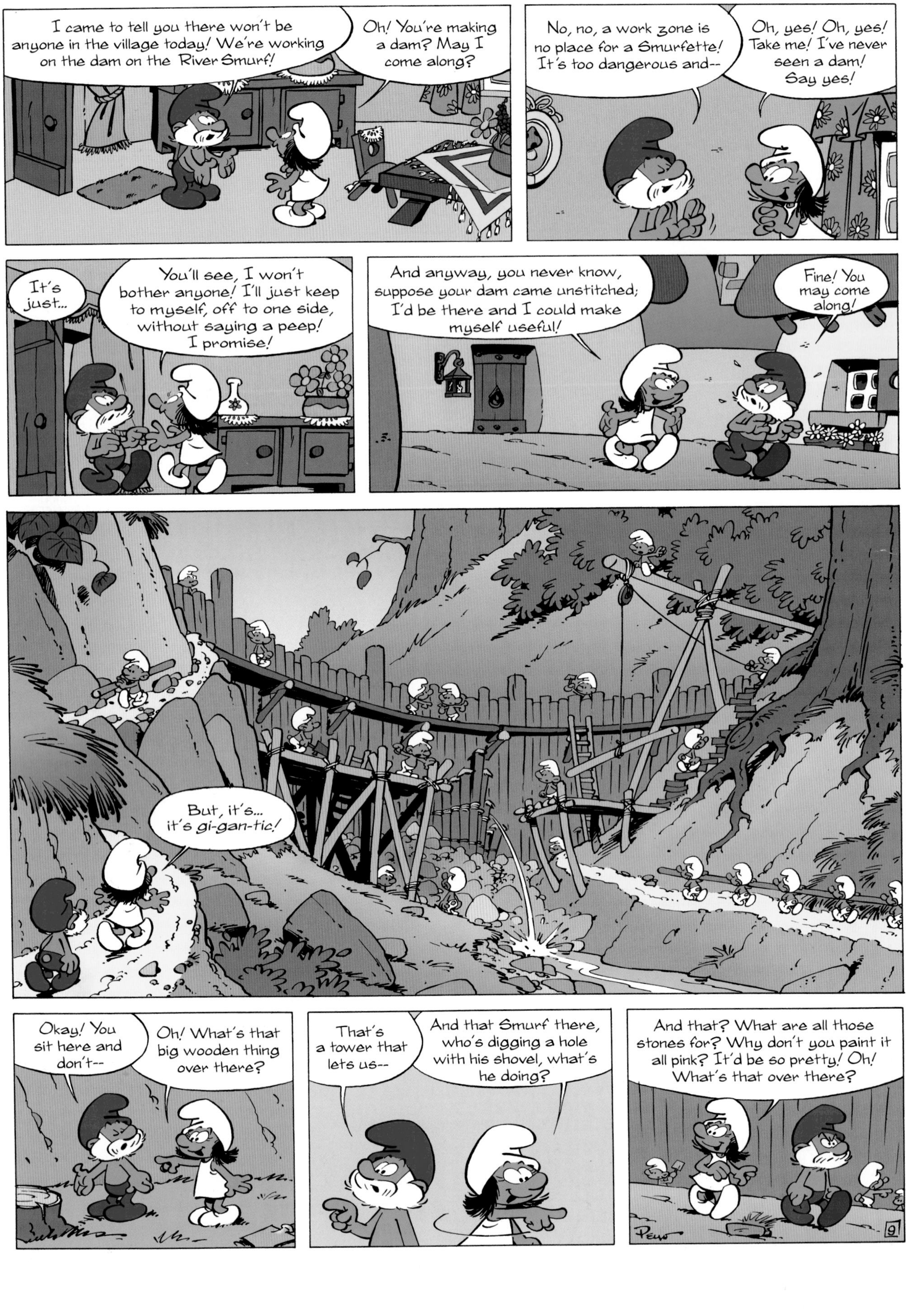
I came to tell you there won't be anyone in the village today! We're working on the dam on the River Smurf!
Oh! You're making a dam? May I come along?
No, no, a work zone is no place for a Smurfette! It's too dangerous and--
Oh, yes! Oh, yes! Take me! I've never seen a dam! Say yes!
It's just...
You'll see, I won't bother anyone! I'll just keep to myself, off to one side, without saying a peep! I promise!
And anyway, you never know, suppose your dam came unstitched; I'd be there and I could make myself useful!
Fine! You may come along!
But, it's... it's gi-gan-tic!
Okay! You sit here and don't--
Oh! What's that big wooden thing over there?
That's a tower that lets us--
And that Smurf there, who's digging a hole with his shovel, what's he doing?
And that? What are all those stones for? Why don't you paint it all pink? It'd be so pretty! Oh! What's that over there?
9

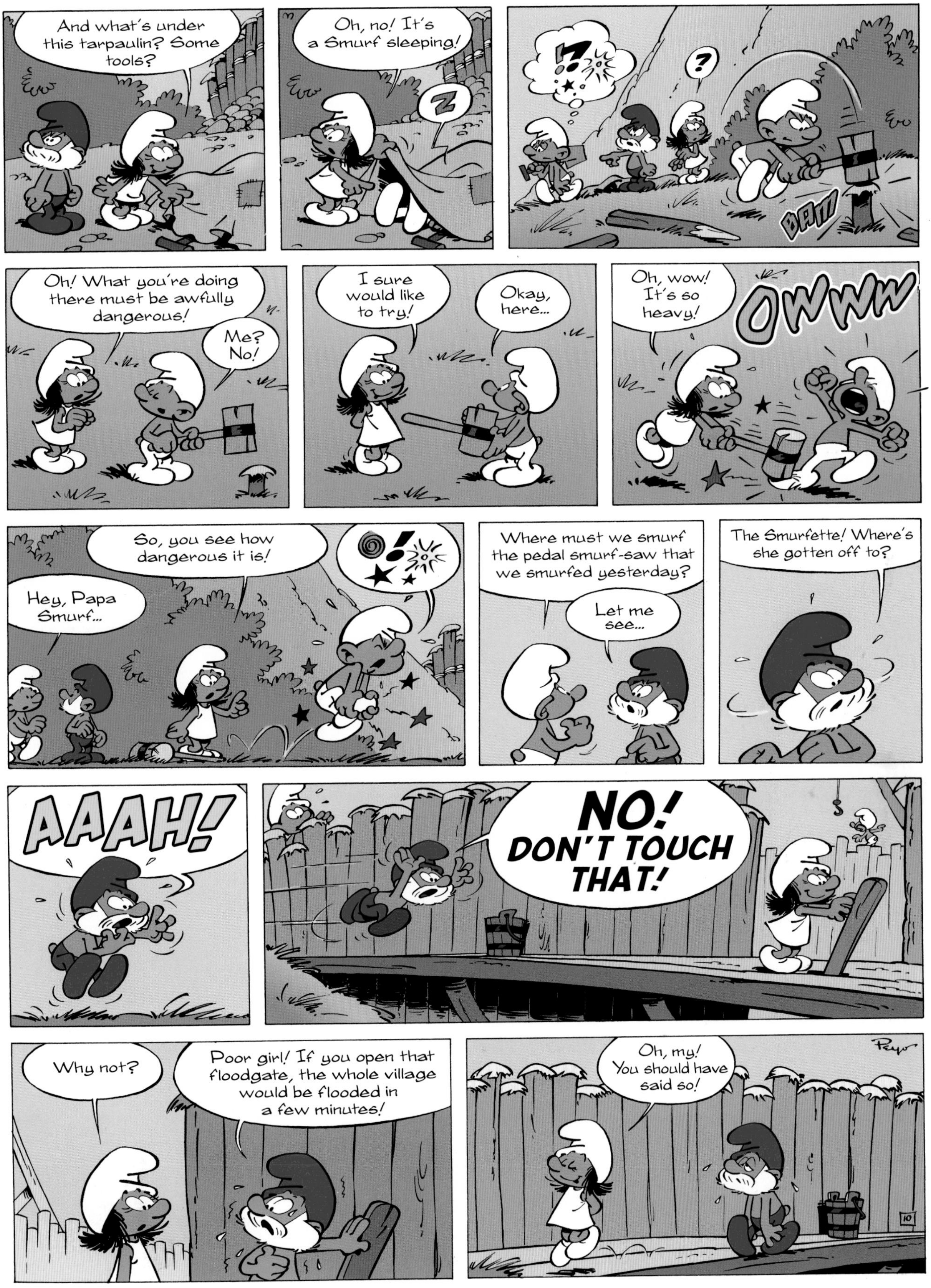
And what's under this tarpaulin? Some tools?
Oh, no! It's a Smurf sleeping!
Z
?
BAM!
Oh! What you're doing there must be awfully dangerous!
Me? No!
I sure would like to try!
Okay, here...
Oh, wow! It's so heavy!
OWWW
So, you see how dangerous it is!
Hey, Papa Smurf...
Where must we smurf the pedal smurf-saw that we smurfed yesterday?
Let me see...
The Smurfette! Where's she gotten off to?
AAAH!
NO! DON'T TOUCH THAT!
Why not?
Poor girl! If you open that floodgate, the whole village would be flooded in a few minutes!
Oh, my! You should have said so!
Peyo
10

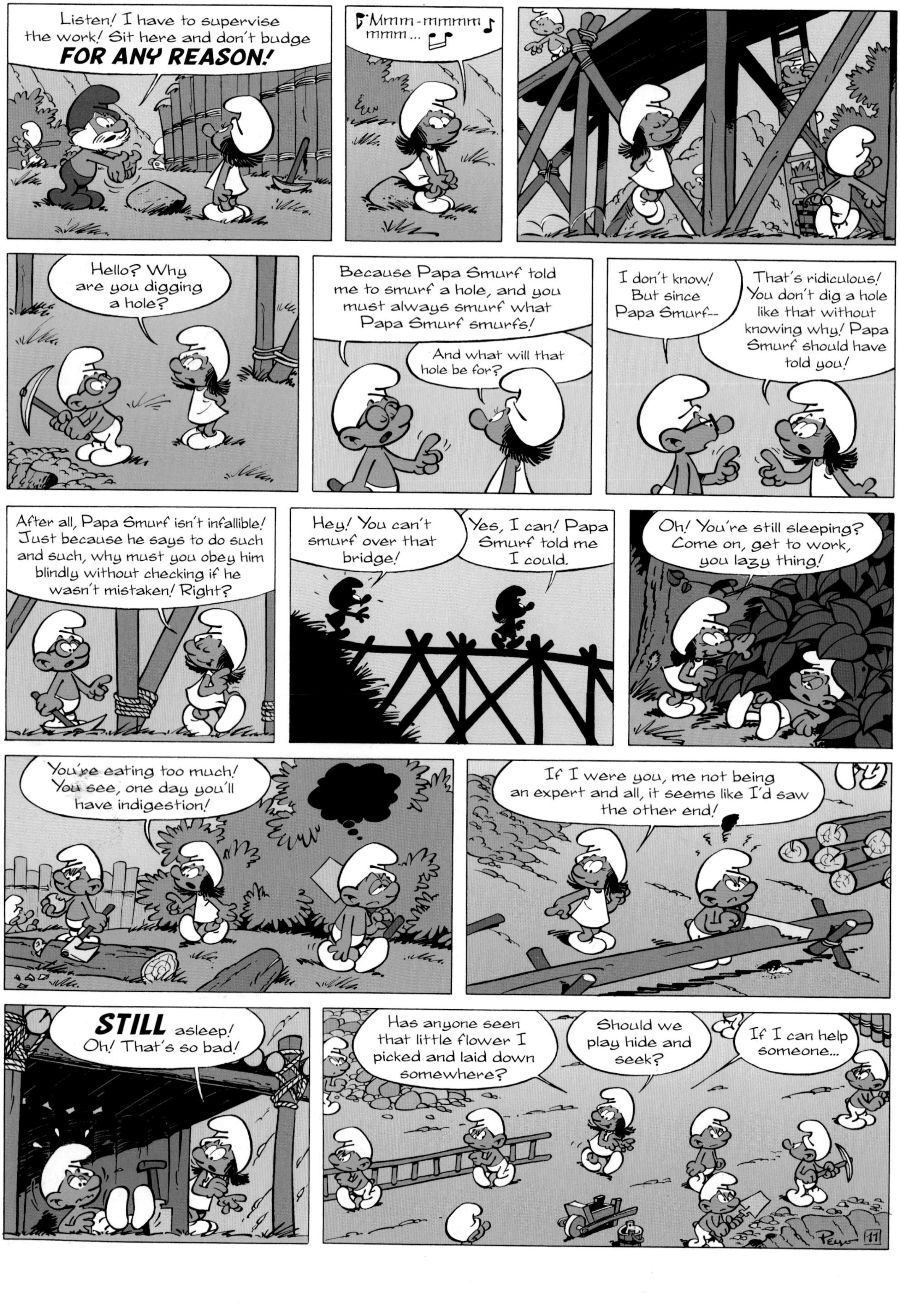

Listen! I have to supervise the work! Sit here and don't budge FOR ANY REASON!
Mmm-mmmm mmm...
Hello? Why are you digging a hole?
Because Papa Smurf told me to smurf a hole, and you must always smurf what Papa Smurf smurfs!
And what will that hole be for?
I don't know! But since Papa Smurf--
That's ridiculous! You don't dig a hole like that without knowing why! Papa Smurf should have told you!
After all, Papa Smurf isn't infallible! Just because he says to do such and such, why must you obey him blindly without checking if he wasn't mistaken! Right?
Hey! You can't smurf over that bridge!
Yes, I can! Papa Smurf told me I could.
Oh! You're still sleeping? Come on, get to work, you lazy thing!
You're eating too much! You see, one day you'll have indigestion!
If I were you, me not being an expert and all, it seems like I'd saw the other end!
STILL asleep! Oh! That's so bad!
Has anyone seen that little flower I picked and laid down somewhere?
Should we play hide and seek?
If I can help someone...
Peyo
11

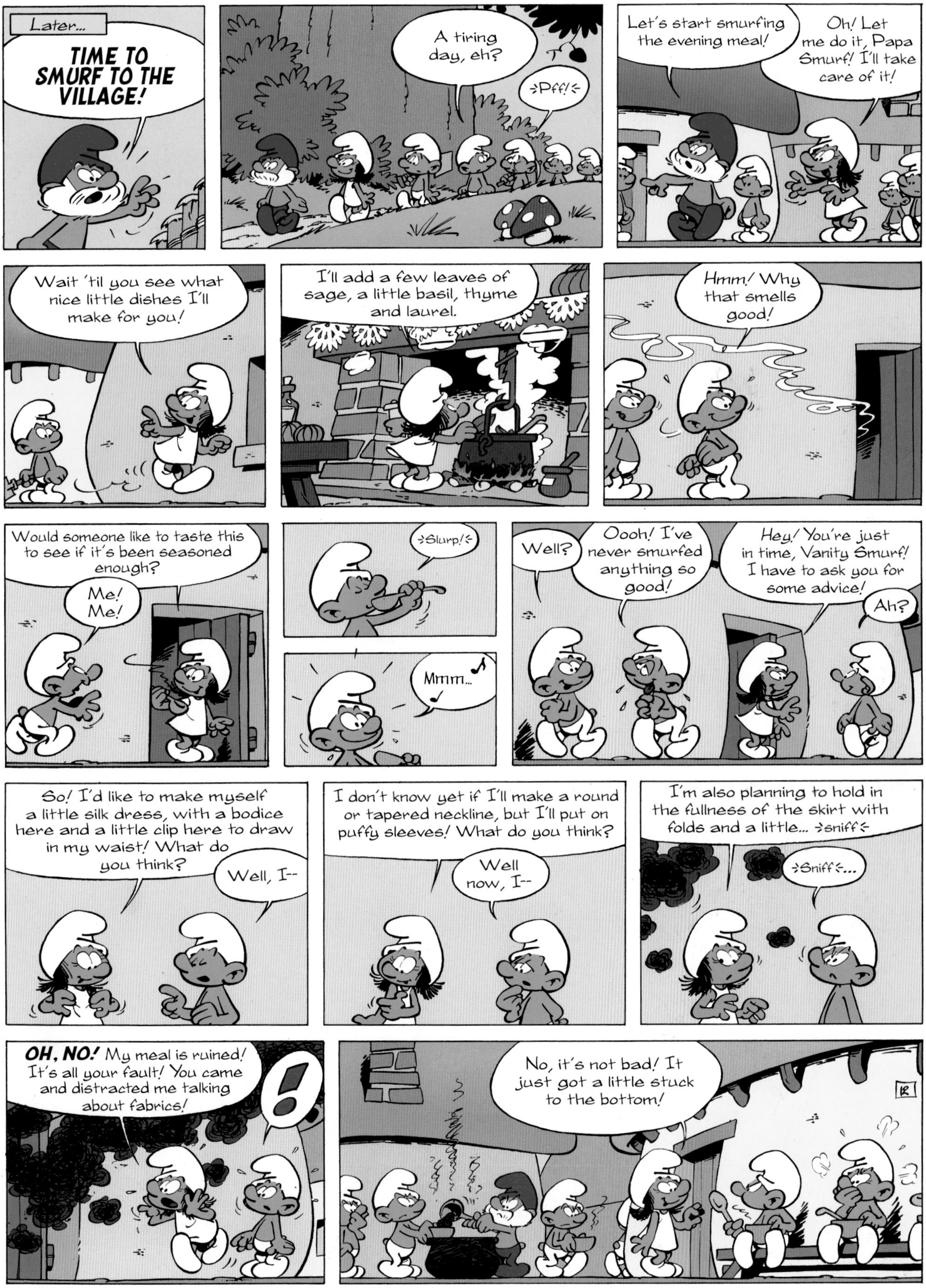
Later...
TIME TO SMURF TO THE VILLAGE!
A tiring day, eh?
Pff!
Let's start smurfing the evening meal!
Oh! Let me do it, Papa Smurf! I'll take care of it!
Wait 'til you see what nice little dishes I'll make for you!
I'll add a few leaves of sage, a little basil, thyme and laurel.
Hmm! Why that smells good!
Would someone like to taste this to see if it's been seasoned enough?
Me! Me!
Slurp!
Mmm...
Well?
Oooh! I've never smurfed anything so good!
Hey! You're just in time, Vanity Smurf! I have to ask you for some advice!
Ah?
So! I'd like to make myself a little silk dress, with a bodice here and a little clip here to draw in my waist! What do you think?
Well, I--
I don't know yet if I'll make a round or tapered neckline, but I'll put on puffy sleeves! What do you think?
Well now, I--
I'm also planning to hold in the fullness of the skirt with folds and a little... sniff
Sniff...
OH, NO! My meal is ruined! It's all your fault! You came and distracted me talking about fabrics!
No, it's not bad! It just got a little stuck to the bottom!

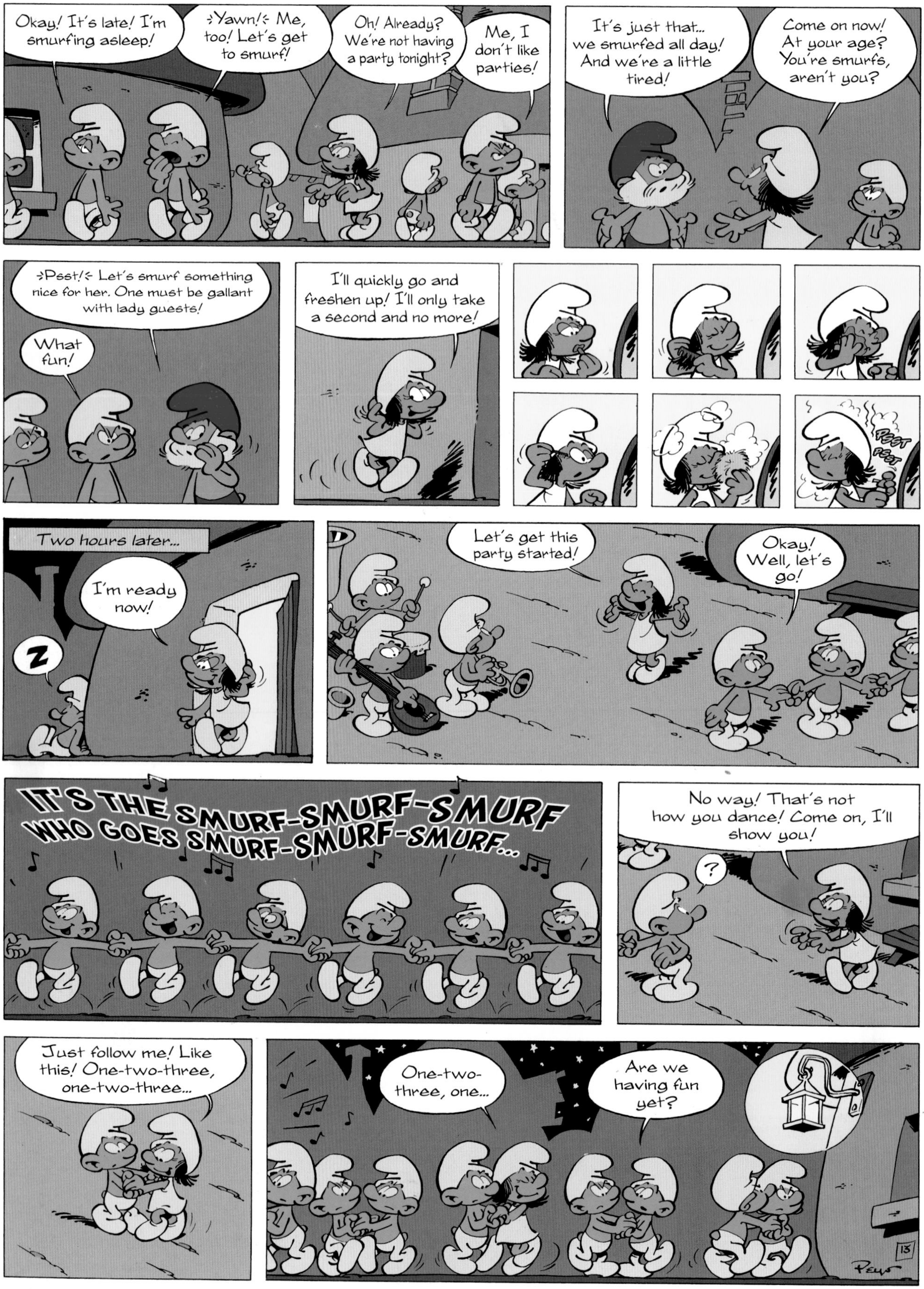
Okay! It's late! I'm smurfing asleep!
>Yawn!< Me, too! Let's get to smurf!
Oh! Already? We're not having a party tonight?
Me, I don't like parties!
It's just that... we smurfed all day! And we're a little tired!
Come on now! At your age? You're smurfs, aren't you?
>Psst!< Let's smurf something nice for her. One must be gallant with lady guests!
What fun!
I'll quickly go and freshen up! I'll only take a second and no more!
PSST PSST
Two hours later...
Z
I'm ready now!
Let's get this party started!
Okay! Well, let's go!
IT'S THE SMURF-SMURF-SMURF WHO GOES SMURF-SMURF-SMURF...
No way! That's not how you dance! Come on, I'll show you!
?
Just follow me! Like this! One-two-three, one-two-three...
One-two-three, one...
Are we having fun yet?

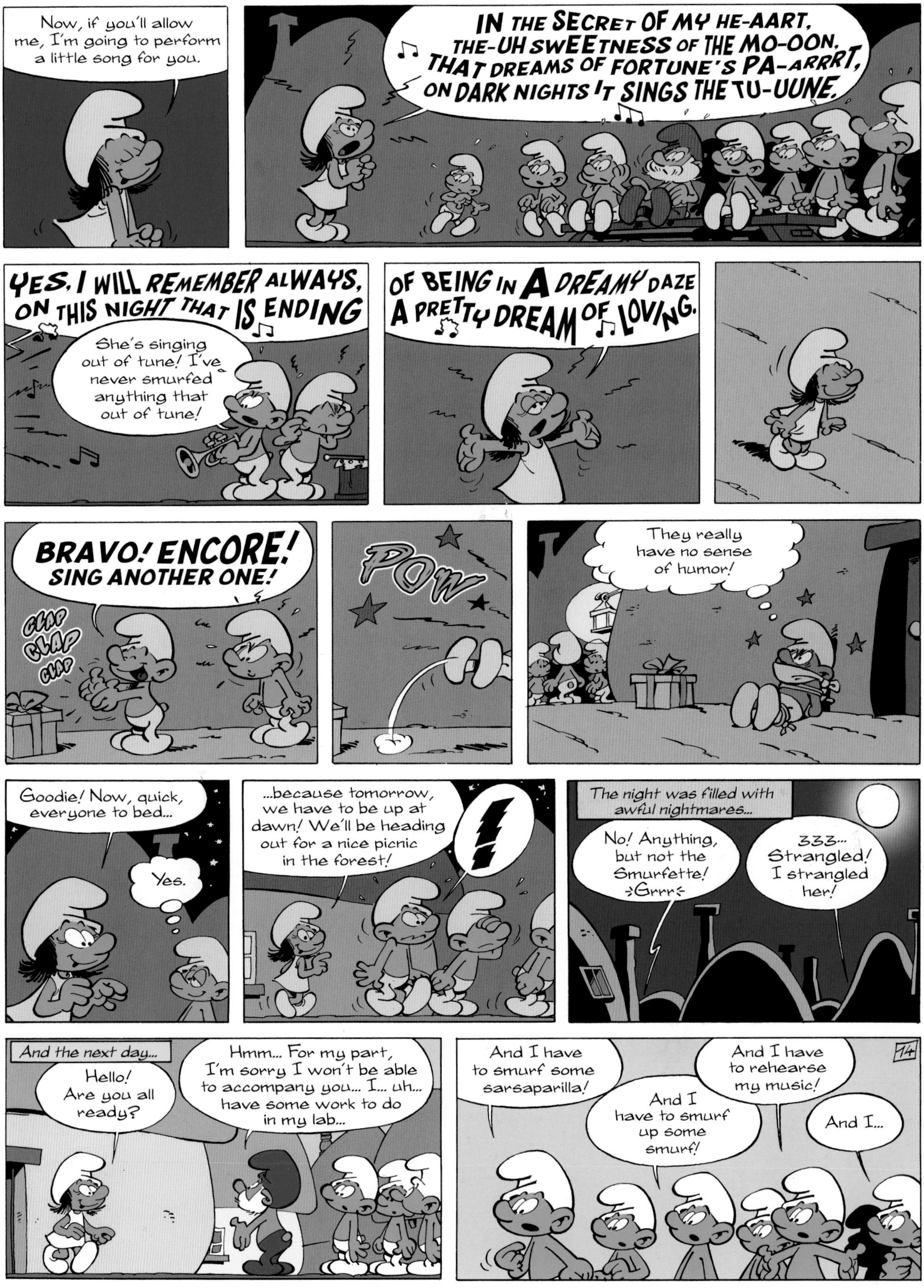
Now, if you'll allow me, I'm going to perform a little song for you.
IN THE SECRET OF MY HE-AART, THE-UH SWEETNESS OF THE MO-OON, THAT DREAMS OF FORTUNE'S PA-ARRRT, ON DARK NIGHTS IT SINGS THE TU-UUNE.
YES, I WILL REMEMBER ALWAYS, ON THIS NIGHT THAT IS ENDING
She's singing out of tune! I've never smurfed anything that out of tune!
OF BEING IN A DREAMY DAZE A PRETTY DREAM OF LOVING.
BRAVO! ENCORE! SING ANOTHER ONE!
CLAP CLAP CLAP
POW
They really have no sense of humor!
Goodie! Now, quick, everyone to bed...
Yes.
...because tomorrow, we have to be up at dawn! We'll be heading out for a nice picnic in the forest!
The night was filled with awful nightmares...
No! Anything, but not the Smurfette! Grrr
ZZZ... Strangled! I strangled her!
And the next day...
Hello! Are you all ready?
Hmm... For my part, I'm sorry I won't be able to accompany you... I... uh... have some work to do in my lab...
14
And I have to smurf some sarsaparilla!
And I have to smurf up some smurf!
And I have to rehearse my music!
And I...

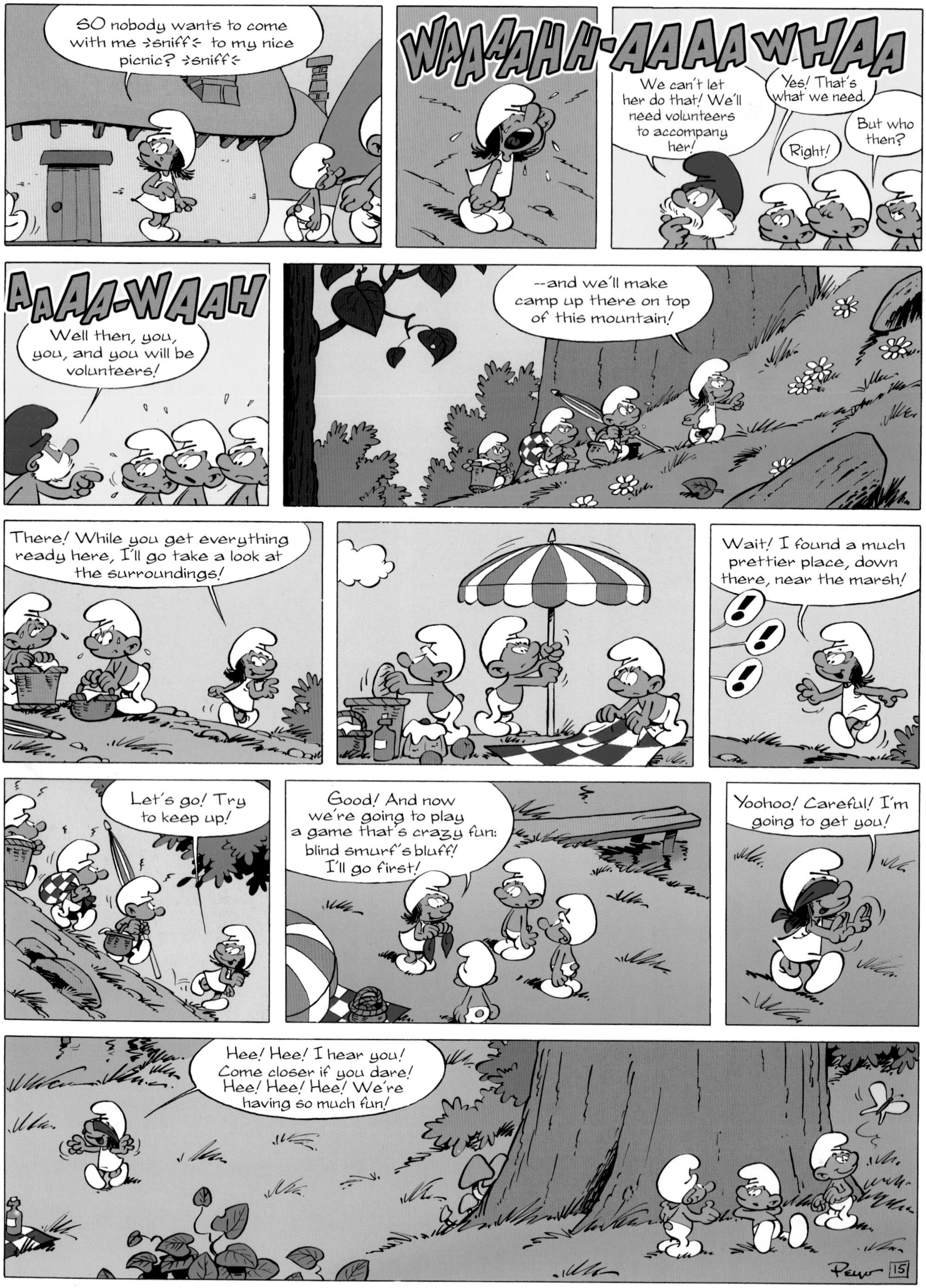
SO nobody wants to come with me >sniff< to my nice picnic? >sniff<
WAAAAHH-AAAAWHAA
We can't let her do that! We'll need volunteers to accompany her!
Yes! That's what we need.
Right!
But who then?
AAAA-WAAAH
Well then, you, you, and you will be volunteers!
--and we'll make camp up there on top of this mountain!
There! While you get everything ready here, I'll go take a look at the surroundings!
Wait! I found a much prettier place, down there, near the marsh!
!
!
!
Let's go! Try to keep up!
Good! And now we're going to play a game that's crazy fun: blind smurf's bluff! I'll go first!
Yoohoo! Careful! I'm going to get you!
Hee! Hee! I hear you! Come closer if you dare! Hee! Hee! Hee! We're having so much fun!
Peyo
15

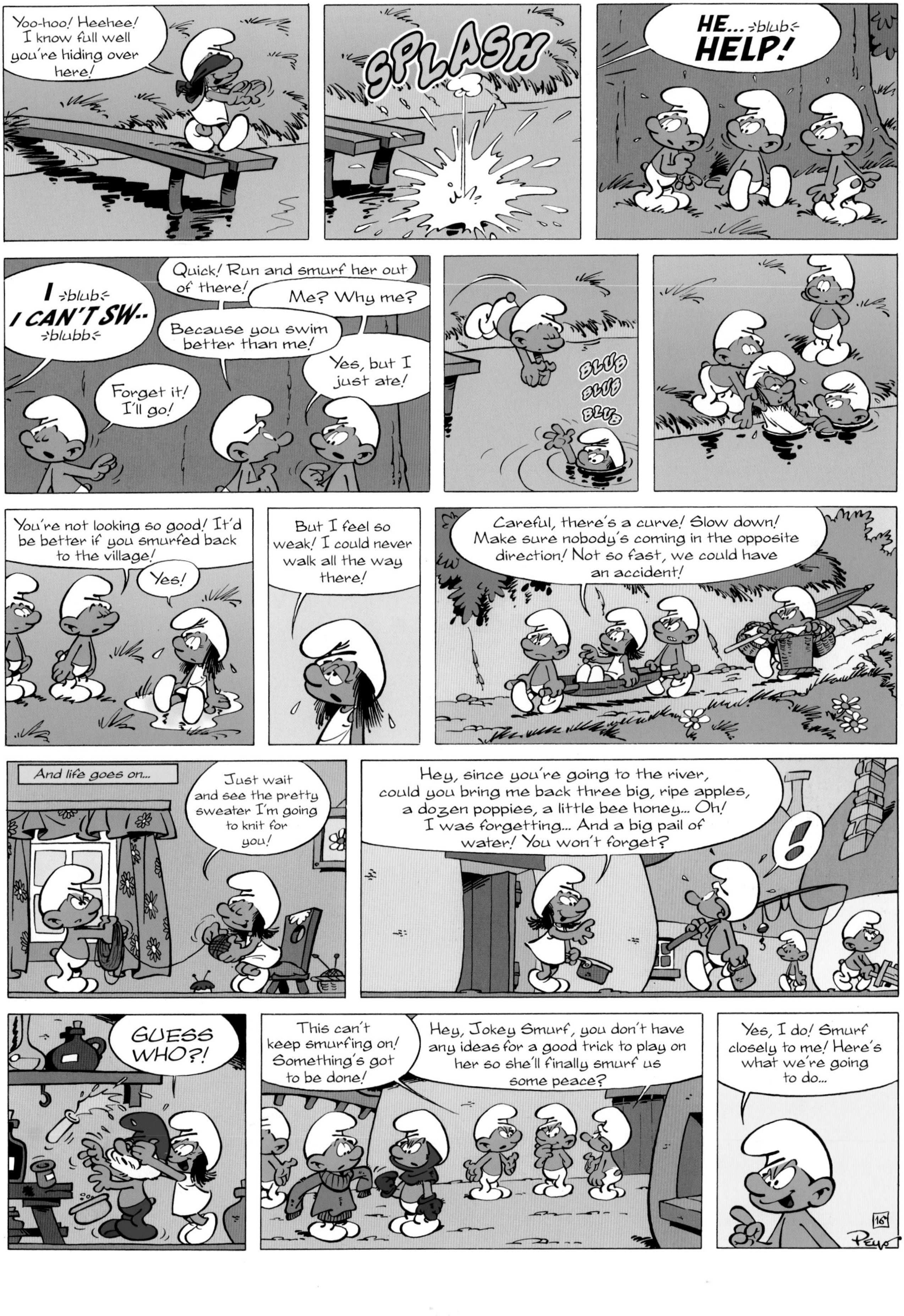

Yoo-hoo! Heehee! I know full well you're hiding over here!
SPLASH
HE... blub HELP!
I blub I CAN'T SW-- blubb
Quick! Run and smurf her out of there!
Me? Why me?
Because you swim better than me!
Yes, but I just ate!
Forget it! I'll go!
BLUB BLUB BLUB
You're not looking so good! It'd be better if you smurfed back to the village!
Yes!
But I feel so weak! I could never walk all the way there!
Careful, there's a curve! Slow down! Make sure nobody's coming in the opposite direction! Not so fast, we could have an accident!
And life goes on...
Just wait and see the pretty sweater I'm going to knit for you!
Hey, since you're going to the river, could you bring me back three big, ripe apples, a dozen poppies, a little bee honey... Oh! I was forgetting... And a big pail of water! You won't forget?
!
GUESS WHO?!
This can't keep smurfing on! Something's got to be done!
Hey, Jokey Smurf, you don't have any ideas for a good trick to play on her so she'll finally smurf us some peace?
Yes, I do! Smurf closely to me! Here's what we're going to do...
16
Peyo

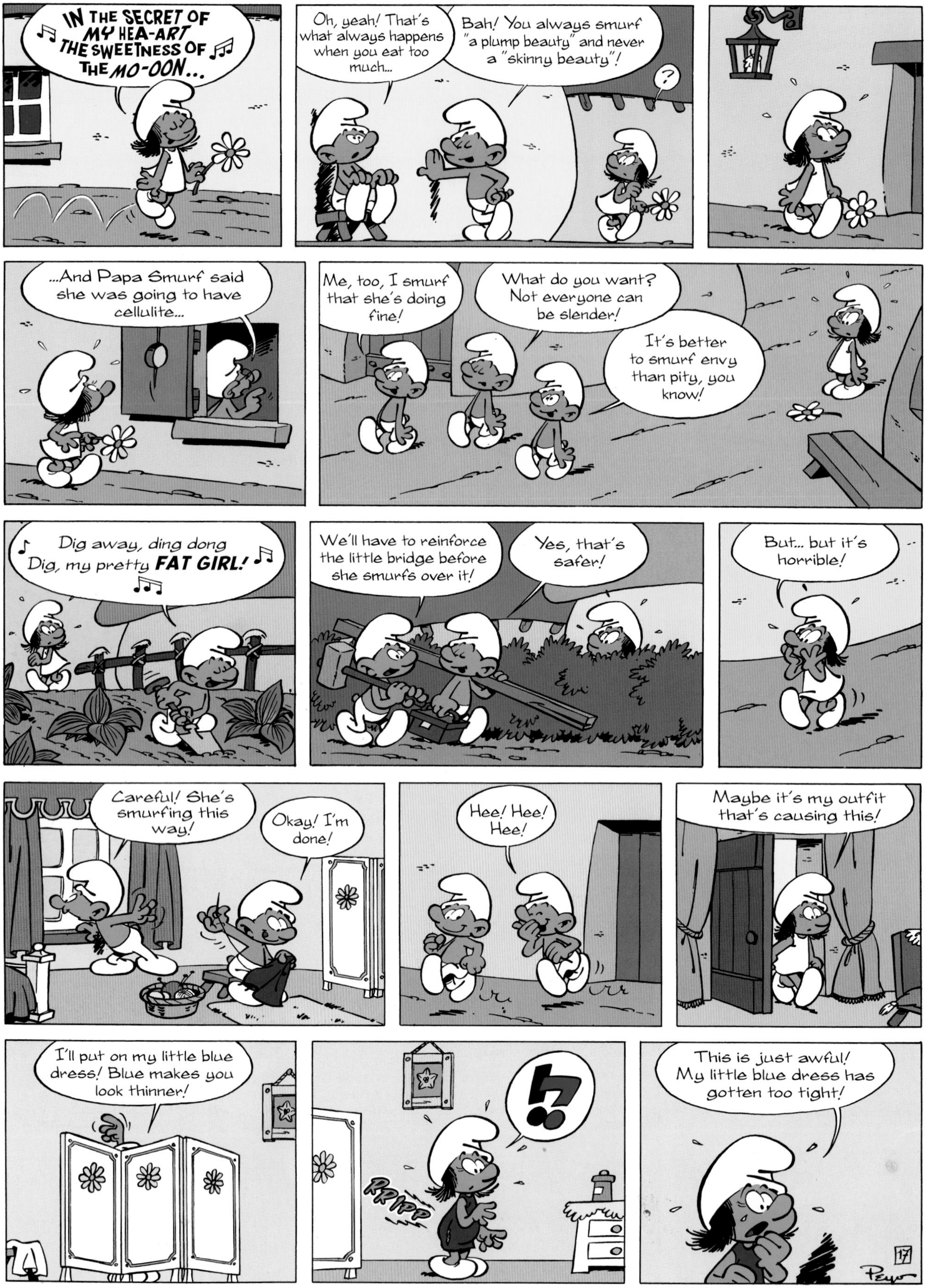
IN THE SECRET OF MY HEA-ART THE SWEETNESS OF THE MO-OON...
Oh, yeah! That's what always happens when you eat too much...
Bah! You always smurf "a plump beauty" and never a "skinny beauty"!
?
...And Papa Smurf said she was going to have cellulite...
Me, too, I smurf that she's doing fine!
What do you want? Not everyone can be slender!
It's better to smurf envy than pity, you know!
Dig away, ding dong Dig, my pretty FAT GIRL!
We'll have to reinforce the little bridge before she smurfs over it!
Yes, that's safer!
But... but it's horrible!
Careful! She's smurfing this way!
Okay! I'm done!
Hee! Hee! Hee!
Maybe it's my outfit that's causing this!
I'll put on my little blue dress! Blue makes you look thinner!
RRIPP
This is just awful! My little blue dress has gotten too tight!
17
Peyo

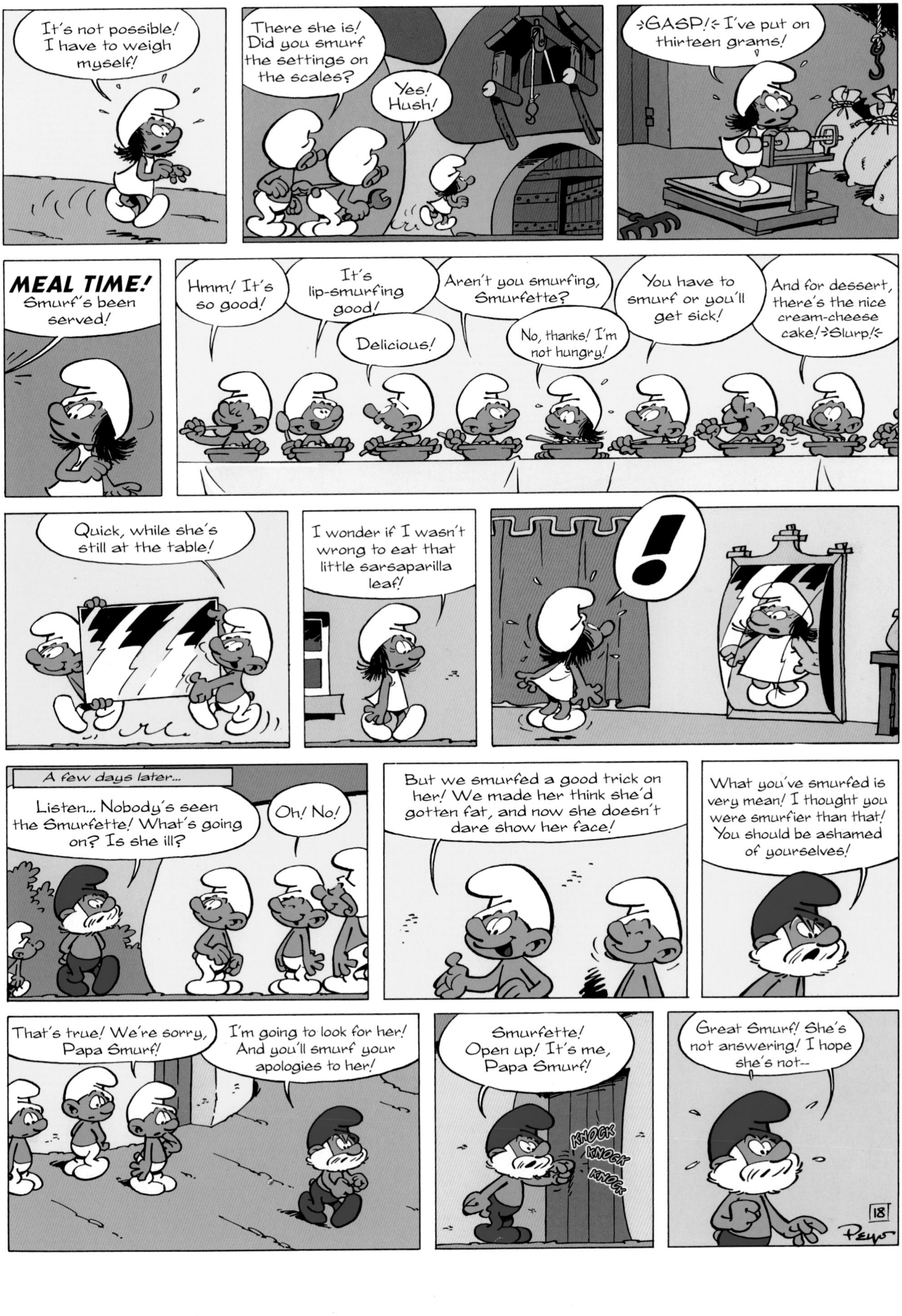

It's not possible! I have to weigh myself!
There she is! Did you smurf the settings on the scales?
Yes! Hush!
GASP! I've put on thirteen grams!
MEAL TIME! Smurf's been served!
Hmm! It's so good!
It's lip-smurfing good!
Delicious!
Aren't you smurfing, Smurfette?
No, thanks! I'm not hungry!
You have to smurf or you'll get sick!
And for dessert, there's the nice cream-cheese cake! Slurp!
Quick, while she's still at the table!
I wonder if I wasn't wrong to eat that little sarsaparilla leaf!
!
A few days later...
Listen... Nobody's seen the Smurfette! What's going on? Is she ill?
Oh! No!
But we smurfed a good trick on her! We made her think she'd gotten fat, and now she doesn't dare show her face!
What you've smurfed is very mean! I thought you were smurfier than that! You should be ashamed of yourselves!
That's true! We're sorry, Papa Smurf!
I'm going to look for her! And you'll smurf your apologies to her!
Smurfette! Open up! It's me, Papa Smurf!
KNOCK KNOCK KNOCK
Great Smurf! She's not answering! I hope she's not--
18
Peyo

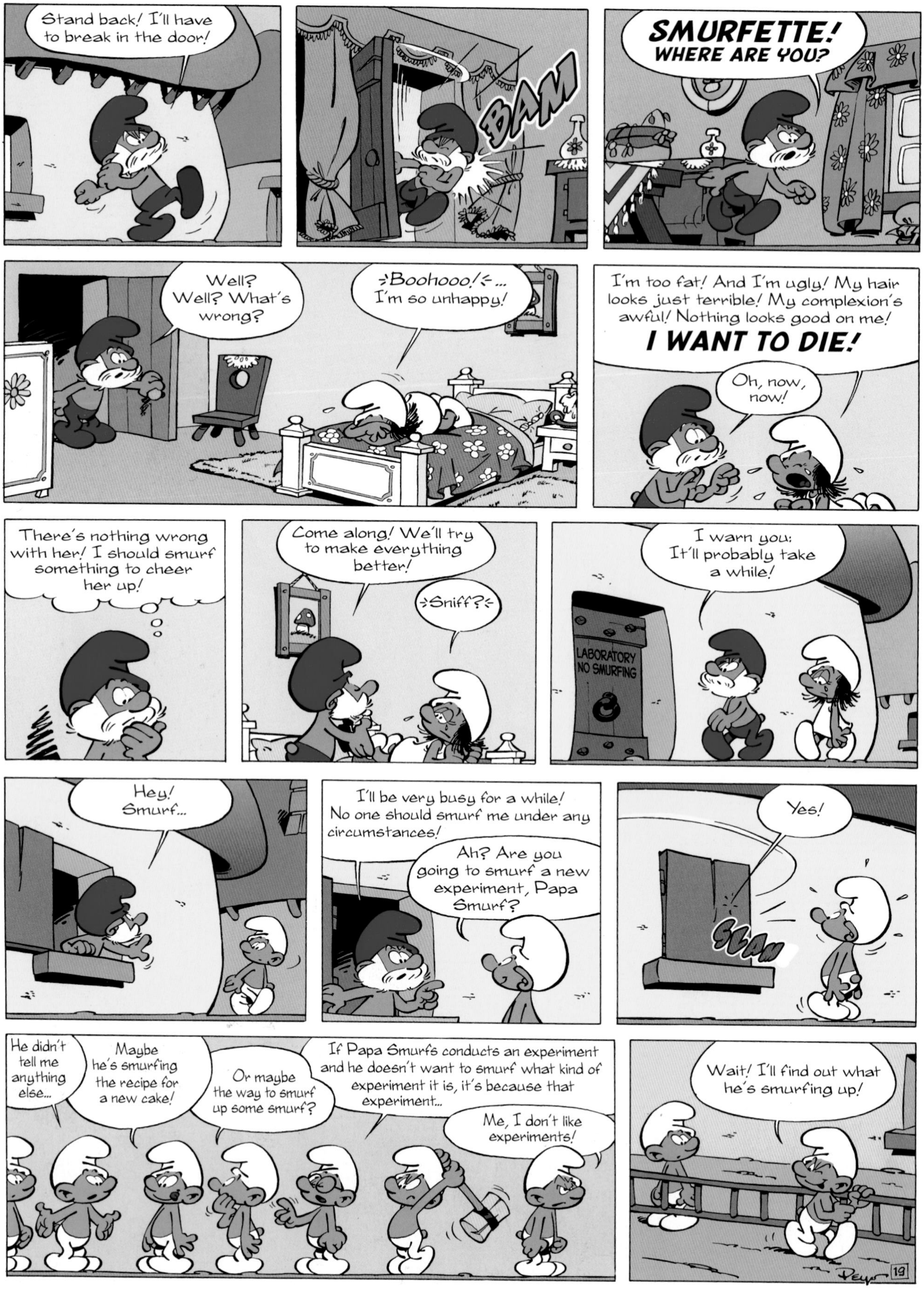

Stand back! I'll have to break in the door!
BAM
SMURFETTE! WHERE ARE YOU?
Well? Well? What's wrong?
Boohooo! ... I'm so unhappy!
I'm too fat! And I'm ugly! My hair looks just terrible! My complexion's awful! Nothing looks good on me! I WANT TO DIE!
Oh, now, now!
There's nothing wrong with her! I should smurf something to cheer her up!
Come along! We'll try to make everything better!
Sniff?
I warn you: It'll probably take a while!
LABORATORY NO SMURFING
Hey! Smurf...
I'll be very busy for a while! No one should smurf me under any circumstances!
Ah? Are you going to smurf a new experiment, Papa Smurf?
Yes!
SLAM
He didn't tell me anything else...
Maybe he's smurfing the recipe for a new cake!
Or maybe the way to smurf up some smurf?
If Papa Smurfs conducts an experiment and he doesn't want to smurf what kind of experiment it is, it's because that experiment...
Me, I don't like experiments!
Wait! I'll find out what he's smurfing up!
19

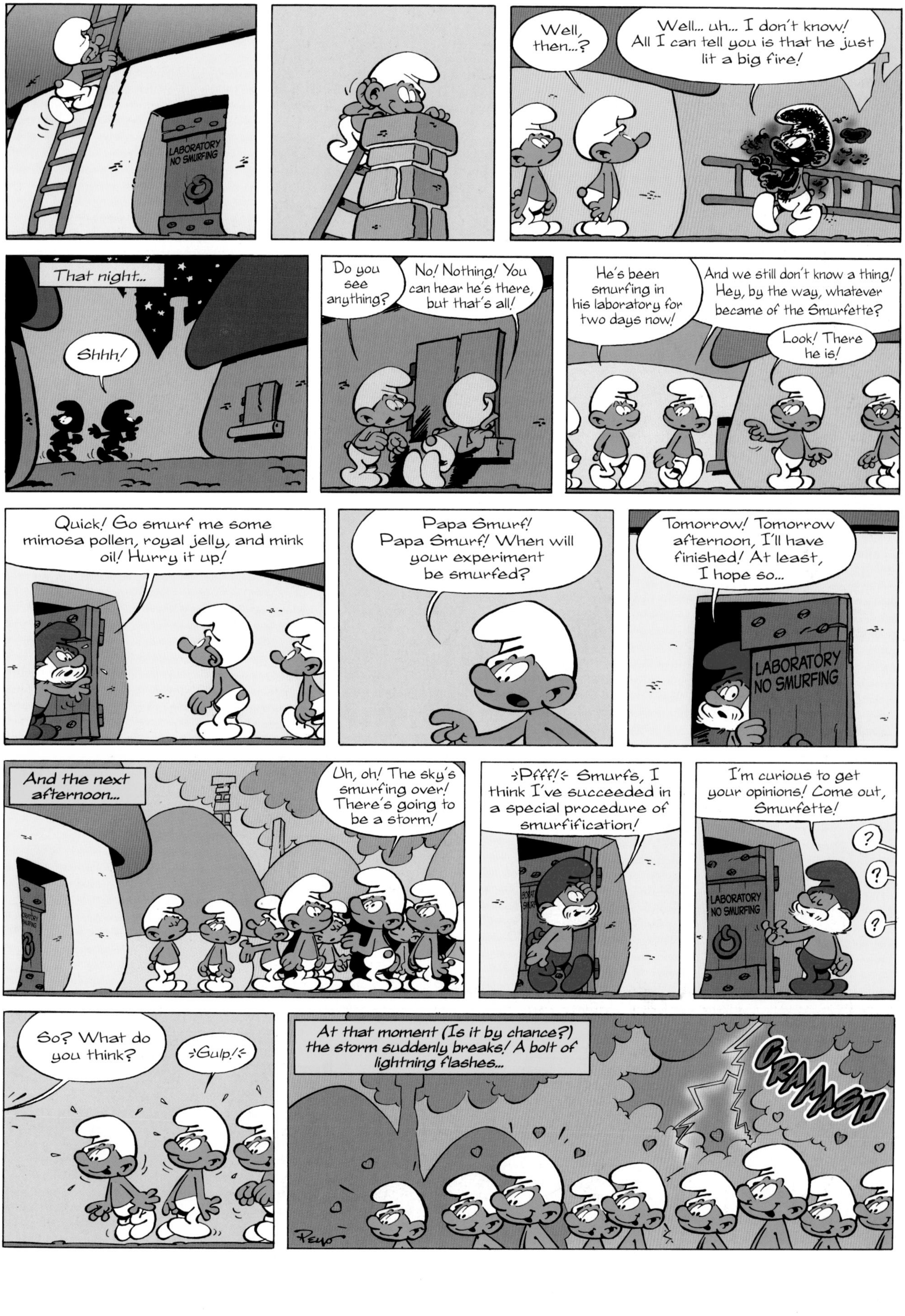
LABORATORY NO SMURFING
Well, then...?
Well... uh... I don't know! All I can tell you is that he just lit a big fire!
That night...
Shhh!
Do you see anything?
No! Nothing! You can hear he's there, but that's all!
He's been smurfing in his laboratory for two days now!
And we still don't know a thing! Hey, by the way, whatever became of the Smurfette?
Look! There he is!
Quick! Go smurf me some mimosa pollen, royal jelly, and mink oil! Hurry it up!
Papa Smurf! Papa Smurf! When will your experiment be smurfed?
Tomorrow! Tomorrow afternoon, I'll have finished! At least, I hope so...
LABORATORY NO SMURFING
And the next afternoon...
Uh, oh! The sky's smurfing over! There's going to be a storm!
Pfff! Smurfs, I think I've succeeded in a special procedure of smurfification!
I'm curious to get your opinions! Come out, Smurfette!
LABORATORY NO SMURFING
?
?
?
So? What do you think?
Gulp!
At that moment (Is it by chance?) the storm suddenly breaks! A bolt of lightning flashes...
CRAAAASH

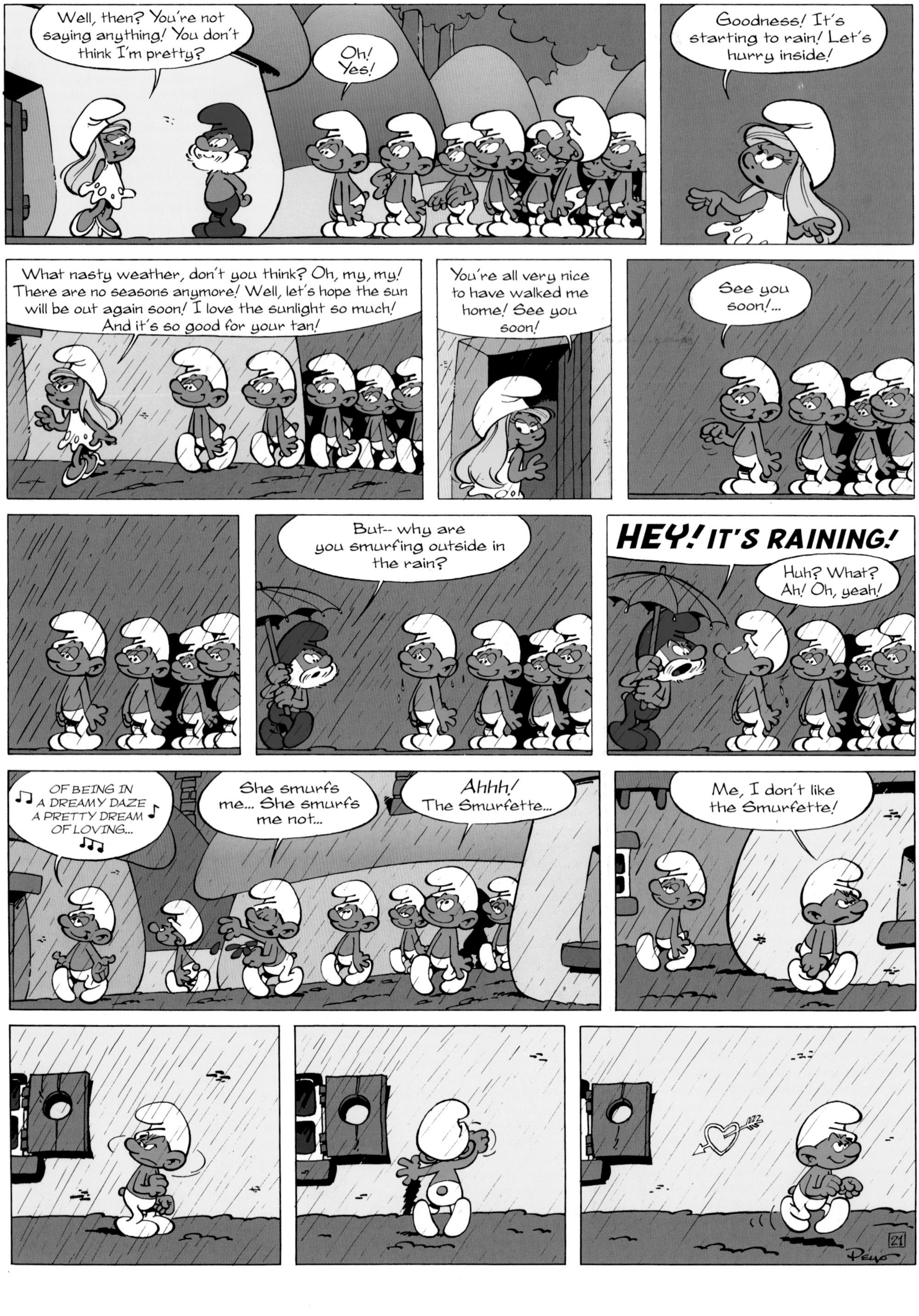

Well, then? You're not saying anything! You don't think I'm pretty?
Oh! Yes!
Goodness! It's starting to rain! Let's hurry inside!
What nasty weather, don't you think? Oh, my, my! There are no seasons anymore! Well, let's hope the sun will be out again soon! I love the sunlight so much! And it's so good for your tan!
You're all very nice to have walked me home! See you soon!
See you soon!...
But-- why are you smurfing outside in the rain?
HEY! IT'S RAINING!
Huh? What? Ah! Oh, yeah!
OF BEING IN A DREAMY DAZE A PRETTY DREAM OF LOVING...
She smurfs me... She smurfs me not...
Ahhh! The Smurfette...
Me, I don't like the Smurfette!
21

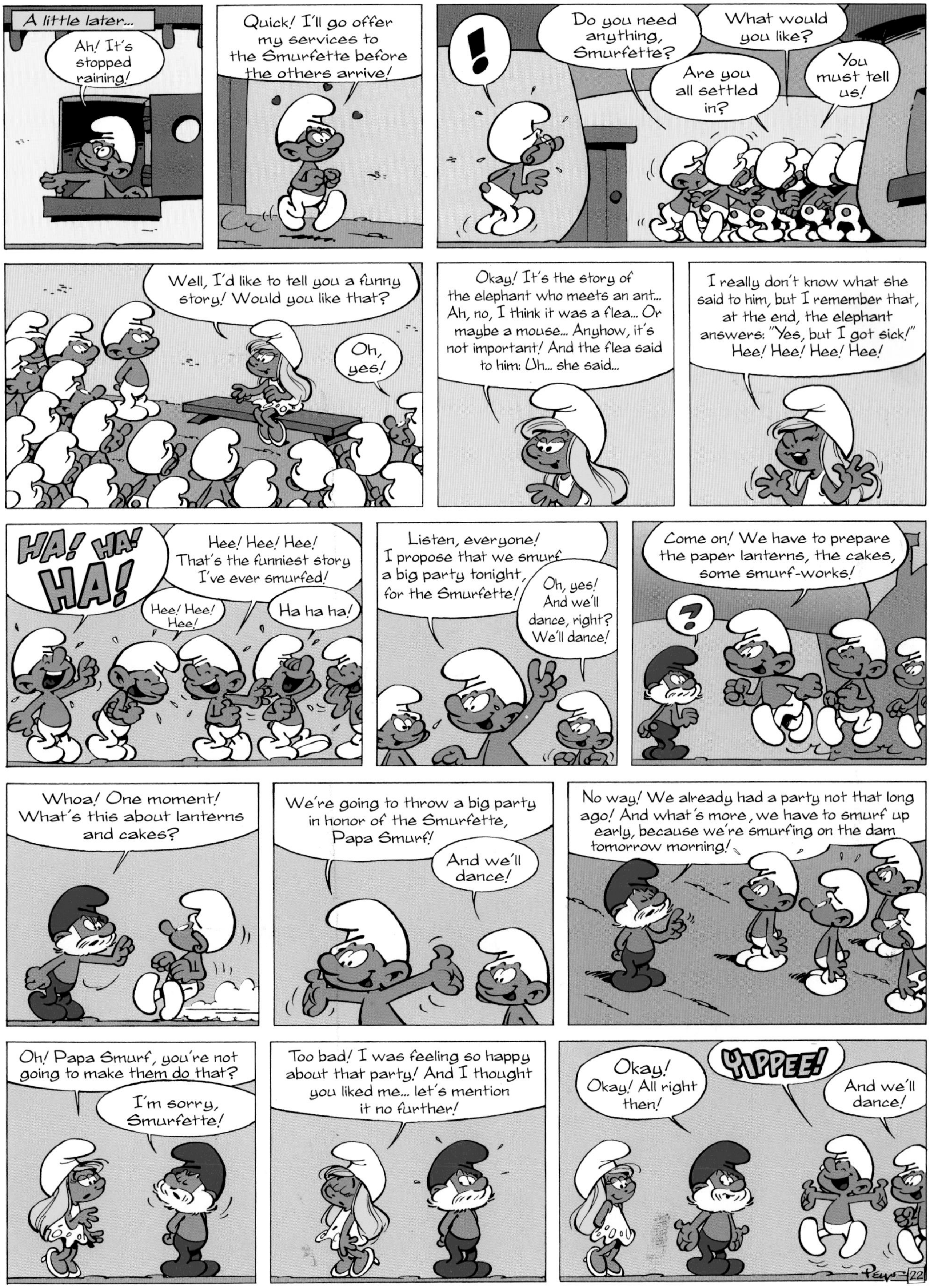
A little later...
Ah! It's stopped raining!
Quick! I'll go offer my services to the Smurfette before the others arrive!
!
Do you need anything, Smurfette?
What would you like?
Are you all settled in?
You must tell us!
Well, I'd like to tell you a funny story! Would you like that?
Oh, yes!
Okay! It's the story of the elephant who meets an ant... Ah, no, I think it was a flea... Or maybe a mouse... Anyhow, it's not important! And the flea said to him: Uh... she said...
I really don't know what she said to him, but I remember that, at the end, the elephant answers: "Yes, but I got sick!" Hee! Hee! Hee! Hee!
HA! HA! HA!
Hee! Hee! Hee! That's the funniest story I've ever smurfed!
Hee! Hee! Hee!
Ha ha ha!
Listen, everyone! I propose that we smurf a big party tonight, for the Smurfette!
Oh, yes! And we'll dance, right? We'll dance!
Come on! We have to prepare the paper lanterns, the cakes, some smurf-works!
?
Whoa! One moment! What's this about lanterns and cakes?
We're going to throw a big party in honor of the Smurfette, Papa Smurf!
And we'll dance!
No way! We already had a party not that long ago! And what's more, we have to smurf up early, because we're smurfing on the dam tomorrow morning!
Oh! Papa Smurf, you're not going to make them do that?
I'm sorry, Smurfette!
Too bad! I was feeling so happy about that party! And I thought you liked me... let's mention it no further!
Okay! Okay! All right then!
YIPPEE!
And we'll dance!
22

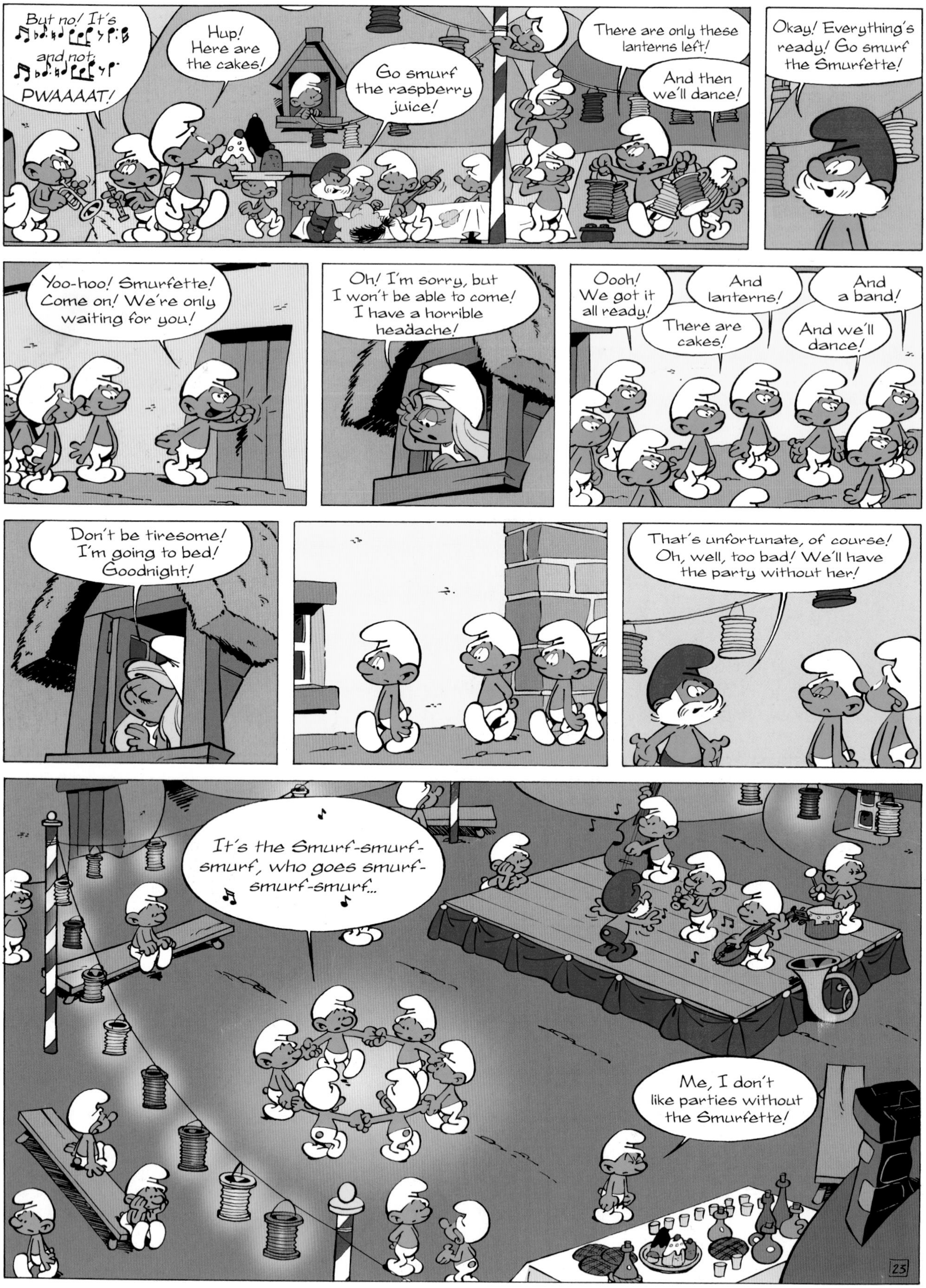
But no! It's
and not
PWAAAAT!
Hup! Here are the cakes!
Go smurf the raspberry juice!
There are only these lanterns left!
And then we'll dance!
Okay! Everything's ready! Go smurf the Smurfette!
Yoo-hoo! Smurfette! Come on! We're only waiting for you!
Oh! I'm sorry, but I won't be able to come! I have a horrible headache!
Oooh! We got it all ready!
And lanterns!
And a band!
There are cakes!
And we'll dance!
Don't be tiresome! I'm going to bed! Goodnight!
That's unfortunate, of course! Oh, well, too bad! We'll have the party without her!
It's the Smurf-smurf-smurf, who goes smurf-smurf-smurf...
Me, I don't like parties without the Smurfette!
23

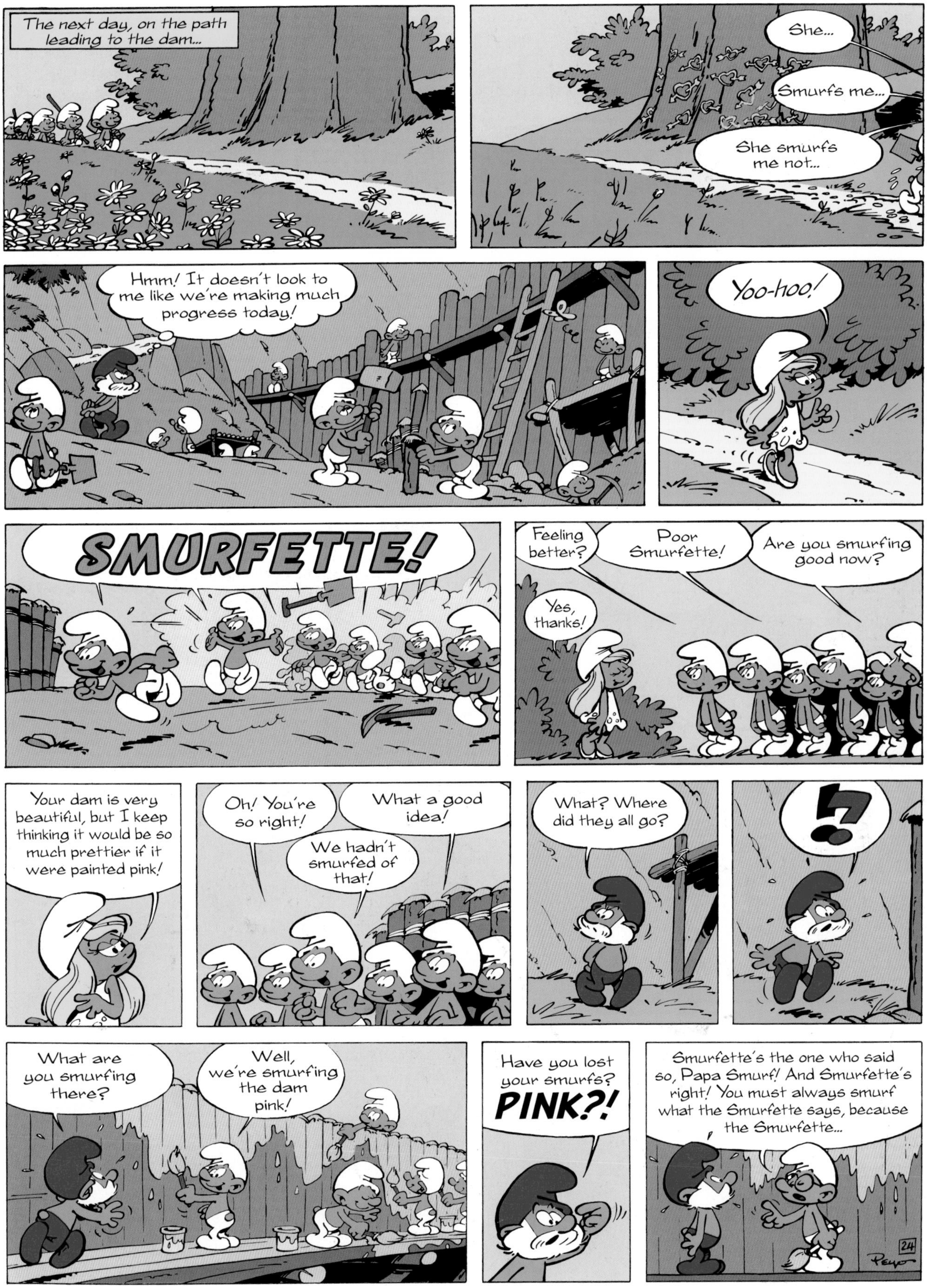
The next day, on the path leading to the dam...
She...
Smurfs me...
She smurfs me not...
Hmm! It doesn't look to me like we're making much progress today!
Yoo-hoo!
SMURFETTE!
Feeling better?
Poor Smurfette!
Are you smurfing good now?
Yes, thanks!
Your dam is very beautiful, but I keep thinking it would be so much prettier if it were painted pink!
Oh! You're so right!
What a good idea!
We hadn't smurfed of that!
What? Where did they all go?
?!
What are you smurfing there?
Well, we're smurfing the dam pink!
Have you lost your smurfs? PINK?!
Smurfette's the one who said so, Papa Smurf! And Smurfette's right! You must always smurf what the Smurfette says, because the Smurfette...
24
Peyo

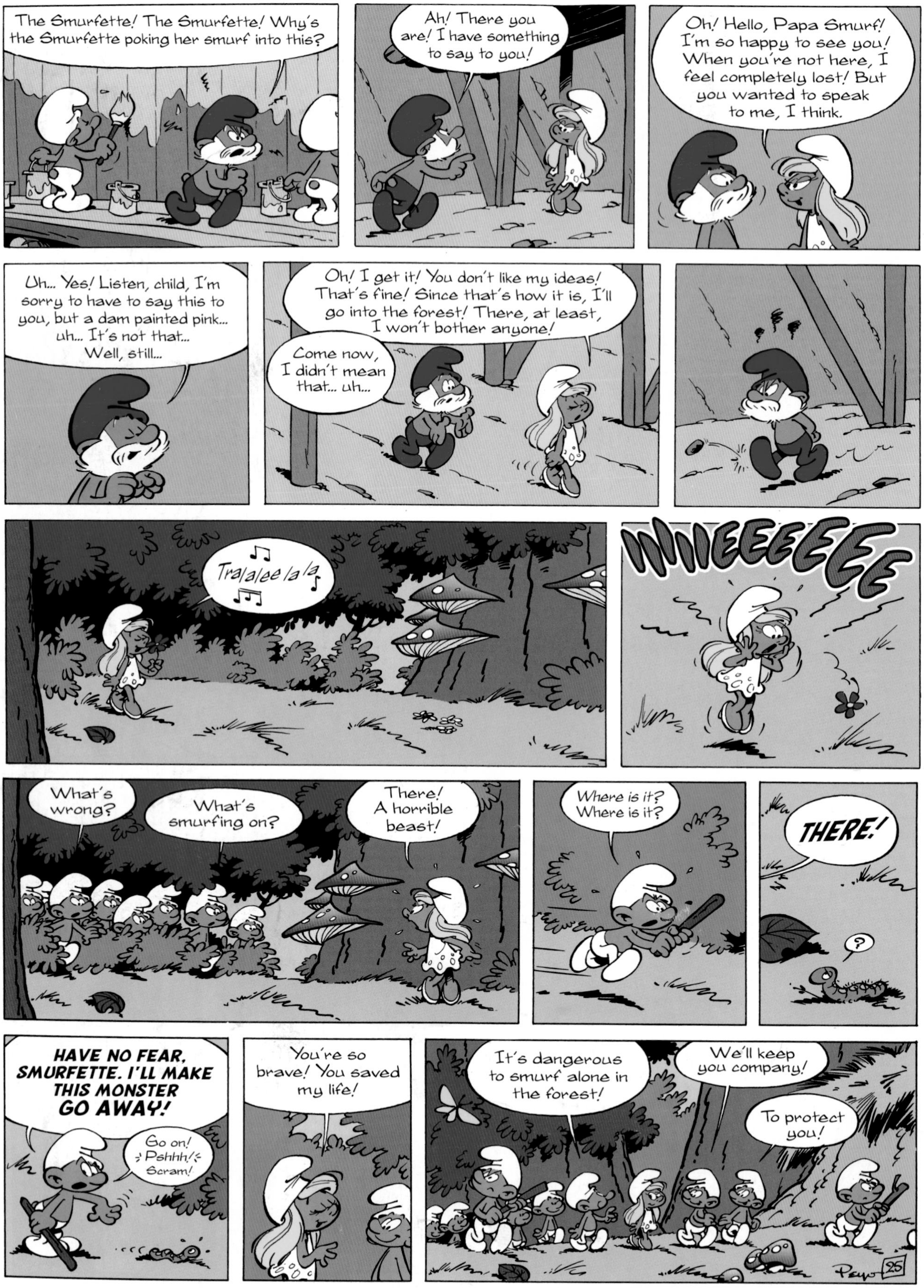
The Smurfette! The Smurfette! Why's the Smurfette poking her smurf into this?
Ah! There you are! I have something to say to you!
Oh! Hello, Papa Smurf! I'm so happy to see you! When you're not here, I feel completely lost! But you wanted to speak to me, I think.
Uh... Yes! Listen, child, I'm sorry to have to say this to you, but a dam painted pink... uh... It's not that... Well, still...
Oh! I get it! You don't like my ideas! That's fine! Since that's how it is, I'll go into the forest! There, at least, I won't bother anyone!
Come now, I didn't mean that... uh...
Tralalee lala
WIIIEEEEEEE
What's wrong?
What's smurfing on?
There! A horrible beast!
Where is it? Where is it?
THERE!
HAVE NO FEAR, SMURFETTE. I'LL MAKE THIS MONSTER GO AWAY!
Go on! Pshhh! Scram!
You're so brave! You saved my life!
It's dangerous to smurf alone in the forest!
We'll keep you company!
To protect you!
Peyo
25

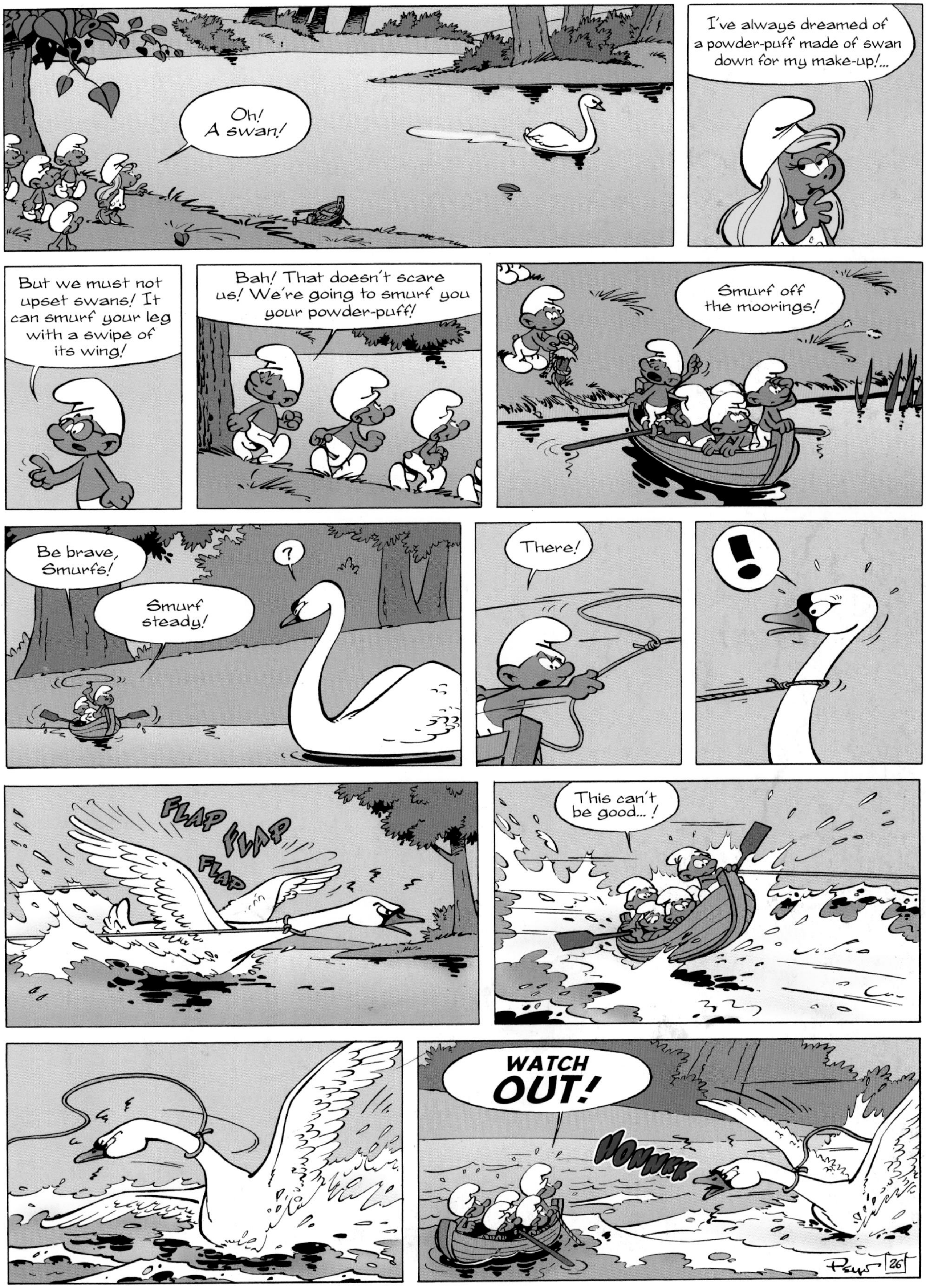
Oh! A swan!
I've always dreamed of a powder-puff made of swan down for my make-up!...
But we must not upset swans! It can smurf your leg with a swipe of its wing!
Bah! That doesn't scare us! We're going to smurf you your powder-puff!
Smurf off the moorings!
Be brave, Smurfs!
Smurf steady!
?
There!
!
FLAP FLAP FLAP
This can't be good... !
WATCH OUT!
HONNKK
26

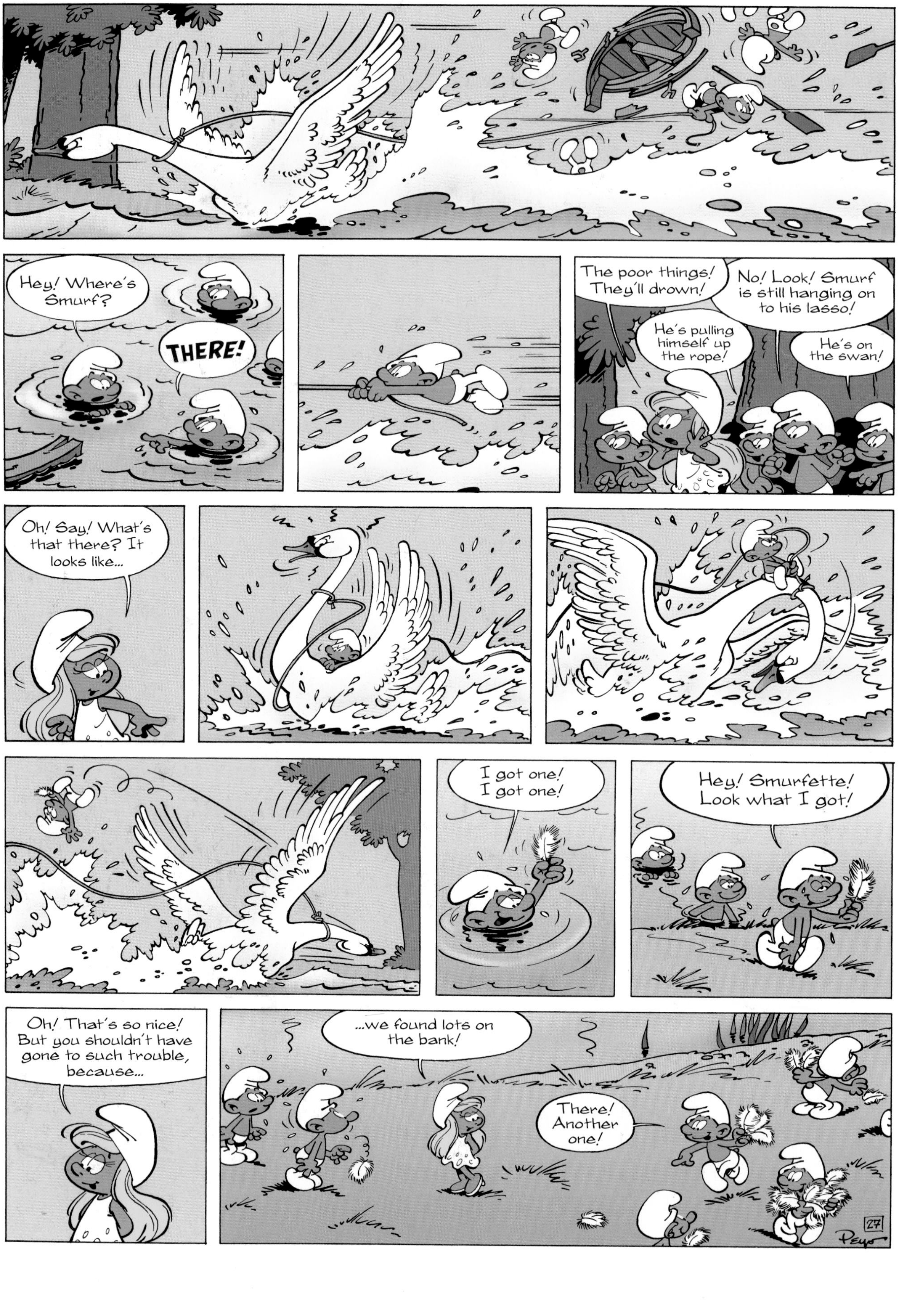
Hey! Where's Smurf?
THERE!
The poor things! They'll drown!
No! Look! Smurf is still hanging on to his lasso!
He's pulling himself up the rope!
He's on the swan!
Oh! Say! What's that there? It looks like...
I got one! I got one!
Hey! Smurfette! Look what I got!
Oh! That's so nice! But you shouldn't have gone to such trouble, because...
...we found lots on the bank!
There! Another one!
27
Peyo

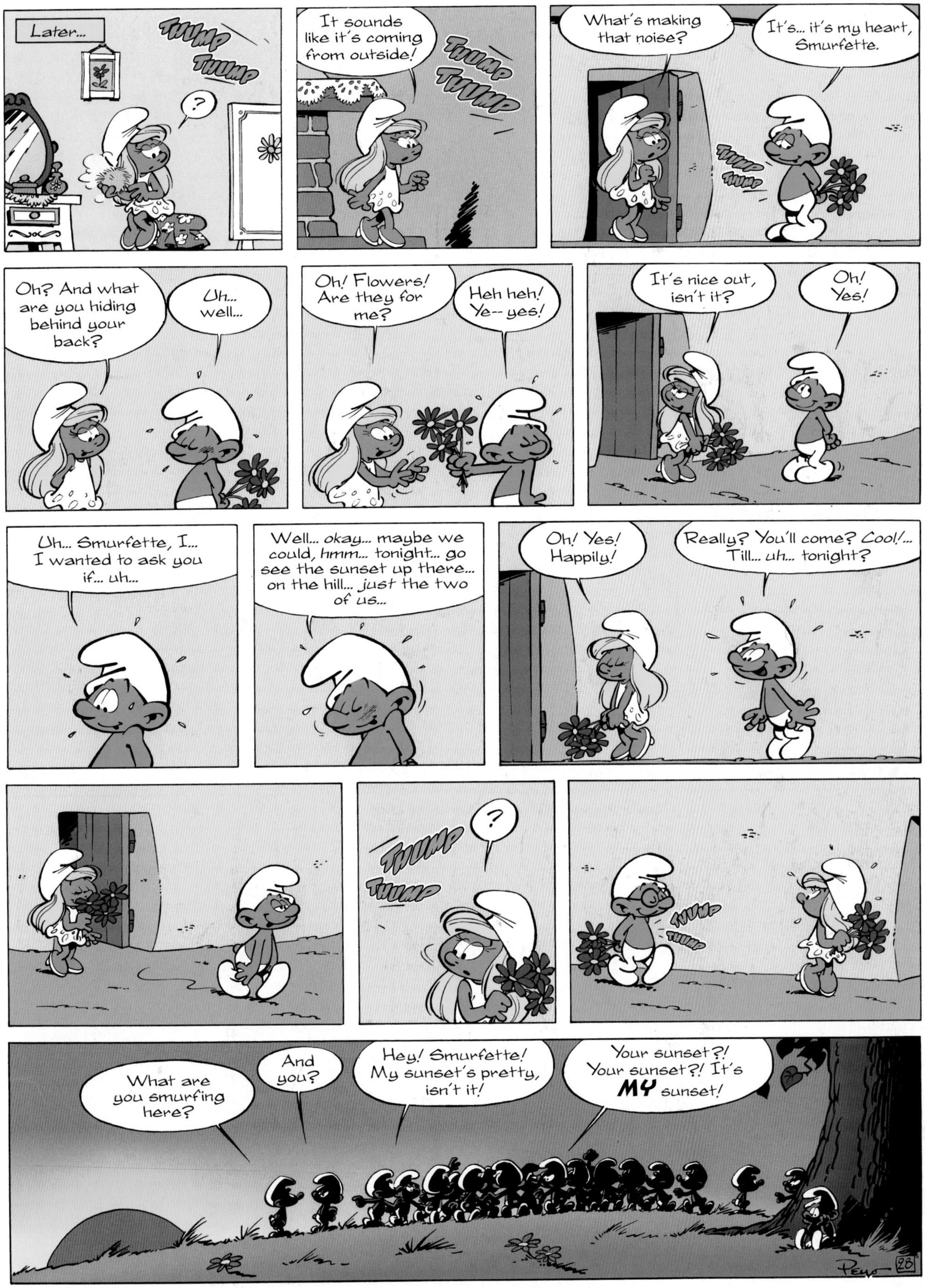
Later...
THUMP THUMP
?
It sounds like it's coming from outside!
THUMP THUMP
What's making that noise?
It's... it's my heart, Smurfette.
THUMP THUMP
Oh? And what are you hiding behind your back?
Uh... well...
Oh! Flowers! Are they for me?
Heh heh! Ye-- yes!
It's nice out, isn't it?
Oh! Yes!
Uh... Smurfette, I... I wanted to ask you if... uh...
Well... okay... maybe we could, hmm... tonight... go see the sunset up there... on the hill... just the two of us...
Oh! Yes! Happily!
Really? You'll come? Cool!... Till... uh... tonight?
THUMP THUMP
?
THUMP THUMP
What are you smurfing here?
And you?
Hey! Smurfette! My sunset's pretty, isn't it!
Your sunset?! Your sunset?! It's MY sunset!
Peyo 28

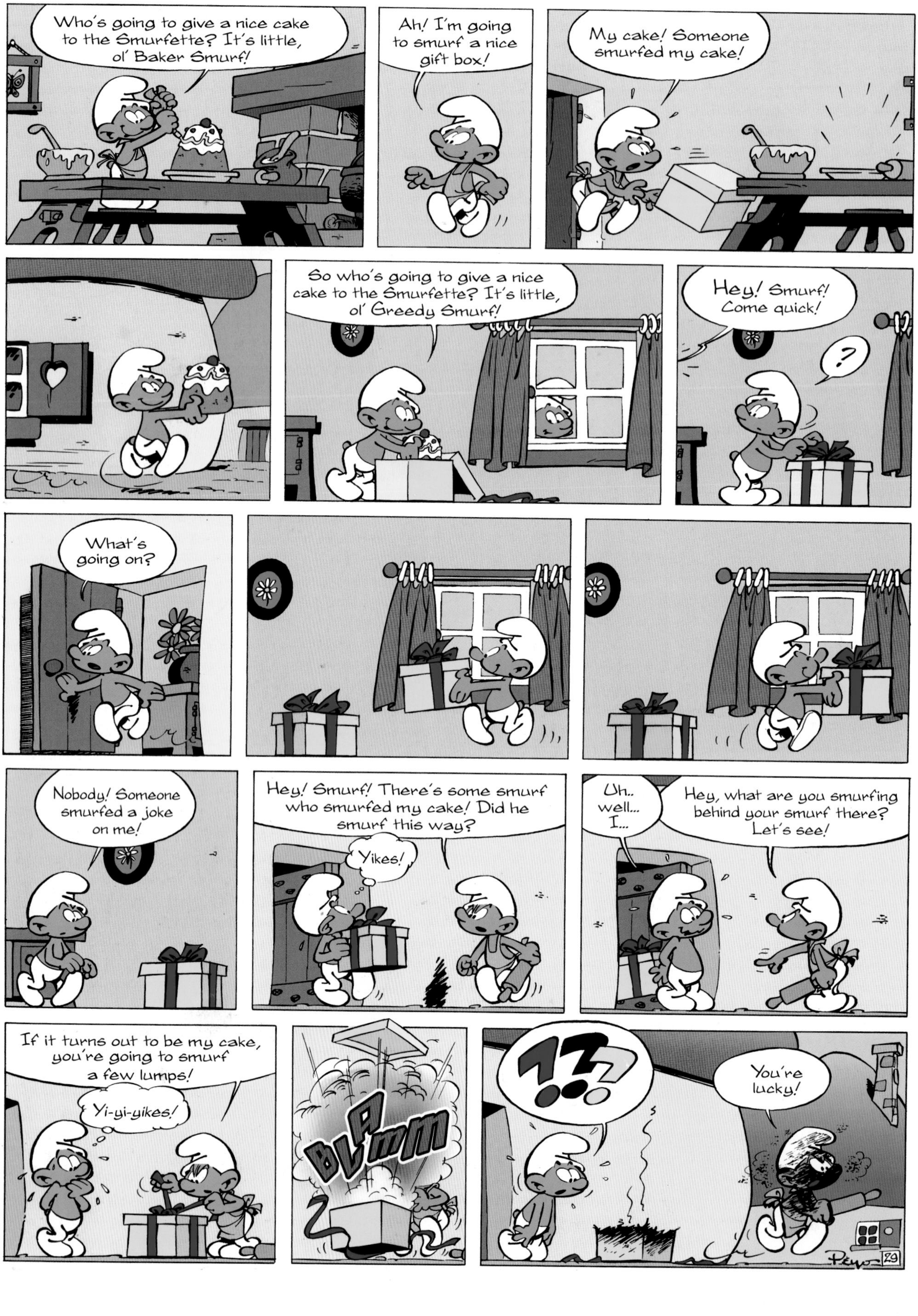
Who's going to give a nice cake to the Smurfette? It's little, ol' Baker Smurf!
Ah! I'm going to smurf a nice gift box!
My cake! Someone smurfed my cake!
So who's going to give a nice cake to the Smurfette? It's little, ol' Greedy Smurf!
Hey! Smurf! Come quick!
?
What's going on?
Nobody! Someone smurfed a joke on me!
Hey! Smurf! There's some smurf who smurfed my cake! Did he smurf this way?
Yikes!
Uh.. well... I...
Hey, what are you smurfing behind your smurf there? Let's see!
If it turns out to be my cake, you're going to smurf a few lumps!
Yi-yi-yikes!
BLAMM
?!?
You're lucky!
Peyo
29

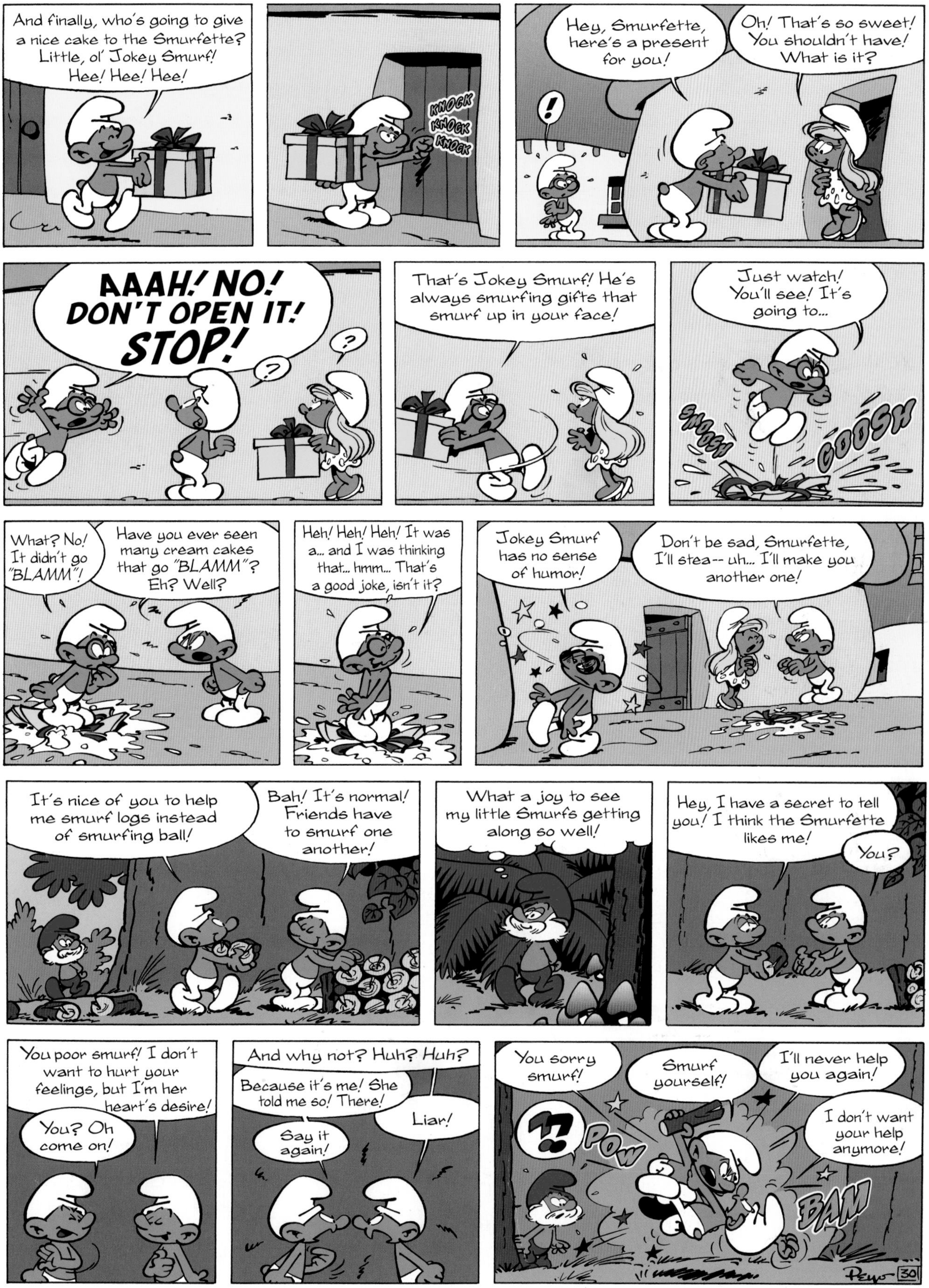
And finally, who's going to give a nice cake to the Smurfette? Little, ol' Jokey Smurf! Hee! Hee! Hee!
KNOCK KNOCK KNOCK
Hey, Smurfette, here's a present for you!
Oh! That's so sweet! You shouldn't have! What is it?
!
AAAH! NO! DON'T OPEN IT! STOP!
?
?
That's Jokey Smurf! He's always smurfing gifts that smurf up in your face!
Just watch! You'll see! It's going to...
SPLOOSH
COOSH
What? No! It didn't go "BLAMM"!
Have you ever seen many cream cakes that go "BLAMM"? Eh? Well?
Heh! Heh! Heh! It was a... and I was thinking that... hmm... That's a good joke, isn't it?
Jokey Smurf has no sense of humor!
Don't be sad, Smurfette, I'll stea-- uh... I'll make you another one!
It's nice of you to help me smurf logs instead of smurfing ball!
Bah! It's normal! Friends have to smurf one another!
What a joy to see my little Smurfs getting along so well!
Hey, I have a secret to tell you! I think the Smurfette likes me!
You?
You poor smurf! I don't want to hurt your feelings, but I'm her heart's desire!
You? Oh come on!
And why not? Huh? Huh?
Because it's me! She told me so! There!
Liar!
Say it again!
You sorry smurf!
Smurf yourself!
I'll never help you again!
I don't want your help anymore!
POW
BAM
Peyo
30

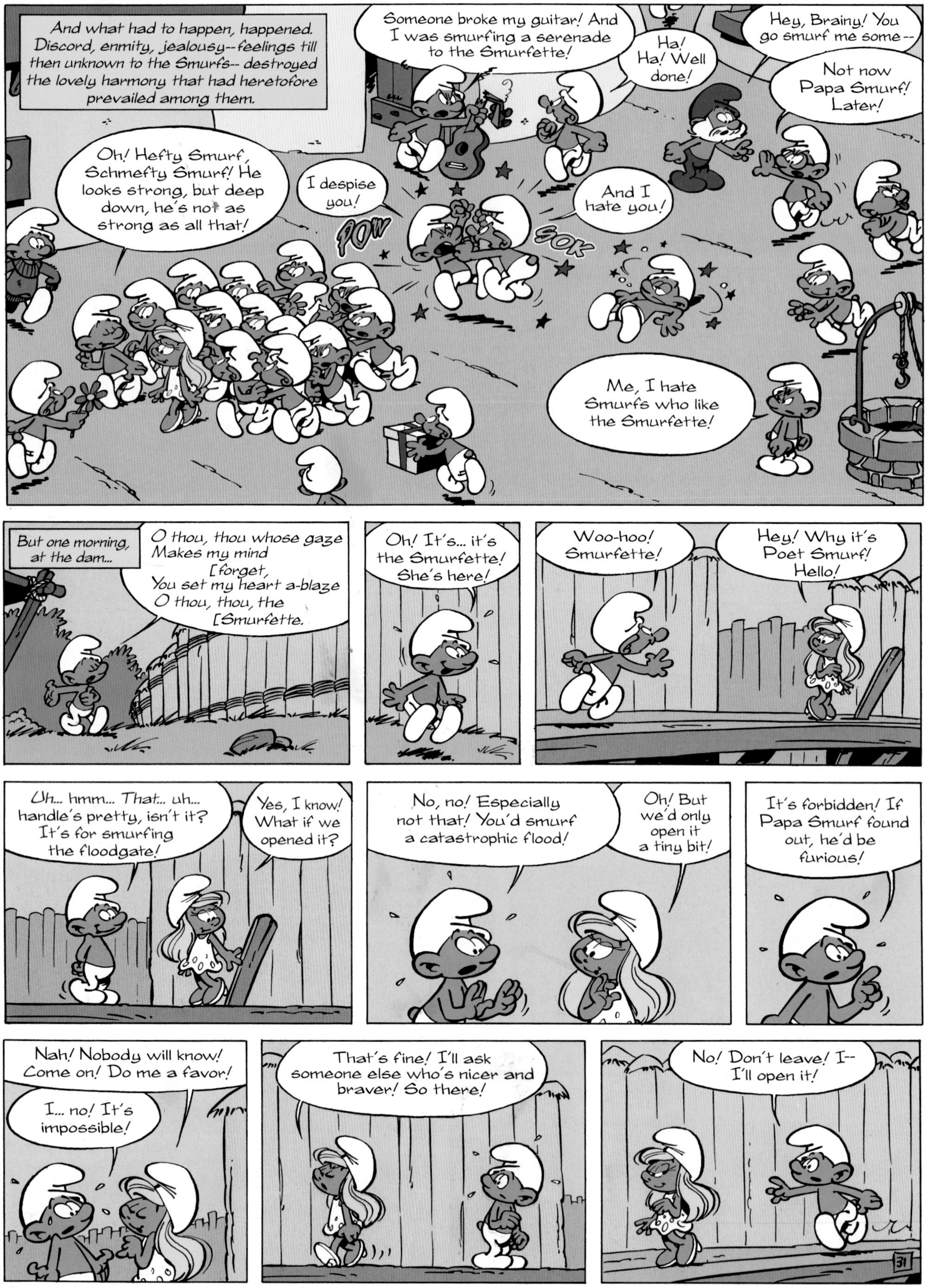
And what had to happen, happened. Discord, enmity, jealousy--feelings till then unknown to the Smurfs-- destroyed the lovely harmony that had heretofore prevailed among them.
Someone broke my guitar! And I was smurfing a serenade to the Smurfette!
Ha! Ha! Well done!
Hey, Brainy! You go smurf me some--
Not now Papa Smurf! Later!
Oh! Hefty Smurf, Schmefty Smurf! He looks strong, but deep down, he's not as strong as all that!
I despise you!
POW
And I hate you!
SOK
Me, I hate Smurfs who like the Smurfette!
But one morning, at the dam...
O thou, thou whose gaze Makes my mind [forget, You set my heart a-blaze O thou, thou, the [Smurfette.
Oh! It's... it's the Smurfette! She's here!
Woo-hoo! Smurfette!
Hey! Why it's Poet Smurf! Hello!
Uh... hmm... That... uh... handle's pretty, isn't it? It's for smurfing the floodgate!
Yes, I know! What if we opened it?
No, no! Especially not that! You'd smurf a catastrophic flood!
Oh! But we'd only open it a tiny bit!
It's forbidden! If Papa Smurf found out, he'd be furious!
Nah! Nobody will know! Come on! Do me a favor!
I... no! It's impossible!
That's fine! I'll ask someone else who's nicer and braver! So there!
No! Don't leave! I-- I'll open it!
31

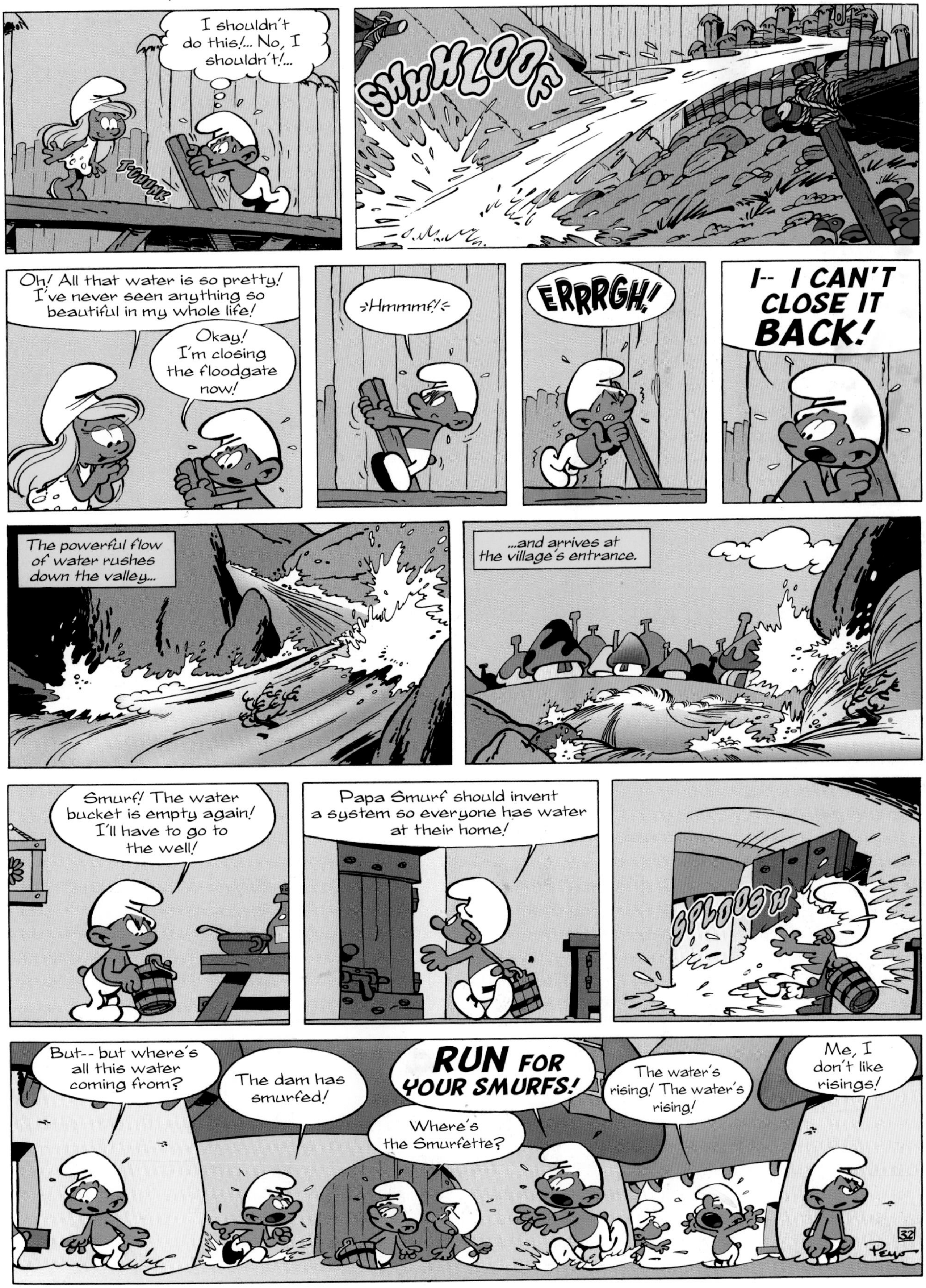
I shouldn't do this!... No, I shouldn't!...
T-CHUNK
SHHHLOOF
Oh! All that water is so pretty! I've never seen anything so beautiful in my whole life!
Okay! I'm closing the floodgate now!
Hmmmf!
ERRRGH!
I-- I CAN'T CLOSE IT BACK!
The powerful flow of water rushes down the valley...
...and arrives at the village's entrance.
Smurf! The water bucket is empty again! I'll have to go to the well!
Papa Smurf should invent a system so everyone has water at their home!
SPLOOSH
But-- but where's all this water coming from?
The dam has smurfed!
RUN FOR YOUR SMURFS!
Where's the Smurfette?
The water's rising! The water's rising!
Me, I don't like risings!
32
Peyo

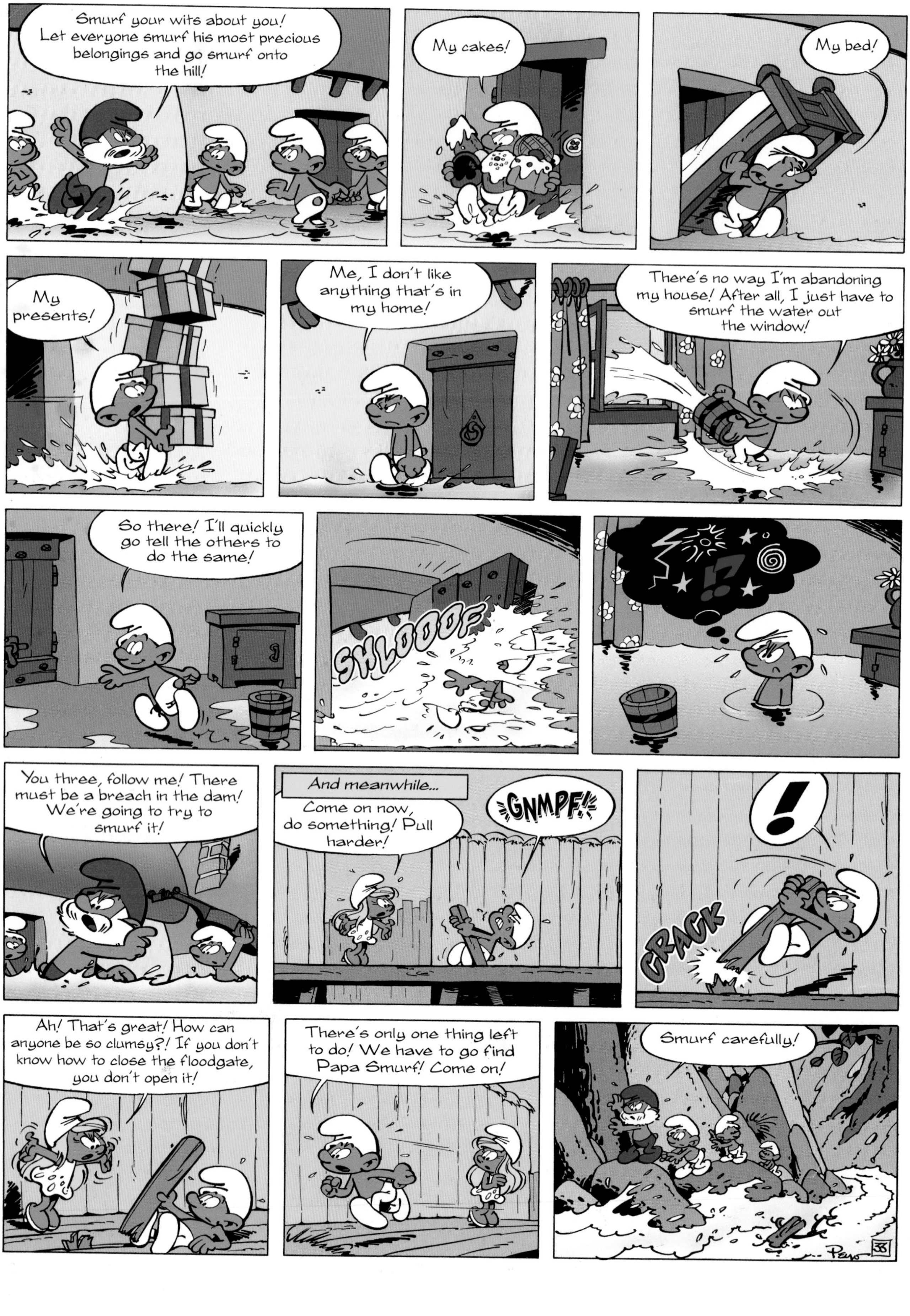
Smurf your wits about you! Let everyone smurf his most precious belongings and go smurf onto the hill!
My cakes!
My bed!
My presents!
Me, I don't like anything that's in my home!
There's no way I'm abandoning my house! After all, I just have to smurf the water out the window!
So there! I'll quickly go tell the others to do the same!
SHLOOOF
You three, follow me! There must be a breach in the dam! We're going to try to smurf it!
And meanwhile...
Come on now, do something! Pull harder!
GNMPF!
!
CRACK
Ah! That's great! How can anyone be so clumsy?! If you don't know how to close the floodgate, you don't open it!
There's only one thing left to do! We have to go find Papa Smurf! Come on!
Smurf carefully!
Peyo
38

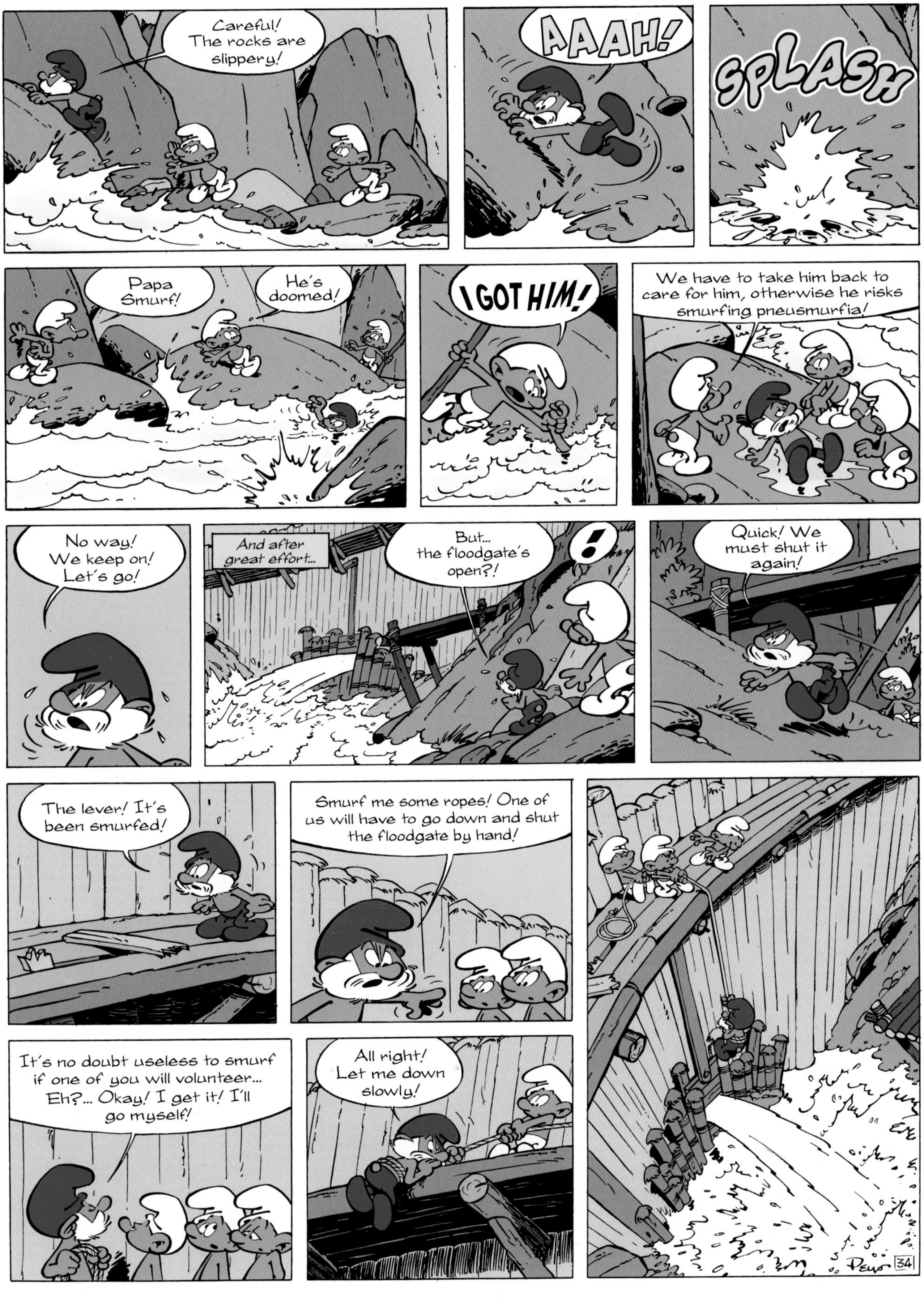
Careful! The rocks are slippery!
AAAH!
SPLASH
Papa Smurf!
He's doomed!
I GOT HIM!
We have to take him back to care for him, otherwise he risks smurfing pneusmurfia!
No way! We keep on! Let's go!
And after great effort...
But... the floodgate's open?!
!
Quick! We must shut it again!
The lever! It's been smurfed!
Smurf me some ropes! One of us will have to go down and shut the floodgate by hand!
It's no doubt useless to smurf if one of you will volunteer... Eh?... Okay! I get it! I'll go myself!
All right! Let me down slowly!
34

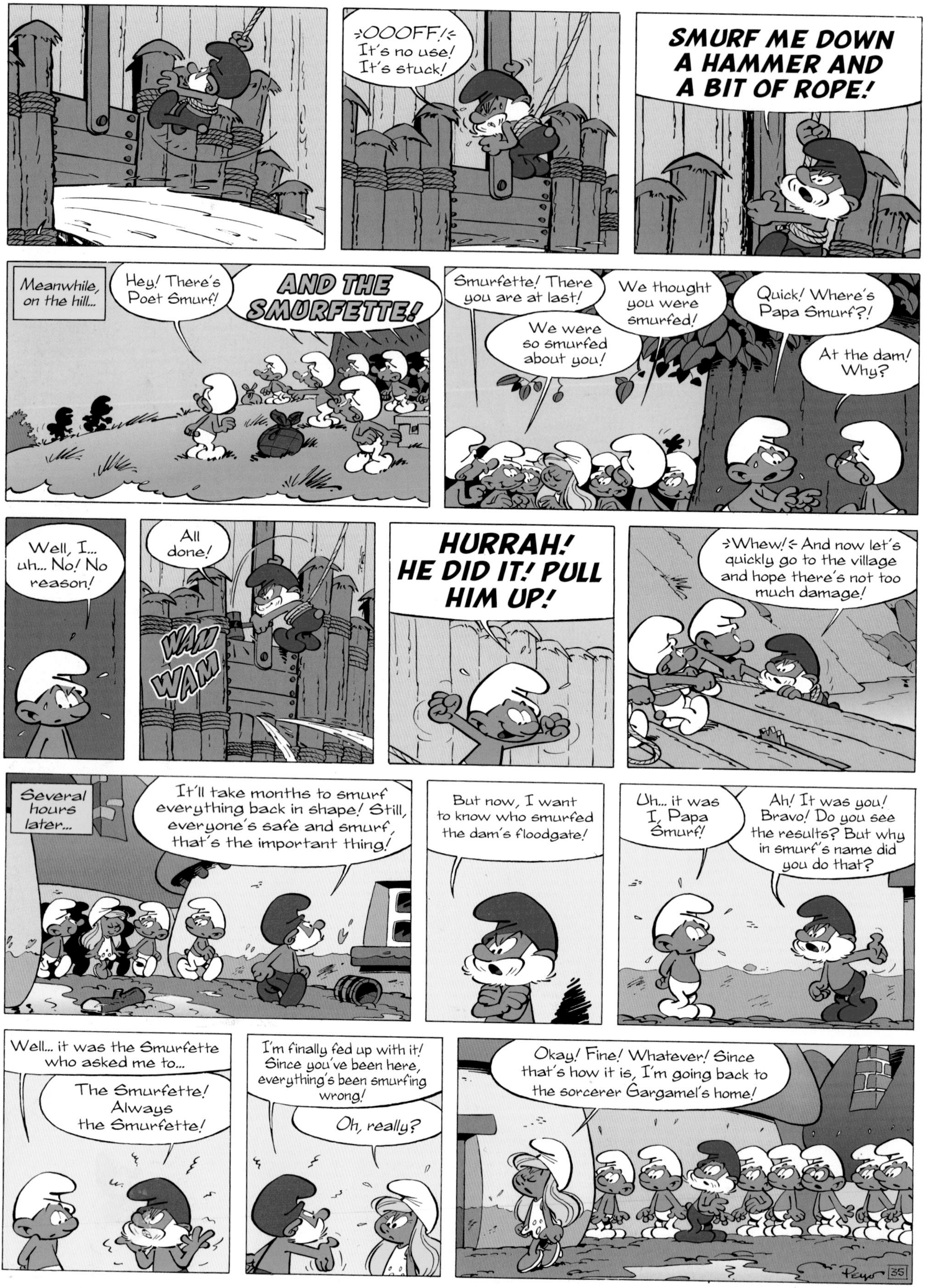

>OOOFF!<
It's no use! It's stuck!
SMURF ME DOWN A HAMMER AND A BIT OF ROPE!
Meanwhile, on the hill...
Hey! There's Poet Smurf!
AND THE SMURFETTE!
Smurfette! There you are at last!
We were so smurfed about you!
We thought you were smurfed!
Quick! Where's Papa Smurf?!
At the dam! Why?
Well, I... uh... No! No reason!
All done!
WAM WAM
HURRAH! HE DID IT! PULL HIM UP!
>Whew!< And now let's quickly go to the village and hope there's not too much damage!
Several hours later...
It'll take months to smurf everything back in shape! Still, everyone's safe and smurf, that's the important thing!
But now, I want to know who smurfed the dam's floodgate!
Uh... it was I, Papa Smurf!
Ah! It was you! Bravo! Do you see the results? But why in smurf's name did you do that?
Well... it was the Smurfette who asked me to...
The Smurfette! Always the Smurfette!
I'm finally fed up with it! Since you've been here, everything's been smurfing wrong!
Oh, really?
Okay! Fine! Whatever! Since that's how it is, I'm going back to the sorcerer Gargamel's home!
Peyo 35

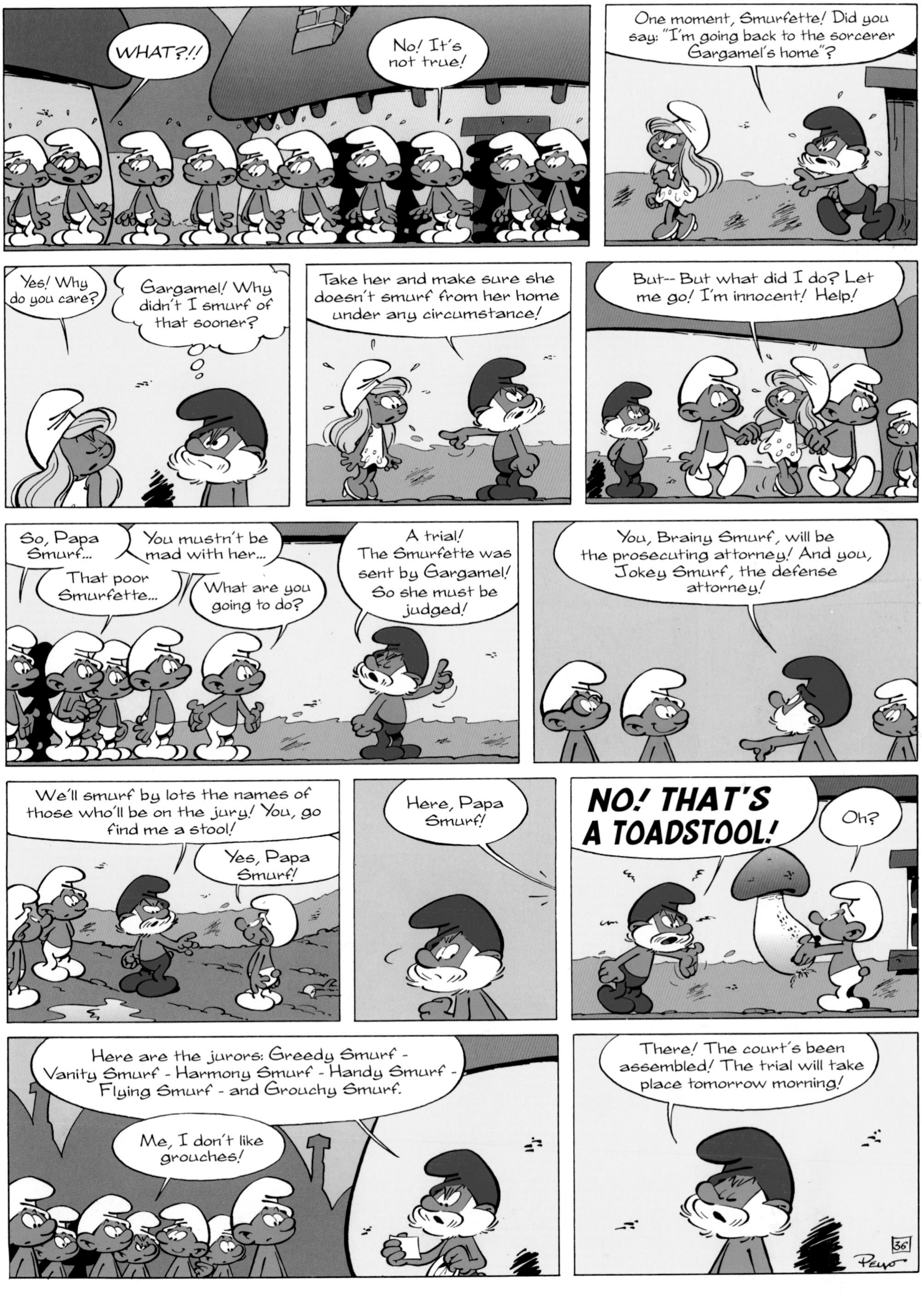
WHAT?!!
No! It's not true!
One moment, Smurfette! Did you say: "I'm going back to the sorcerer Gargamel's home"?
Yes! Why do you care?
Gargamel! Why didn't I smurf of that sooner?
Take her and make sure she doesn't smurf from her home under any circumstance!
But-- But what did I do? Let me go! I'm innocent! Help!
So, Papa Smurf...
You mustn't be mad with her...
That poor Smurfette...
What are you going to do?
A trial! The Smurfette was sent by Gargamel! So she must be judged!
You, Brainy Smurf, will be the prosecuting attorney! And you, Jokey Smurf, the defense attorney!
We'll smurf by lots the names of those who'll be on the jury! You, go find me a stool!
Yes, Papa Smurf!
Here, Papa Smurf!
NO! THAT'S A TOADSTOOL!
Oh?
Here are the jurors: Greedy Smurf - Vanity Smurf - Harmony Smurf - Handy Smurf - Flying Smurf - and Grouchy Smurf.
Me, I don't like grouches!
There! The court's been assembled! The trial will take place tomorrow morning!
36
Peyo

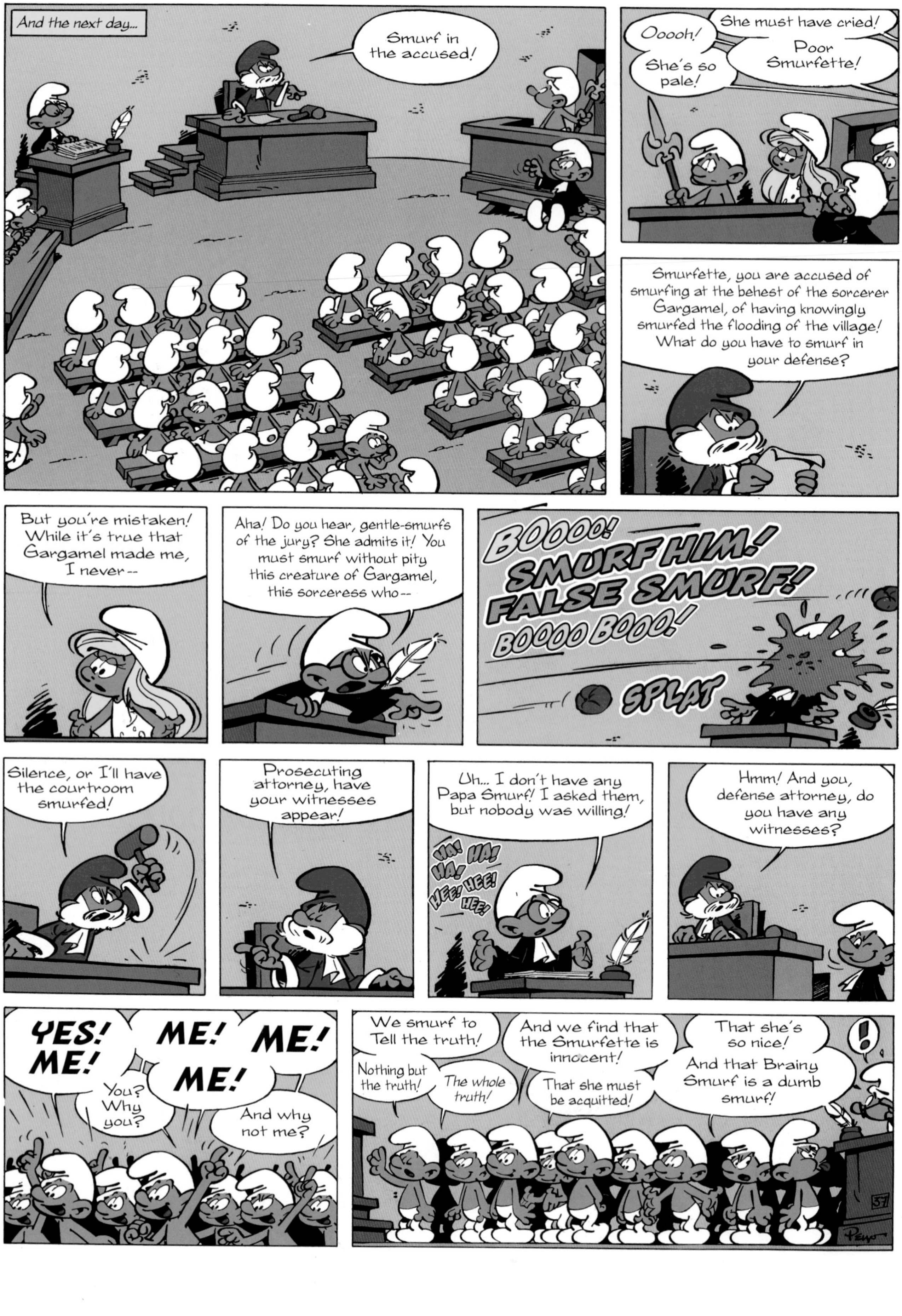
And the next day...
Smurf in the accused!
Ooooh!
She must have cried!
She's so pale!
Poor Smurfette!
Smurfette, you are accused of smurfing at the behest of the sorcerer Gargamel, of having knowingly smurfed the flooding of the village! What do you have to smurf in your defense?
But you're mistaken! While it's true that Gargamel made me, I never--
Aha! Do you hear, gentle-smurfs of the jury? She admits it! You must smurf without pity this creature of Gargamel, this sorceress who--
BOOOO!
SMURF HIM!
FALSE SMURF!
BOOOO BOOO!
SPLAT
Silence, or I'll have the courtroom smurfed!
Prosecuting attorney, have your witnesses appear!
Uh... I don't have any Papa Smurf! I asked them, but nobody was willing!
HA! HA! HA!
HEE! HEE! HEE!
Hmm! And you, defense attorney, do you have any witnesses?
YES! ME!
ME!
ME!
ME!
You? Why you?
And why not me?
We smurf to Tell the truth!
Nothing but the truth!
The whole truth!
And we find that the Smurfette is innocent!
That she must be acquitted!
That she's so nice!
And that Brainy Smurf is a dumb smurf!
!

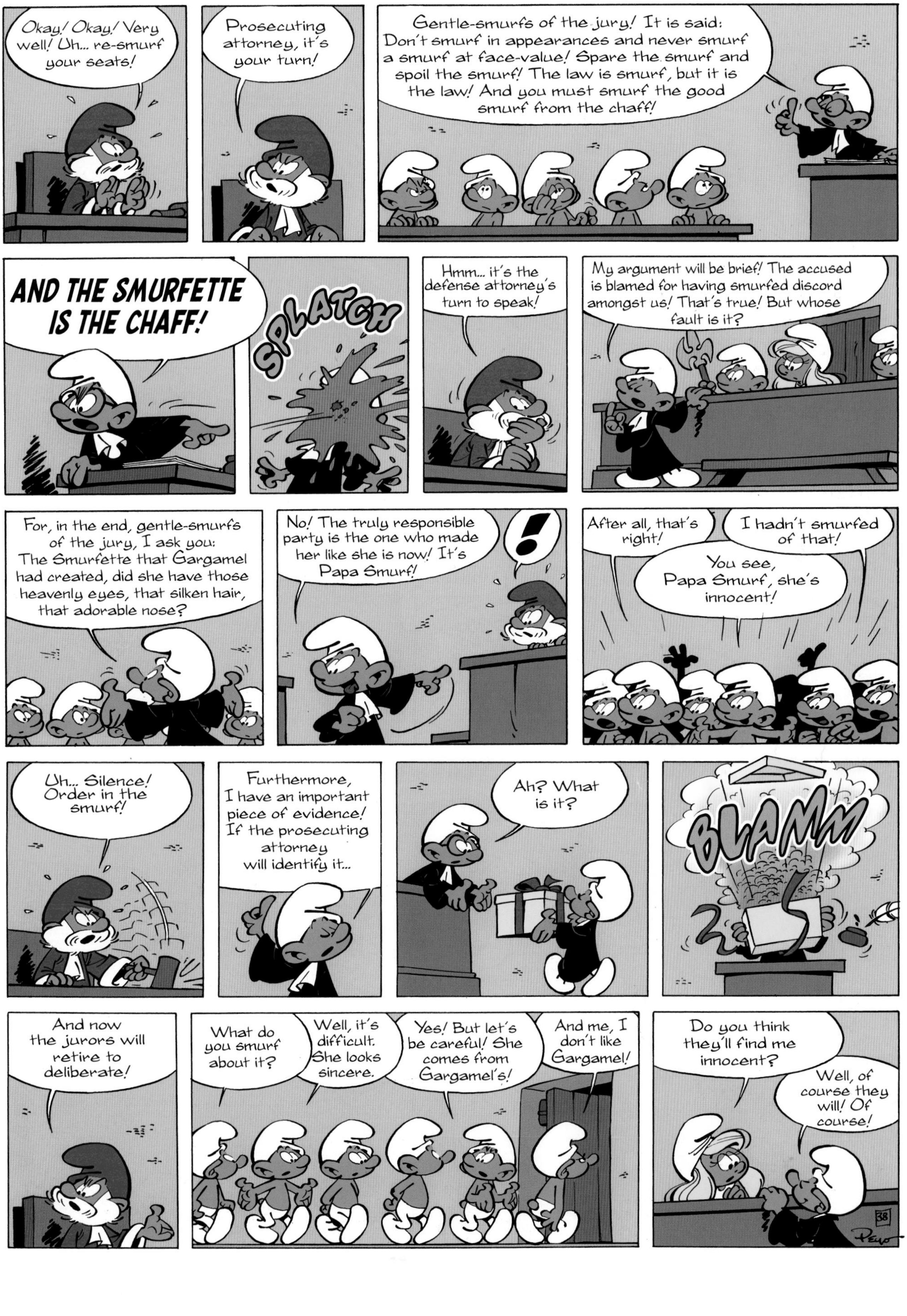

Okay! Okay! Very well! Uh... re-smurf your seats!
Prosecuting attorney, it's your turn!
Gentle-smurfs of the jury! It is said: Don't smurf in appearances and never smurf a smurf at face-value! Spare the smurf and spoil the smurf! The law is smurf, but it is the law! And you must smurf the good smurf from the chaff!
AND THE SMURFETTE IS THE CHAFF!
SPLATCH
Hmm... it's the defense attorney's turn to speak!
My argument will be brief! The accused is blamed for having smurfed discord amongst us! That's true! But whose fault is it?
For, in the end, gentle-smurfs of the jury, I ask you: The Smurfette that Gargamel had created, did she have those heavenly eyes, that silken hair, that adorable nose?
No! The truly responsible party is the one who made her like she is now! It's Papa Smurf!
!
After all, that's right!
I hadn't smurfed of that!
You see, Papa Smurf, she's innocent!
Uh... Silence! Order in the smurf!
Furthermore, I have an important piece of evidence! If the prosecuting attorney will identify it...
Ah? What is it?
BLAMM
And now the jurors will retire to deliberate!
What do you smurf about it?
Well, it's difficult. She looks sincere.
Yes! But let's be careful! She comes from Gargamel's!
And me, I don't like Gargamel!
Do you think they'll find me innocent?
Well, of course they will! Of course!
38
Peyo

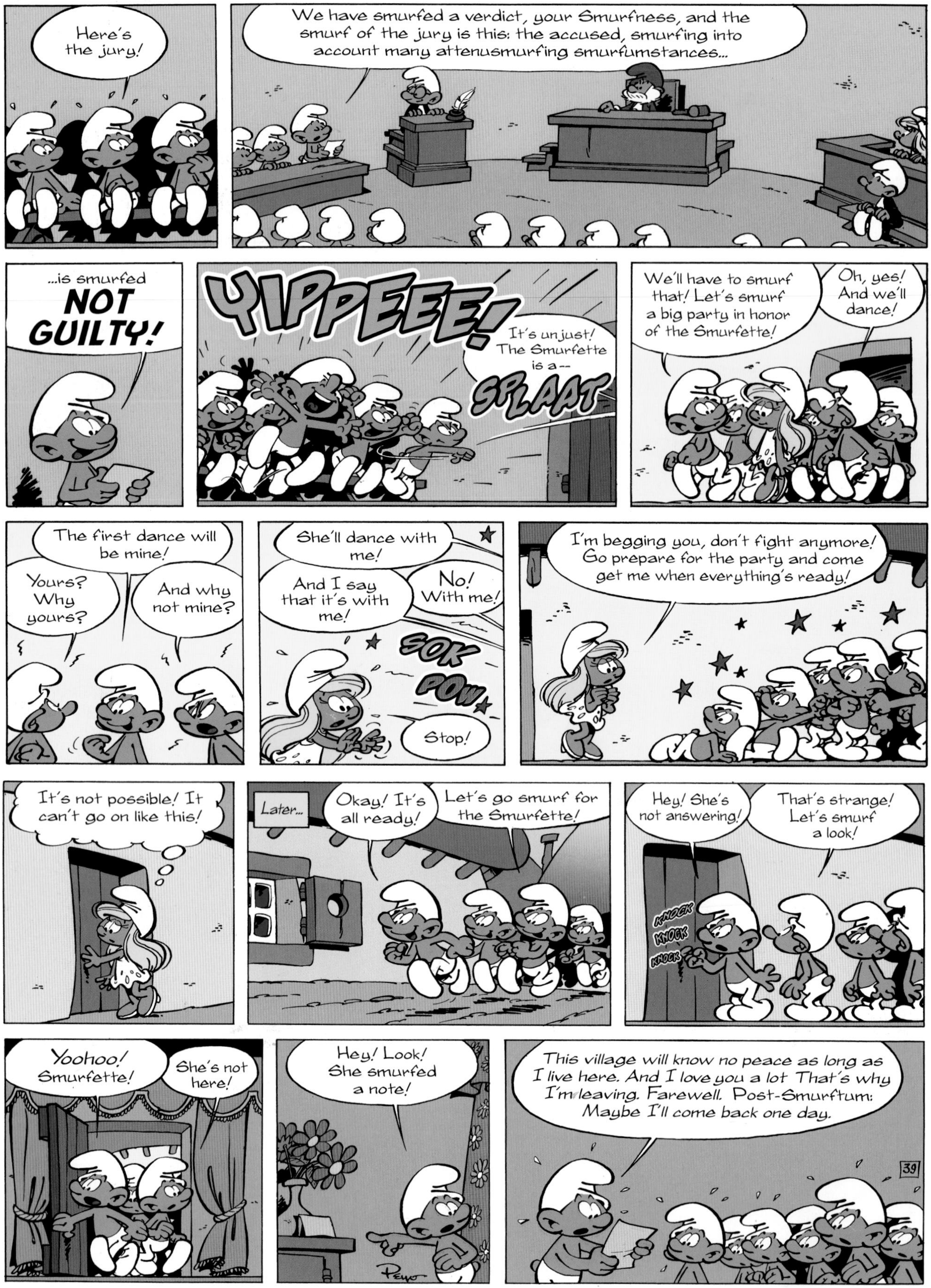
Here's the jury!
We have smurfed a verdict, your Smurfness, and the smurf of the jury is this: the accused, smurfing into account many attenusmurfing smurfumstances...
...is smurfed NOT GUILTY!
YIPPEEE!
It's unjust! The Smurfette is a--
SPLAAT
We'll have to smurf that! Let's smurf a big party in honor of the Smurfette!
Oh, yes! And we'll dance!
The first dance will be mine!
Yours? Why yours?
And why not mine?
She'll dance with me!
And I say that it's with me!
No! With me!
SOK
POW
Stop!
I'm begging you, don't fight anymore! Go prepare for the party and come get me when everything's ready!
It's not possible! It can't go on like this!
Later...
Okay! It's all ready!
Let's go smurf for the Smurfette!
Hey! She's not answering!
KNOCK
KNOCK
KNOCK
That's strange! Let's smurf a look!
Yoohoo! Smurfette!
She's not here!
Hey! Look! She smurfed a note!
This village will know no peace as long as I live here. And I love you a lot That's why I'm leaving. Farewell. Post-Smurftum: Maybe I'll come back one day.
39
Peyo

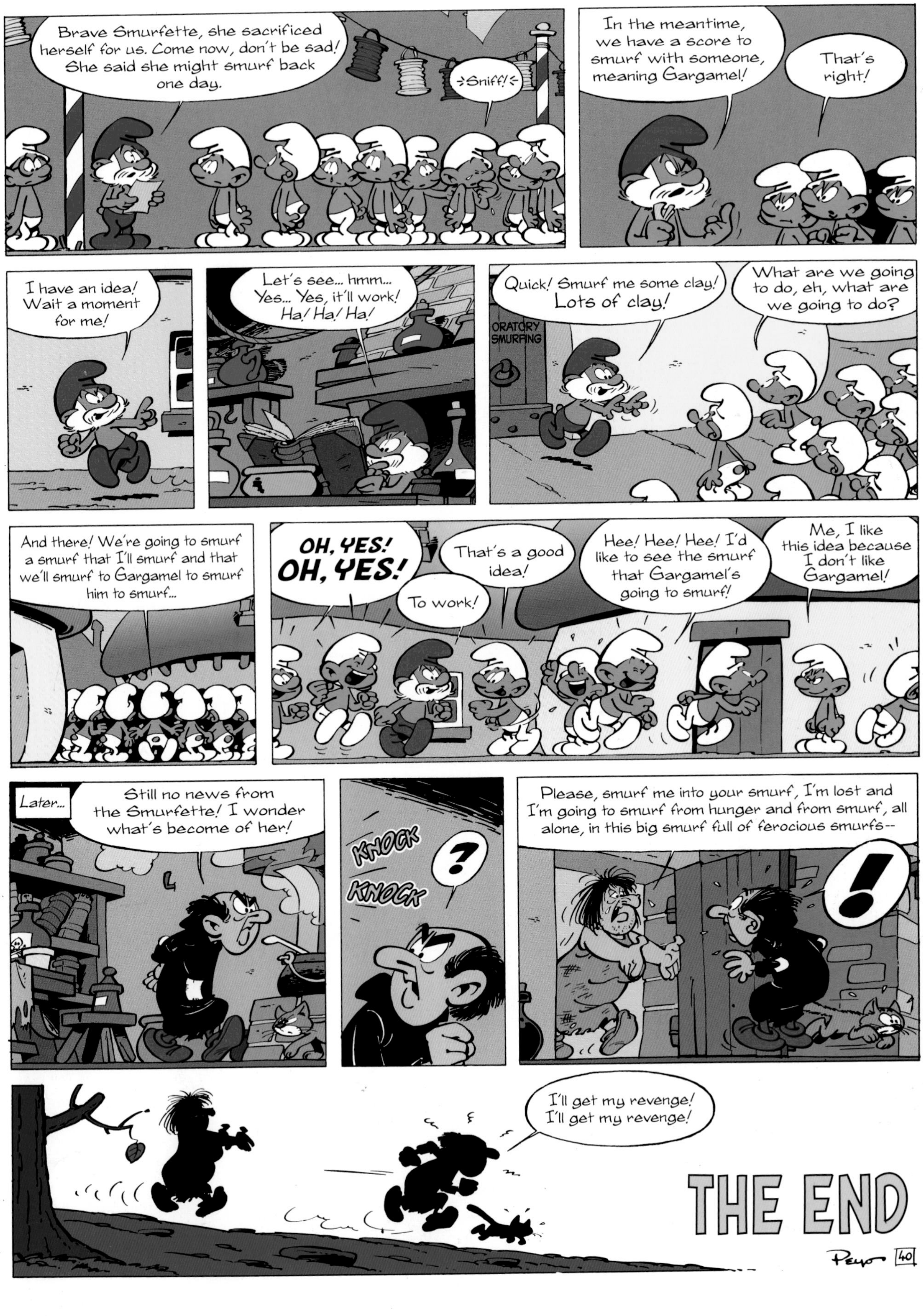
Brave Smurfette, she sacrificed herself for us. Come now, don't be sad! She said she might smurf back one day.
Sniff!
In the meantime, we have a score to smurf with someone, meaning Gargamel!
That's right!
I have an idea! Wait a moment for me!
Let's see... hmm... Yes... Yes, it'll work! Ha! Ha! Ha!
ORATORY SMURFING
Quick! Smurf me some clay! Lots of clay!
What are we going to do, eh, what are we going to do?
And there! We're going to smurf a smurf that I'll smurf and that we'll smurf to Gargamel to smurf him to smurf...
OH, YES! OH, YES!
That's a good idea!
To work!
Hee! Hee! Hee! I'd like to see the smurf that Gargamel's going to smurf!
Me, I like this idea because I don't like Gargamel!
Later...
Still no news from the Smurfette! I wonder what's become of her!
KNOCK
KNOCK
?
Please, smurf me into your smurf, I'm lost and I'm going to smurf from hunger and from smurf, all alone, in this big smurf full of ferocious smurfs--
!
I'll get my revenge! I'll get my revenge!
THE END
Peyo
40

THE HUNGRY SMURFS

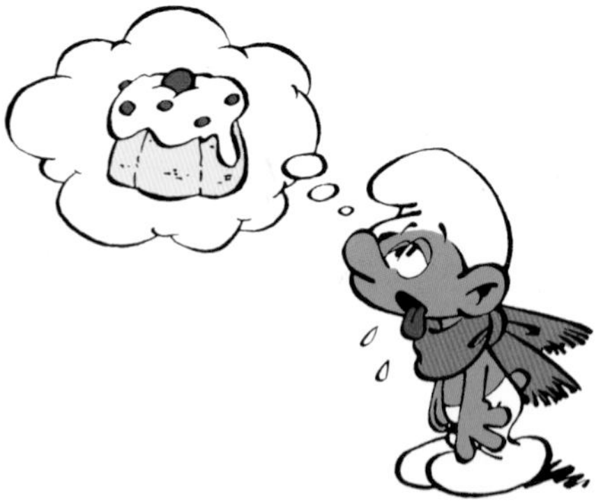

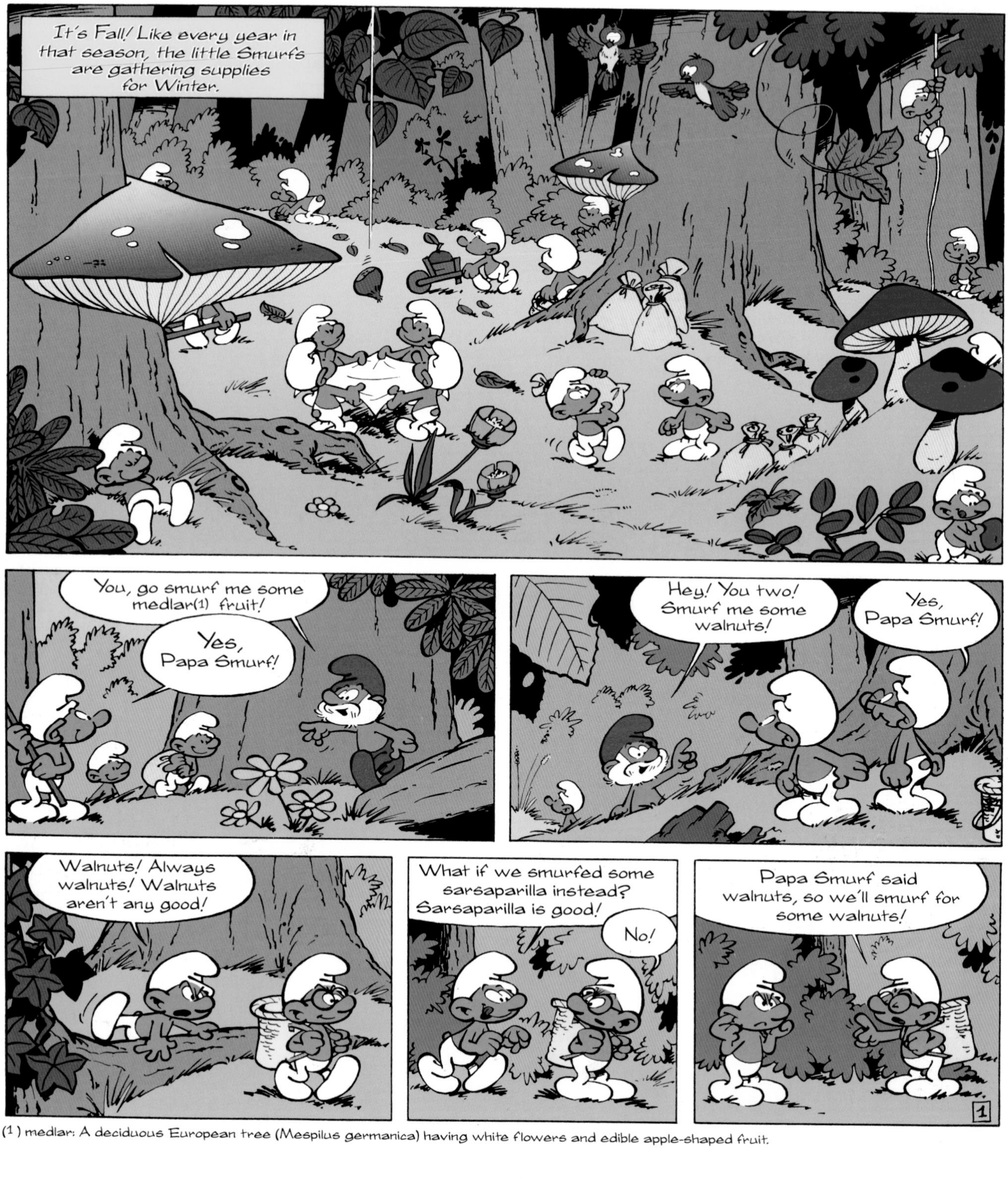

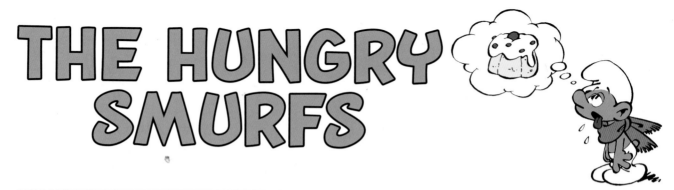

It's Fall! Like every year in that season, the little Smurfs are gathering supplies for Winter.
You, go smurf me some medlar(1) fruit!
Yes, Papa Smurf!
Hey! You two! Smurf me some walnuts!
Yes, Papa Smurf!
Walnuts! Always walnuts! Walnuts aren't any good!
What if we smurfed some sarsaparilla instead? Sarsaparilla is good!
No!
Papa Smurf said walnuts, so we'll smurf for some walnuts!
1

(1) medlar: A deciduous European tree (Mespilus germanica) having white flowers and edible apple-shaped fruit.

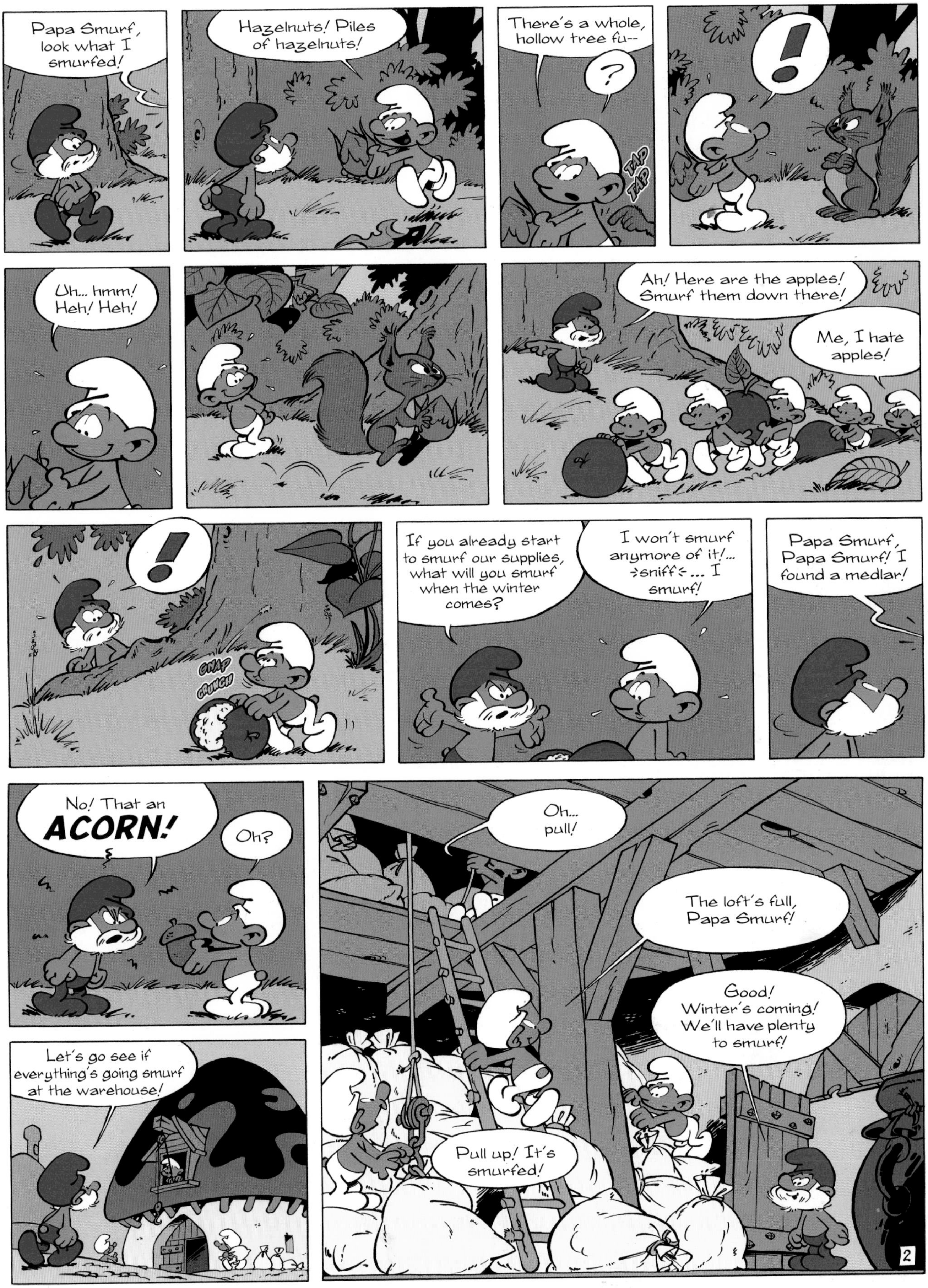

Papa Smurf, look what I smurfed!
Hazelnuts! Piles of hazelnuts!
There's a whole, hollow tree fu--
?
TAP TAP
!
Uh... hmm! Heh! Heh!
Ah! Here are the apples! Smurf them down there!
Me, I hate apples!
!
CHAP CRUNCH
If you already start to smurf our supplies, what will you smurf when the winter comes?
I won't smurf anymore of it!... >sniff<... I smurf!
Papa Smurf, Papa Smurf! I found a medlar!
No! That an ACORN!
Oh?
Let's go see if everything's going smurf at the warehouse!
Oh... pull!
The loft's full, Papa Smurf!
Good! Winter's coming! We'll have plenty to smurf!
Pull up! It's smurfed!
2

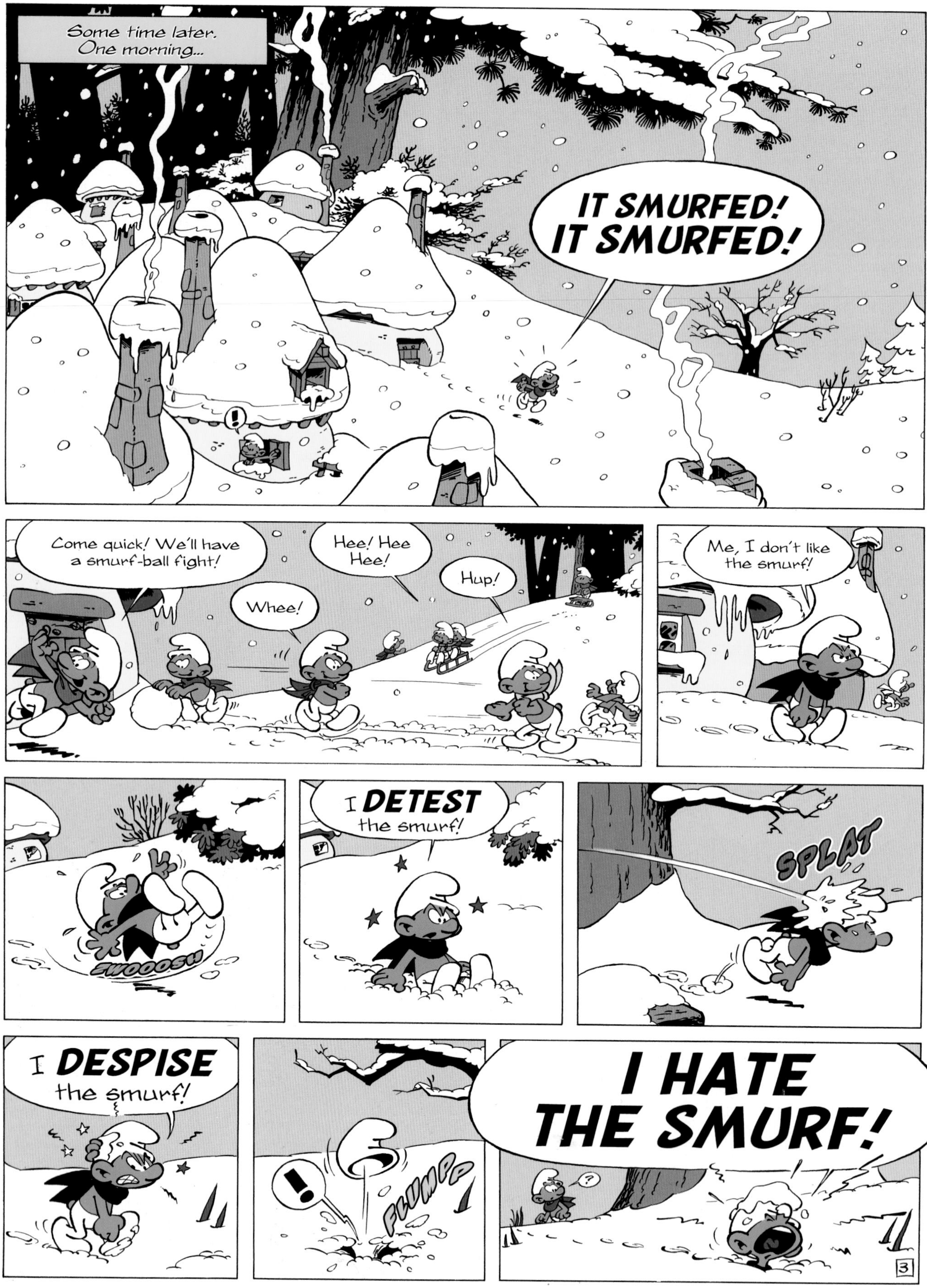

Some time later.
One morning...
IT SMURFED! IT SMURFED!
Come quick! We'll have a smurf-ball fight!
Hee! Hee Hee!
Whee!
Hup!
Me, I don't like the smurf!
ZWOOOSH
I DETEST the smurf!
SPLAT
I DESPISE the smurf!
FLUMPP
I HATE THE SMURF!
3

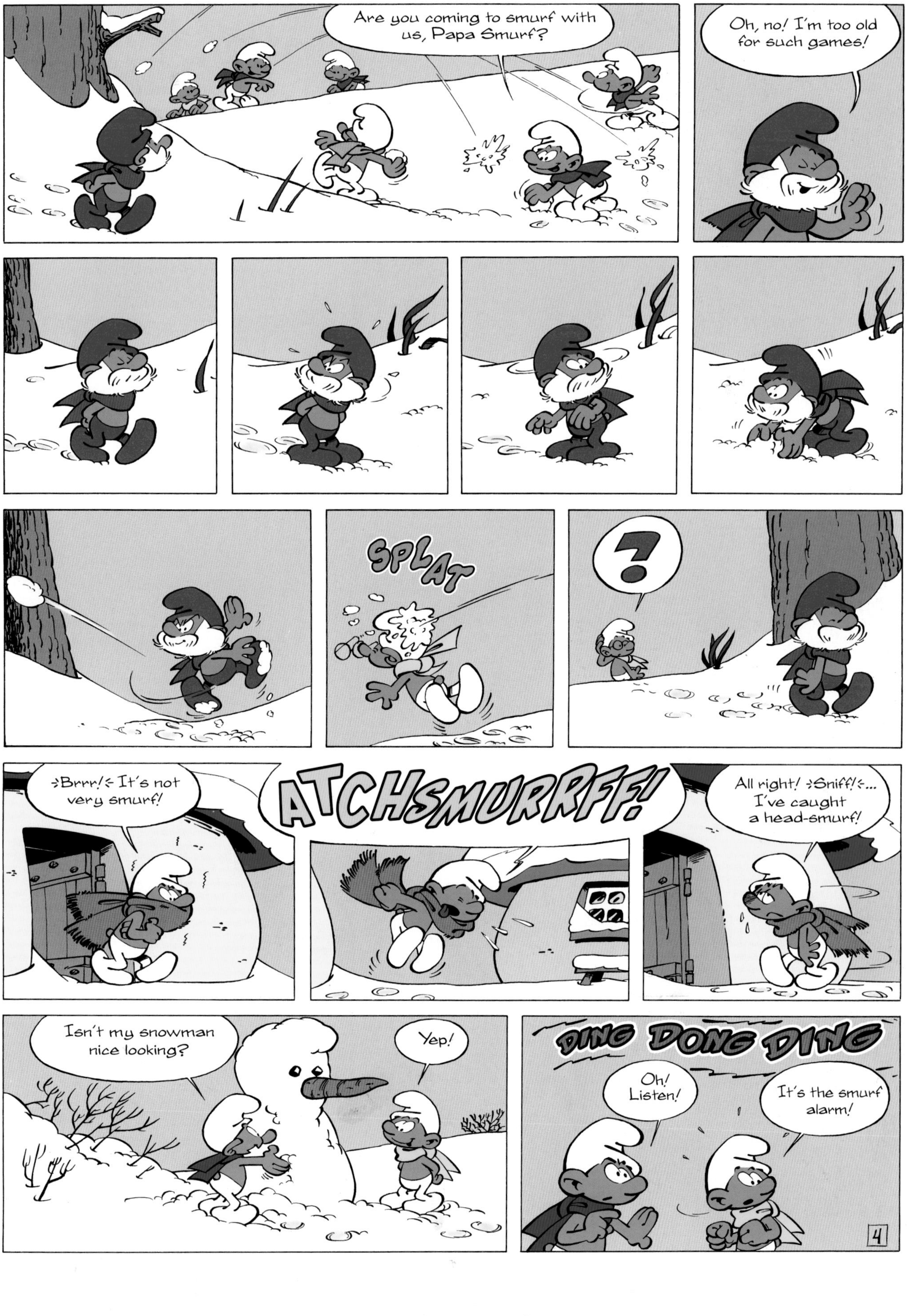

Are you coming to smurf with us, Papa Smurf?
Oh, no! I'm too old for such games!
?
SPLAT
⇒Brrr!⇐ It's not very smurf!
ATCHSMURRFF!
All right! ⇒Sniff!⇐... I've caught a head-smurf!
Isn't my snowman nice looking?
Yep!
DING DONG DING
Oh! Listen!
It's the smurf alarm!
4

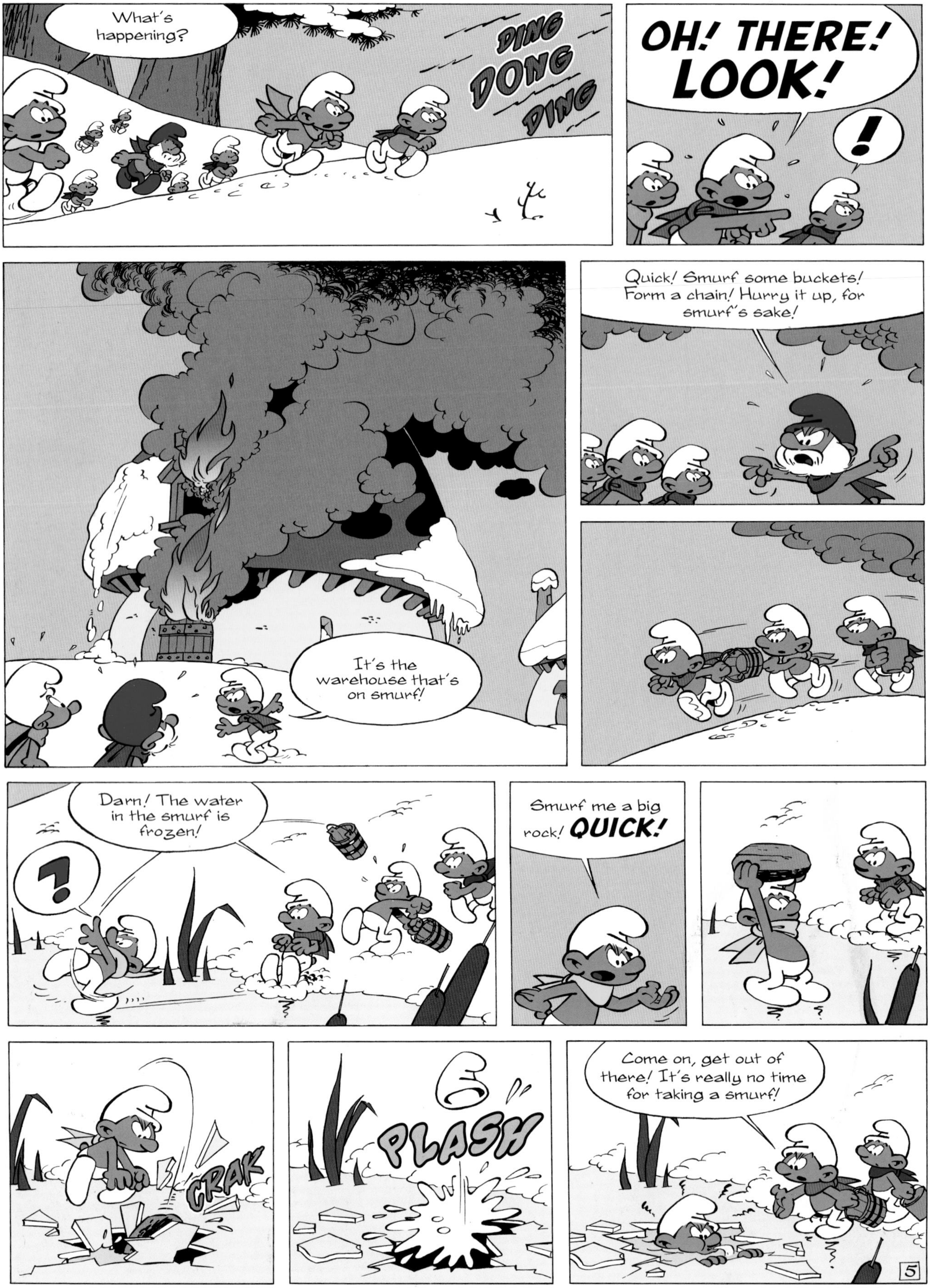
What's happening?
DING DONG DING
OH! THERE! LOOK!
!
Quick! Smurf some buckets! Form a chain! Hurry it up, for smurf's sake!
It's the warehouse that's on smurf!
Darn! The water in the smurf is frozen!
?
Smurf me a big rock! QUICK!
CRAK
PLASH
Come on, get out of there! It's really no time for taking a smurf!
5

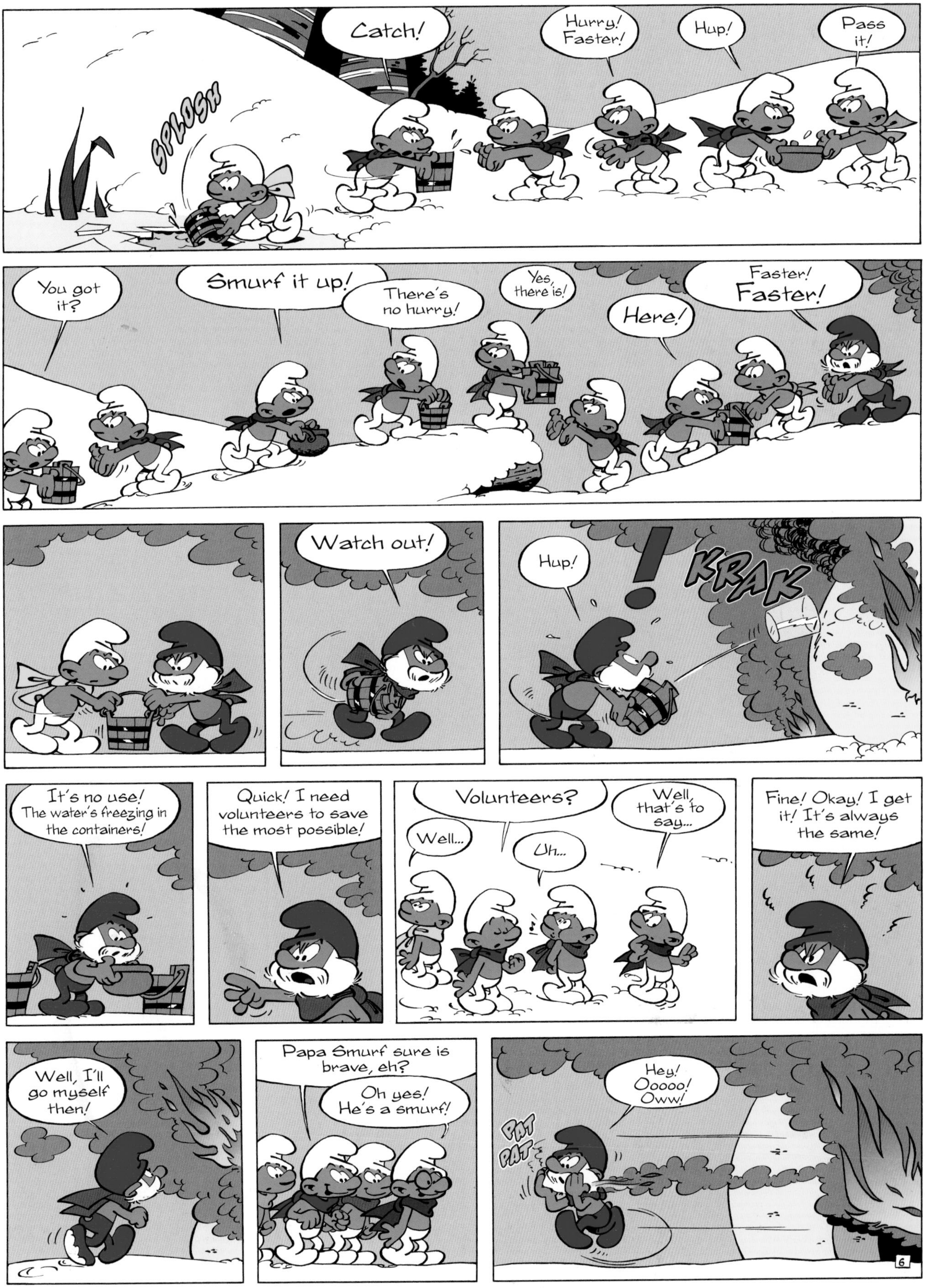
SPLOSH
Catch!
Hurry! Faster!
Hup!
Pass it!
You got it?
Smurf it up!
There's no hurry!
Yes, there is!
Here!
Faster! Faster!
Watch out!
Hup!
!
KRAK
It's no use! The water's freezing in the containers!
Quick! I need volunteers to save the most possible!
Volunteers?
Well...
Uh...
Well, that's to say...
Fine! Okay! I get it! It's always the same!
Well, I'll go myself then!
Papa Smurf sure is brave, eh?
Oh yes! He's a smurf!
Hey! Ooooo! Oww!
PAT PAT
6

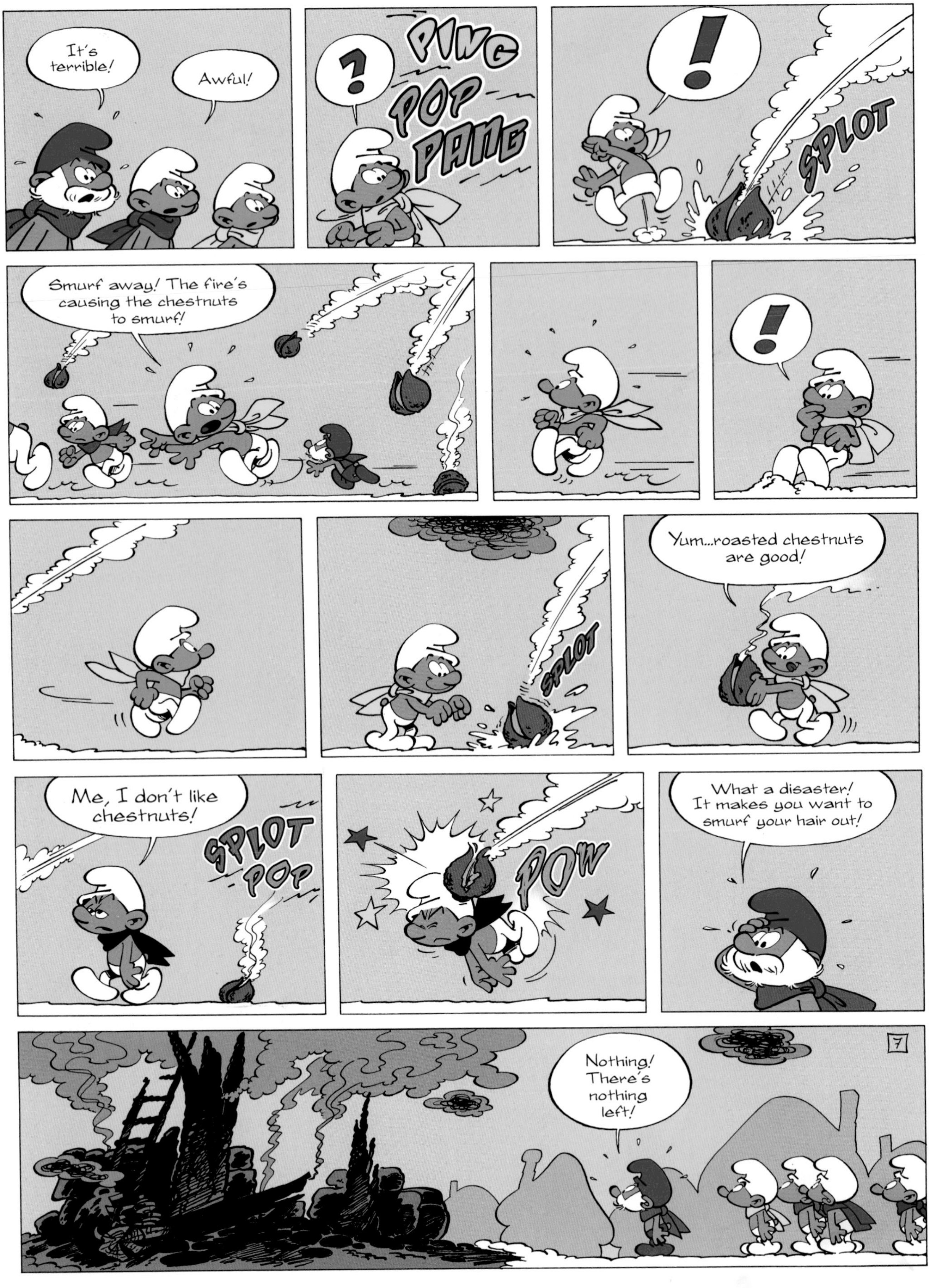
It's terrible!
Awful!
?
PING
POP
PANG
!
SPLOT
Smurf away! The fire's causing the chestnuts to smurf!
!
SPLOT
Yum...roasted chestnuts are good!
Me, I don't like chestnuts!
SPLOT
POP
POW
What a disaster! It makes you want to smurf your hair out!
7
Nothing! There's nothing left!

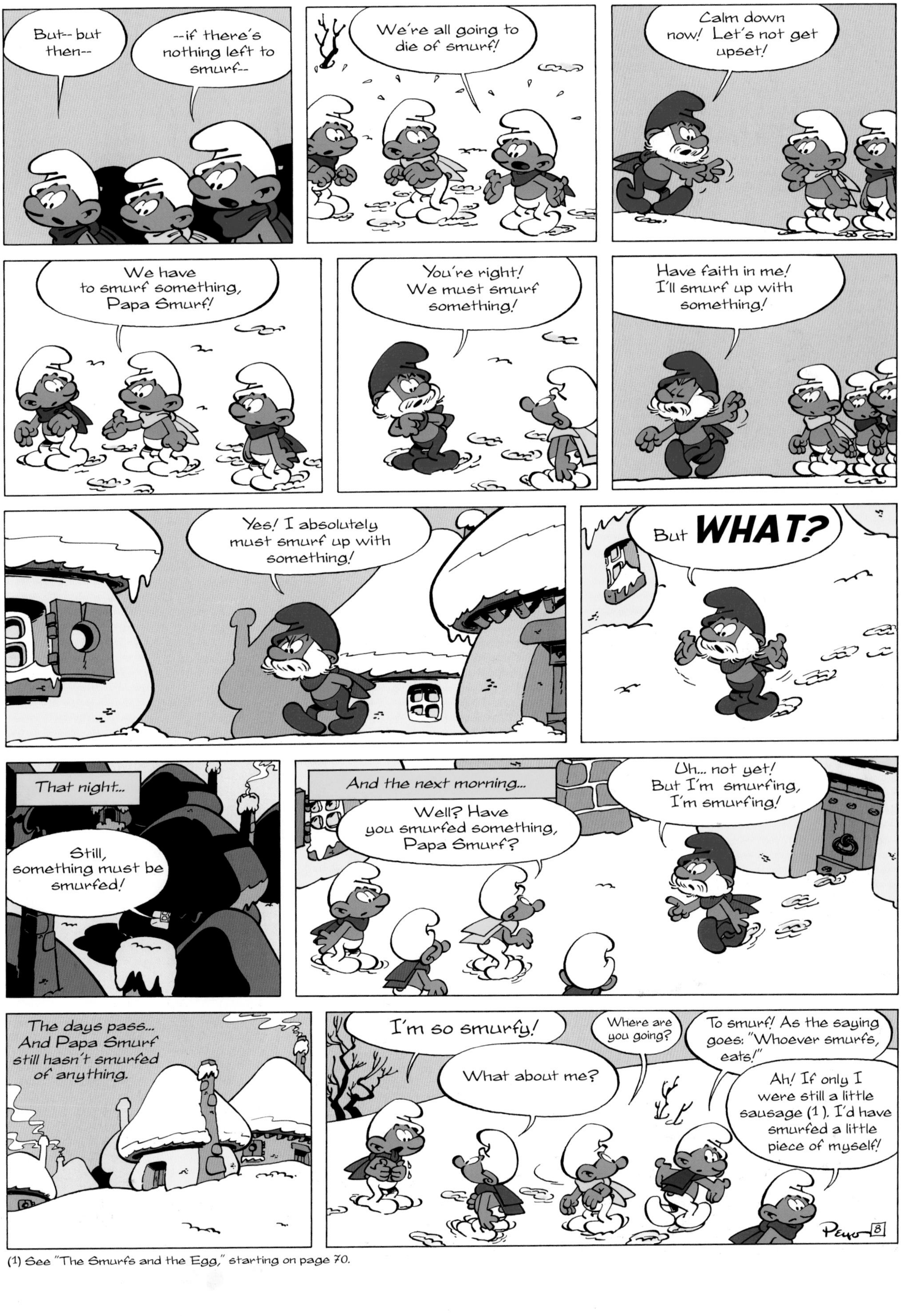

But-- but then--
--if there's nothing left to smurf--
We're all going to die of smurf!
Calm down now! Let's not get upset!
We have to smurf something, Papa Smurf!
You're right! We must smurf something!
Have faith in me! I'll smurf up with something!
Yes! I absolutely must smurf up with something!
But WHAT?
That night...
Still, something must be smurfed!
And the next morning...
Well? Have you smurfed something, Papa Smurf?
Uh... not yet! But I'm smurfing, I'm smurfing!
The days pass... And Papa Smurf still hasn't smurfed of anything.
I'm so smurfy!
What about me?
Where are you going?
To smurf! As the saying goes: "Whoever smurfs, eats!"
Ah! If only I were still a little sausage (1). I'd have smurfed a little piece of myself!
Peyo 8

(1) See "The Smurfs and the Egg," starting on page 70.

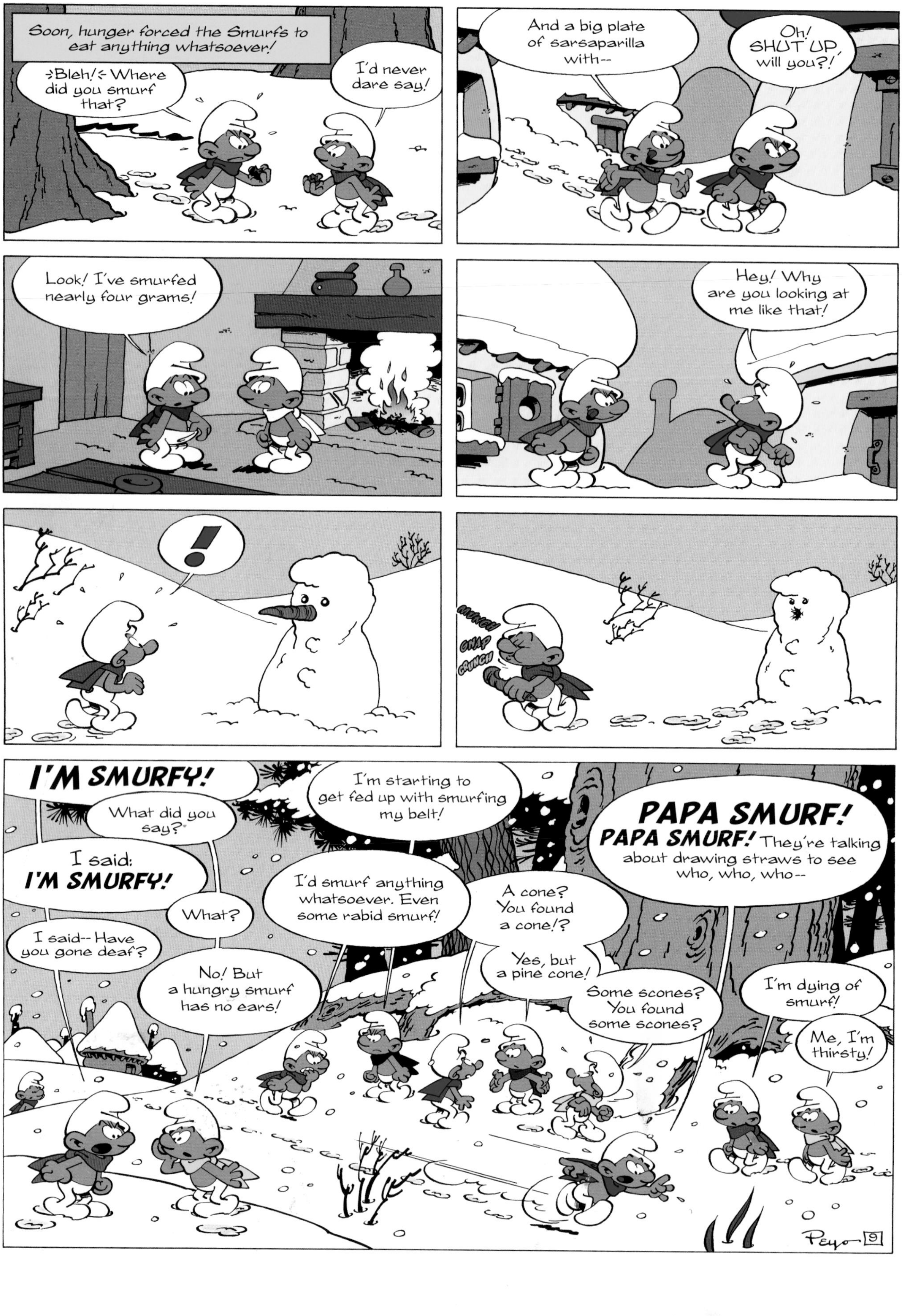
Soon, hunger forced the Smurfs to eat anything whatsoever!
>Bleh!< Where did you smurf that?
I'd never dare say!
And a big plate of sarsaparilla with--
Oh! SHUT UP, will you?!
Look! I've smurfed nearly four grams!
Hey! Why are you looking at me like that!
!
MUNCH
GNAP
CRUNCH
I'M SMURFY!
What did you say?
I said: I'M SMURFY!
What?
I said-- Have you gone deaf?
No! But a hungry smurf has no ears!
I'm starting to get fed up with smurfing my belt!
I'd smurf anything whatsoever. Even some rabid smurf!
A cone? You found a cone!?
Yes, but a pine cone!
Some scones? You found some scones?
PAPA SMURF! PAPA SMURF! They're talking about drawing straws to see who, who, who--
I'm dying of smurf!
Me, I'm thirsty!
Peyo
9

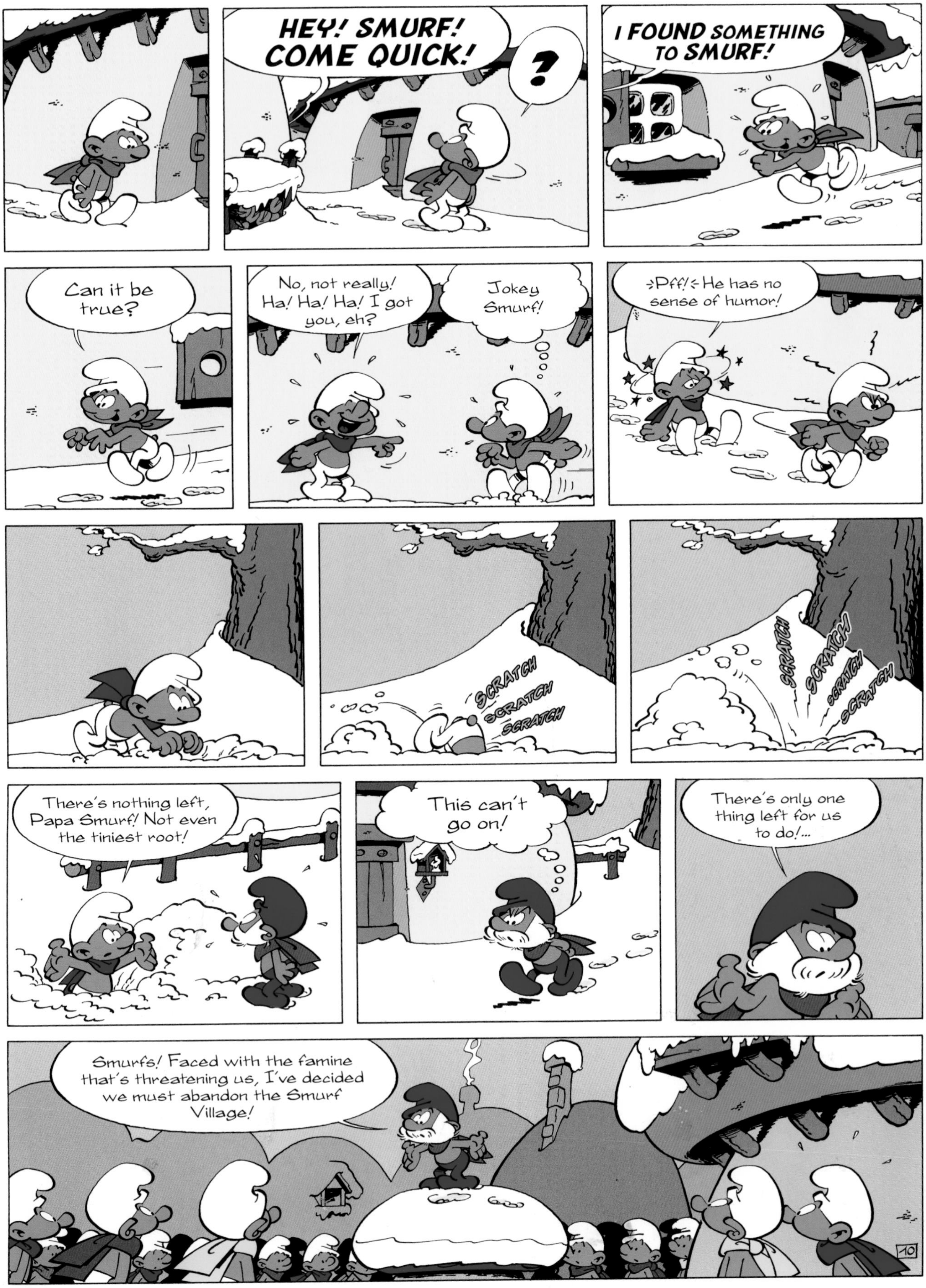
HEY! SMURF! COME QUICK!
?
I FOUND SOMETHING TO SMURF!
Can it be true?
No, not really! Ha! Ha! Ha! I got you, eh?
Jokey Smurf!
Pff! He has no sense of humor!
SCRATCH SCRATCH SCRATCH
SCRATCH SCRATCH SCRATCH SCRATCH
There's nothing left, Papa Smurf! Not even the tiniest root!
This can't go on!
There's only one thing left for us to do!...
Smurfs! Faced with the famine that's threatening us, I've decided we must abandon the Smurf Village!
10

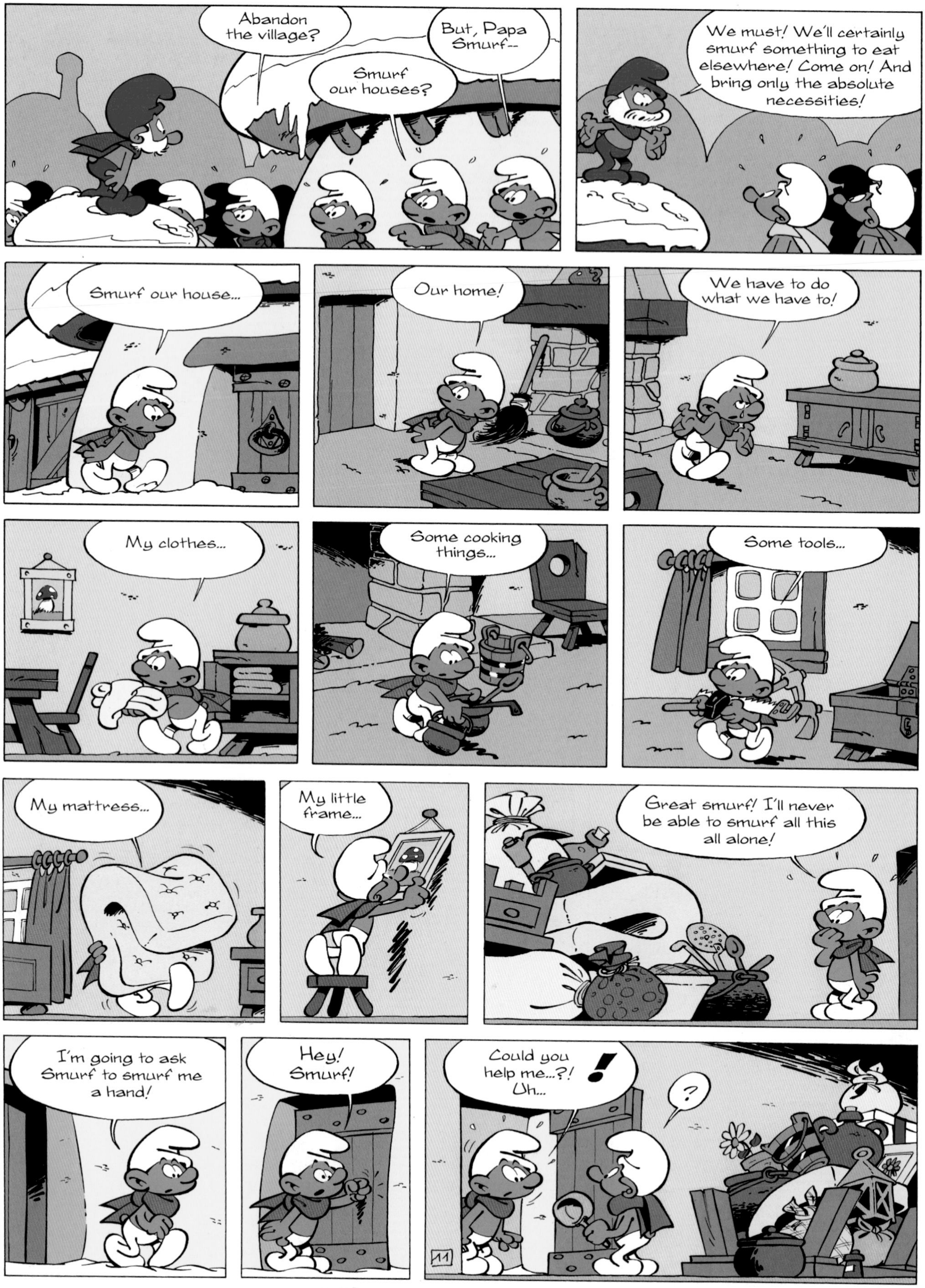
Abandon the village?
Smurf our houses?
But, Papa Smurf--
We must! We'll certainly smurf something to eat elsewhere! Come on! And bring only the absolute necessities!
Smurf our house...
Our home!
We have to do what we have to!
My clothes...
Some cooking things...
Some tools...
My mattress...
My little frame...
Great smurf! I'll never be able to smurf all this all alone!
I'm going to ask Smurf to smurf me a hand!
Hey! Smurf!
Could you help me...?! Uh...
!
?
11

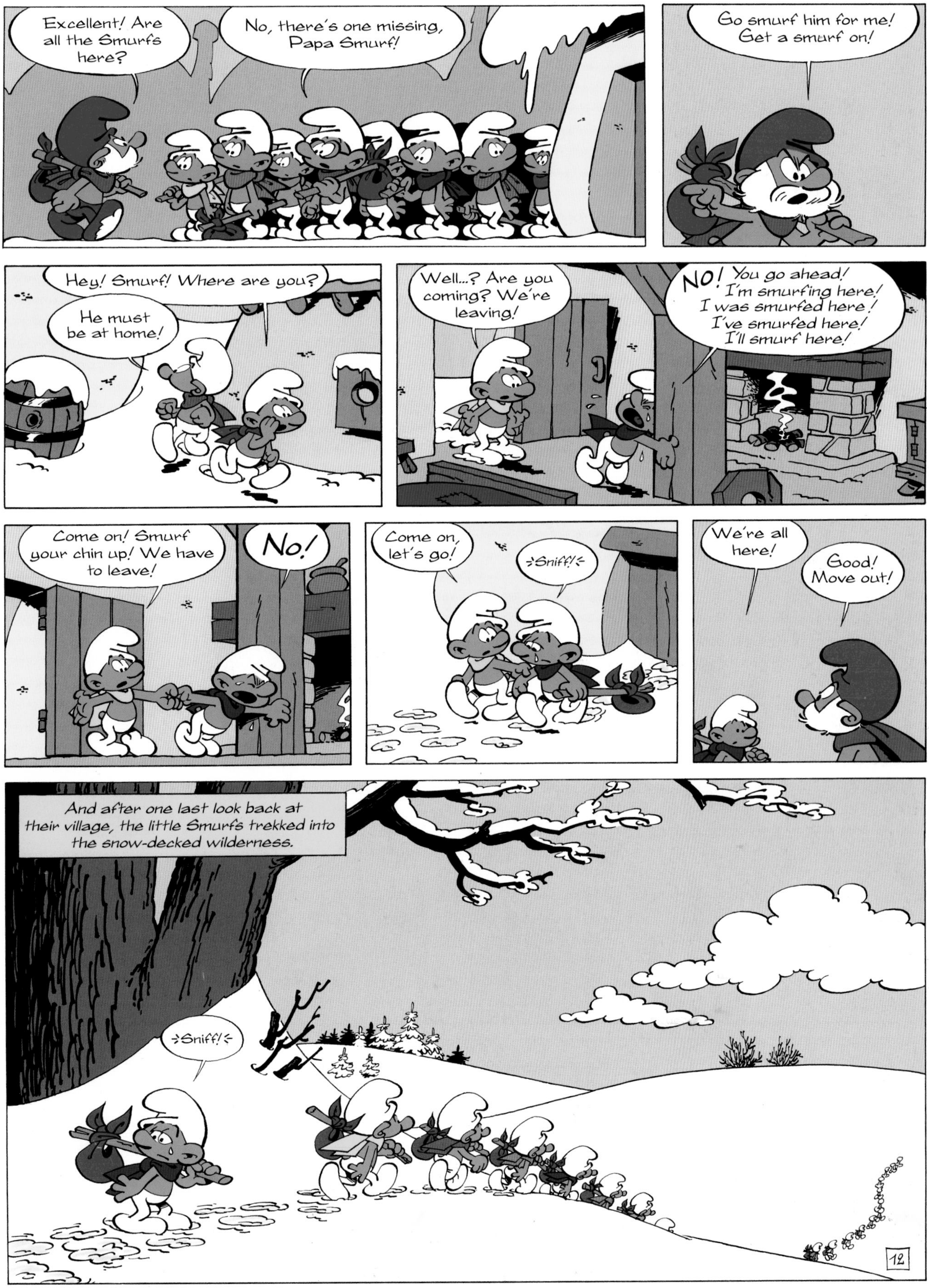
Excellent! Are all the Smurfs here?
No, there's one missing, Papa Smurf!
Go smurf him for me! Get a smurf on!
Hey! Smurf! Where are you?
He must be at home!
Well...? Are you coming? We're leaving!
NO! You go ahead! I'm smurfing here! I was smurfed here! I've smurfed here! I'll smurf here!
Come on! Smurf your chin up! We have to leave!
No!
Come on, let's go!
Sniff!
We're all here!
Good! Move out!
And after one last look back at their village, the little Smurfs trekked into the snow-decked wilderness.
Sniff!
12

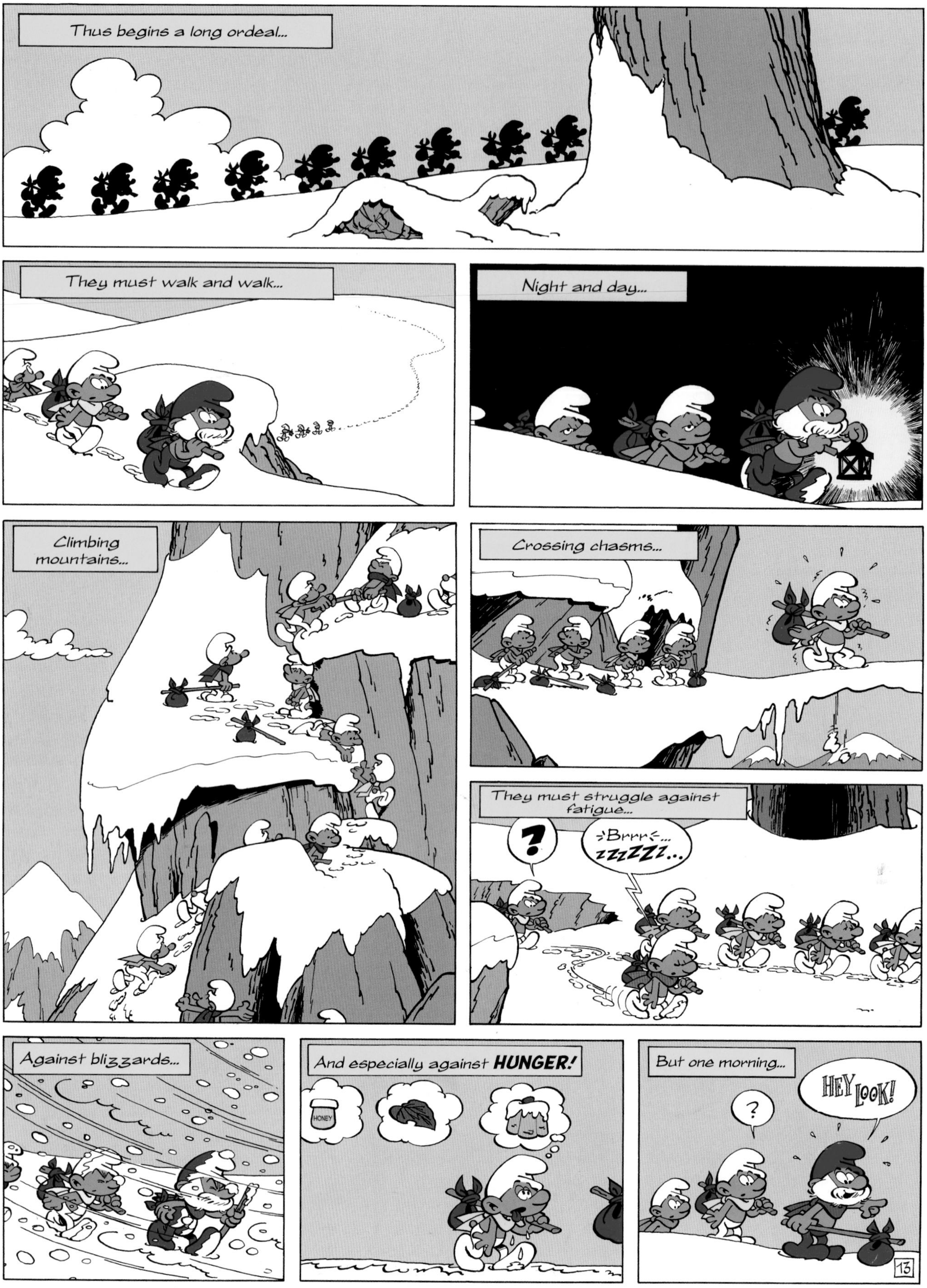

Thus begins a long ordeal...
They must walk and walk...
Night and day...
Climbing mountains...
Crossing chasms...
They must struggle against fatigue...
?
Brrr...
ZZZZZZ...
Against blizzards...
And especially against HUNGER!
HONEY
But one morning...
?
HEY LOOK!
13

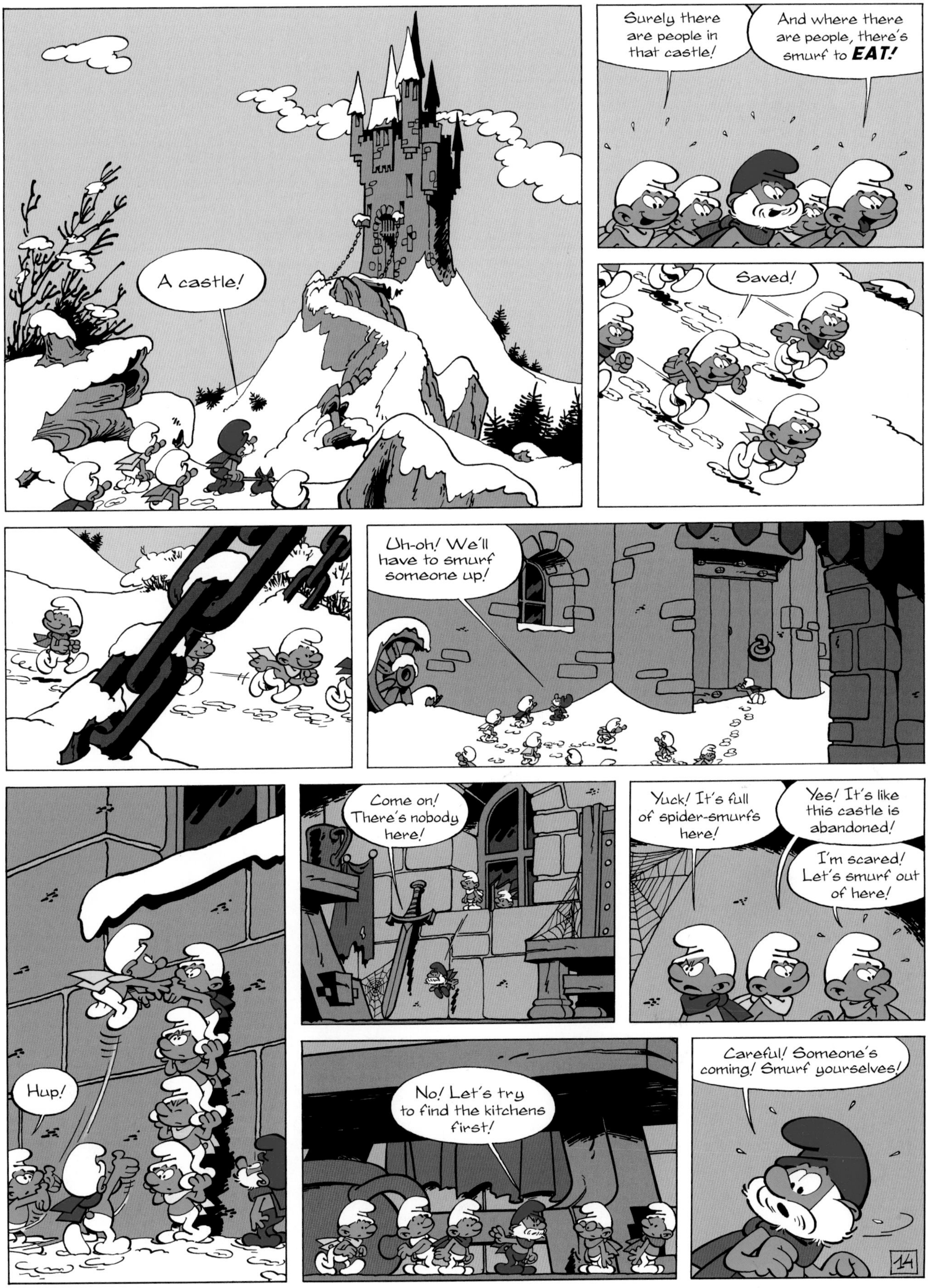
A castle!
Surely there are people in that castle!
And where there are people, there's smurf to EAT!
Saved!
Uh-oh! We'll have to smurf someone up!
Hup!
Come on! There's nobody here!
Yuck! It's full of spider-smurfs here!
Yes! It's like this castle is abandoned!
I'm scared! Let's smurf out of here!
No! Let's try to find the kitchens first!
Careful! Someone's coming! Smurf yourselves!
14

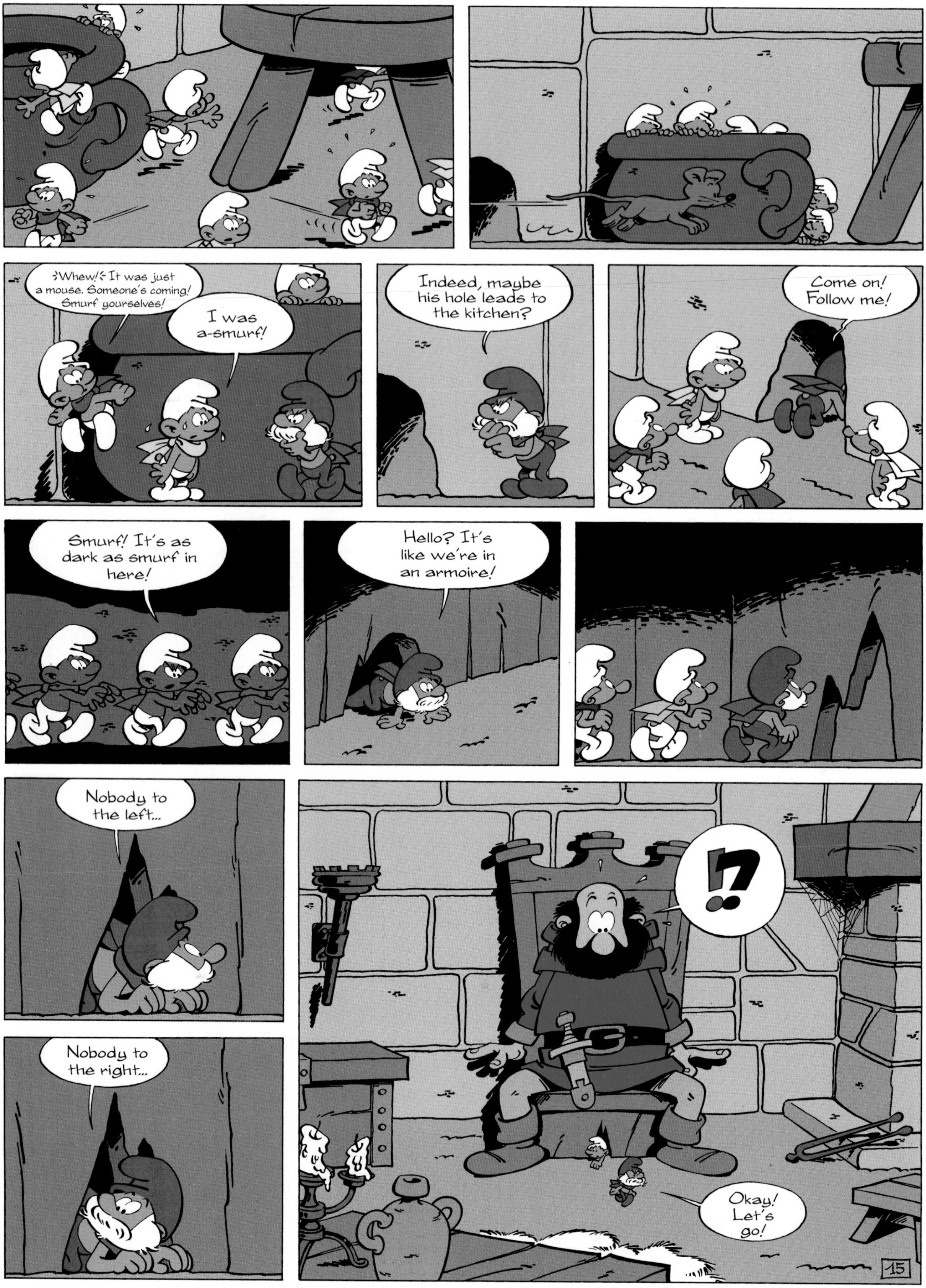

Whew! It was just a mouse. Someone's coming! Smurf yourselves!
I was a-smurf!
Indeed, maybe his hole leads to the kitchen?
Come on! Follow me!
Smurf! It's as dark as smurf in here!
Hello? It's like we're in an armoire!
Nobody to the left...
Nobody to the right...
!?
Okay! Let's go!
15

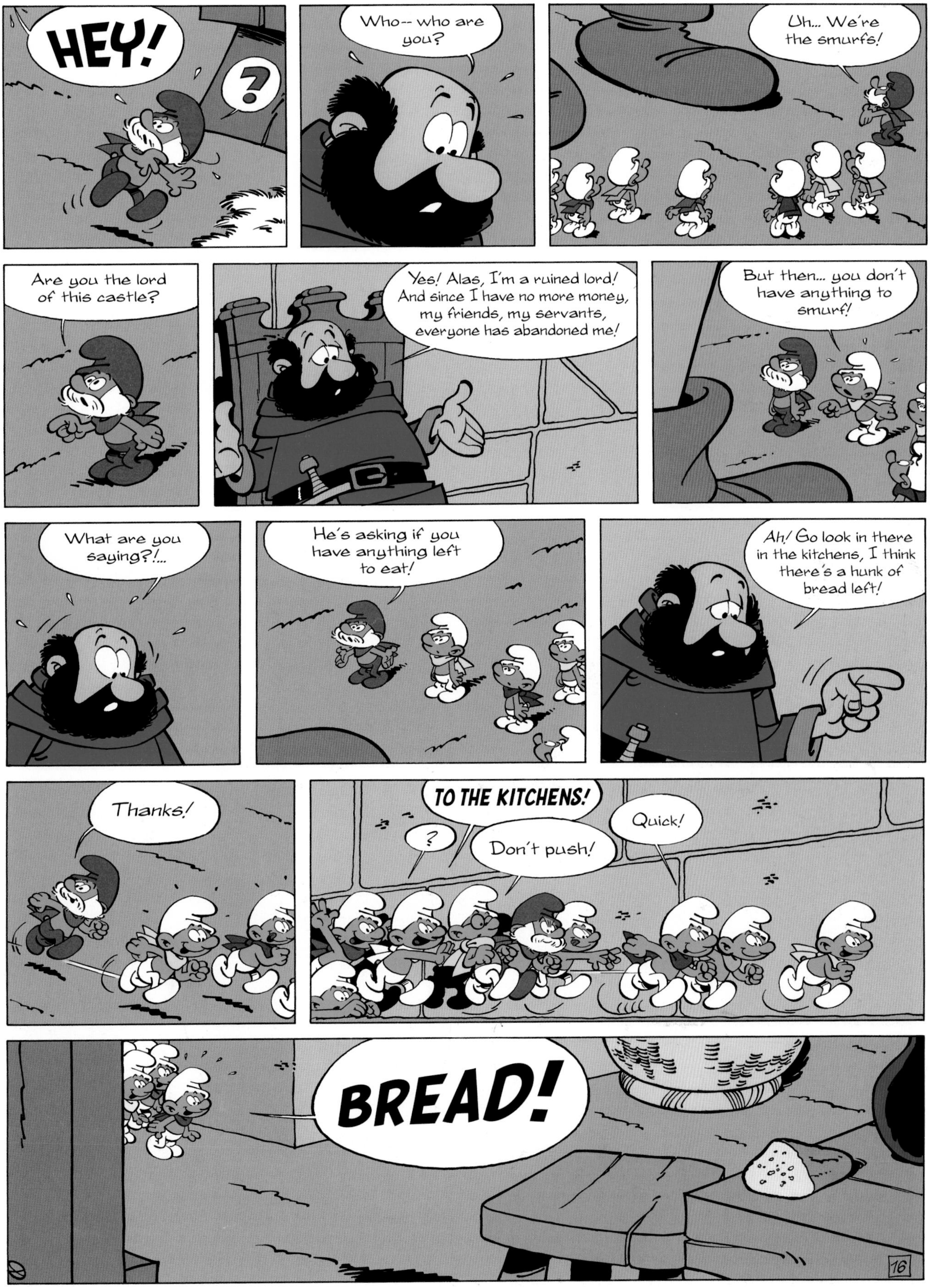

HEY!
?
Who-- who are you?
Uh... We're the smurfs!
Are you the lord of this castle?
Yes! Alas, I'm a ruined lord! And since I have no more money, my friends, my servants, everyone has abandoned me!
But then... you don't have anything to smurf!
What are you saying?!...
He's asking if you have anything left to eat!
Ah! Go look in there in the kitchens, I think there's a hunk of bread left!
Thanks!
TO THE KITCHENS!
?
Don't push!
Quick!
BREAD!
16

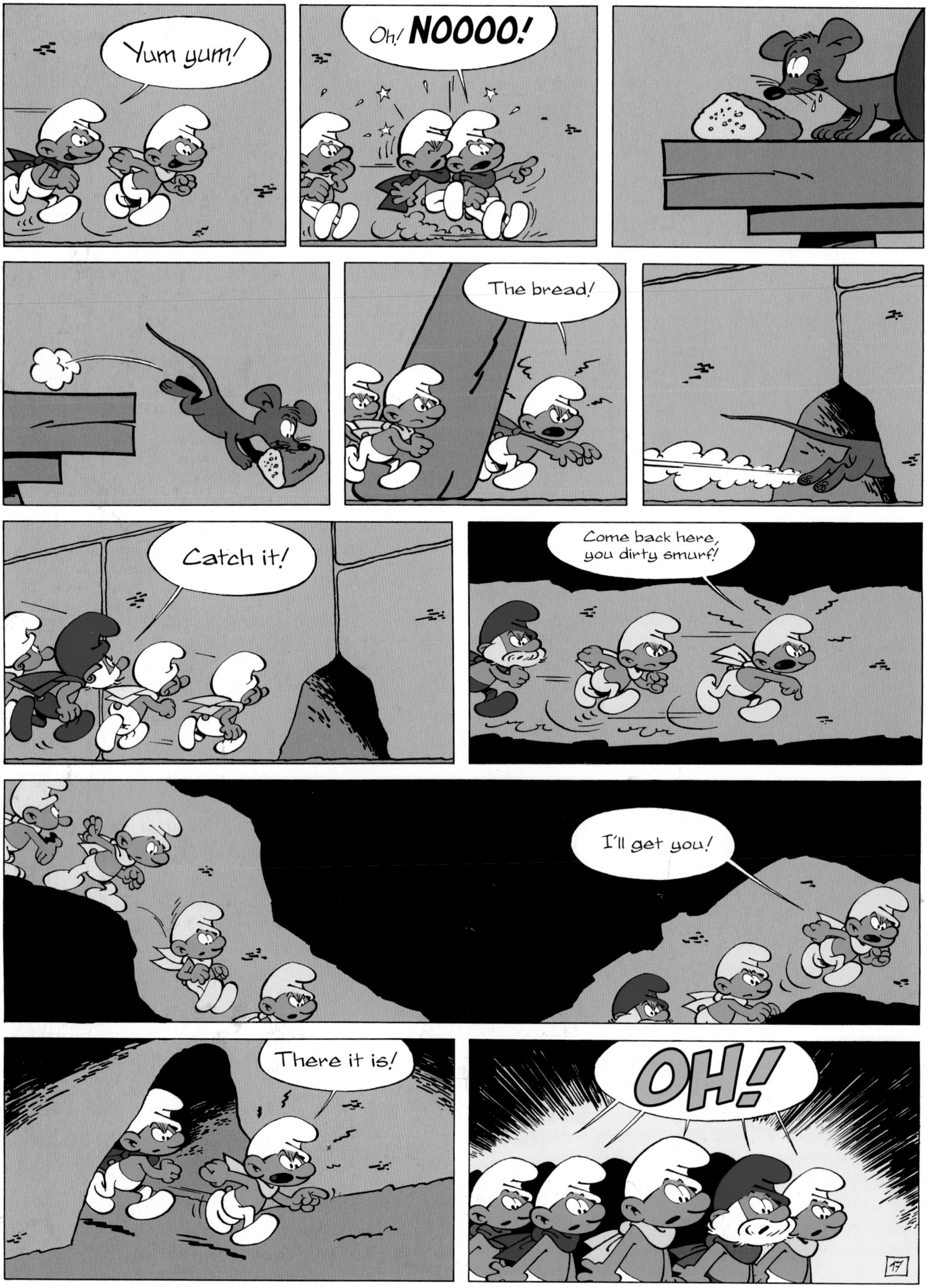
Yum yum!
Oh! NOOOO!
The bread!
Catch it!
Come back here, you dirty smurf!
I'll get you!
There it is!
OH!
17

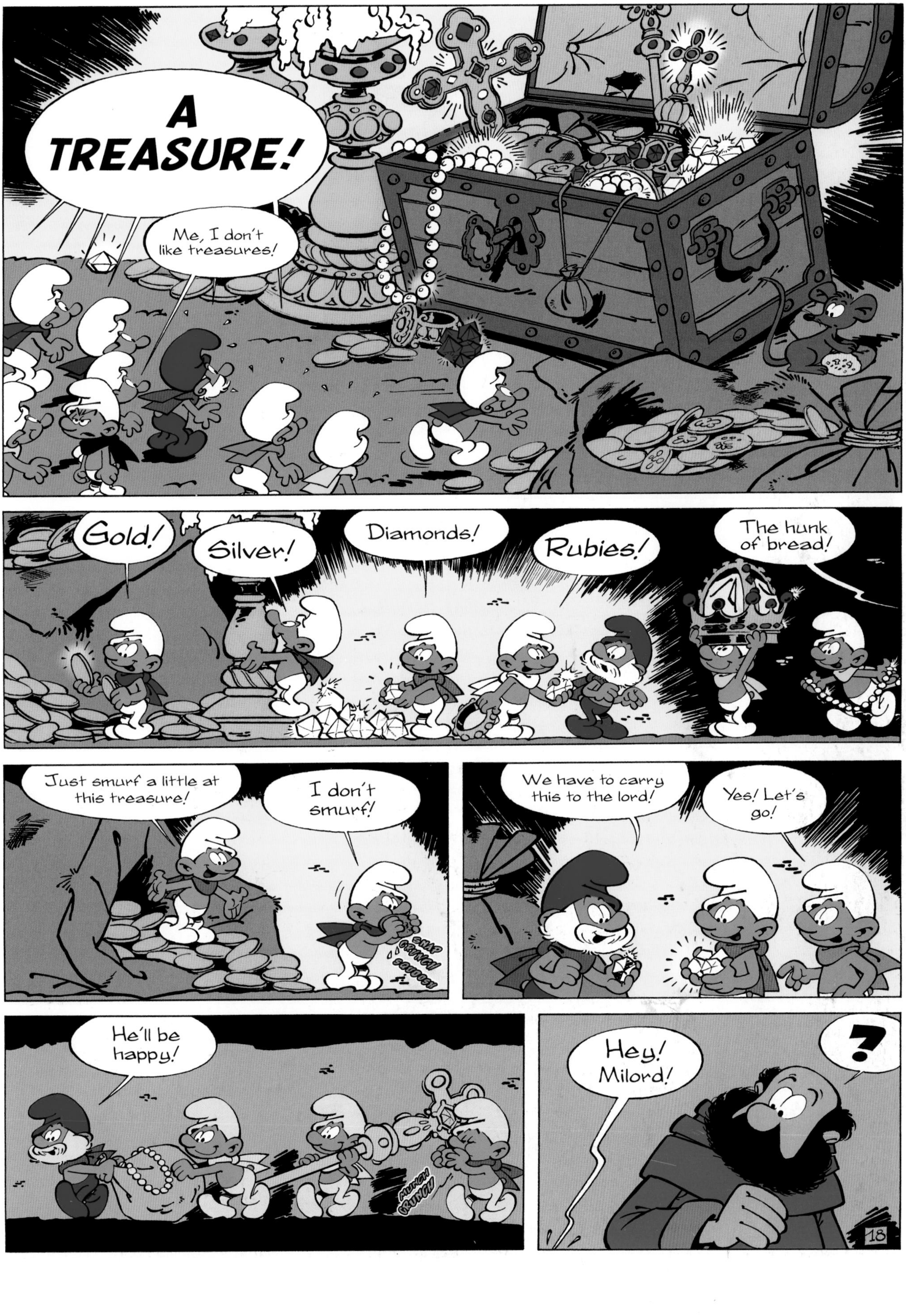
A TREASURE!
Me, I don't like treasures!
Gold!
Silver!
Diamonds!
Rubies!
The hunk of bread!
Just smurf a little at this treasure!
I don't smurf!
SNAP
CRUNCH
SQUOOSH
We have to carry this to the lord!
Yes! Let's go!
He'll be happy!
MUNCH
CRUNCH
Hey! Milord!
?
18

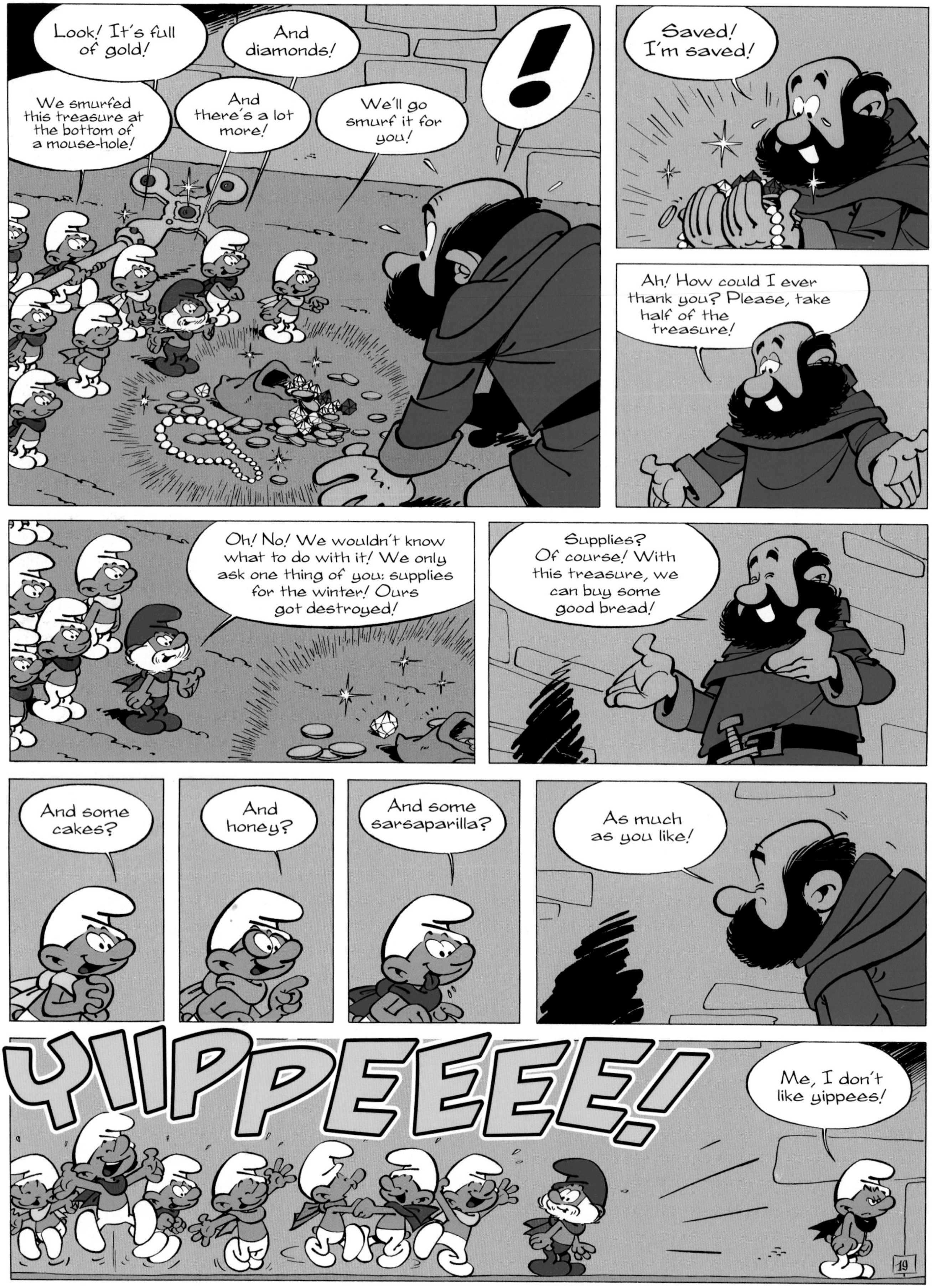
Look! It's full of gold!
And diamonds!
We smurfed this treasure at the bottom of a mouse-hole!
And there's a lot more!
We'll go smurf it for you!
!
Saved! I'm saved!
Ah! How could I ever thank you? Please, take half of the treasure!
Oh! No! We wouldn't know what to do with it! We only ask one thing of you: supplies for the winter! Ours got destroyed!
Supplies? Of course! With this treasure, we can buy some good bread!
And some cakes?
And honey?
And some sarsaparilla?
As much as you like!
YIIPPEEEE!
Me, I don't like yippees!
19

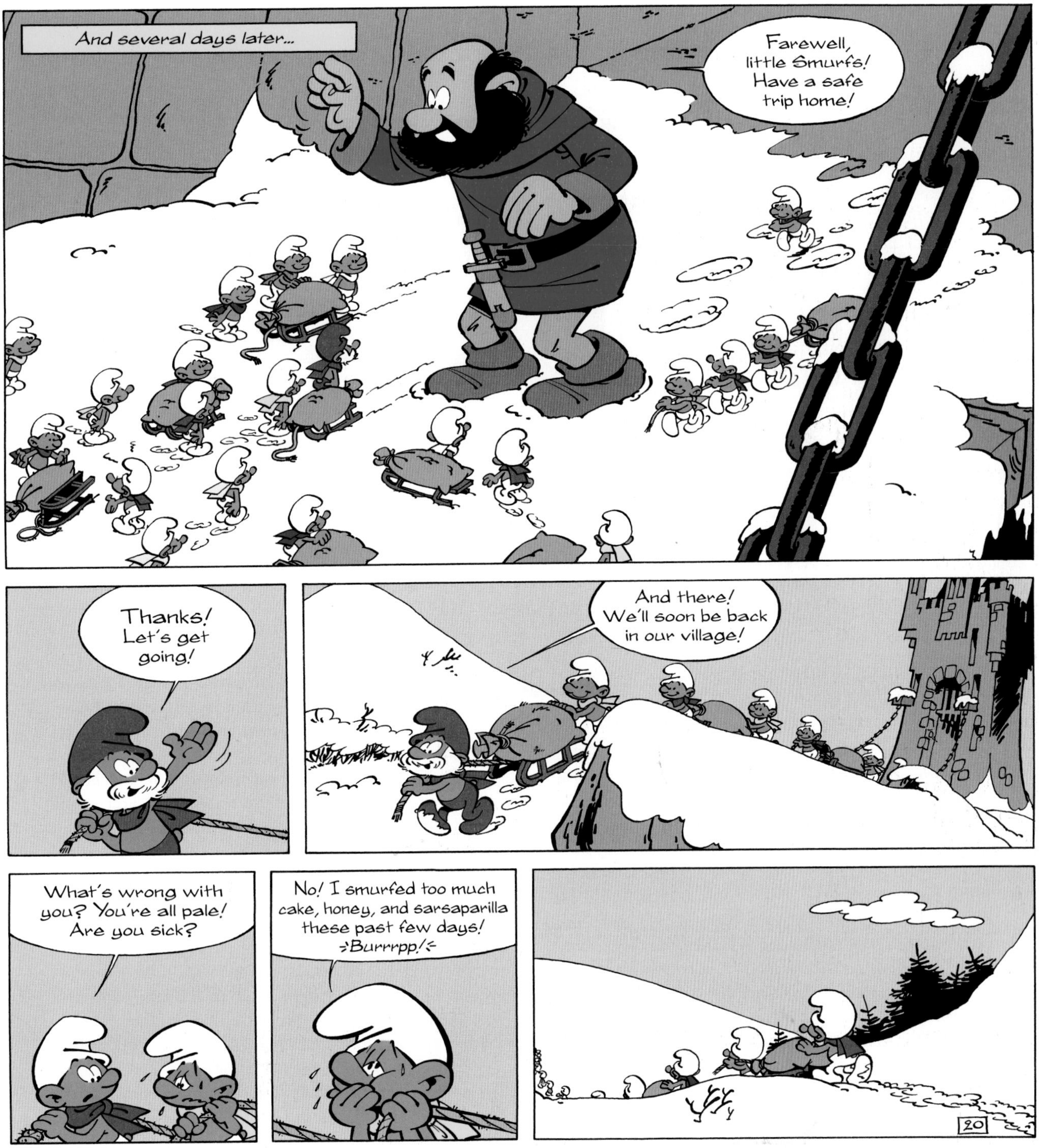
And several days later...
Farewell, little Smurfs! Have a safe trip home!
Thanks! Let's get going!
And there! We'll soon be back in our village!
What's wrong with you? You're all pale! Are you sick?
No! I smurfed too much cake, honey, and sarsaparilla these past few days! >Burrrpp!<
20

And that was the **END** of the Hungry Smurfs.

CRISIS ON INFINITE SMURFS

BY MATT. MURRAY, SMURFOLOGIST

The early publication history of THE SMURFS can seem strange and a bit convoluted to the casual Smurfologist.

As mentioned in THE SMURFS ANTHOLOGY #1, they first appeared in 1958 in the pages of the Franco-Belgian comics anthology *Le Journal de Spirou*'s serial adventure strip "*Johan et Pirlouit*." Their popularity led to their own spin-off series which initially came in the form of pull-out *mini-recits* (mini-comics) created and drawn by *Johan*'s artist, Peyo, with the assistance of his editor and co-writer Yvan Delporte.

Although the publishers of *Spirou* had little faith in the initial proposition, THE SMURFS *mini-recits* were a big hit with the magazine's fans, and between 1959 and 1962, six short stories saw publication including: "*Les Schtroumpfs noirs*," "*Le voleur des Schtroumpfs*," "*L'oeuf et les Schtroumpfs*," "*Le faux Schtroumpf*," "*La faim des Schtroumpfs*," and "*Le centième Schtroumpf*." During this time, the Smurfs continued to make appearances in the serialized adventures of "*Johan et Pirlouit*" including a cameo in 1959's "*Les sept fontaines*" (which is featured in this volume.)

After "*fontaines*" Peyo and *Spirou* published a Smurf-less *Johan et Pirlouit* adventure called "*L'anneau de Castellac*" (1960), but found that without the little blue leprechauns, Johan and Peewit (as he's called in English) didn't have as much selling power, which is why the Smurfs returned in full force in 1961's "*Le pays maudit*" -- which is just as much a SMURFS comic as it is the 12th feature-length *Johan et Pirlouit* adventure. Although he loved Johan and Peewit, Peyo couldn't ignore the fact that their popularity had been eclipsed by that of the Smurfs and neither could the publishers of *Spirou*, who petitioned the artist to transition the characters out of the pull-out *mini-récit* format and into

the large-format pages of the magazine proper. The larger format also allowed for easy reprints in hardcover "albums" (the large "board book" format in which these comics remain in print to this day throughout the French-speaking world). Assembling a magazine serial into a collected album was the intended publishing goal for most of the comics featured in anthologies such as *Spirou*, as it increased the popularity and visibility of the title, as well as the publisher's revenue.

While Peyo and his studio (which now included a number of art assistants including Will, who collaborated with Peyo on "*Benoit Brisefer*" -- published by Papercutz as BENNY BREAKIRON) started with shorter original stories for the new arrangement, Peyo also decided to have the original *mini-recits* re-drawn by his staff to the new size, allowing him to focus the bulk of his attention on his four other comics (the aforementioned "*Johan*" and "*Benoit*," in addition to the adolescent adventure comic "*Jacky et Celestin*" and the comedy strip "*Poussy*") as well as the business of the Smurfs, which now included merchandising and a series of black and white animated shorts which were being produced for Belgian television.

In 1963, *Éditions Dupuis* (which owned *Spirou*) published the first Smurfs album, which debuted the re-drawn versions of "*Les Schtroumpfs noirs*" and "*Le voleur des Schtroumpfs*" as well as a reprint of "*Le Schtroumpf volant*" the first of the new stories from the magazine. Meanwhile, Peyo's studio continued to rework their older comics while developing new long form Smurfs adventures such as "*Le Schtroumpfissime*" and "*La Schtroumpfette*." Publication of new and old strips, long form and short, was alternated in the pages of *Spirou* until there was enough material to collect in a hardcover album (which worked out to every year or two, depending on the scope of the narratives within).

The "*Le Schtroumpfissime*" album (1965) featured "*Schtroumpfonie en ut,*" (direct from the pages of *Spirou* proper) and was followed by "*La Schtroumpfette*" (1966) which featured the re-drawn "*La faim des Schtroumpfs*" as back-up. In 1968, all loose ends in regards to the *mini-recit*s were tied-up with the album "*L'œuf et les Schtroumpfs*" which featured the re-drawn versions of the title tale, as well as "*Le faux Schtroumpf*" and "*Le centième Schtroumpf.*"

The journey you're about to embark upon with "The Smurfs and the Egg," was started in 1960, as the pull-out mini-comic "*L'oeuf et les Schtroumpfs,*" but the edition herein was re-drawn, expanded and published in the pages of *Spirou* in 1966. The back-up stories "The Fake Smurf" and "The Hundredth Smurf" began their lives in 1961 and 1962 respectively, and while the "new" "Fake Smurf" appeared in the pages of *Spirou* in 1968, the re-drawn "Hundredth Smurf" didn't see print until the publication of the album.

Confused yet?

Fear not, Blue Believers, even the most seasoned Smurfologists have to whip out a chart to figure things out for the introductions they're charged to write. Which is why it's best to follow two rules when trying to trace the publishing history, and in some cases, the "continuity" of THE SMURFS (which is loose at best): 1) when in doubt, forget everything else but the order of the original albums (yes, that means the recent Papercutz publication history as well, which saw "*Le voleur des Schtroumpfs*" released as "The Smurfnapper" before "The Purple Smurfs" – our version of "*Les Schtroumpfs noirs*" – which in turn was released before the Smurfs' actual first appearance in "The Smurfs and the Magic Flute;" 2) forget the order of things all together, and just have fun.

While THE SMURFS ANTHOLOGY is Papercutz' attempt to restore the officially recognized order of THE SMURFS graphic novel series, we're still managing to smurf up the works by including the Smurfs' appearances in the *Johan et Pirlouit* albums that either pre-date or run concurrent with some of the stories they share a specific ANTHOLOGY volume with (OR could even be considered their own continuity all together… but should they? *ZUT!* What the smurf?!)

So, you know what? Let us worry about all that smurfy-wurfy timey-wimey stuff. Your assignment in Smurfology for right now, is to sit back, and have fun with this edition of "The Smurf and the Egg." ●

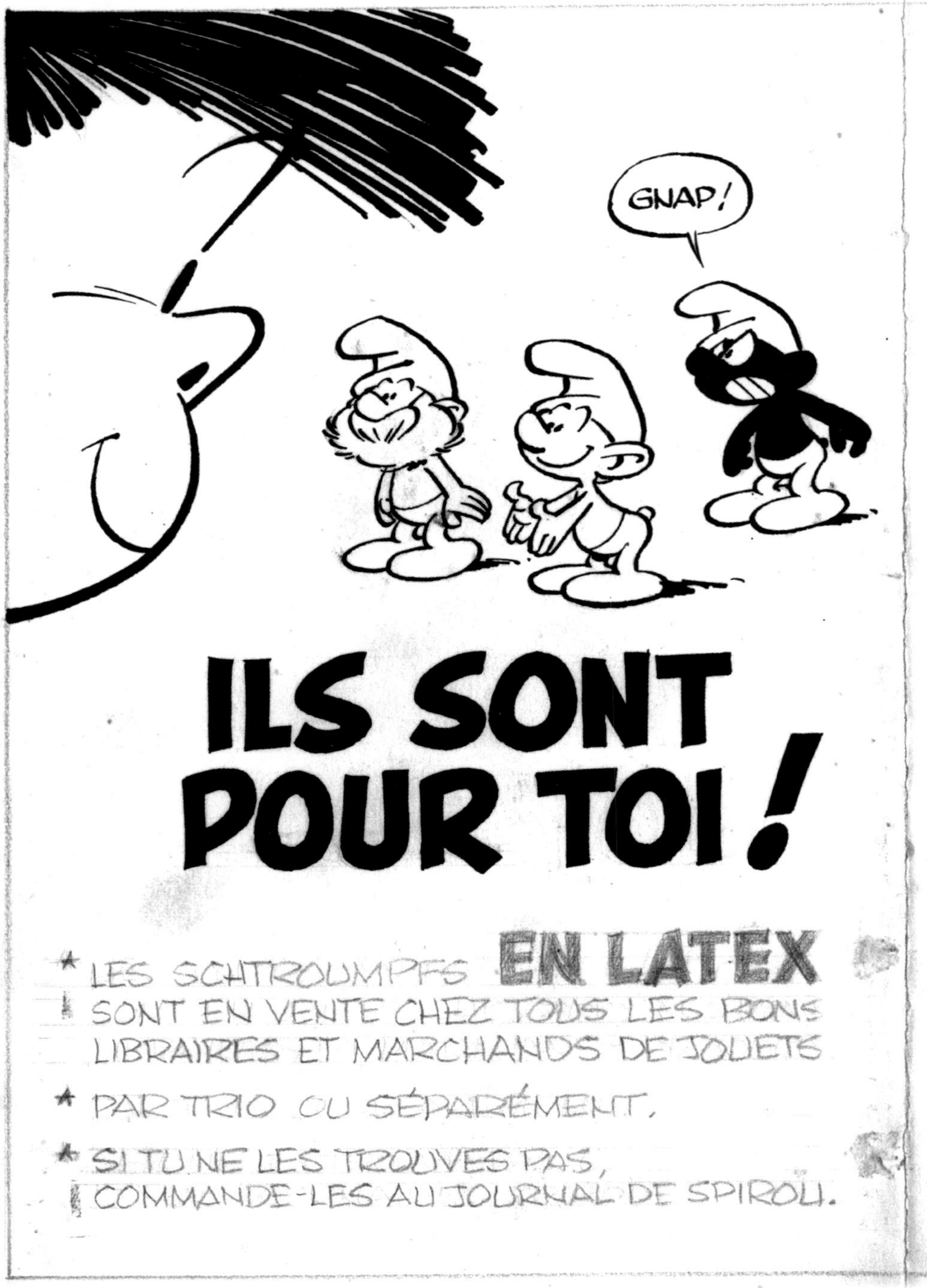
GNAP !
ILS SONT POUR TOI !
★ LES SCHTROUMPFS EN LATEX
SONT EN VENTE CHEZ TOUS LES BONS LIBRAIRES ET MARCHANDS DE JOUETS
★ PAR TRIO OU SÉPARÉMENT.
★ SI TU NE LES TROUVES PAS, COMMANDE-LES AU JOURNAL DE SPIROU.

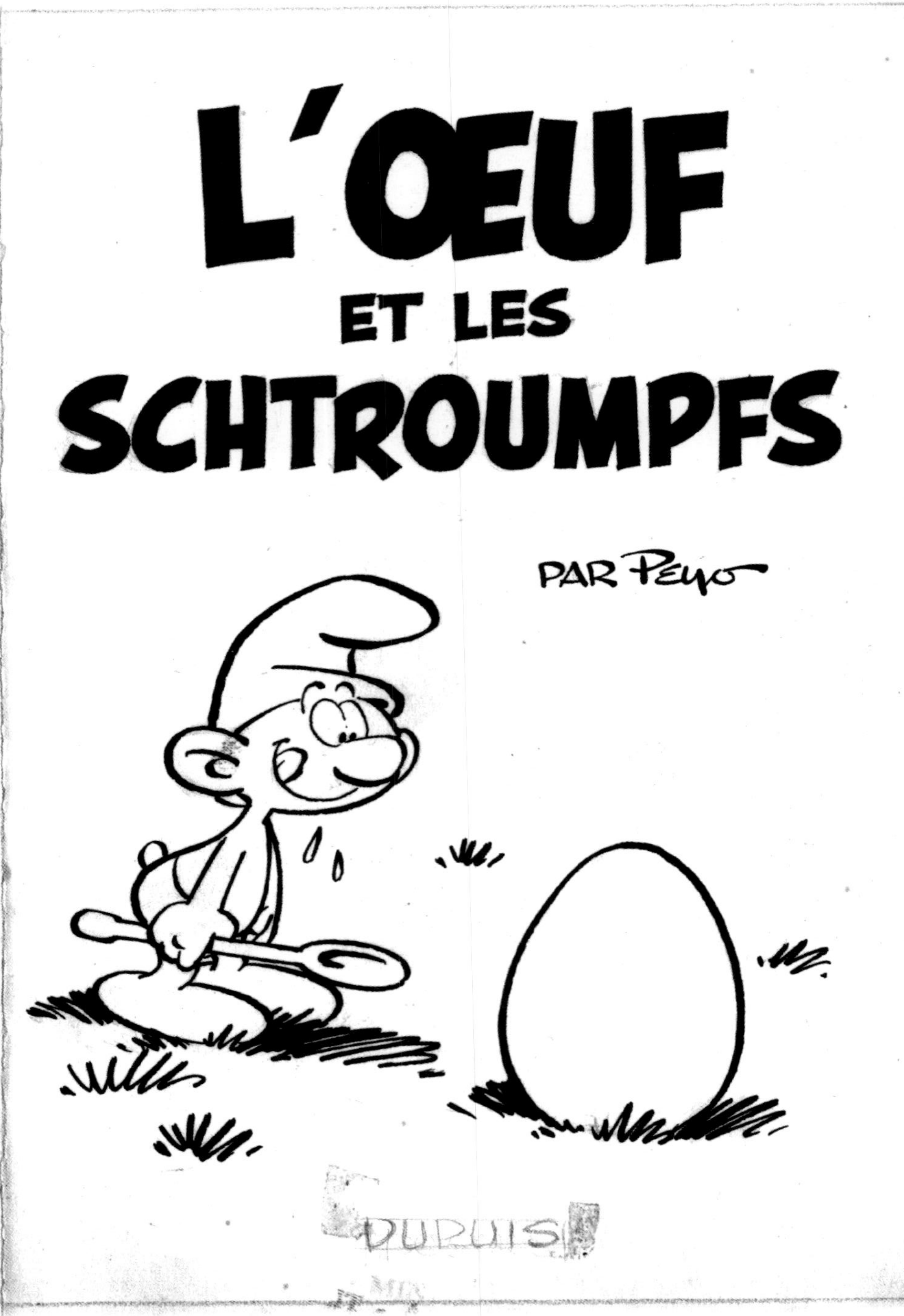
L'OEUF
ET LES
SCHTROUMPFS
PAR PEYO
DUPUIS

4e SERIE

3 Histoires de Schtroumpfs par Peyo

L'OEUF ET LES SCHTROUMPFS

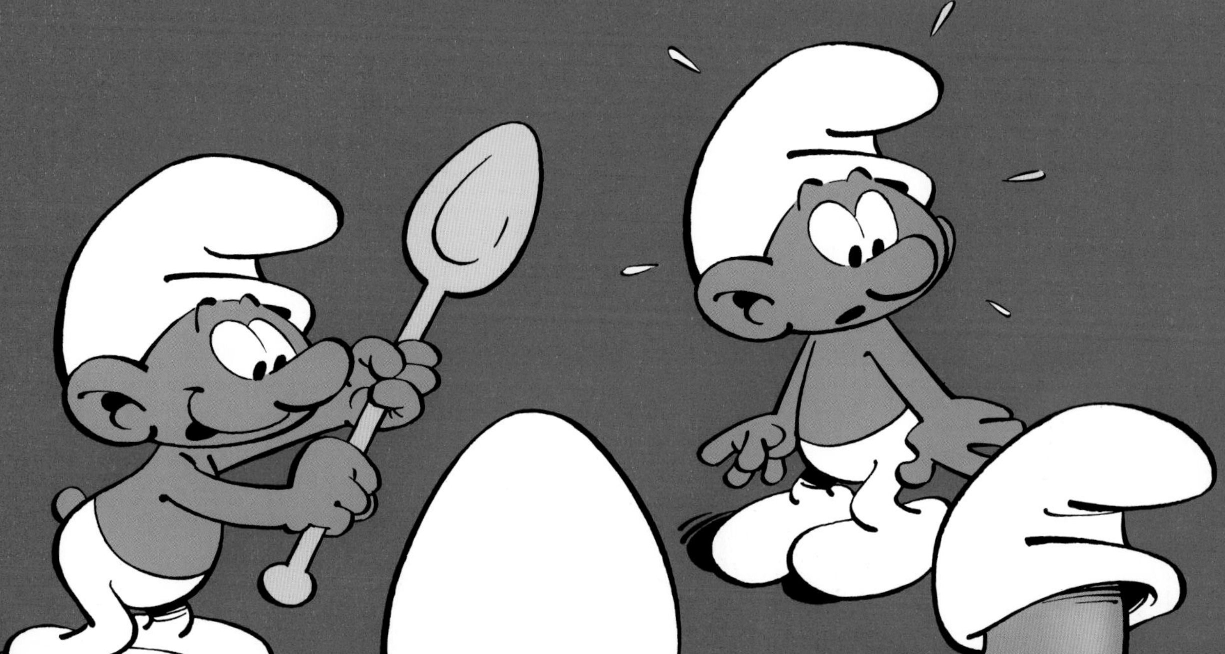

LE FAUX SCHTROUMPF
LE CENTIÈME SCHTROUMPF

THE SMURFS AND THE EGG

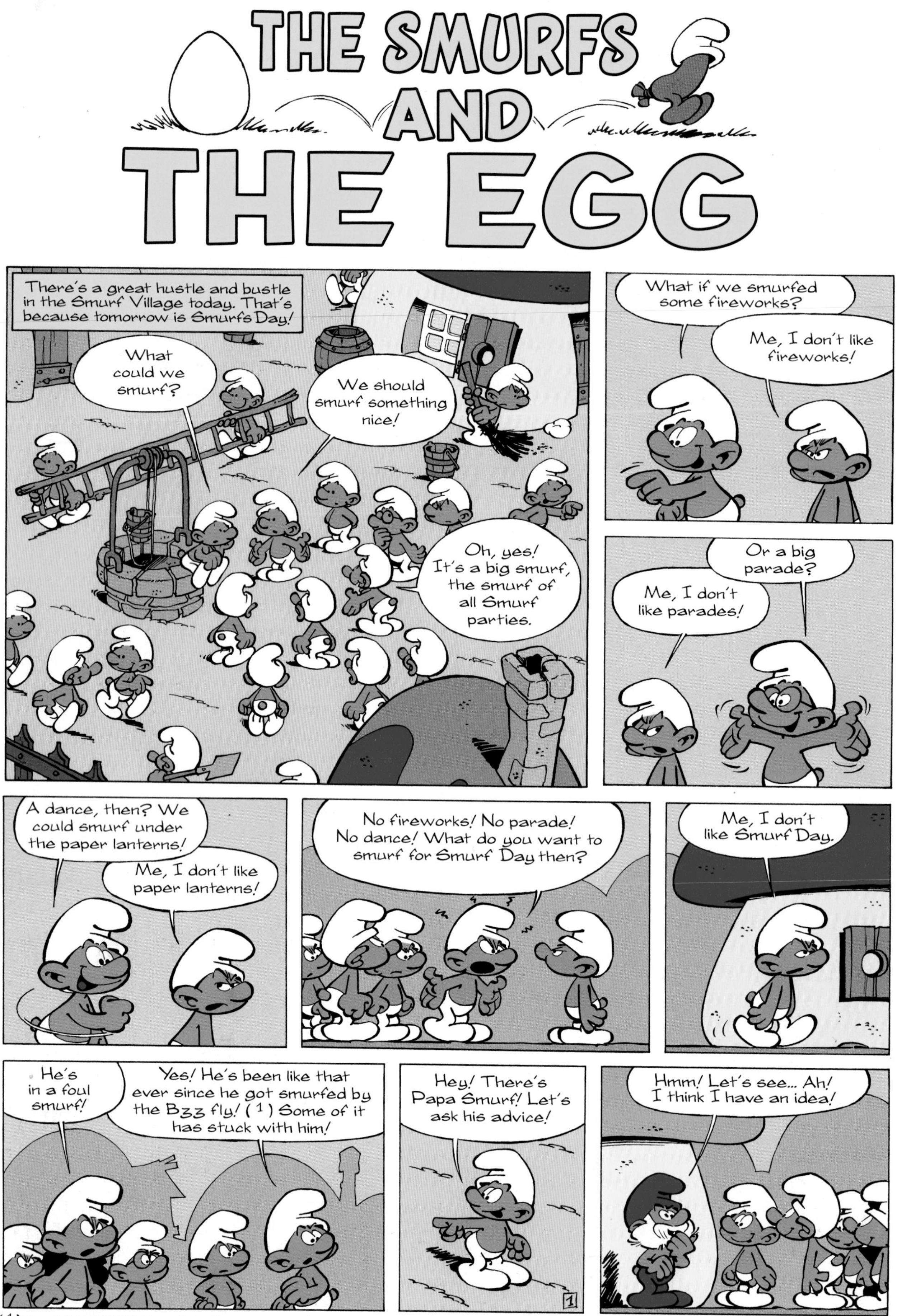

There's a great hustle and bustle in the Smurf Village today. That's because tomorrow is Smurfs Day!
What could we smurf?
We should smurf something nice!
Oh, yes! It's a big smurf, the smurf of all Smurf parties.
What if we smurfed some fireworks?
Me, I don't like fireworks!
Or a big parade?
Me, I don't like parades!
A dance, then? We could smurf under the paper lanterns!
Me, I don't like paper lanterns!
No fireworks! No parade! No dance! What do you want to smurf for Smurf Day then?
Me, I don't like Smurf Day.
He's in a foul smurf!
Yes! He's been like that ever since he got smurfed by the Bzz fly! (1) Some of it has stuck with him!
Hey! There's Papa Smurf! Let's ask his advice!
Hmm! Let's see... Ah! I think I have an idea!
1

(1) See THE SMURFS #1 "The Purple Smurfs" or THE SMURFS ANTHOLOGY Vol. 1.

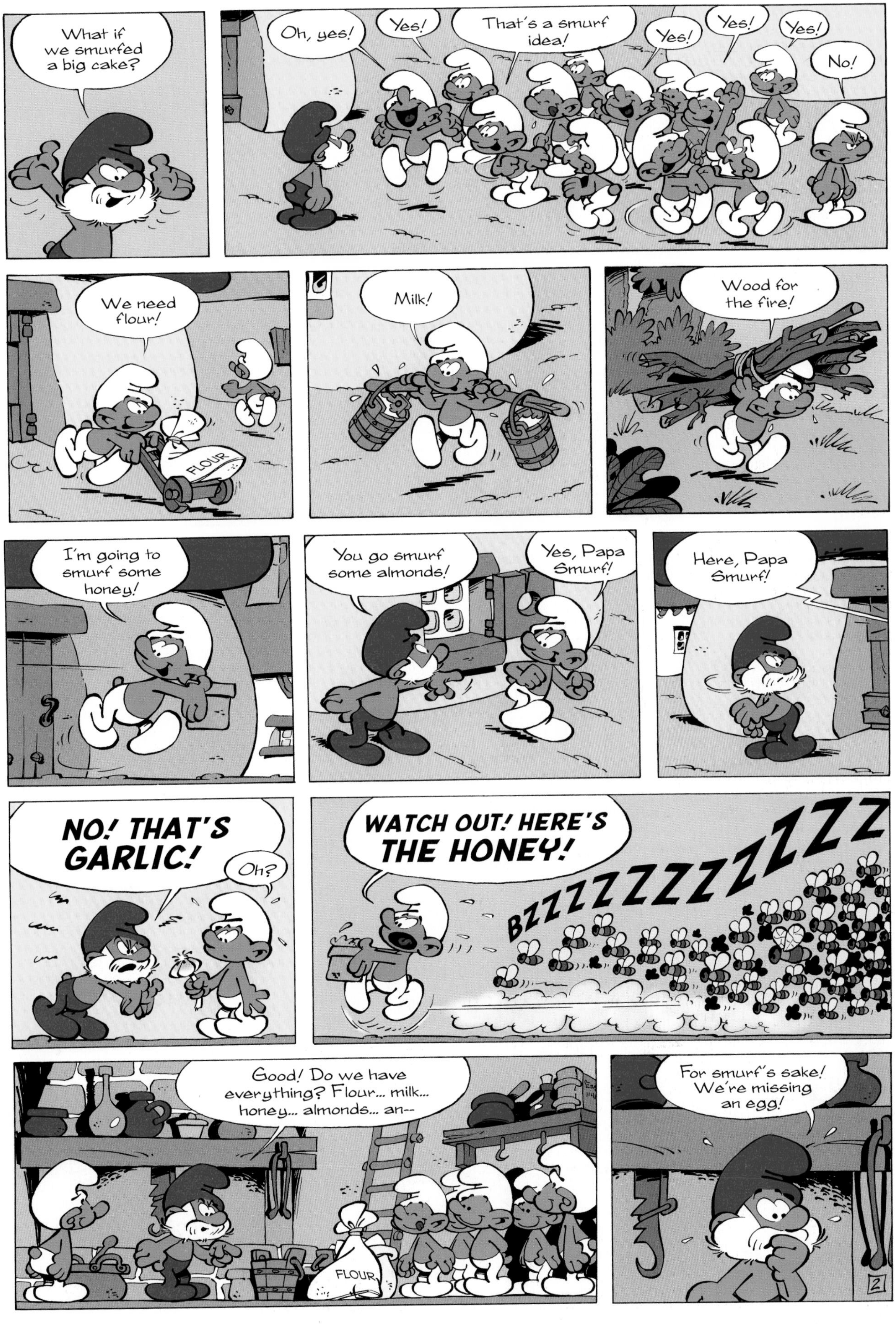

What if we smurfed a big cake?
Oh, yes!
Yes!
That's a smurf idea!
Yes!
Yes!
Yes!
No!
We need flour!
FLOUR
Milk!
Wood for the fire!
I'm going to smurf some honey!
You go smurf some almonds!
Yes, Papa Smurf!
Here, Papa Smurf!
NO! THAT'S GARLIC!
Oh?
WATCH OUT! HERE'S THE HONEY!
BZZZZZZZZZZZZ
Good! Do we have everything? Flour... milk... honey... almonds... an--
FLOUR
For smurf's sake! We're missing an egg!
2

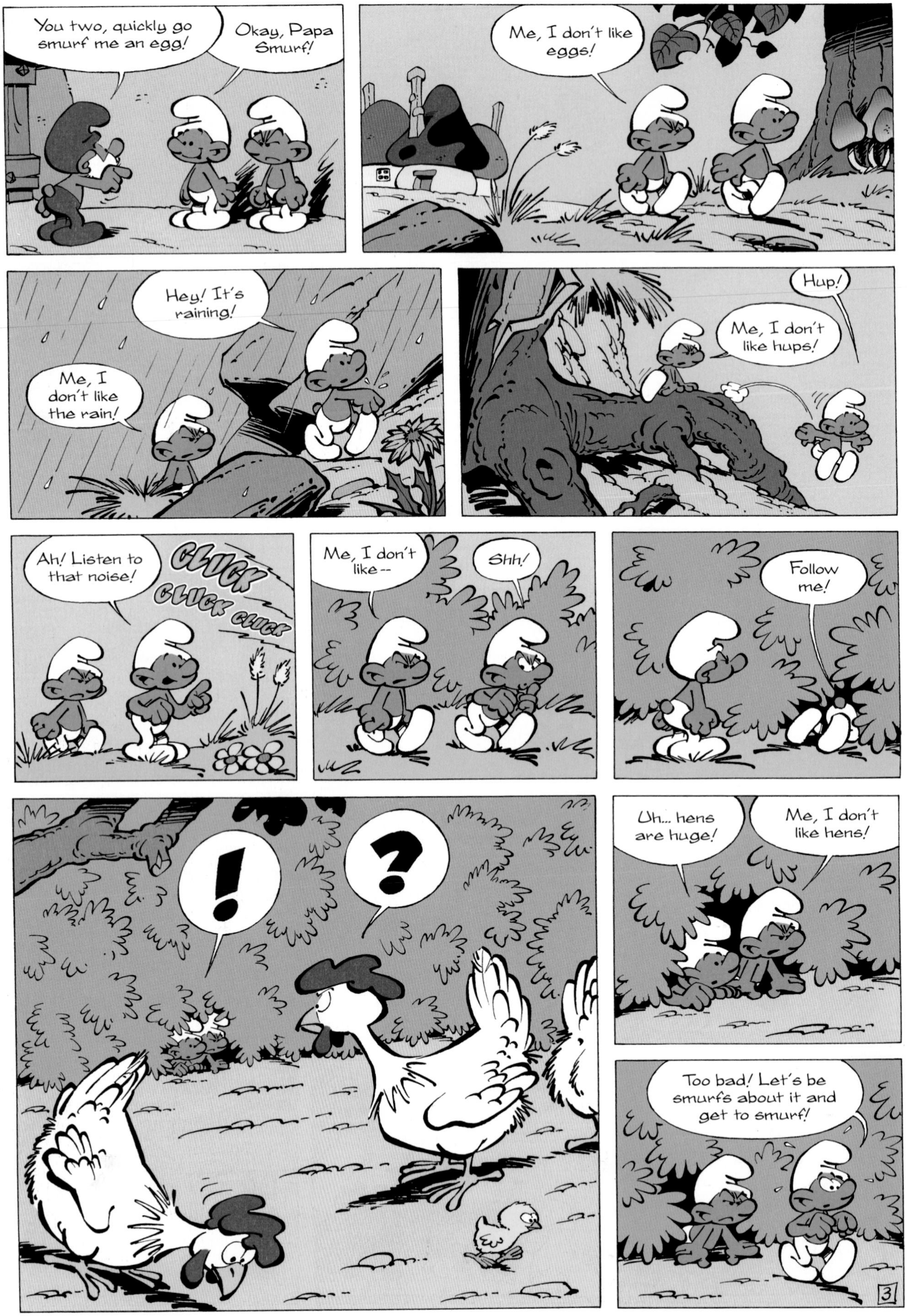
You two, quickly go smurf me an egg!
Okay, Papa Smurf!
Me, I don't like eggs!
Hey! It's raining!
Me, I don't like the rain!
Hup!
Me, I don't like hups!
Ah! Listen to that noise!
CLUCK
CLUCK CLUCK CLUCK
Me, I don't like--
Shh!
Follow me!
!
?
Uh... hens are huge!
Me, I don't like hens!
Too bad! Let's be smurfs about it and get to smurf!
3

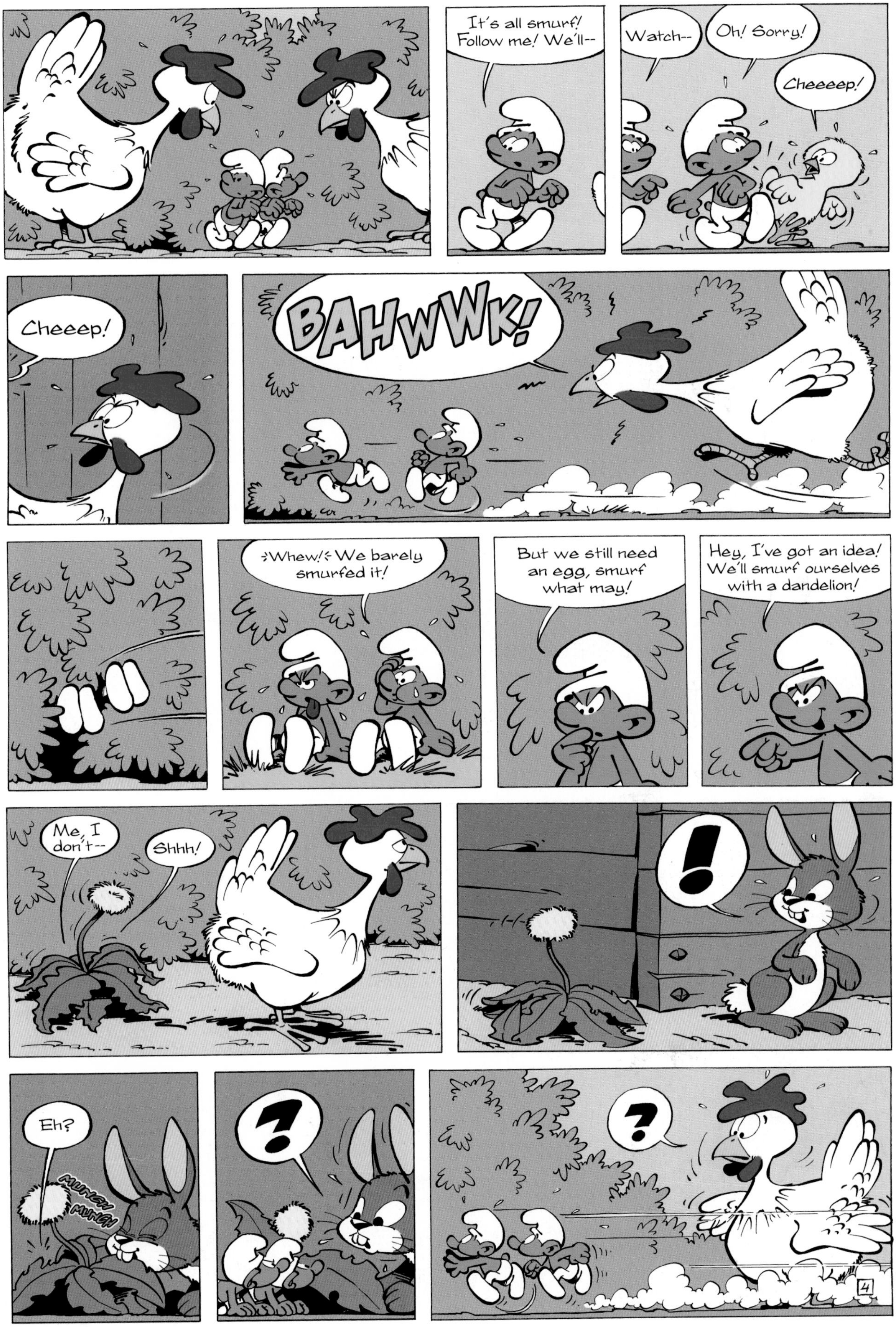
It's all smurf! Follow me! We'll--
Watch--
Oh! Sorry!
Cheeeep!
Cheeeep!
BAHWWK!
Whew! We barely smurfed it!
But we still need an egg, smurf what may!
Hey, I've got an idea! We'll smurf ourselves with a dandelion!
Me, I don't--
Shhh!
!
Eh?
MUNCH
MUNCH
?
?
4

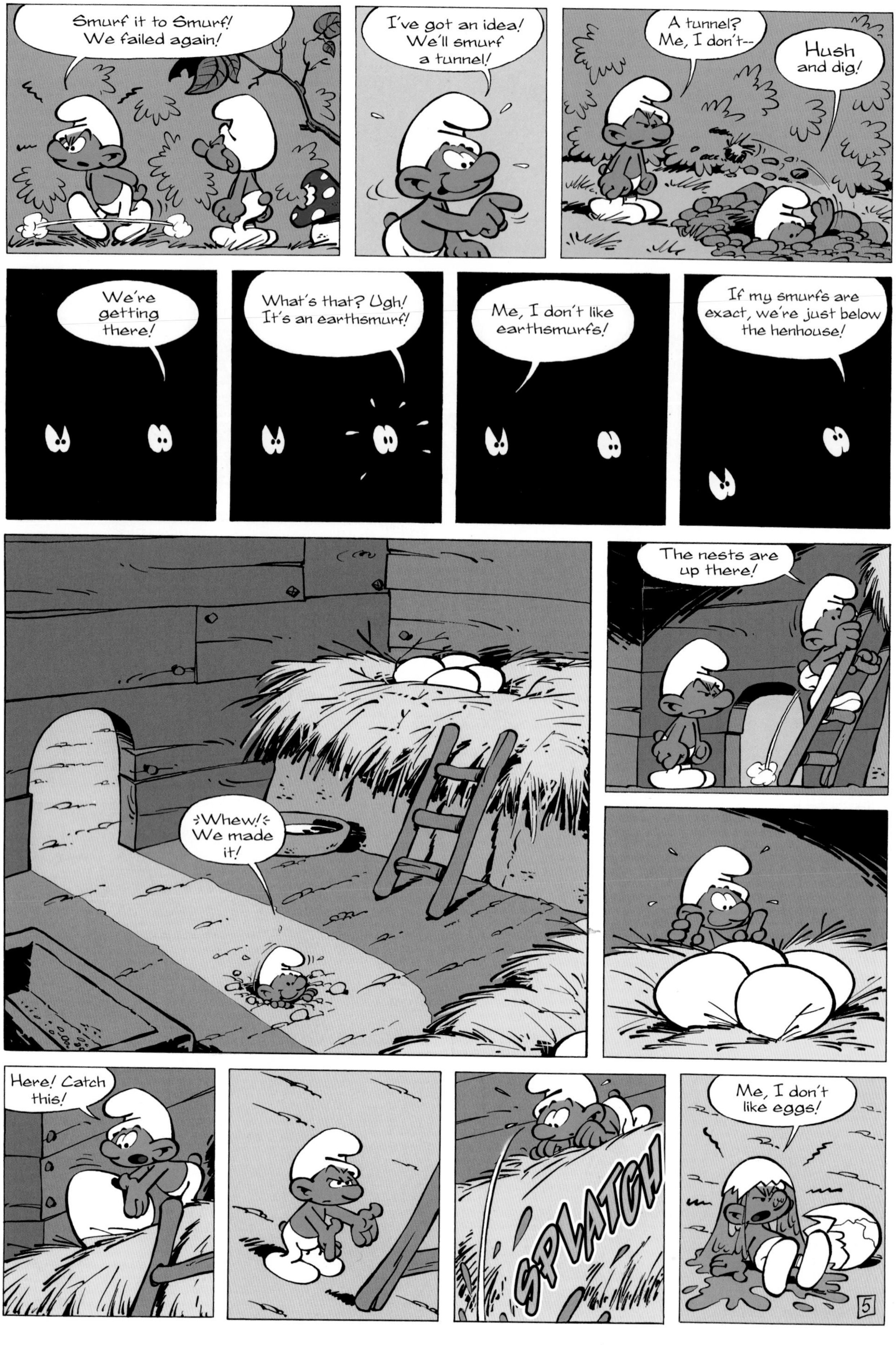

Smurf it to Smurf! We failed again!
I've got an idea! We'll smurf a tunnel!
A tunnel? Me, I don't--
Hush and dig!
We're getting there!
What's that? Ugh! It's an earthsmurf!
Me, I don't like earthsmurfs!
If my smurfs are exact, we're just below the henhouse!
Whew! We made it!
The nests are up there!
Here! Catch this!
SPLATCH
Me, I don't like eggs!
5

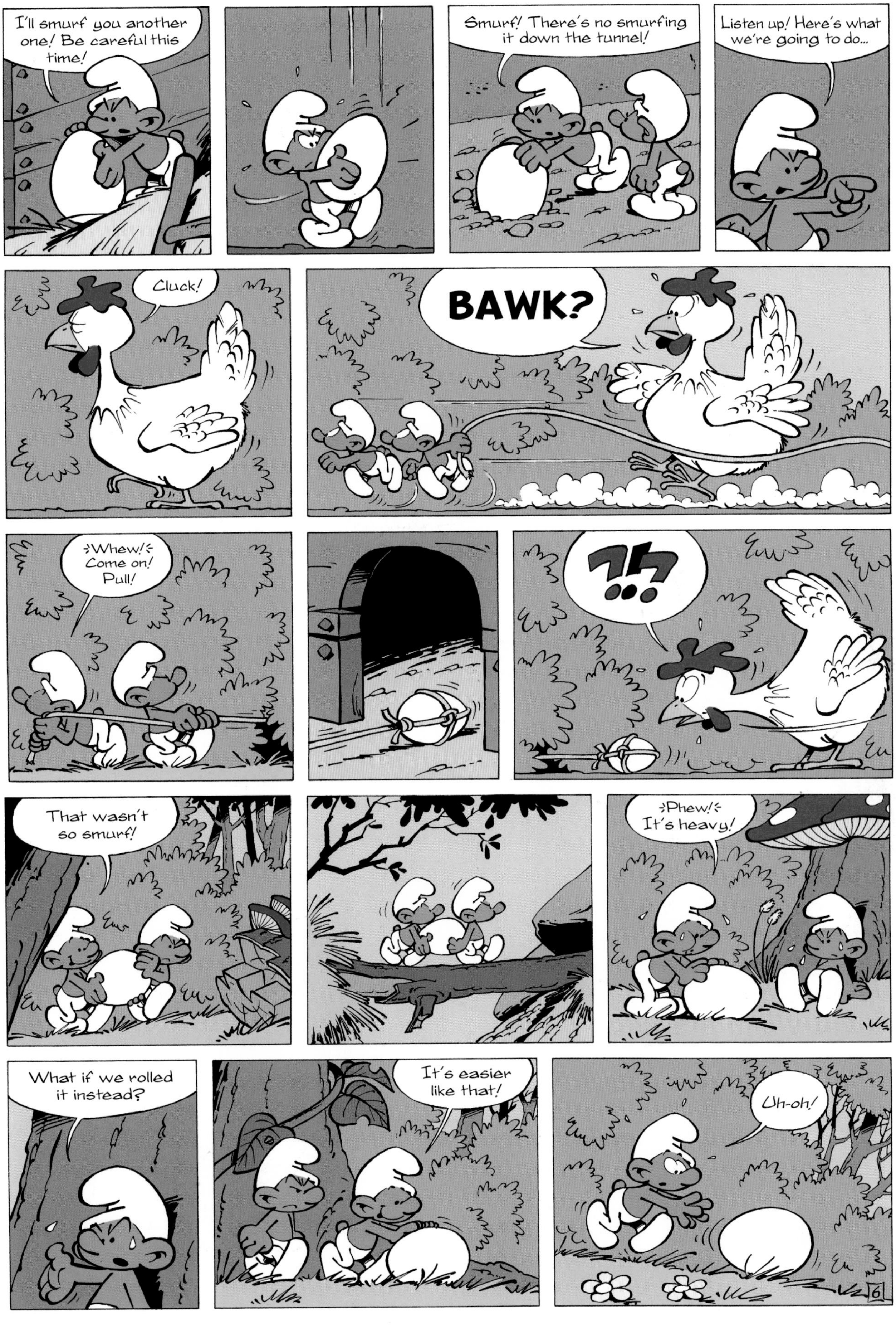
I'll smurf you another one! Be careful this time!
Smurf! There's no smurfing it down the tunnel!
Listen up! Here's what we're going to do...
Cluck!
BAWK?
Whew! Come on! Pull!
?!...
That wasn't so smurf!
Phew! It's heavy!
What if we rolled it instead?
It's easier like that!
Uh-oh!
6

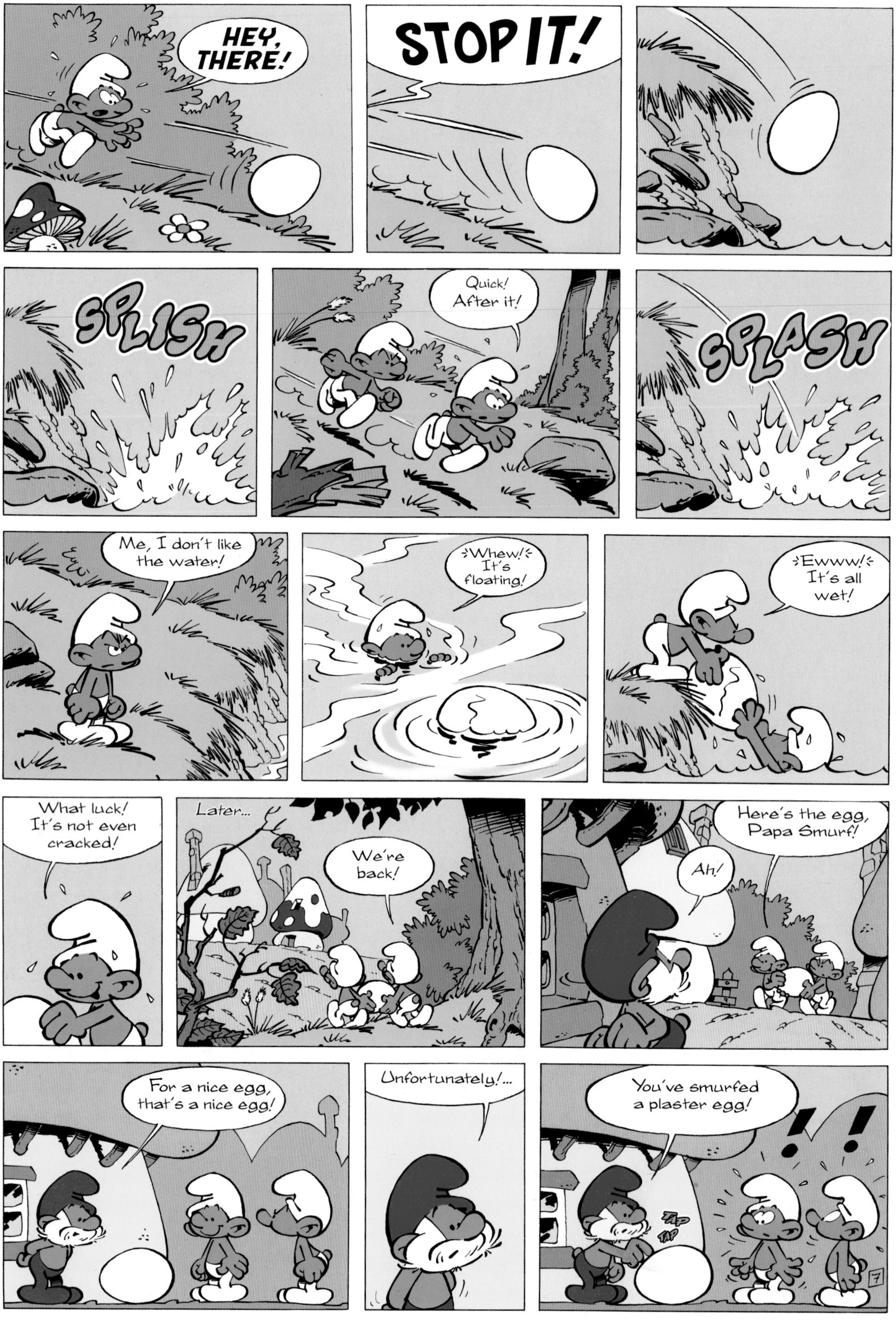
HEY, THERE!
STOP IT!
SPLISH
Quick! After it!
SPLASH
Me, I don't like the water!
Whew! It's floating!
Ewww! It's all wet!
What luck! It's not even cracked!
Later...
We're back!
Here's the egg, Papa Smurf!
Ah!
For a nice egg, that's a nice egg!
Unfortunately!...
You've smurfed a plaster egg!
TAP TAP
!!
7

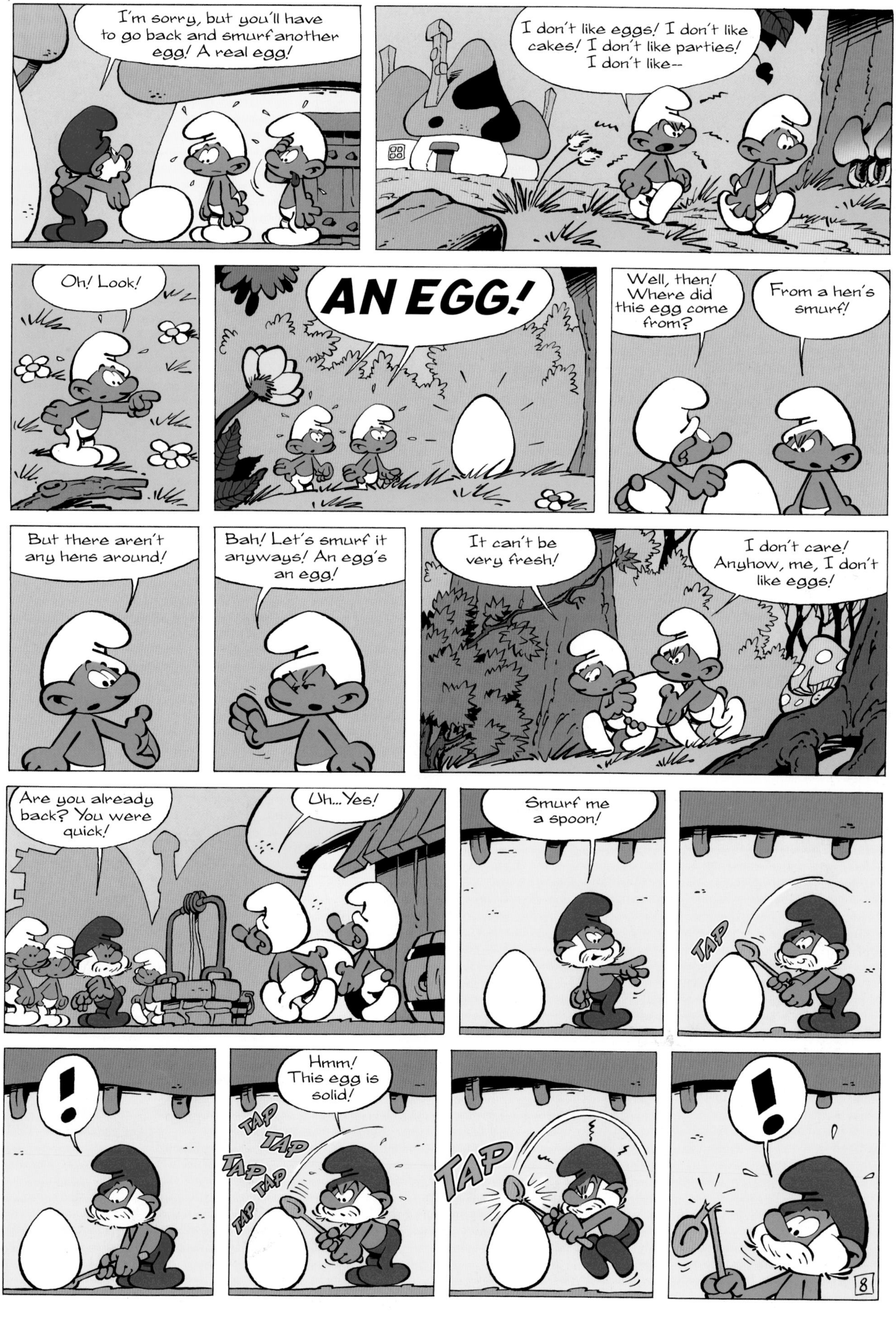
I'm sorry, but you'll have to go back and smurf another egg! A real egg!
I don't like eggs! I don't like cakes! I don't like parties! I don't like--
Oh! Look!
AN EGG!
Well, then! Where did this egg come from?
From a hen's smurf!
But there aren't any hens around!
Bah! Let's smurf it anyways! An egg's an egg!
It can't be very fresh!
I don't care! Anyhow, me, I don't like eggs!
Are you already back? You were quick!
Uh... Yes!
Smurf me a spoon!
TAP
!
Hmm! This egg is solid!
TAP TAP TAP TAP TAP TAP
TAP
!
8

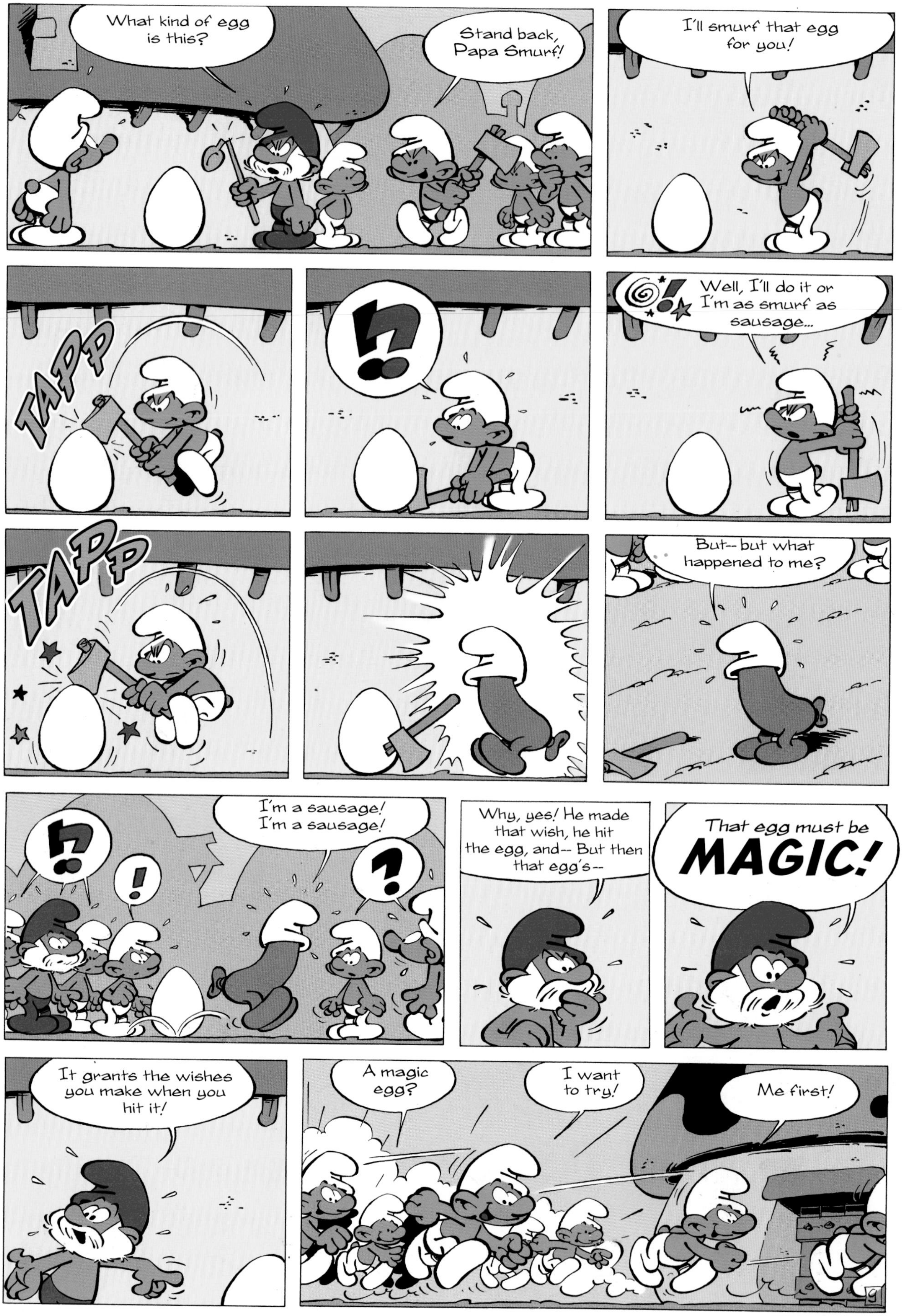

What kind of egg is this?
Stand back, Papa Smurf!
I'll smurf that egg for you!
TAPP
Well, I'll do it or I'm as smurf as sausage...
TAPP
But-- but what happened to me?
I'm a sausage! I'm a sausage!
Why, yes! He made that wish, he hit the egg, and-- But then that egg's--
That egg must be MAGIC!
It grants the wishes you make when you hit it!
A magic egg?
I want to try!
Me first!

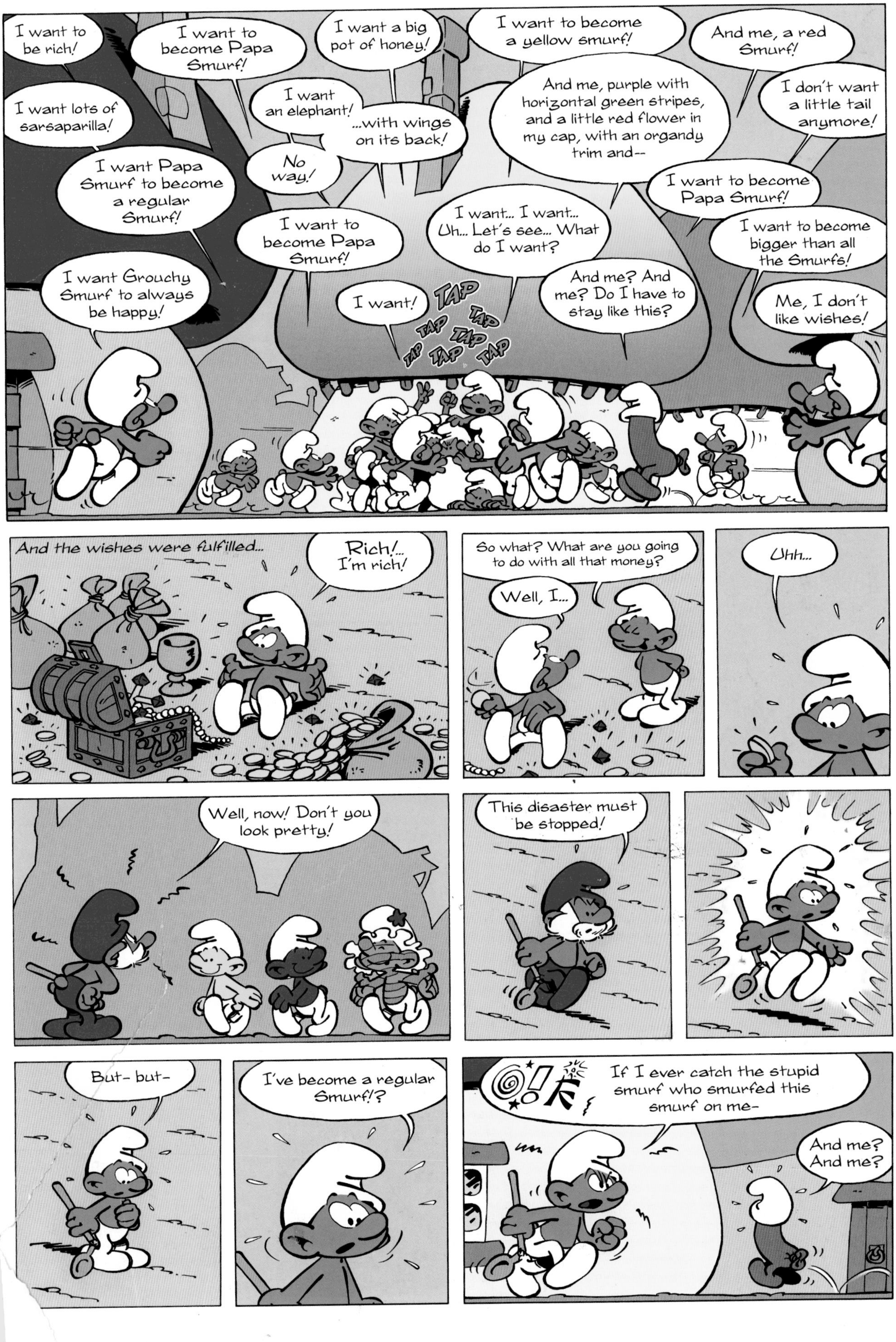
I want to be rich!
I want to become Papa Smurf!
I want a big pot of honey!
I want to become a yellow smurf!
And me, a red Smurf!
I want lots of sarsaparilla!
I want an elephant!
...with wings on its back!
No way!
And me, purple with horizontal green stripes, and a little red flower in my cap, with an organdy trim and--
I don't want a little tail anymore!
I want Papa Smurf to become a regular Smurf!
I want to become Papa Smurf!
I want... I want... Uh... Let's see... What do I want?
I want to become Papa Smurf!
I want to become bigger than all the Smurfs!
I want Grouchy Smurf to always be happy!
I want!
TAP TAP TAP TAP TAP TAP TAP
And me? And me? Do I have to stay like this?
Me, I don't like wishes!
And the wishes were fulfilled...
Rich!... I'm rich!
So what? What are you going to do with all that money?
Well, I...
Uhh...
Well, now! Don't you look pretty!
This disaster must be stopped!
But- but-
I've become a regular Smurf!?
If I ever catch the stupid smurf who smurfed this smurf on me-
And me? And me?

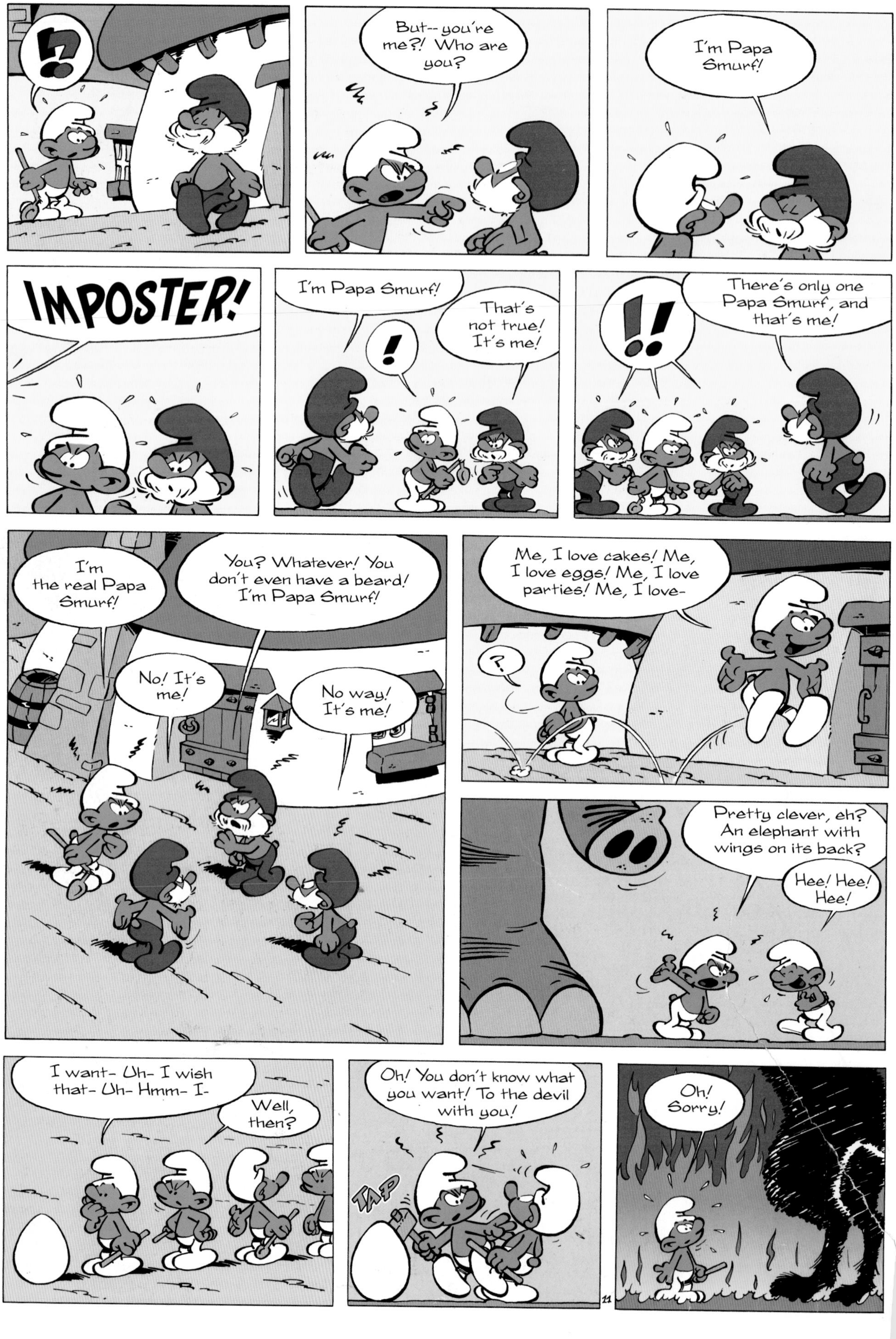

?!
But-- you're me?! Who are you?
I'm Papa Smurf!
IMPOSTER!
I'm Papa Smurf!
!
That's not true! It's me!
!!
There's only one Papa Smurf, and that's me!
I'm the real Papa Smurf!
You? Whatever! You don't even have a beard! I'm Papa Smurf!
No! It's me!
No way! It's me!
Me, I love cakes! Me, I love eggs! Me, I love parties! Me, I love-
?
Pretty clever, eh? An elephant with wings on its back?
Hee! Hee! Hee!
I want- Uh- I wish that- Uh- Hmm- I-
Well, then?
Oh! You don't know what you want! To the devil with you!
TAP
Oh! Sorry!
11

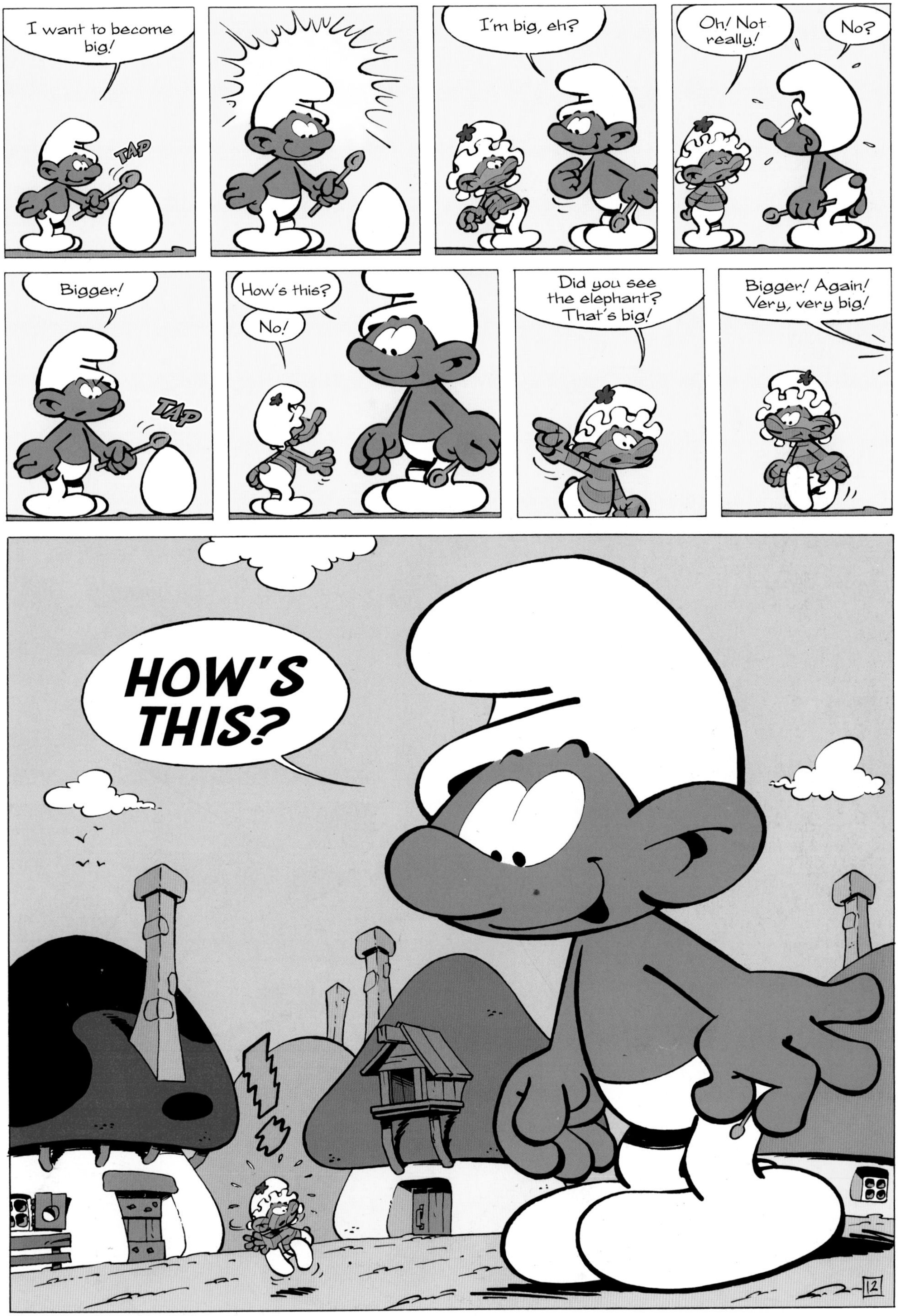
I want to become big!
TAP
I'm big, eh?
Oh! Not really!
No?
Bigger!
TAP
How's this?
No!
Did you see the elephant? That's big!
Bigger! Again! Very, very big!
HOW'S THIS?
12

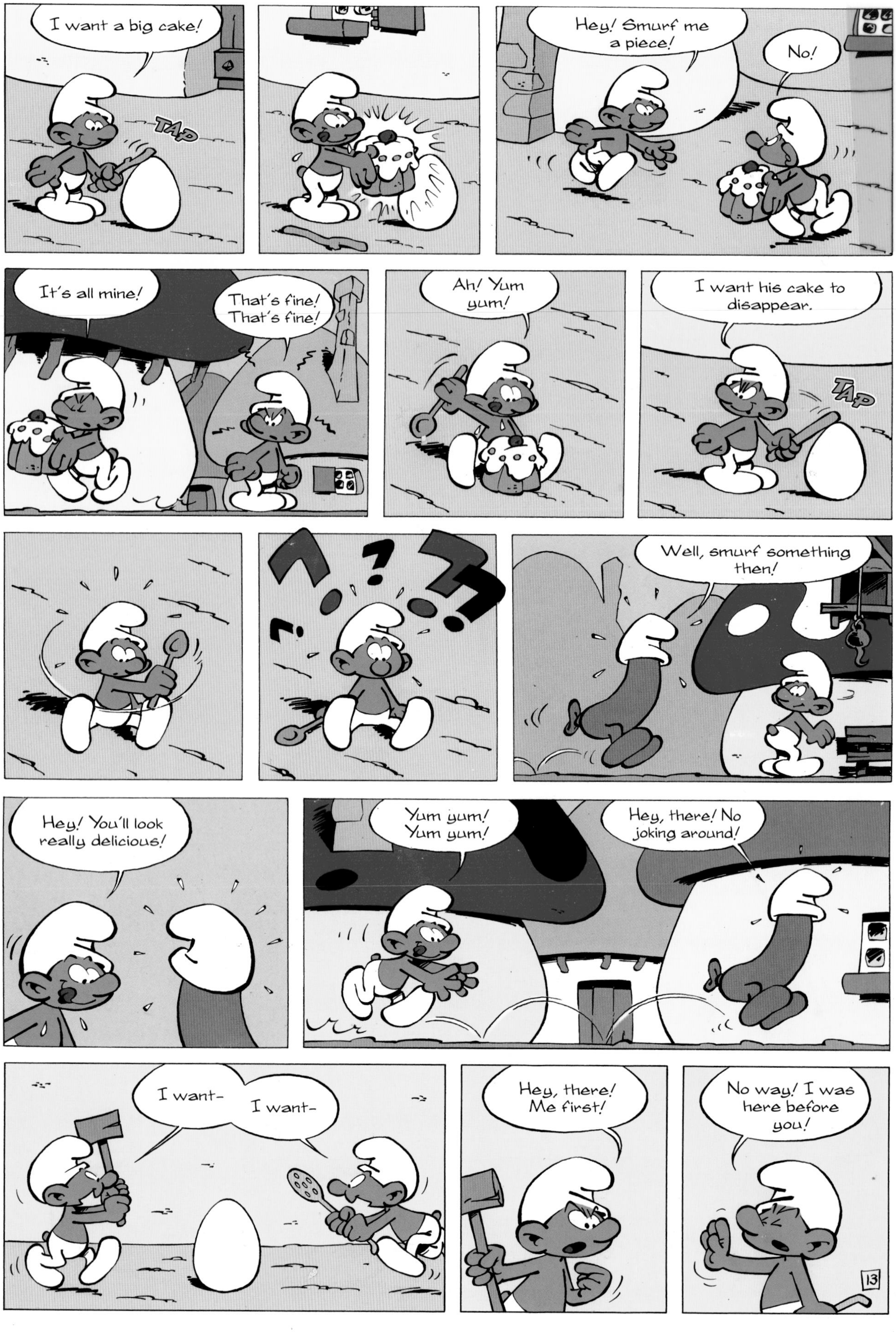
I want a big cake!
TAP
Hey! Smurf me a piece!
No!
It's all mine!
That's fine! That's fine!
Ah! Yum yum!
I want his cake to disappear.
TAP
Well, smurf something then!
Hey! You'll look really delicious!
Yum yum! Yum yum!
Hey, there! No joking around!
I want-
I want-
Hey, there! Me first!
No way! I was here before you!
13

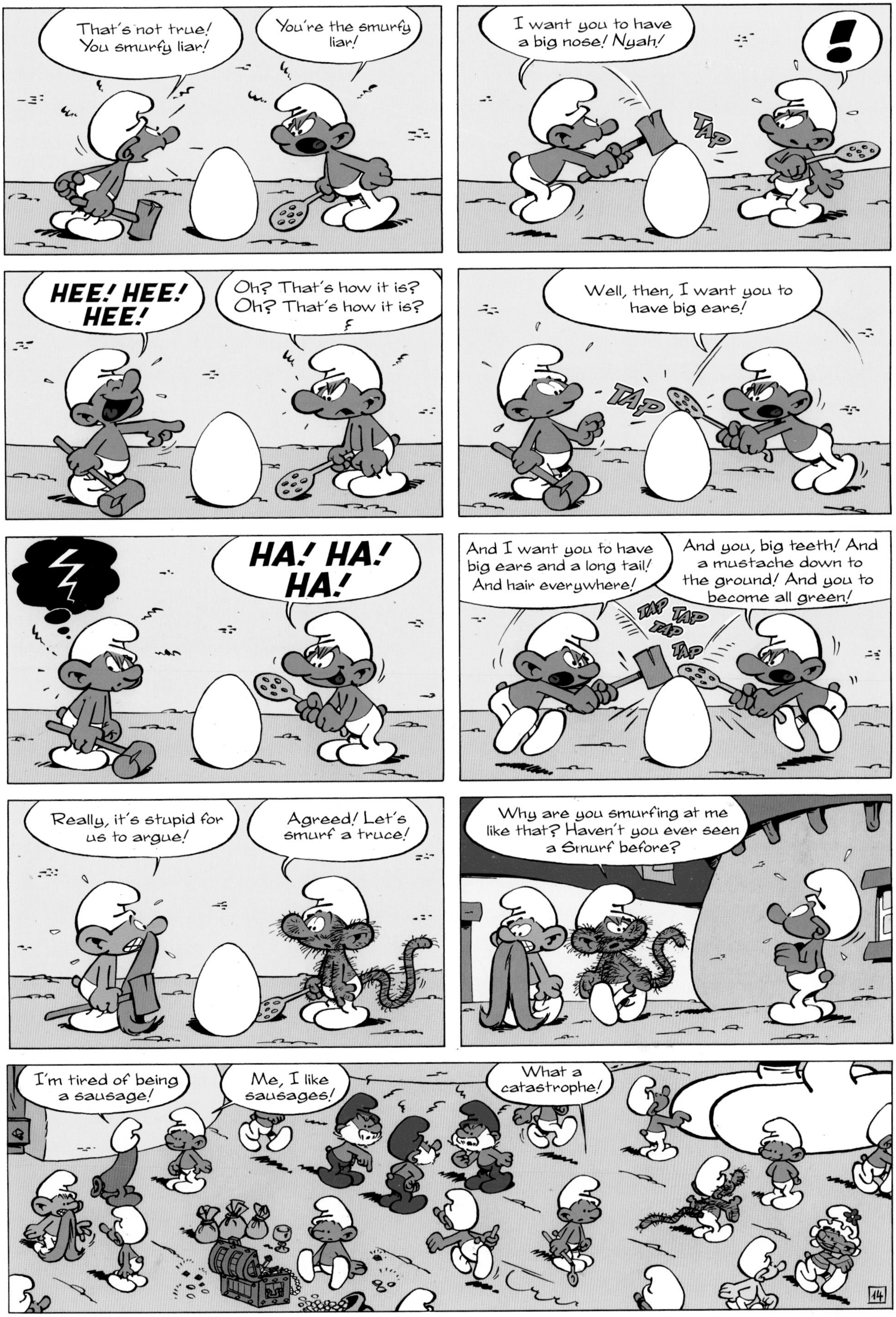
That's not true! You smurfy liar!
You're the smurfy liar!
I want you to have a big nose! Nyah!
TAP
!
HEE! HEE! HEE!
Oh? That's how it is? Oh? That's how it is?
Well, then, I want you to have big ears!
TAP
HA! HA! HA!
And I want you to have big ears and a long tail! And hair everywhere!
And you, big teeth! And a mustache down to the ground! And you to become all green!
TAP TAP TAP TAP
Really, it's stupid for us to argue!
Agreed! Let's smurf a truce!
Why are you smurfing at me like that? Haven't you ever seen a Smurf before?
I'm tired of being a sausage!
Me, I like sausages!
What a catastrophe!
14

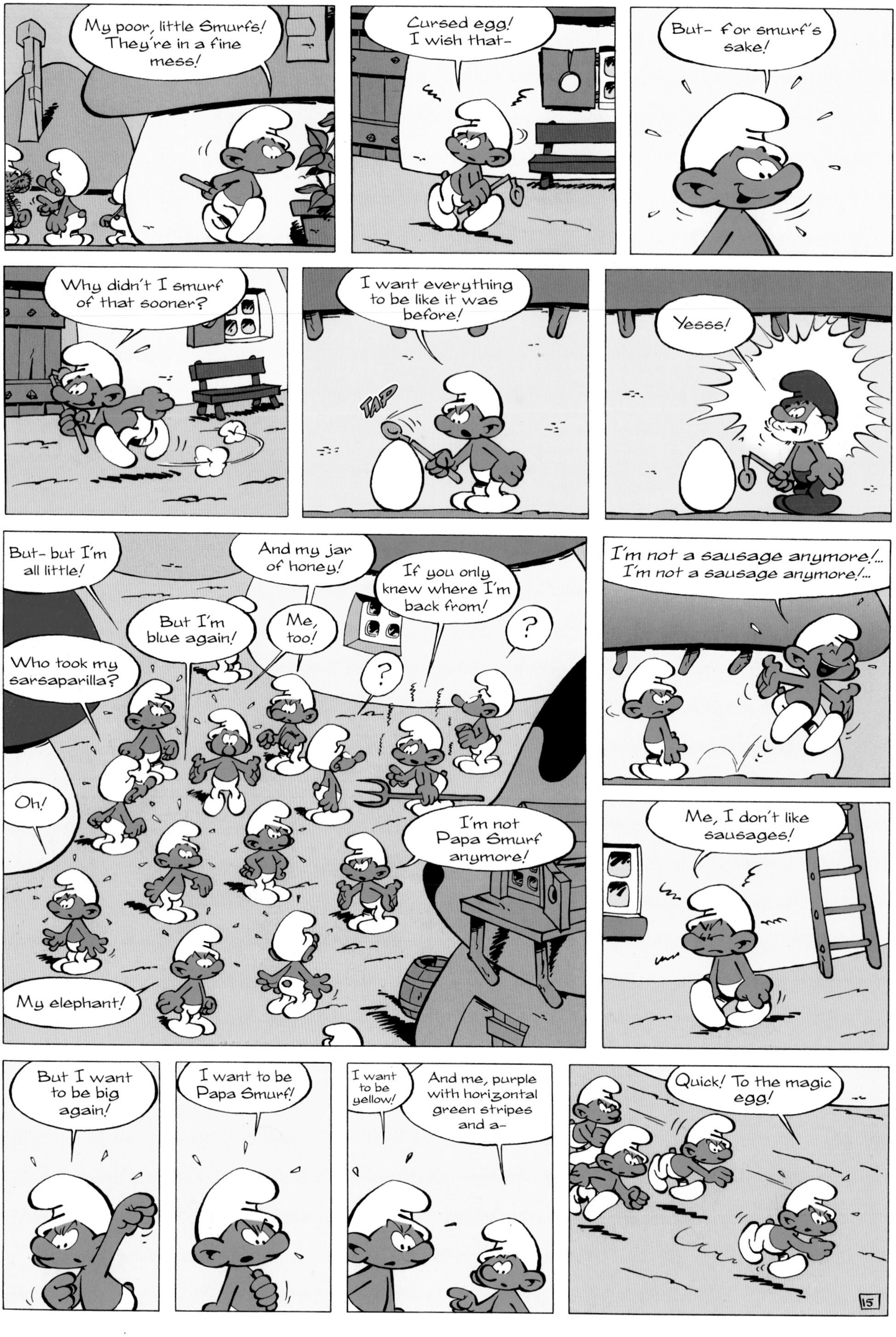

My poor, little Smurfs! They're in a fine mess!
Cursed egg! I wish that-
But- for smurf's sake!
Why didn't I smurf of that sooner?
I want everything to be like it was before!
TAP
Yesss!
But- but I'm all little!
And my jar of honey!
If you only knew where I'm back from!
But I'm blue again!
Me, too!
?
?
Who took my sarsaparilla?
Oh!
I'm not Papa Smurf anymore!
My elephant!
I'm not a sausage anymore!... I'm not a sausage anymore!...
Me, I don't like sausages!
But I want to be big again!
I want to be Papa Smurf!
I want to be yellow!
And me, purple with horizontal green stripes and a-
Quick! To the magic egg!
15

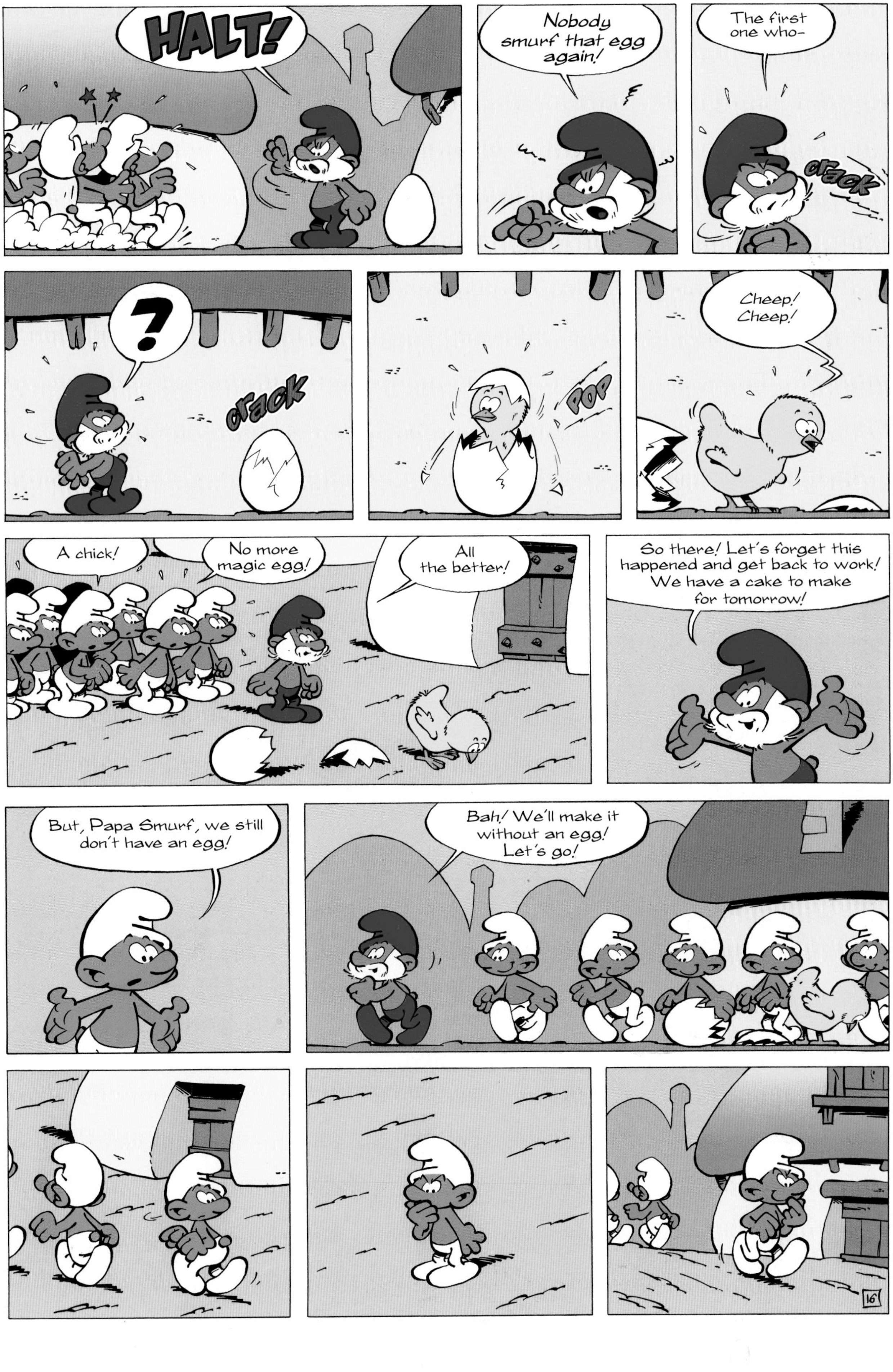
HALT!
Nobody smurf that egg again!
The first one who-
CRACK
?
CRACK
POP
Cheep! Cheep!
A chick!
No more magic egg!
All the better!
So there! Let's forget this happened and get back to work! We have a cake to make for tomorrow!
But, Papa Smurf, we still don't have an egg!
Bah! We'll make it without an egg! Let's go!
16

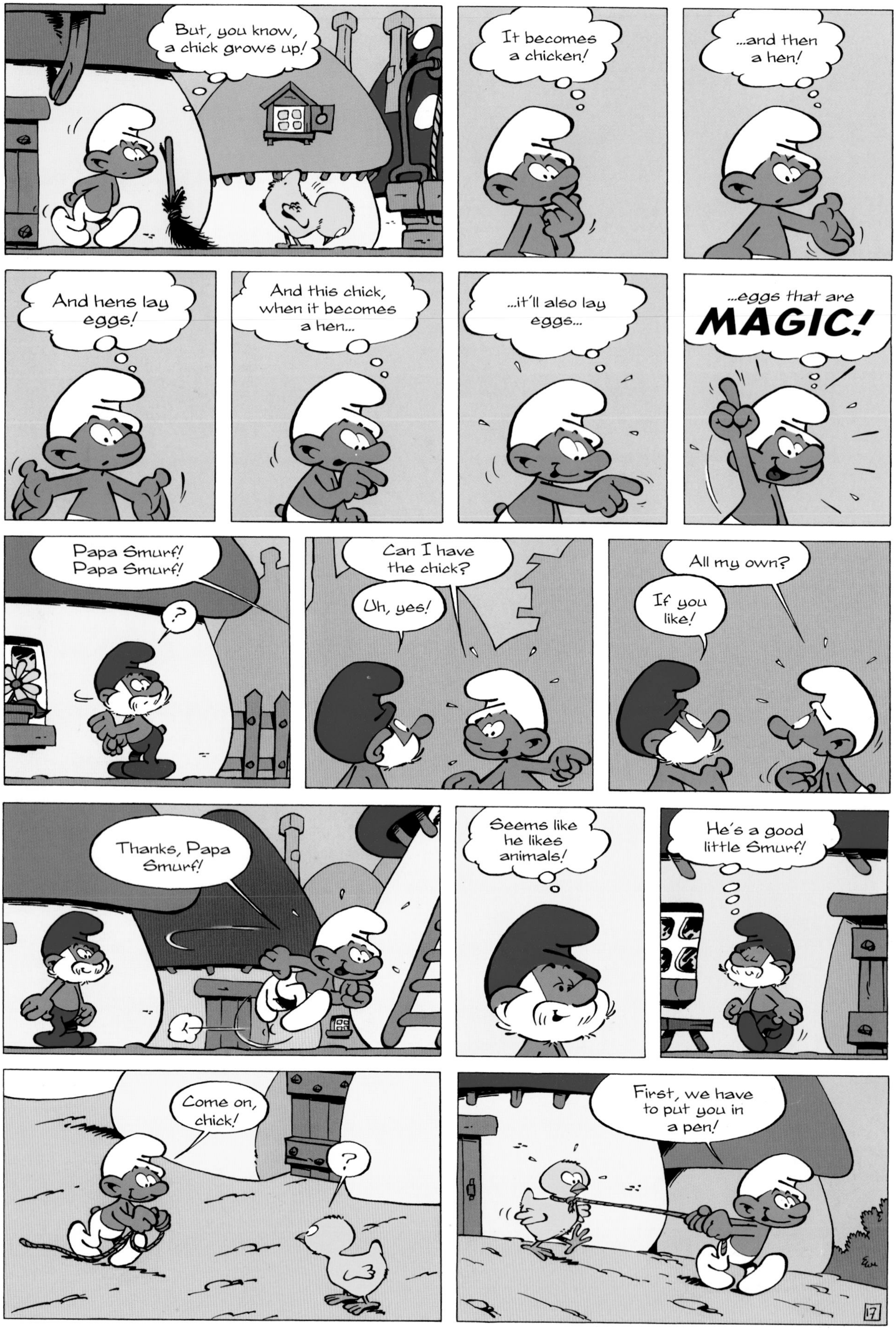

But, you know, a chick grows up!
It becomes a chicken!
...and then a hen!
And hens lay eggs!
And this chick, when it becomes a hen...
...it'll also lay eggs...
...eggs that are MAGIC!
Papa Smurf! Papa Smurf!
?
Can I have the chick?
Uh, yes!
All my own?
If you like!
Thanks, Papa Smurf!
Seems like he likes animals!
He's a good little Smurf!
Come on, chick!
?
First, we have to put you in a pen!
17

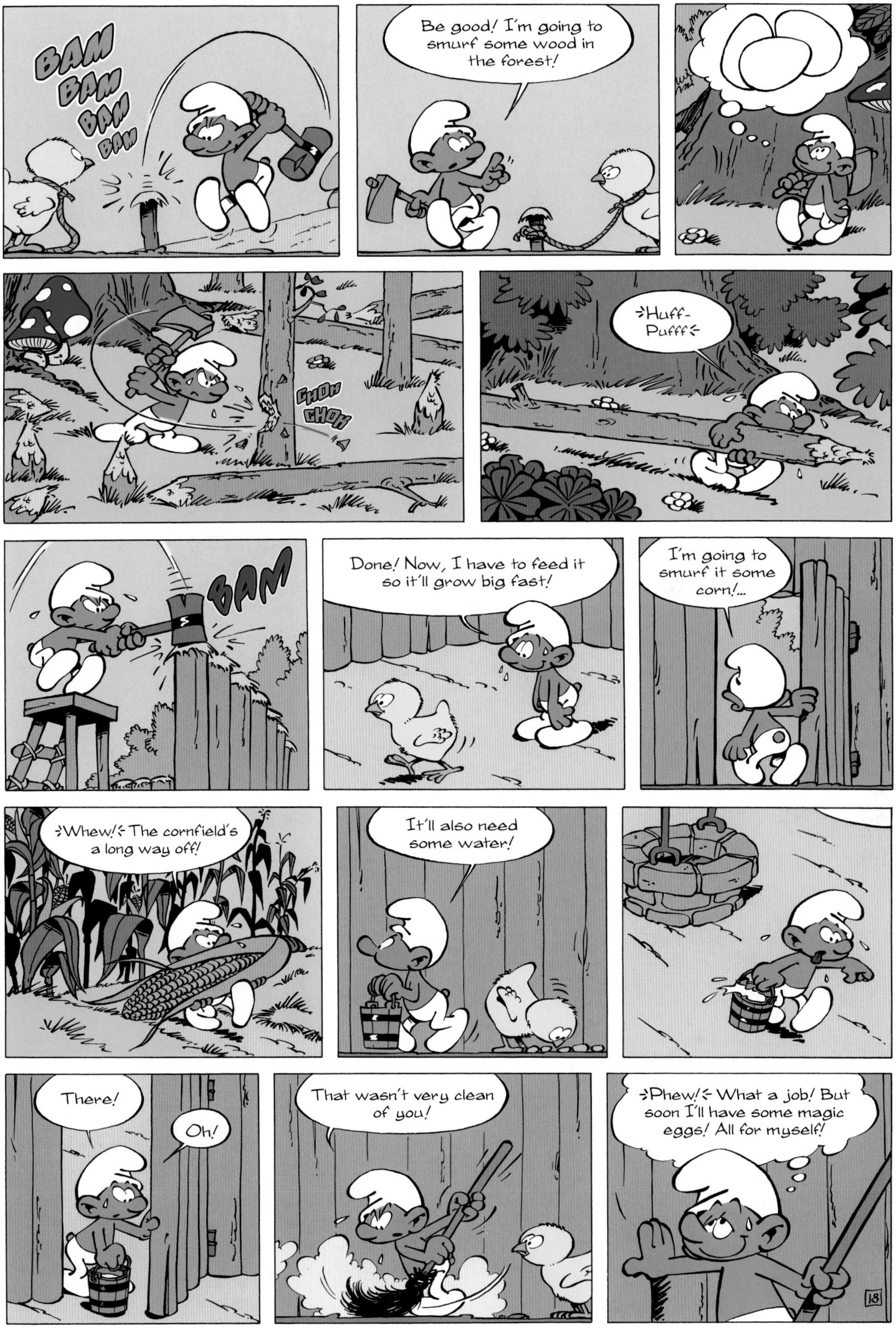
BAM BAM BAM BAM
Be good! I'm going to smurf some wood in the forest!
CHOK CHOK
Huff- Pufff
BAM
Done! Now, I have to feed it so it'll grow big fast!
I'm going to smurf it some corn!...
Whew! The cornfield's a long way off!
It'll also need some water!
There!
Oh!
That wasn't very clean of you!
Phew! What a job! But soon I'll have some magic eggs! All for myself!
18

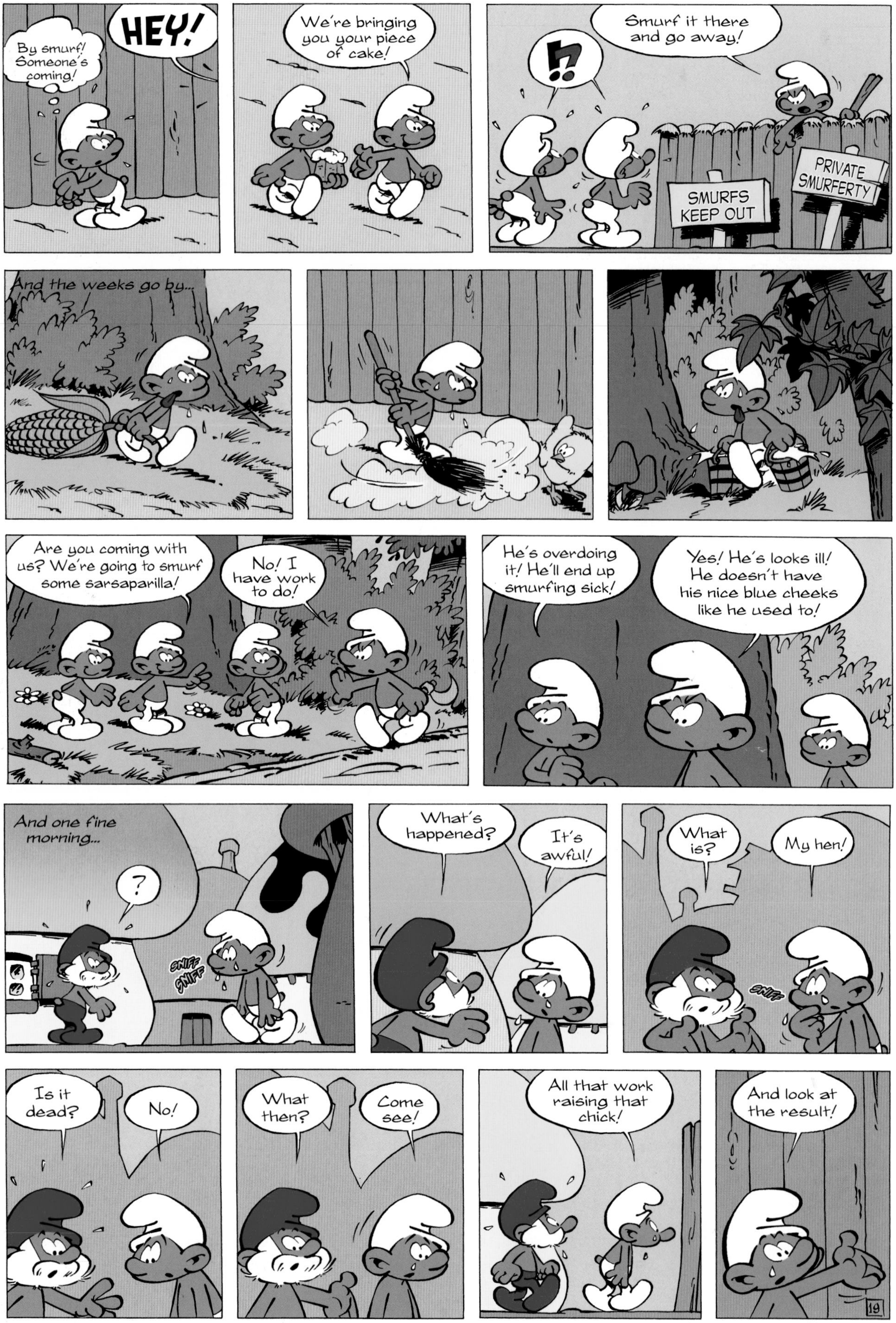
By smurf! Someone's coming!
HEY!
We're bringing you your piece of cake!
!?
Smurf it there and go away!
SMURFS KEEP OUT
PRIVATE SMURFERTY
And the weeks go by...
Are you coming with us? We're going to smurf some sarsaparilla!
No! I have work to do!
He's overdoing it! He'll end up smurfing sick!
Yes! He's looks ill! He doesn't have his nice blue cheeks like he used to!
And one fine morning...
?
SNIFF SNIFF
What's happened?
It's awful!
What is?
My hen!
SNIFF
Is it dead?
No!
What then?
Come see!
All that work raising that chick!
And look at the result!
19

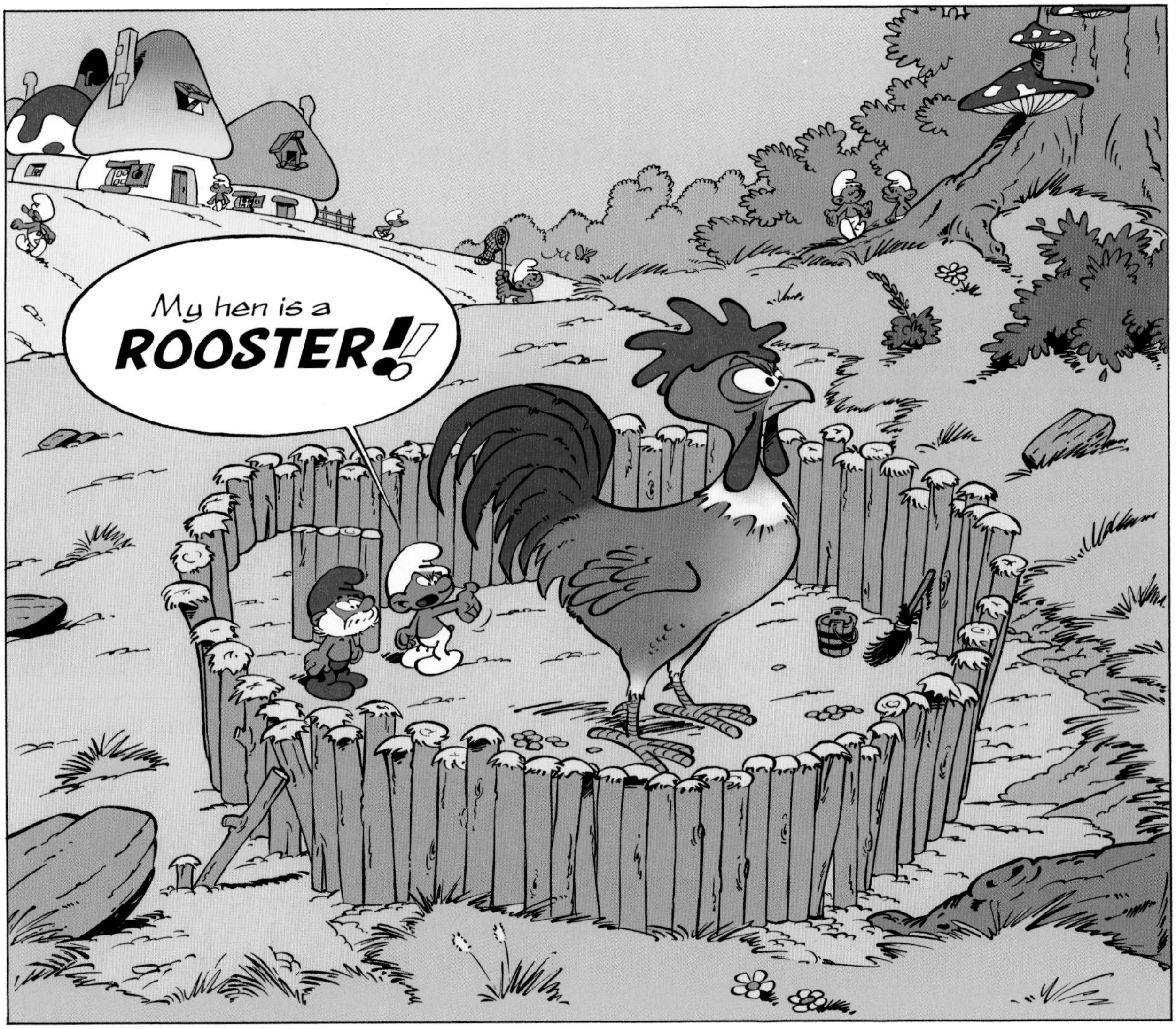
My hen is a ROOSTER!!

THE END

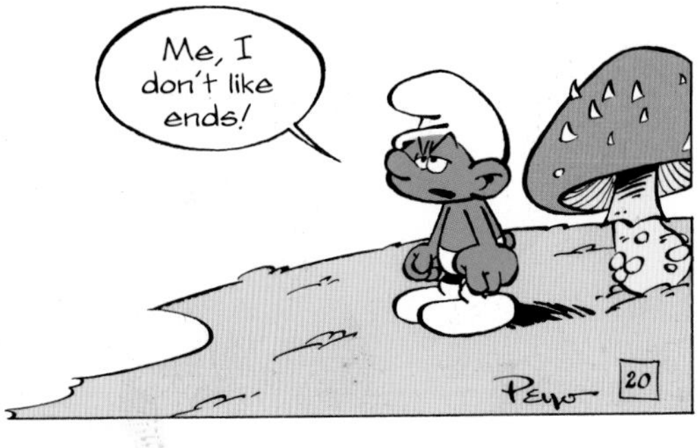
Me, I don't like ends!
Peyo
20

THE FAKE SMURF

by Peyo

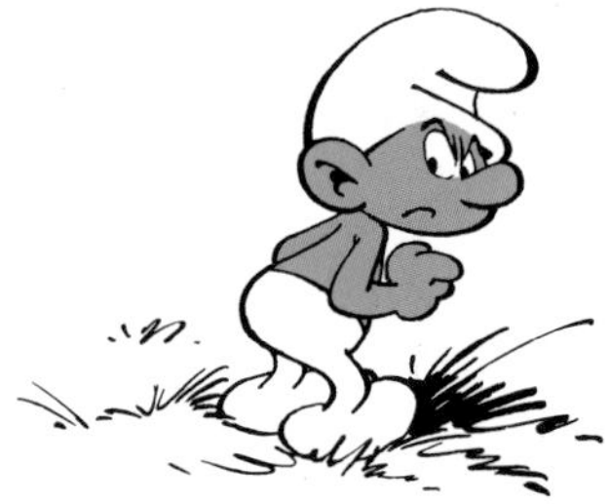

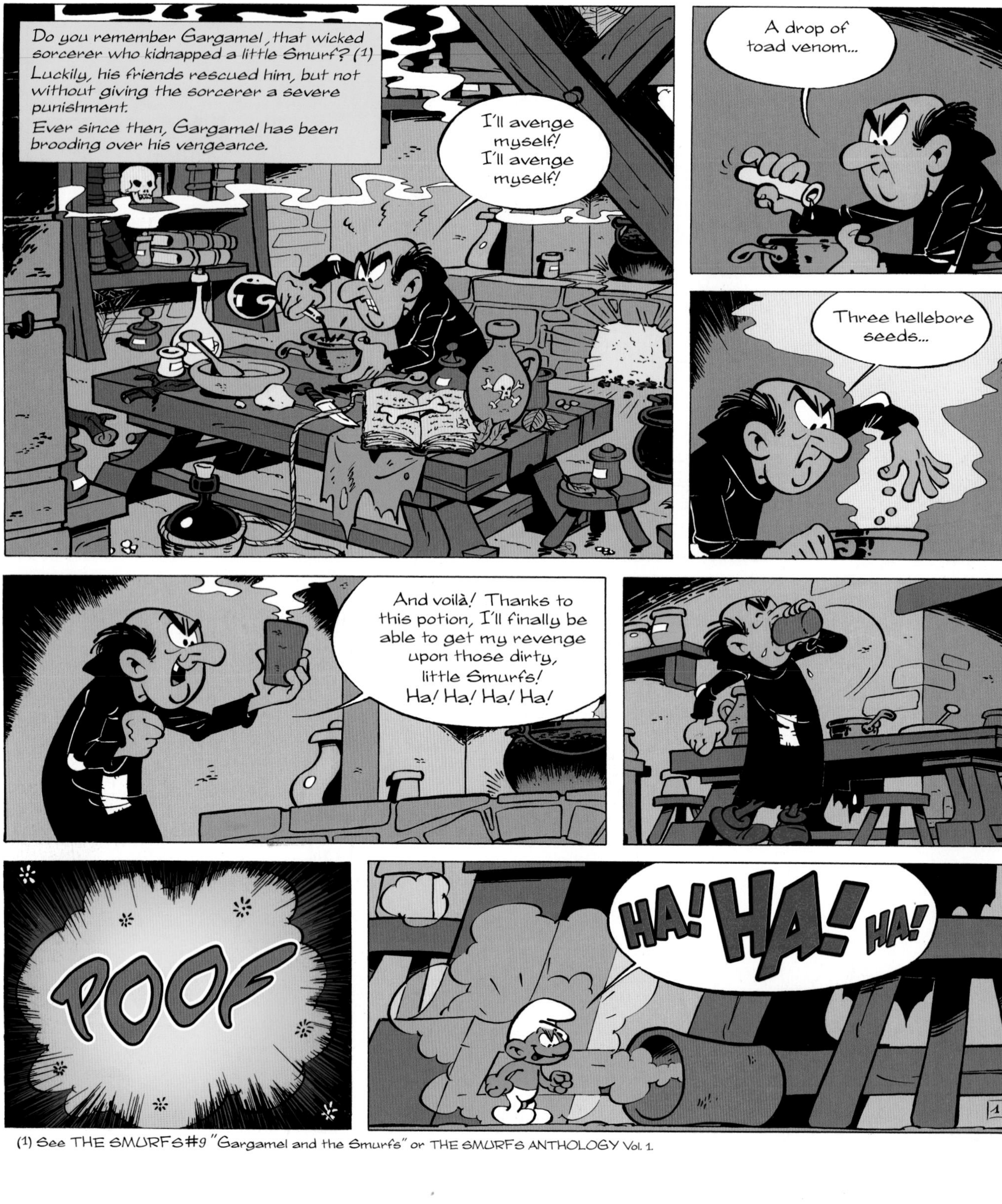

Do you remember Gargamel, that wicked sorcerer who kidnapped a little Smurf? (1) Luckily, his friends rescued him, but not without giving the sorcerer a severe punishment. Ever since then, Gargamel has been brooding over his vengeance.
I'll avenge myself! I'll avenge myself!
A drop of toad venom...
Three hellebore seeds...
And voilà! Thanks to this potion, I'll finally be able to get my revenge upon those dirty, little Smurfs! Ha! Ha! Ha! Ha!
POOF
HA! HA! HA!
1

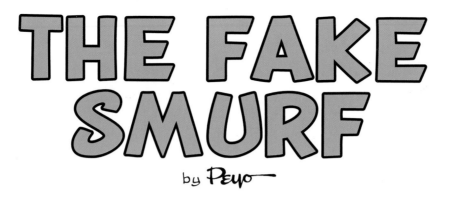

(1) See THE SMURFS #9 "Gargamel and the Smurfs" or THE SMURFS ANTHOLOGY Vol. 1.

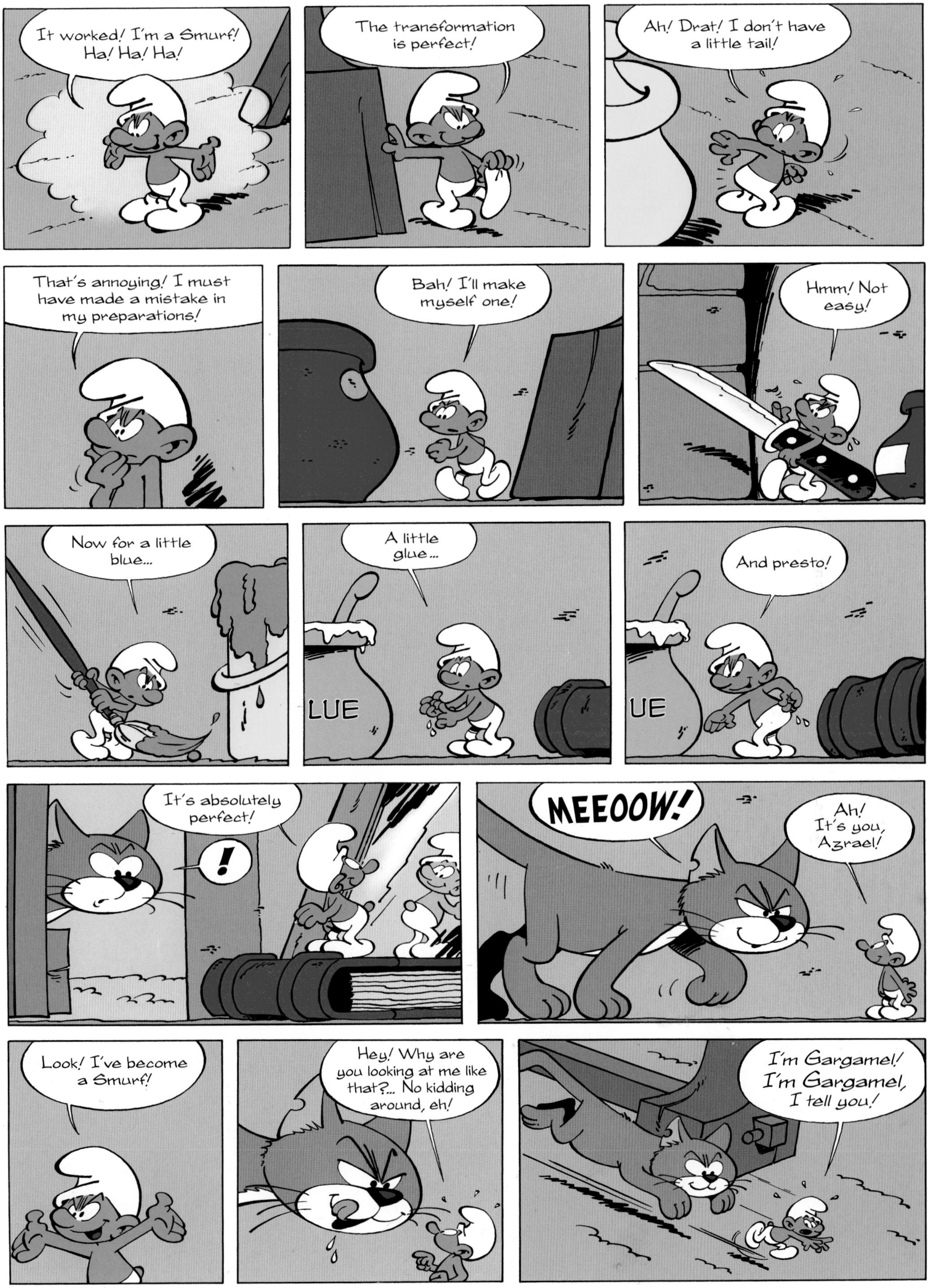
It worked! I'm a Smurf! Ha! Ha! Ha!
The transformation is perfect!
Ah! Drat! I don't have a little tail!
That's annoying! I must have made a mistake in my preparations!
Bah! I'll make myself one!
Hmm! Not easy!
Now for a little blue...
A little glue...
LUE
And presto!
UE
It's absolutely perfect!
!
MEEOOW!
Ah! It's you, Azrael!
Look! I've become a Smurf!
Hey! Why are you looking at me like that?... No kidding around, eh!
I'm Gargamel! I'm Gargamel, I tell you!

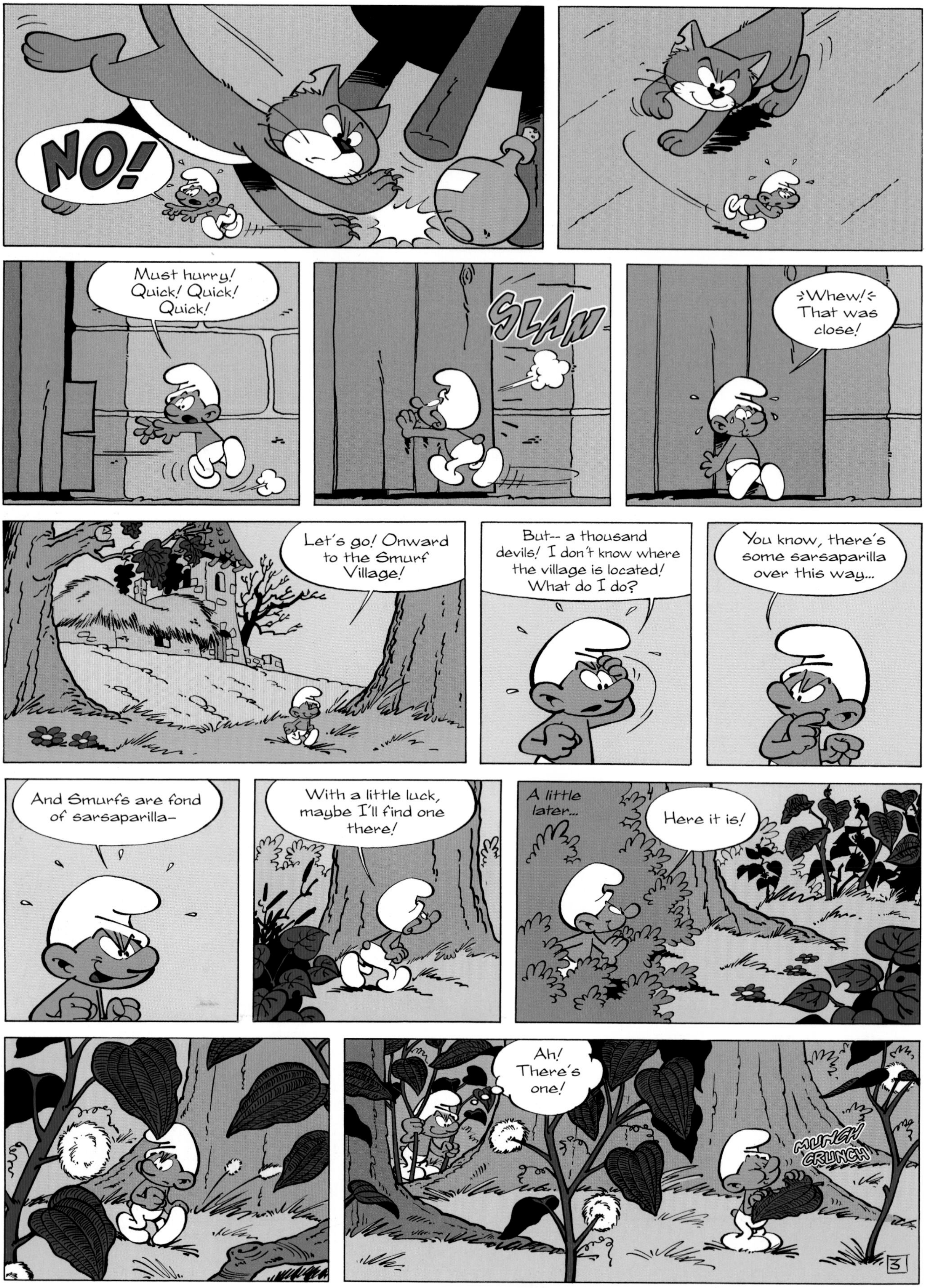
NO!
Must hurry! Quick! Quick! Quick!
SLAM
Whew! That was close!
Let's go! Onward to the Smurf Village!
But-- a thousand devils! I don't know where the village is located! What do I do?
You know, there's some sarsaparilla over this way...
And Smurfs are fond of sarsaparilla-
With a little luck, maybe I'll find one there!
A little later...
Here it is!
Ah! There's one!
MUNCH
CRUNCH
3

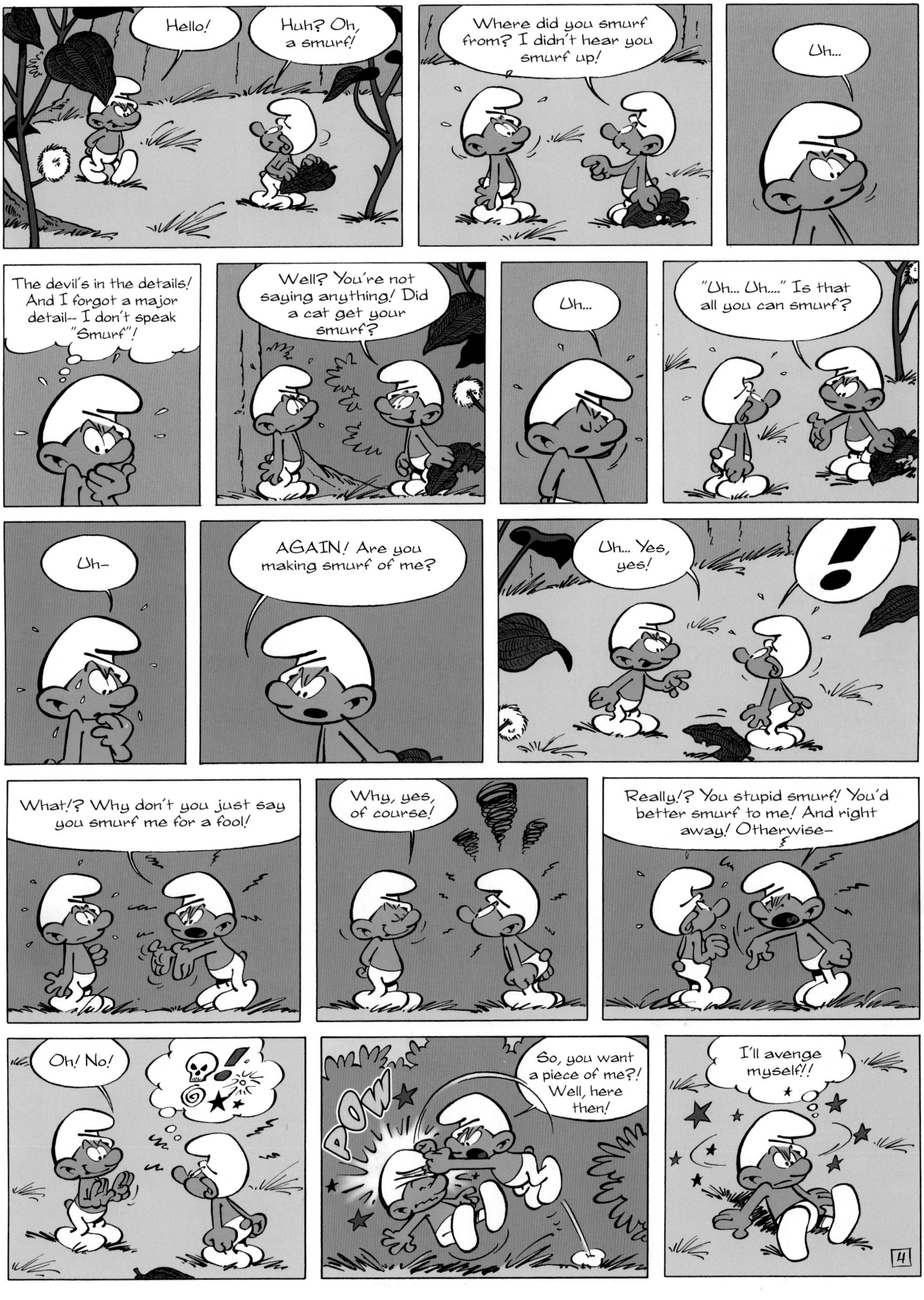
Hello!
Huh? Oh, a smurf!
Where did you smurf from? I didn't hear you smurf up!
Uh...
The devil's in the details! And I forgot a major detail-- I don't speak "Smurf"!
Well? You're not saying anything! Did a cat get your smurf?
Uh...
"Uh... Uh...." Is that all you can smurf?
Uh-
AGAIN! Are you making smurf of me?
Uh... Yes, yes!
!
What!? Why don't you just say you smurf me for a fool!
Why, yes, of course!
Really!? You stupid smurf! You'd better smurf to me! And right away! Otherwise-
Oh! No!
POW
So, you want a piece of me?! Well, here then!
I'll avenge myself!!
4

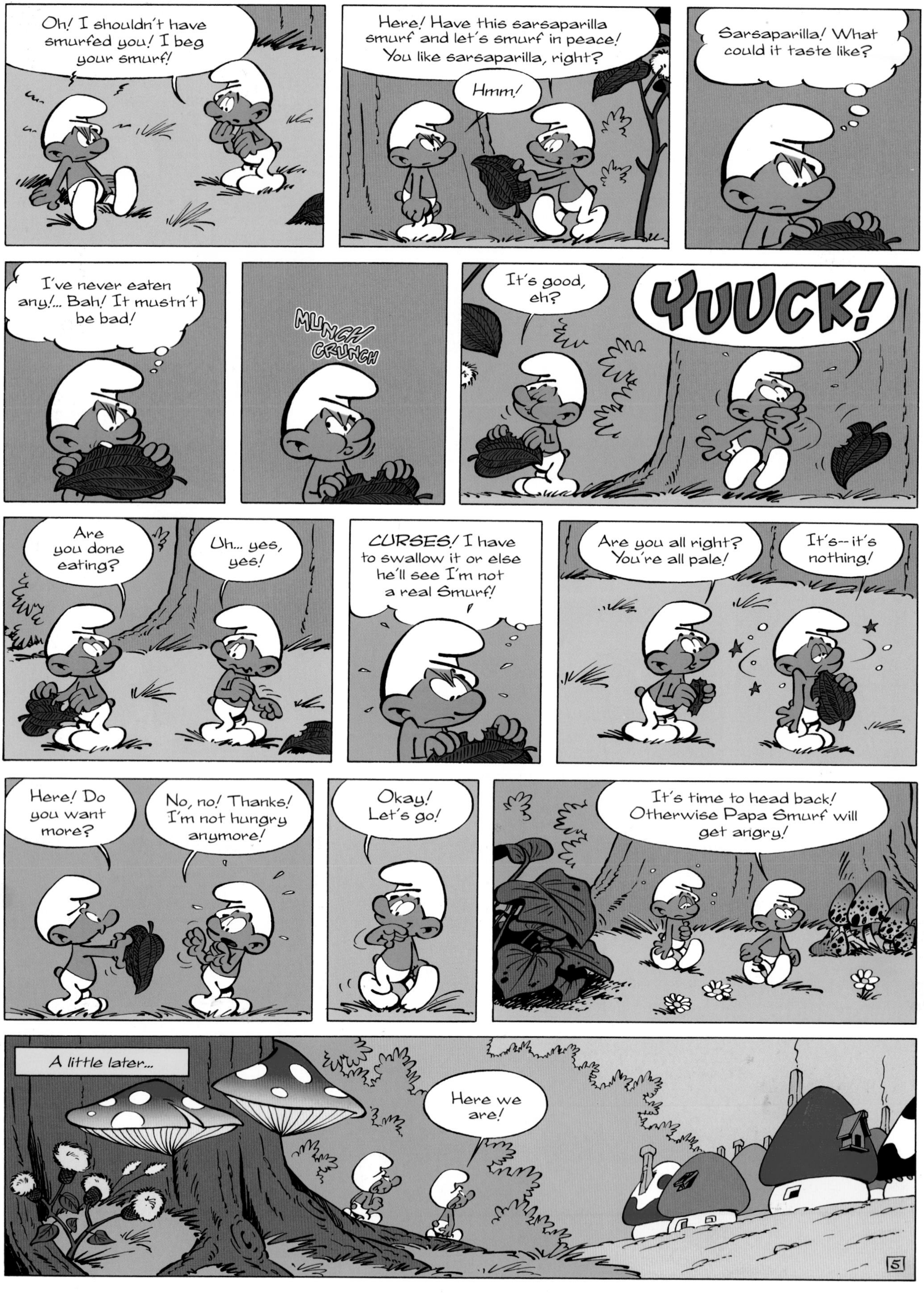
Oh! I shouldn't have smurfed you! I beg your smurf!
Here! Have this sarsaparilla smurf and let's smurf in peace! You like sarsaparilla, right?
Hmm!
Sarsaparilla! What could it taste like?
I've never eaten any!... Bah! It mustn't be bad!
MUNCH CRUNCH
It's good, eh?
YUUCK!
Are you done eating?
Uh... yes, yes!
CURSES! I have to swallow it or else he'll see I'm not a real Smurf!
Are you all right? You're all pale!
It's-- it's nothing!
Here! Do you want more?
No, no! Thanks! I'm not hungry anymore!
Okay! Let's go!
It's time to head back! Otherwise Papa Smurf will get angry!
A little later...
Here we are!
5

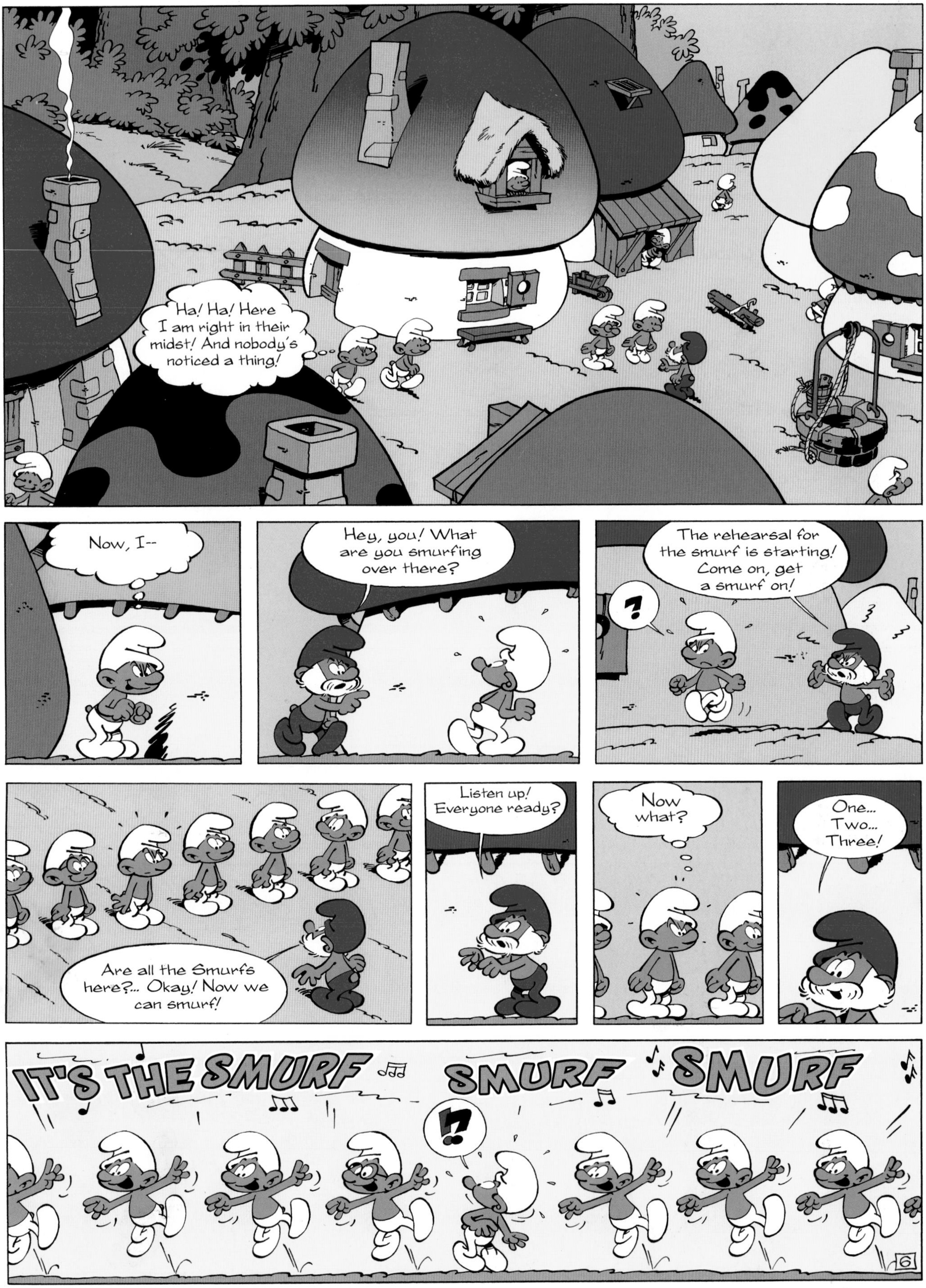
Ha! Ha! Here I am right in their midst! And nobody's noticed a thing!
Now, I--
Hey, you! What are you smurfing over there?
?
The rehearsal for the smurf is starting! Come on, get a smurf on!
Are all the Smurfs here?... Okay! Now we can smurf!
Listen up! Everyone ready?
Now what?
One... Two... Three!
IT'S THE SMURF SMURF SMURF
!?
6

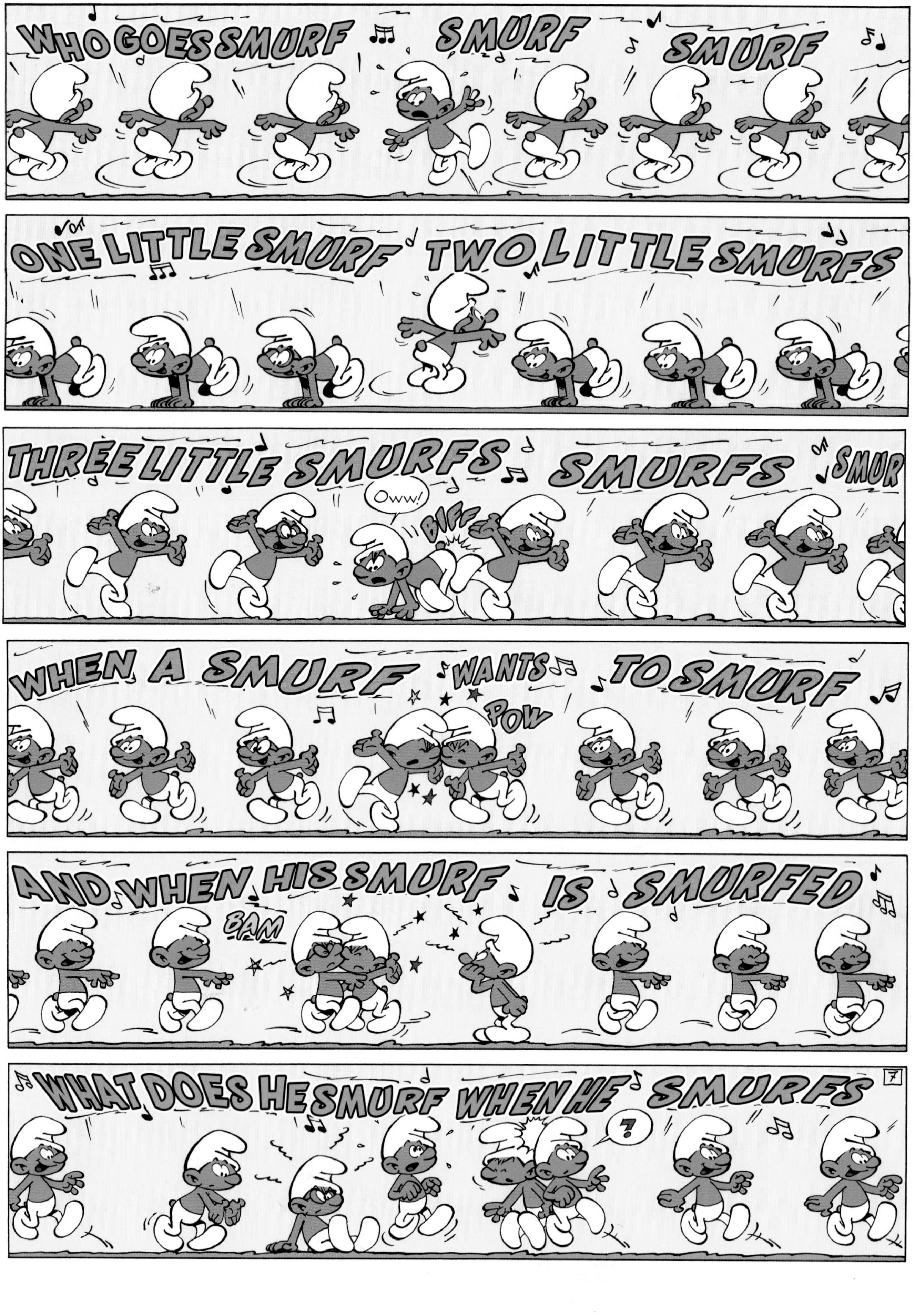
WHO GOES SMURF
SMURF
SMURF
ONE LITTLE SMURF
TWO LITTLE SMURFS
THREE LITTLE SMURFS
SMURFS
SMUR
OWW!
BIFF
WHEN A SMURF
WANTS
TO SMURF
POW
AND WHEN HIS SMURF
IS
SMURFED
BAM
WHAT DOES HE SMURF WHEN HE
SMURFS
7
?

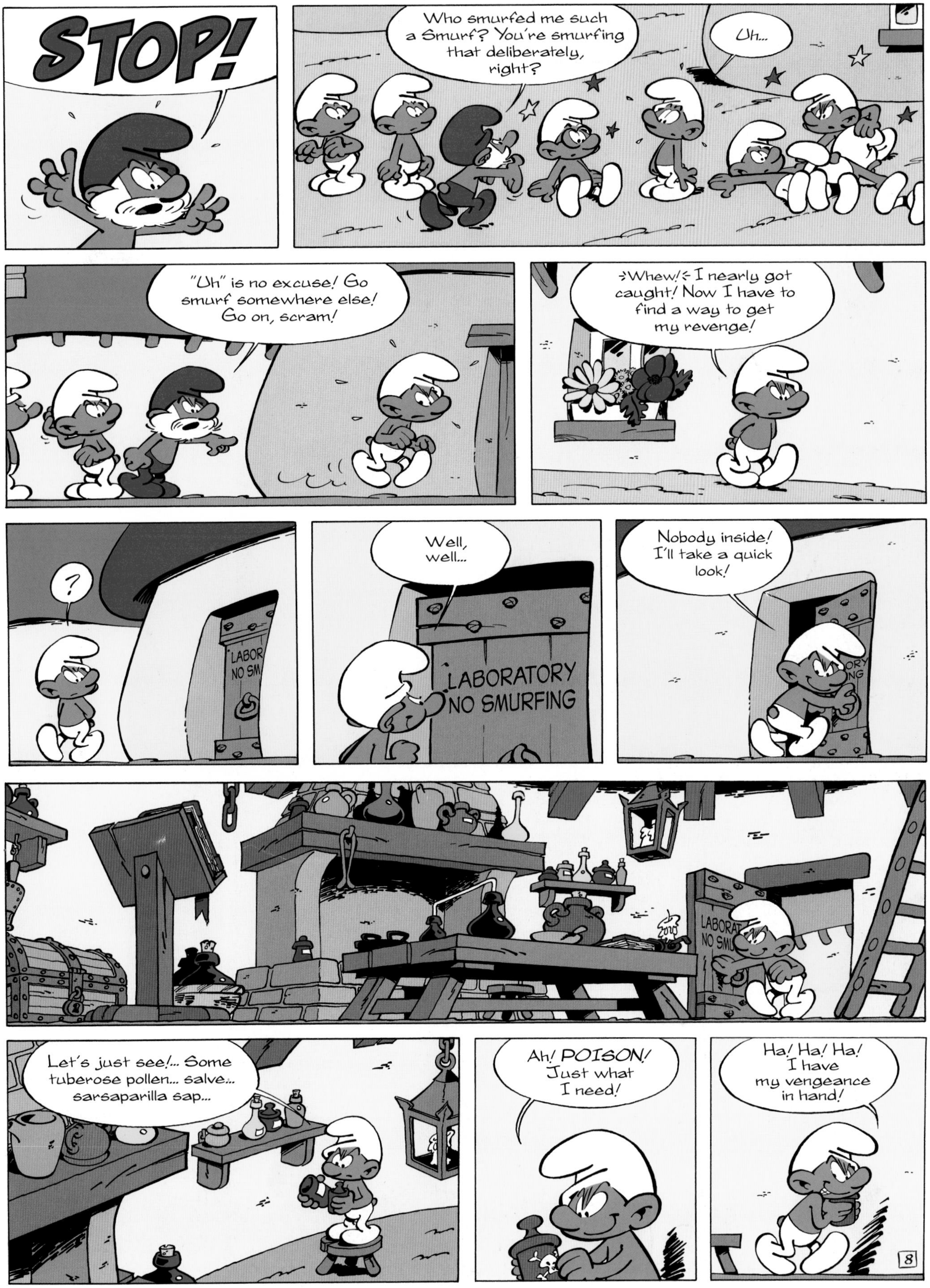
STOP!
Who smurfed me such a Smurf? You're smurfing that deliberately, right?
Uh...
"Uh" is no excuse! Go smurf somewhere else! Go on, scram!
Whew! I nearly got caught! Now I have to find a way to get my revenge!
?
Well, well...
LABORATORY NO SMURFING
Nobody inside! I'll take a quick look!
Let's just see!... Some tuberose pollen... salve... sarsaparilla sap...
Ah! POISON! Just what I need!
Ha! Ha! Ha! I have my vengeance in hand!
8

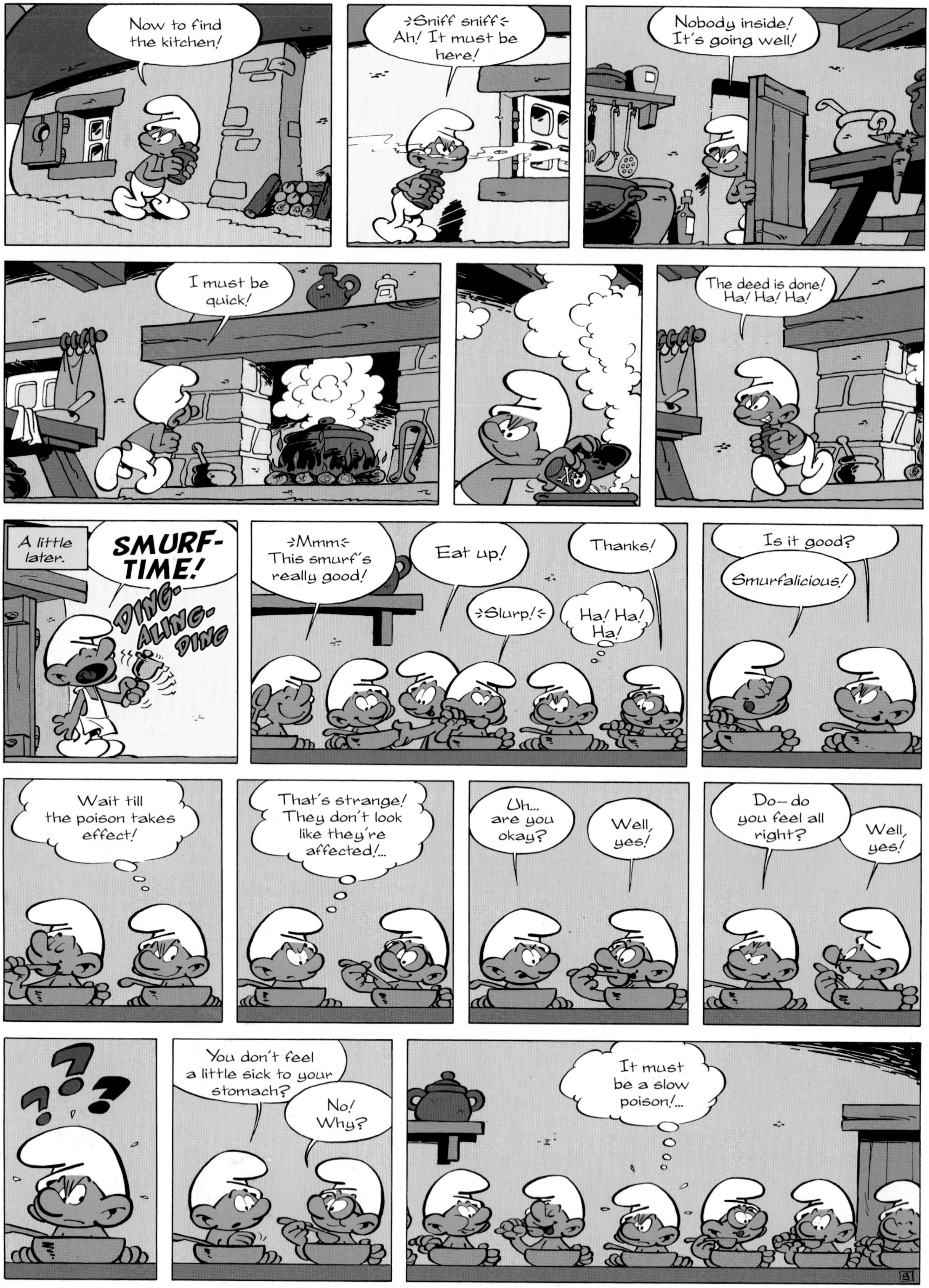
Now to find the kitchen!
Sniff sniff
Ah! It must be here!
Nobody inside! It's going well!
I must be quick!
The deed is done! Ha! Ha! Ha!
A little later.
SMURF-TIME!
DING-ALING-DING
Mmm
This smurf's really good!
Eat up!
Slurp!
Thanks!
Ha! Ha! Ha!
Is it good?
Smurfalicious!
Wait till the poison takes effect!
That's strange! They don't look like they're affected!...
Uh... are you okay?
Well, yes!
Do-- do you feel all right?
Well, yes!
?
?
?
You don't feel a little sick to your stomach?
No! Why?
It must be a slow poison!...

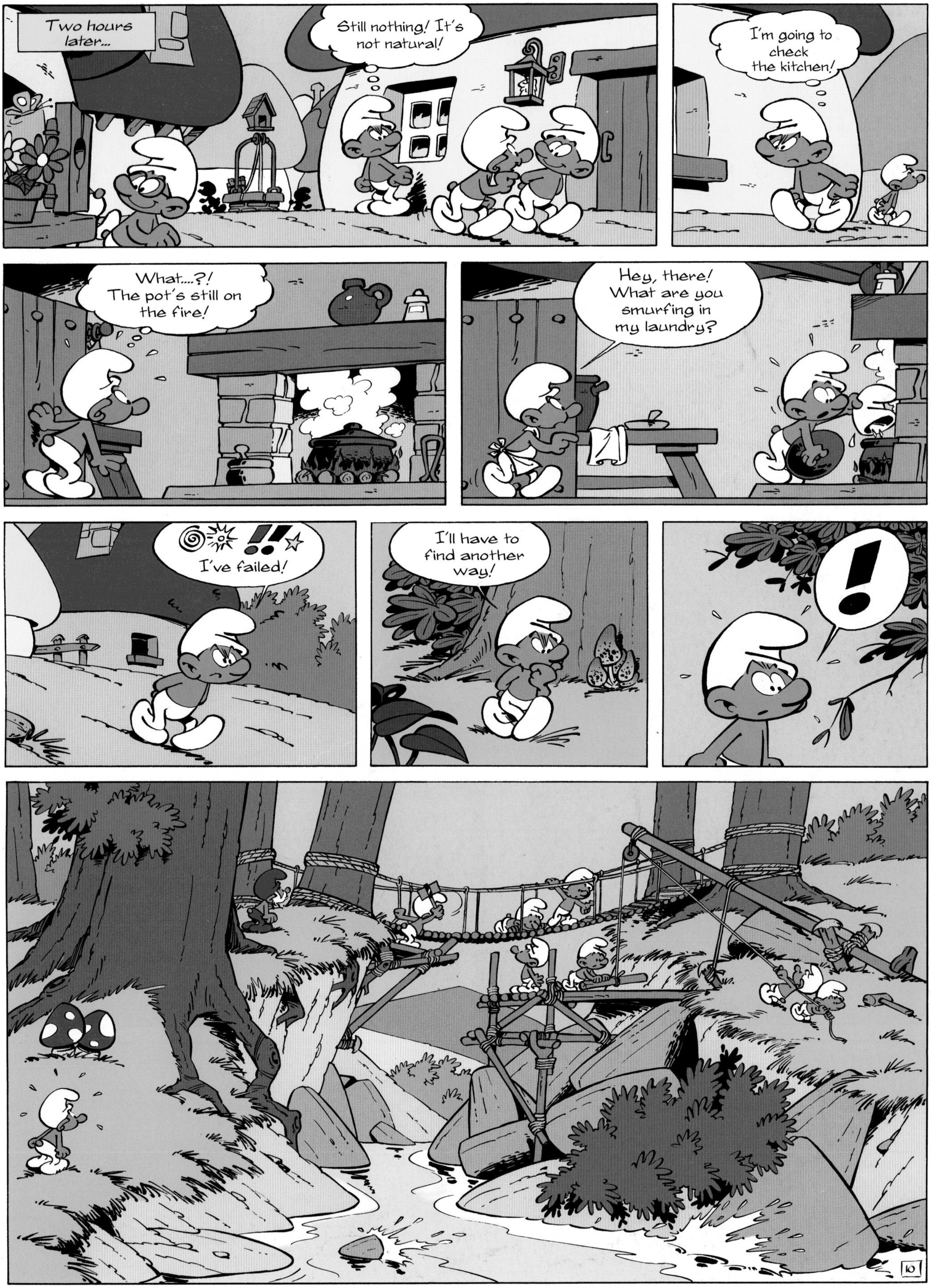
Two hours later...
Still nothing! It's not natural!
I'm going to check the kitchen!
What...?! The pot's still on the fire!
Hey, there! What are you smurfing in my laundry?
!!
I've failed!
I'll have to find another way!
!
10

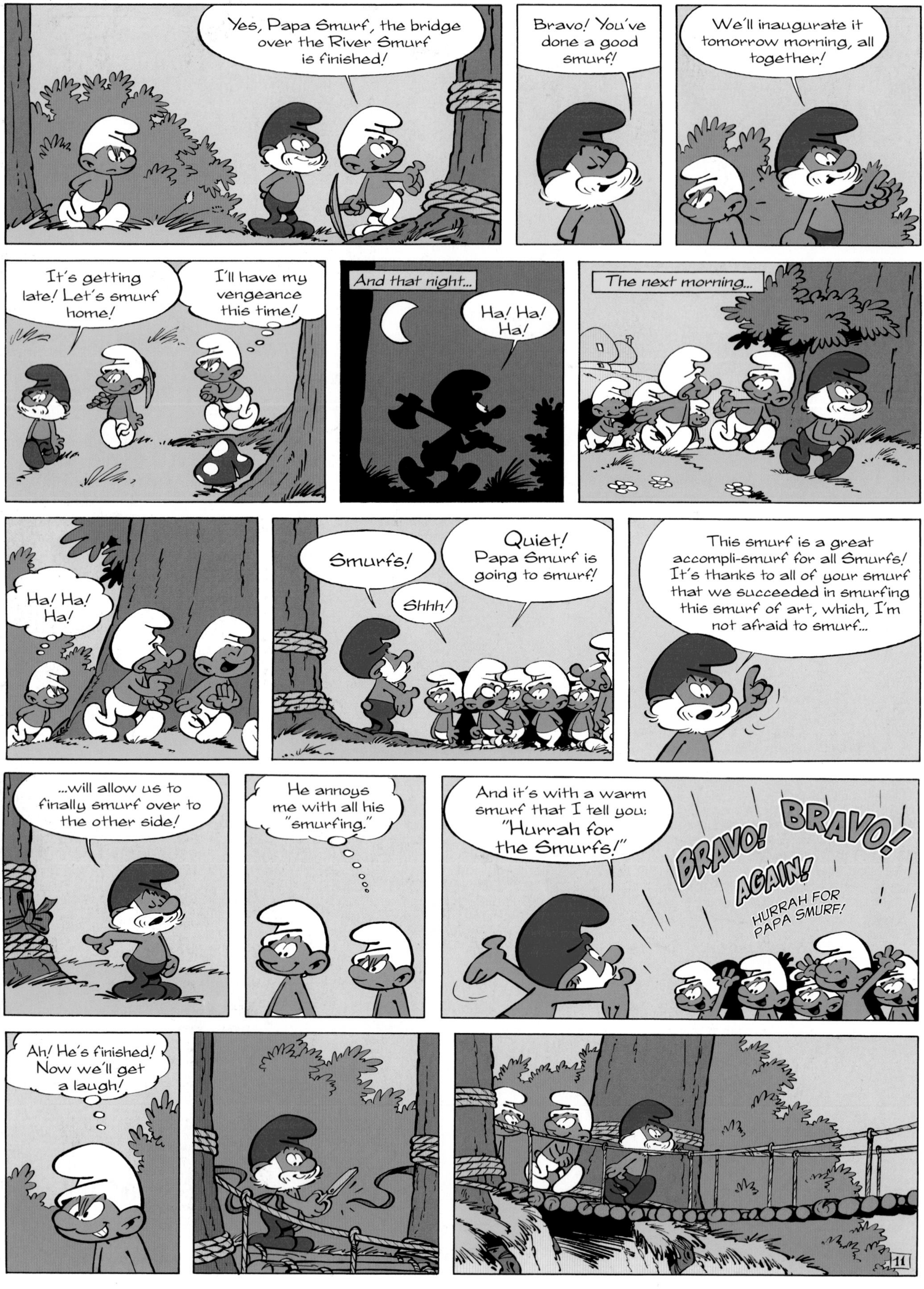

Yes, Papa Smurf, the bridge over the River Smurf is finished!
Bravo! You've done a good smurf!
We'll inaugurate it tomorrow morning, all together!
It's getting late! Let's smurf home!
I'll have my vengeance this time!
And that night...
Ha! Ha! Ha!
The next morning...
Ha! Ha! Ha!
Smurfs!
Shhh!
Quiet! Papa Smurf is going to smurf!
This smurf is a great accompli-smurf for all Smurfs! It's thanks to all of your smurf that we succeeded in smurfing this smurf of art, which, I'm not afraid to smurf...
...will allow us to finally smurf over to the other side!
He annoys me with all his "smurfing."
And it's with a warm smurf that I tell you: "Hurrah for the Smurfs!"
BRAVO!
BRAVO!
AGAIN!
HURRAH FOR PAPA SMURF!
Ah! He's finished! Now we'll get a laugh!
11

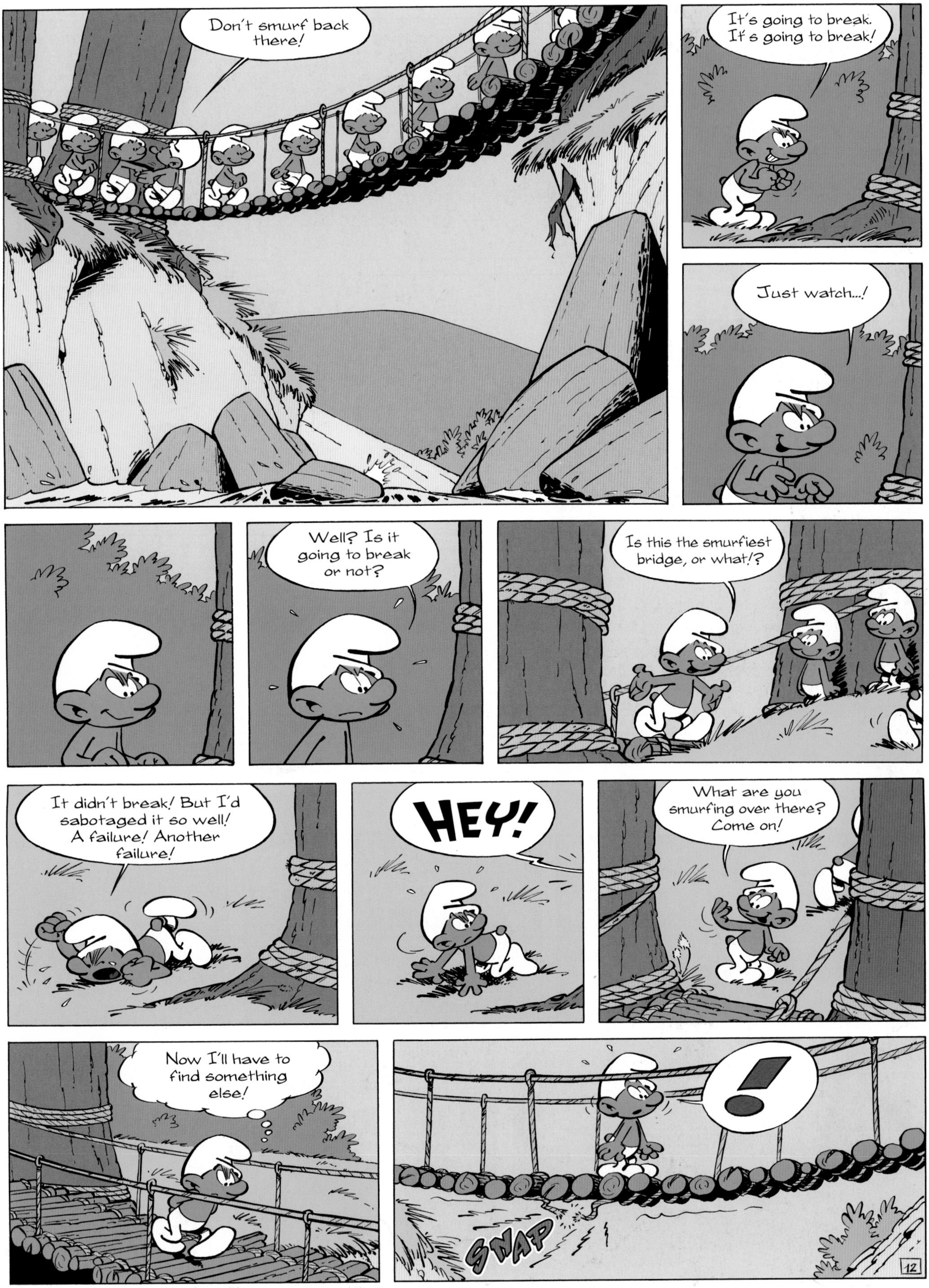

Don't smurf back there!
It's going to break. It's going to break!
Just watch...!
Well? Is it going to break or not?
Is this the smurfiest bridge, or what!?
It didn't break! But I'd sabotaged it so well! A failure! Another failure!
HEY!
What are you smurfing over there? Come on!
Now I'll have to find something else!
!
SNAP
12

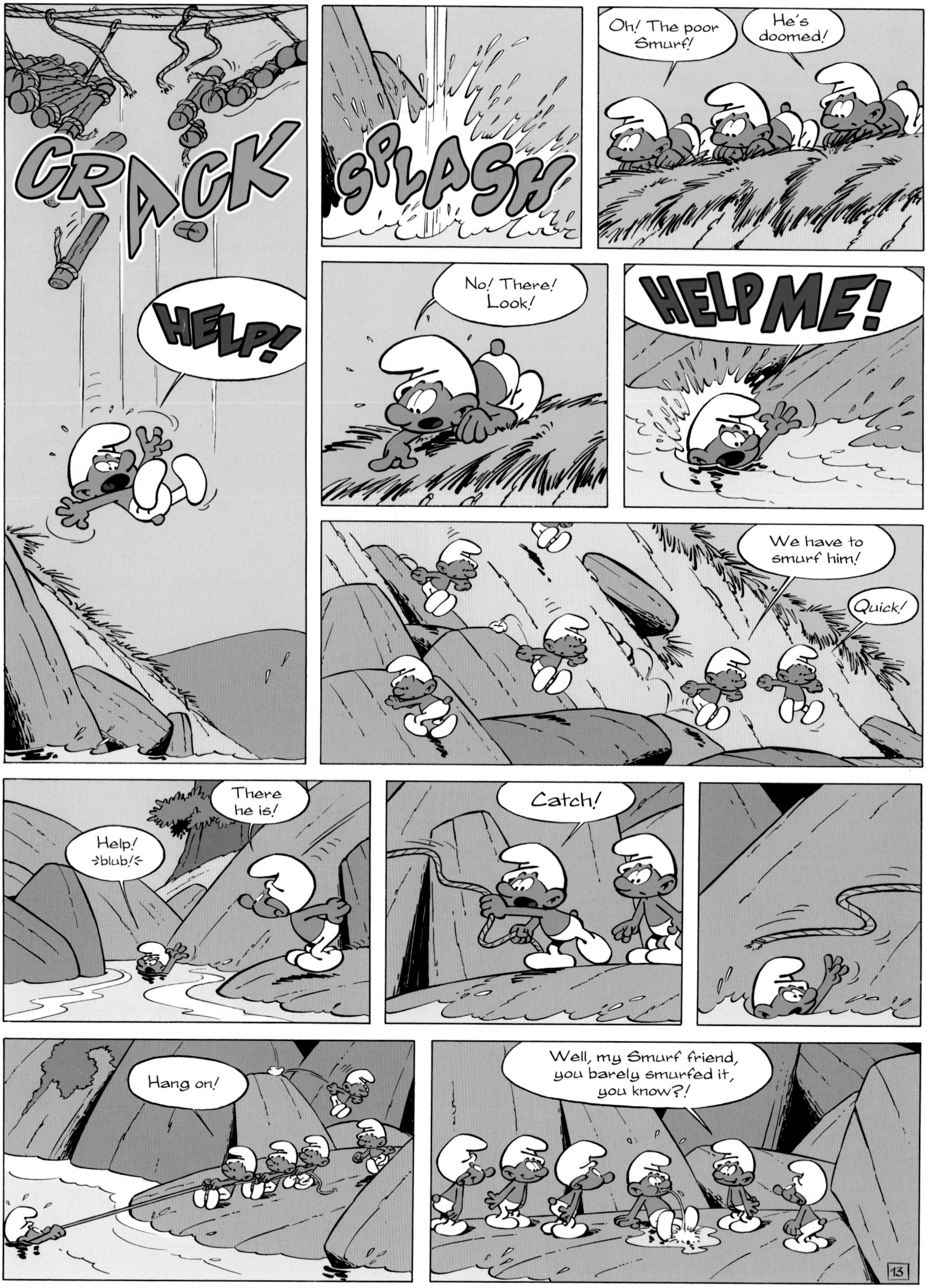
CRACK
HELP!
SPLASH
Oh! The poor Smurf!
He's doomed!
No! There! Look!
HELP ME!
We have to smurf him!
Quick!
There he is!
Help! >blub!<
Catch!
Hang on!
Well, my Smurf friend, you barely smurfed it, you know?!
13

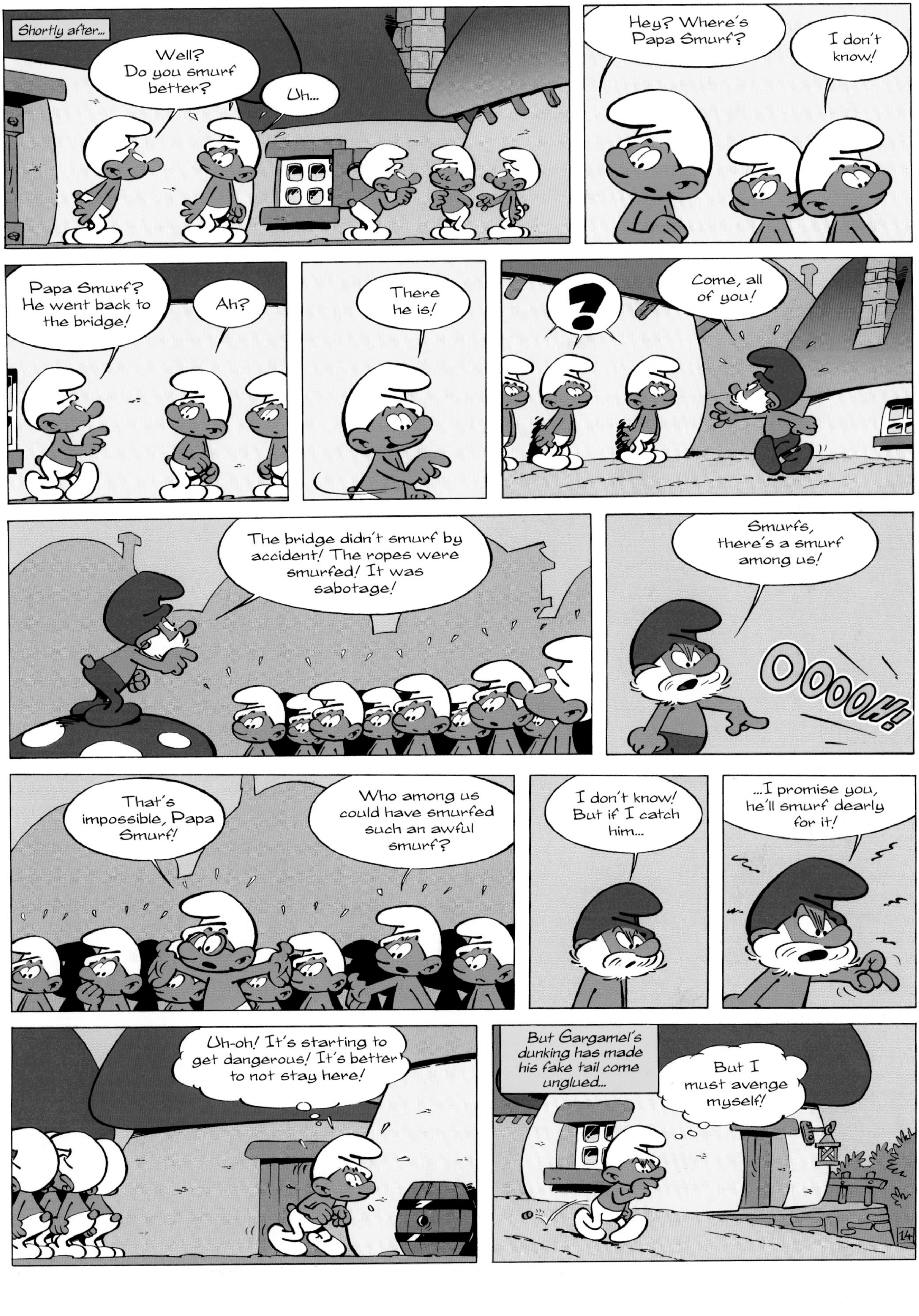
Shortly after...
Well? Do you smurf better?
Uh...
Hey? Where's Papa Smurf?
I don't know!
Papa Smurf? He went back to the bridge!
Ah?
There he is!
?
Come, all of you!
The bridge didn't smurf by accident! The ropes were smurfed! It was sabotage!
Smurfs, there's a smurf among us!
OOOOH!
That's impossible, Papa Smurf!
Who among us could have smurfed such an awful smurf?
I don't know! But if I catch him...
...I promise you, he'll smurf dearly for it!
Uh-oh! It's starting to get dangerous! It's better to not stay here!
But Gargamel's dunking has made his fake tail come unglued...
But I must avenge myself!
14

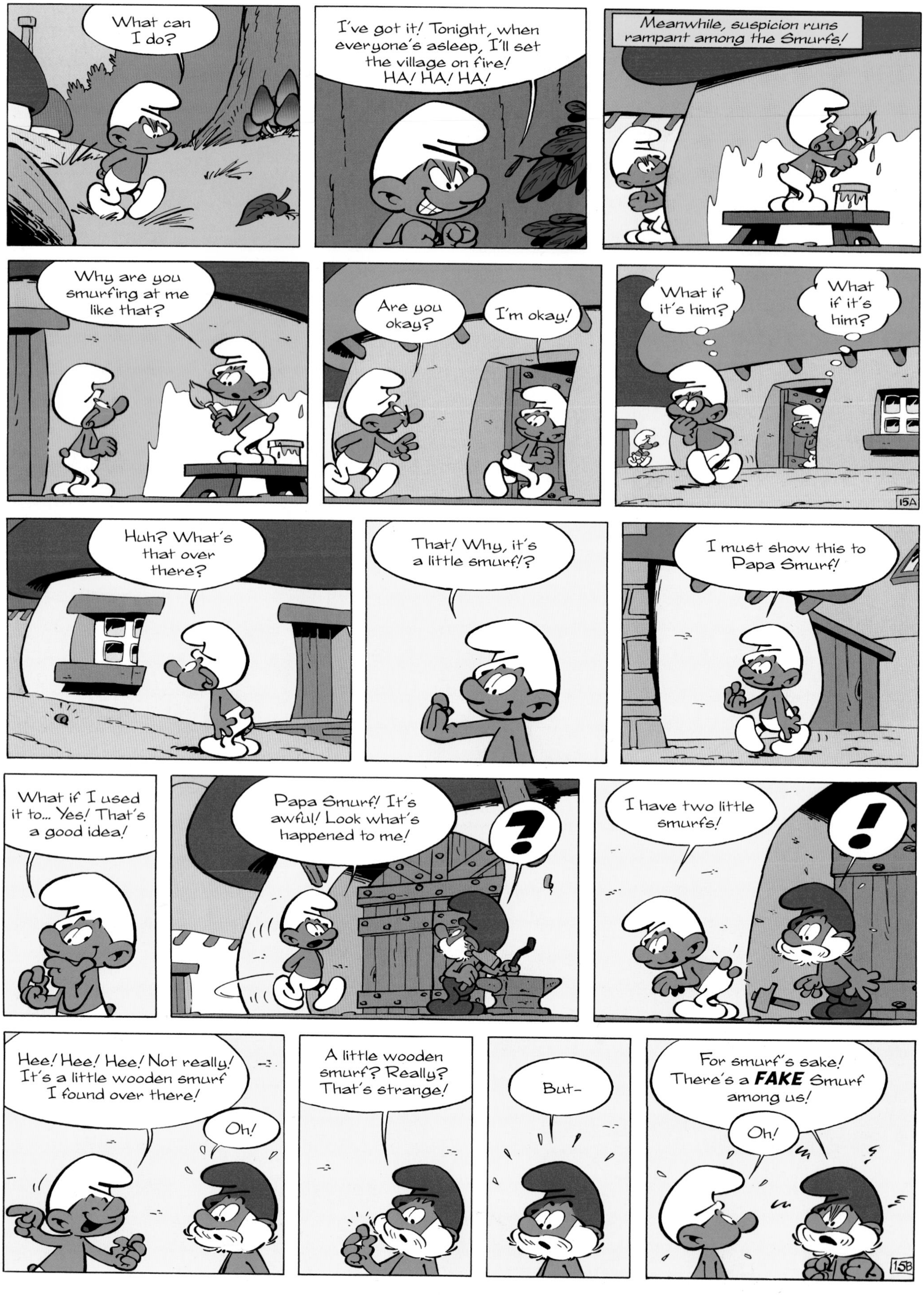
What can I do?
I've got it! Tonight, when everyone's asleep, I'll set the village on fire! HA! HA! HA!
Meanwhile, suspicion runs rampant among the Smurfs!
Why are you smurfing at me like that?
Are you okay?
I'm okay!
What if it's him?
What if it's him?
15A
Huh? What's that over there?
That! Why, it's a little smurf!?
I must show this to Papa Smurf!
What if I used it to... Yes! That's a good idea!
Papa Smurf! It's awful! Look what's happened to me!
?
I have two little smurfs!
!
Hee! Hee! Hee! Not really! It's a little wooden smurf I found over there!
Oh!
A little wooden smurf? Really? That's strange!
But-
For smurf's sake! There's a FAKE Smurf among us!
Oh!
15B

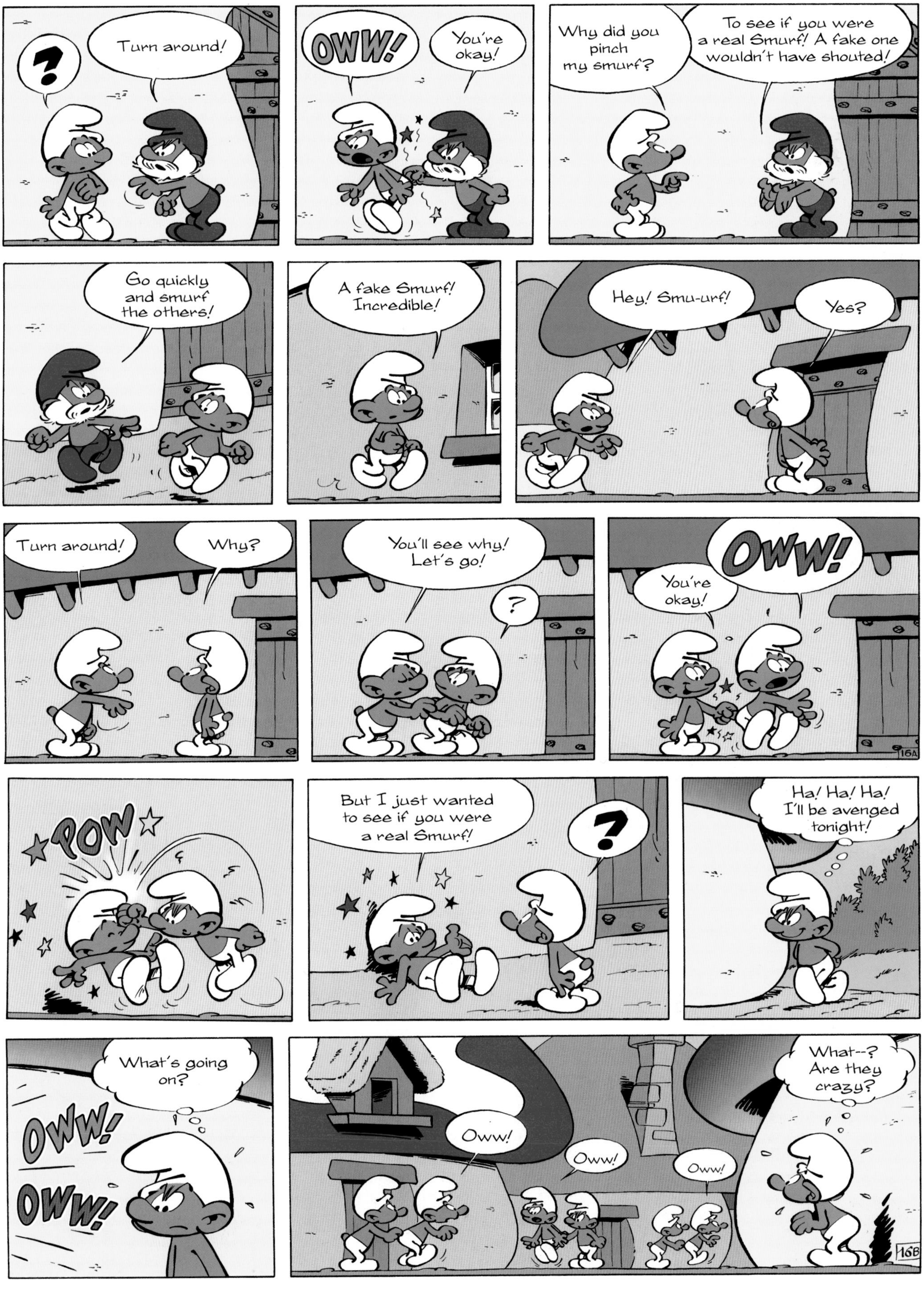
?
Turn around!
OWW!
You're okay!
Why did you pinch my smurf?
To see if you were a real Smurf! A fake one wouldn't have shouted!
Go quickly and smurf the others!
A fake Smurf! Incredible!
Hey! Smu-urf!
Yes?
Turn around!
Why?
You'll see why! Let's go!
?
You're okay!
OWW!
16A
POW
But I just wanted to see if you were a real Smurf!
?
Ha! Ha! Ha! I'll be avenged tonight!
What's going on?
OWW!
OWW!
Oww!
Oww!
Oww!
What--? Are they crazy?
16B

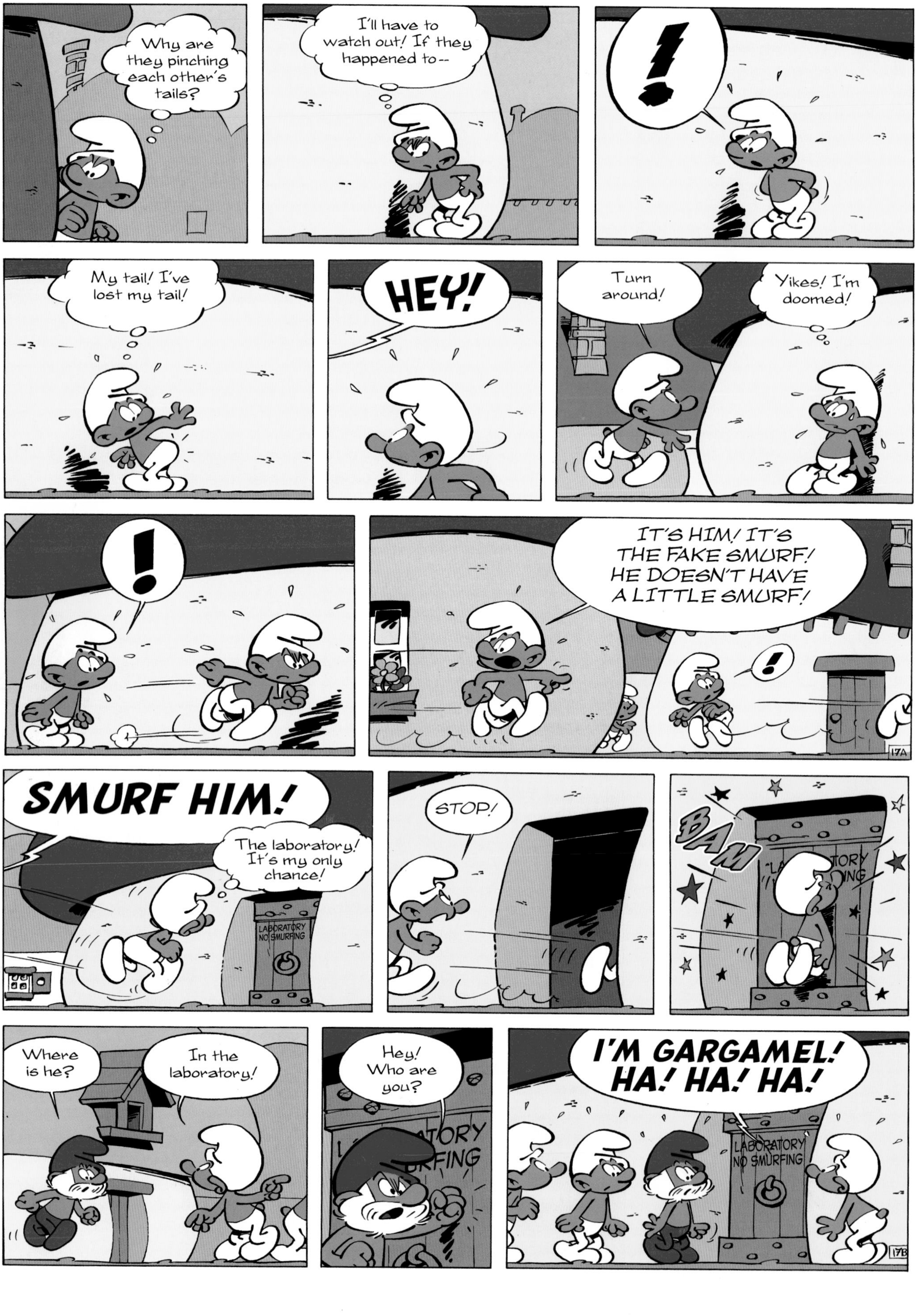
Why are they pinching each other's tails?
I'll have to watch out! If they happened to--
!
My tail! I've lost my tail!
HEY!
Turn around!
Yikes! I'm doomed!
!
IT'S HIM! IT'S THE FAKE SMURF! HE DOESN'T HAVE A LITTLE SMURF!
!
17A
SMURF HIM!
The laboratory! It's my only chance!
LABORATORY NO SMURFING
STOP!
BAM
Where is he?
In the laboratory!
Hey! Who are you?
I'M GARGAMEL! HA! HA! HA!
LABORATORY NO SMURFING
17B

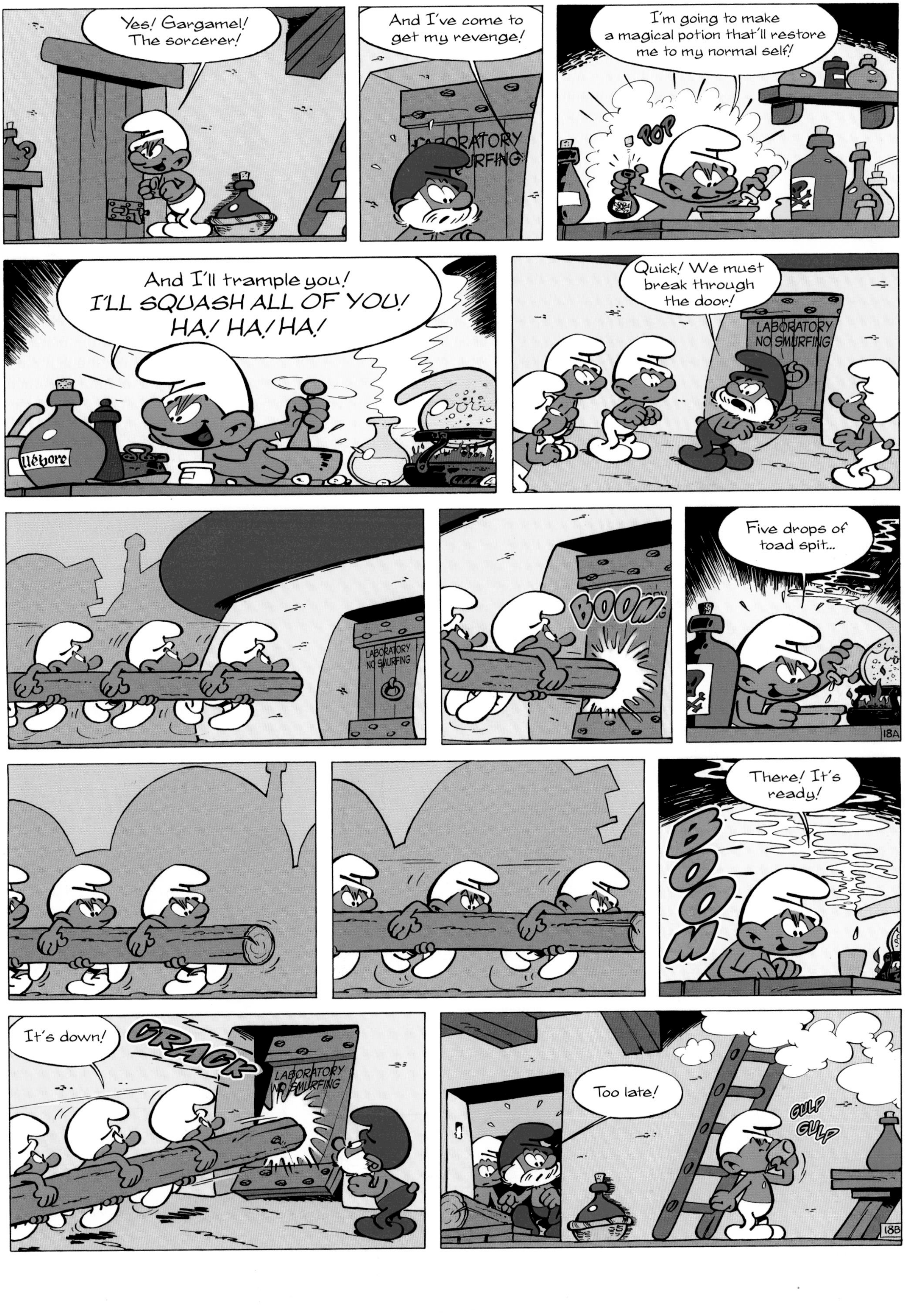
Yes! Gargamel! The sorcerer!
And I've come to get my revenge!
LABORATORY SMURFING
I'm going to make a magical potion that'll restore me to my normal self!
POP
And I'll trample you! I'LL SQUASH ALL OF YOU! HA! HA! HA!
llébore
Quick! We must break through the door!
LABORATORY NO SMURFING
LABORATORY NO SMURFING
BOOM
Five drops of toad spit...
18A
There! It's ready!
BOOM
It's down!
CRACK
LABORATORY NO SMURFING
Too late!
GULP GULP
18B

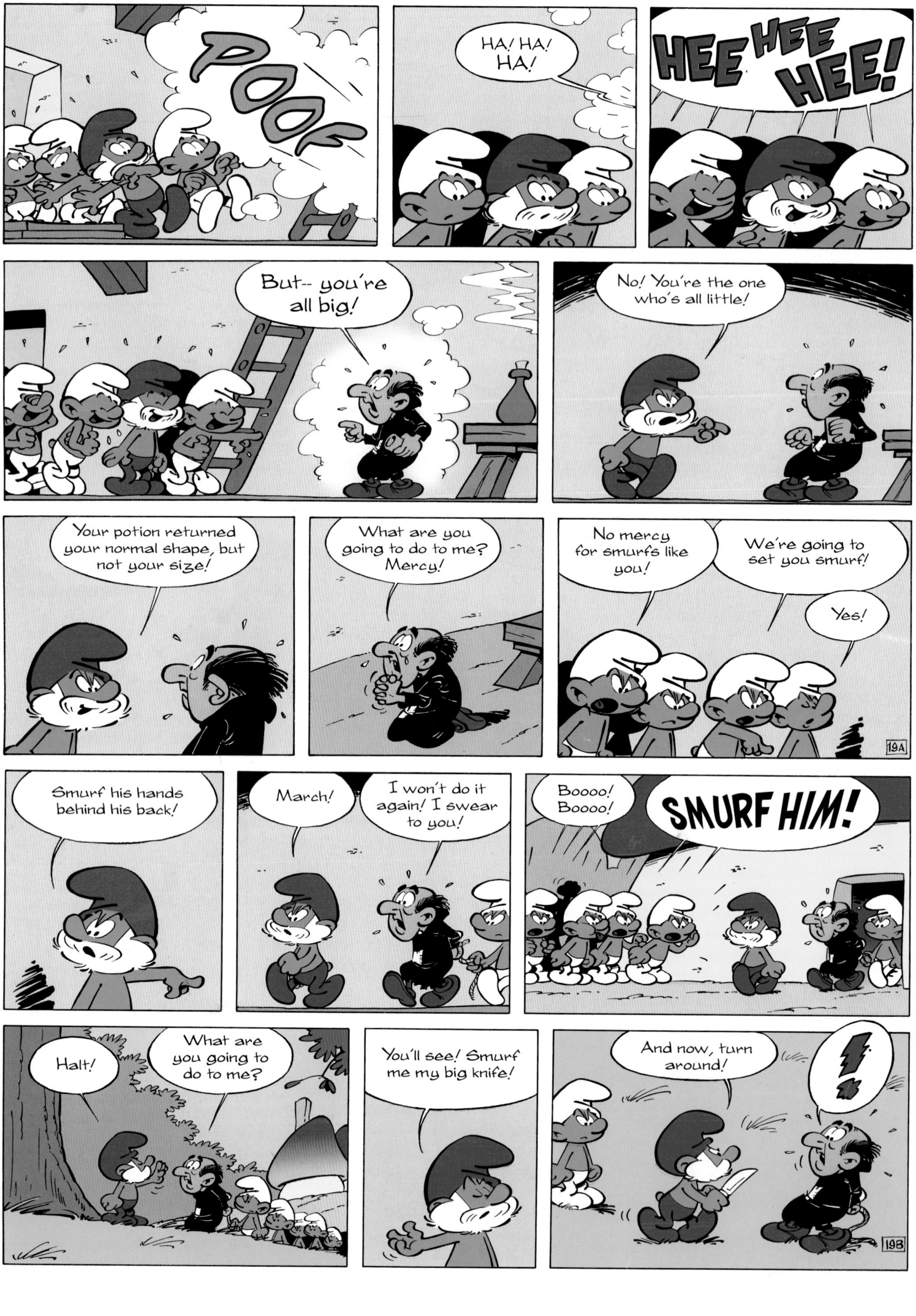
POOF
HA! HA! HA!
HEE HEE HEE HEE!
But-- you're all big!
No! You're the one who's all little!
Your potion returned your normal shape, but not your size!
What are you going to do to me? Mercy!
No mercy for smurfs like you!
We're going to set you smurf!
Yes!
19A
Smurf his hands behind his back!
March!
I won't do it again! I swear to you!
Boooo! Boooo!
SMURF HIM!
Halt!
What are you going to do to me?
You'll see! Smurf me my big knife!
And now, turn around!
19B

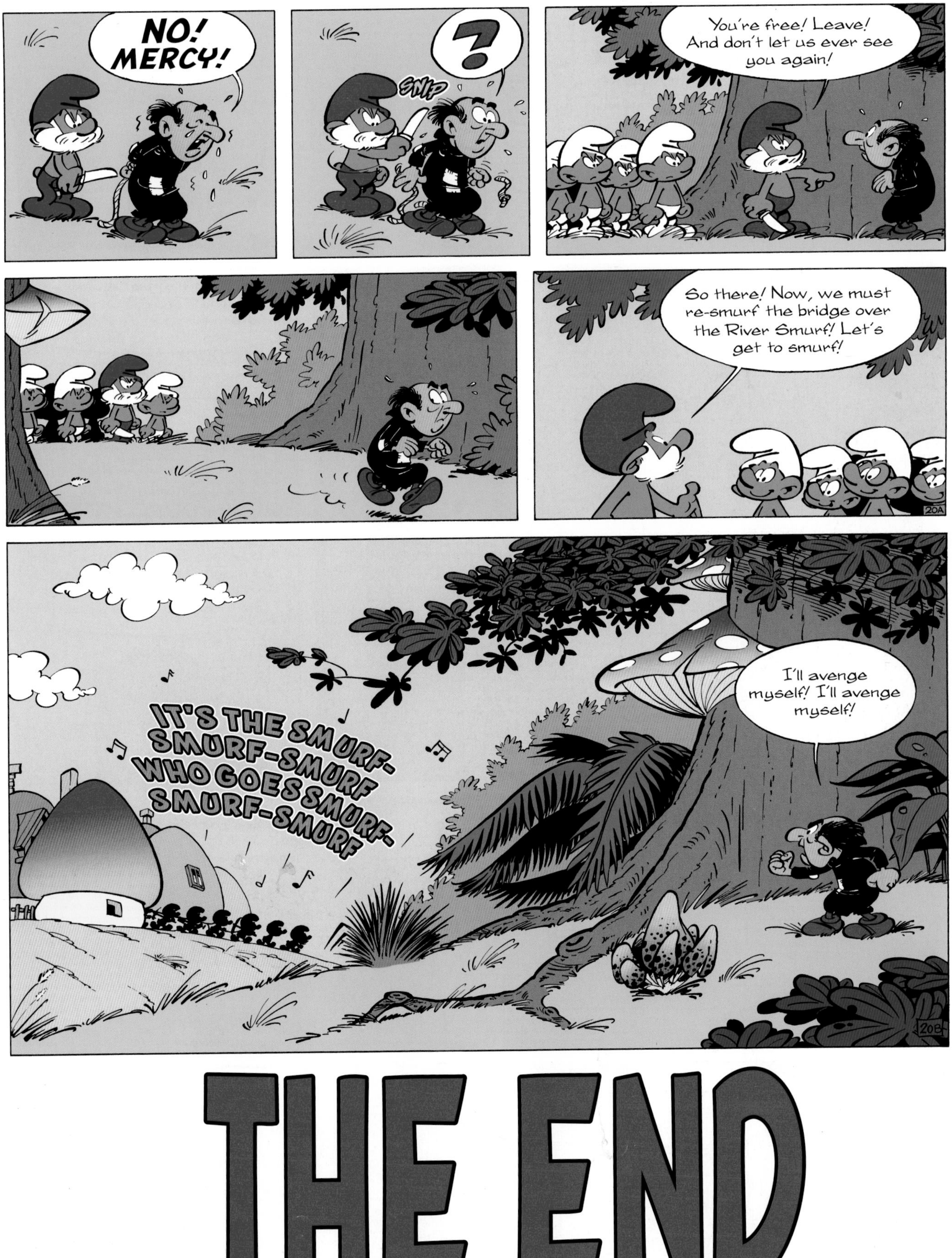
NO! MERCY!
SNIP
?
You're free! Leave! And don't let us ever see you again!
So there! Now, we must re-smurf the bridge over the River Smurf! Let's get to smurf!
20A
IT'S THE SMURF-SMURF-SMURF WHO GOES SMURF-SMURF-SMURF
I'll avenge myself! I'll avenge myself!
20B

THE END

THE HUNDREDTH SMURF

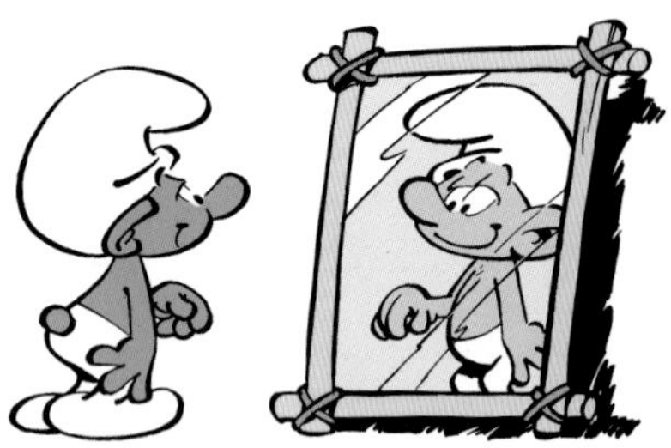

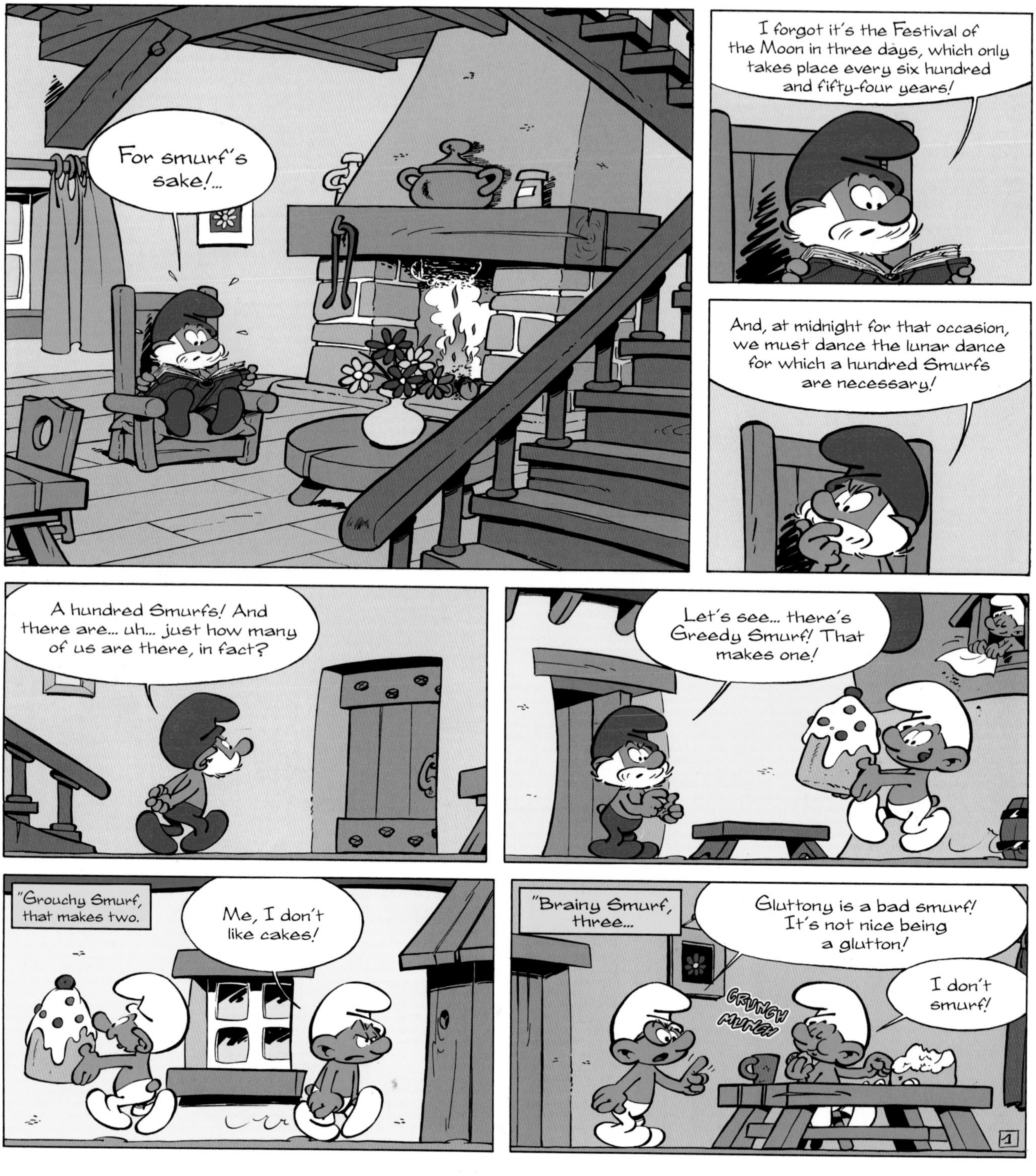
For smurf's sake!...
I forgot it's the Festival of the Moon in three days, which only takes place every six hundred and fifty-four years!
And, at midnight for that occasion, we must dance the lunar dance for which a hundred Smurfs are necessary!
A hundred Smurfs! And there are... uh... just how many of us are there, in fact?
Let's see... there's Greedy Smurf! That makes one!
"Grouchy Smurf, that makes two.
Me, I don't like cakes!
"Brainy Smurf, three...
Gluttony is a bad smurf! It's not nice being a glutton!
GRUNCH
MUNCH
I don't smurf!
1

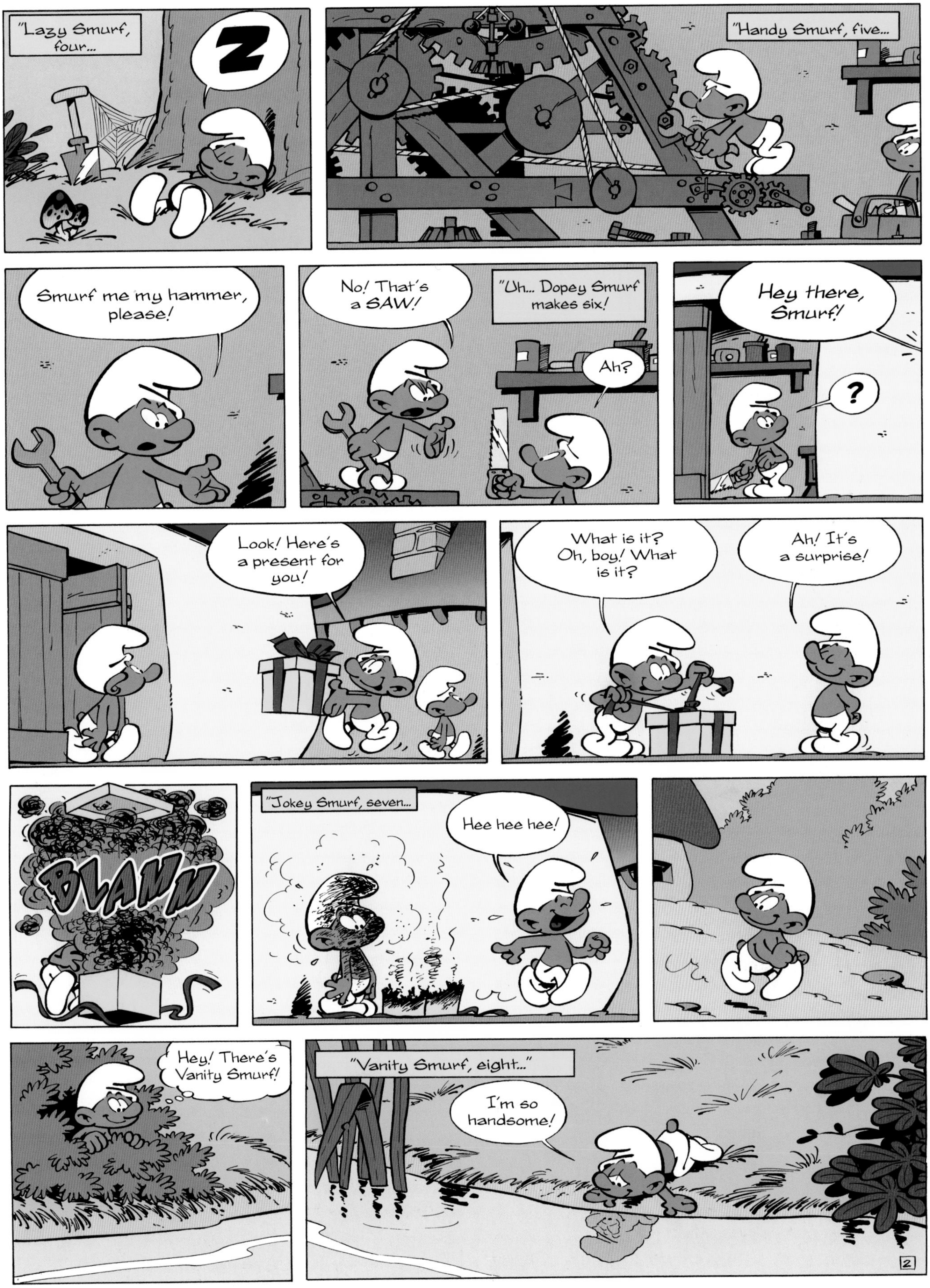
"Lazy Smurf, four...
Z
"Handy Smurf, five...
Smurf me my hammer, please!
No! That's a SAW!
"Uh... Dopey Smurf makes six!
Ah?
Hey there, Smurf!
?
Look! Here's a present for you!
What is it? Oh, boy! What is it?
Ah! It's a surprise!
BLANN
"Jokey Smurf, seven...
Hee hee hee!
Hey! There's Vanity Smurf!
"Vanity Smurf, eight..."
I'm so handsome!
2

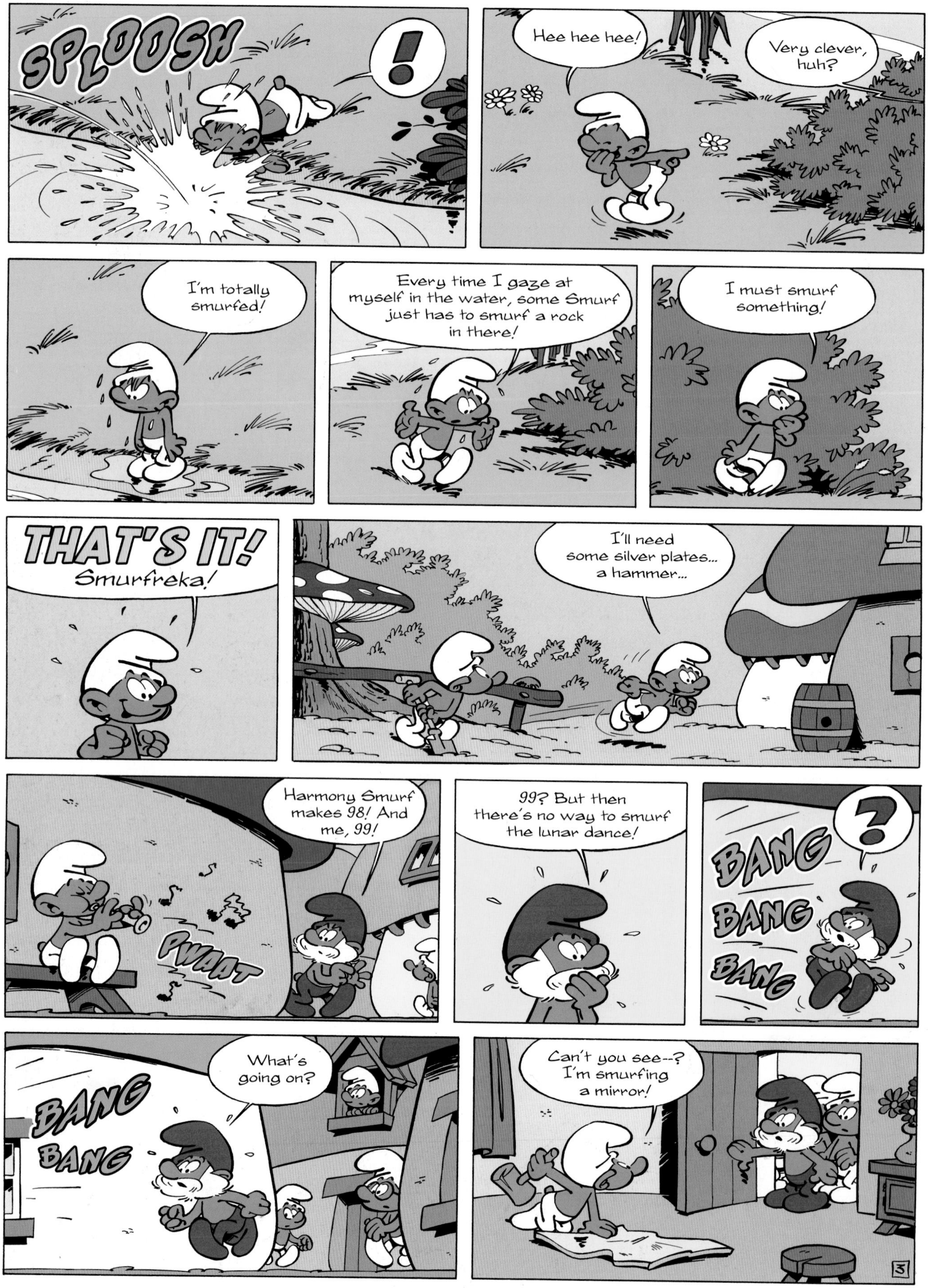
SPLOOSH
!
Hee hee hee!
Very clever, huh?
I'm totally smurfed!
Every time I gaze at myself in the water, some Smurf just has to smurf a rock in there!
I must smurf something!
THAT'S IT! Smurfreka!
I'll need some silver plates... a hammer...
Harmony Smurf makes 98! And me, 99!
PWAAT
99? But then there's no way to smurf the lunar dance!
?
BANG
BANG
BANG
BANG
BANG
What's going on?
Can't you see--? I'm smurfing a mirror!
3

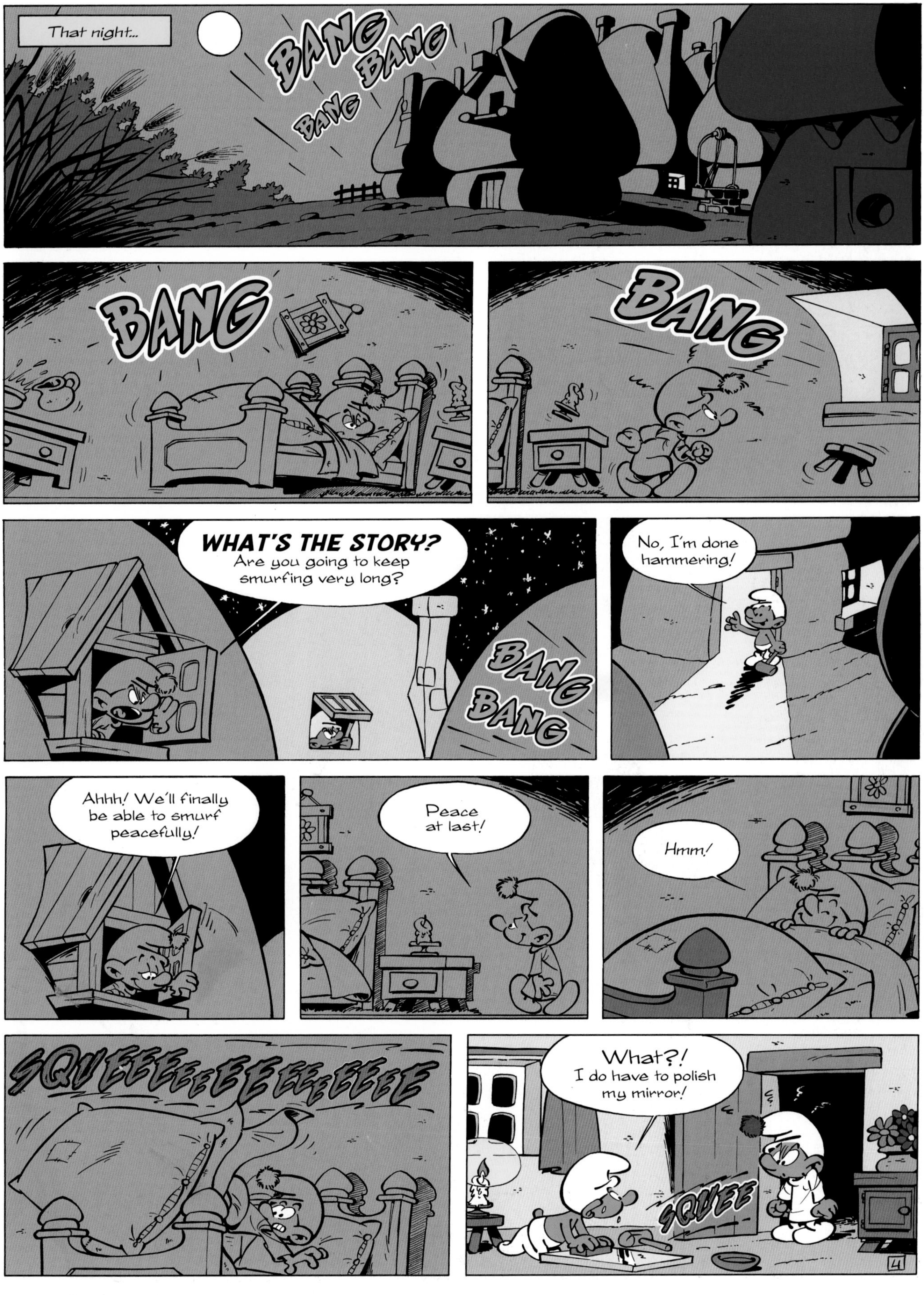
That night...
BANG BANG BANG BANG
BANG
BANG
WHAT'S THE STORY? Are you going to keep smurfing very long?
BANG BANG
No, I'm done hammering!
Ahhh! We'll finally be able to smurf peacefully!
Peace at last!
Hmm!
SQUEEEEEEEEEEEEEEEE
What?! I do have to polish my mirror!
SQUEE
4

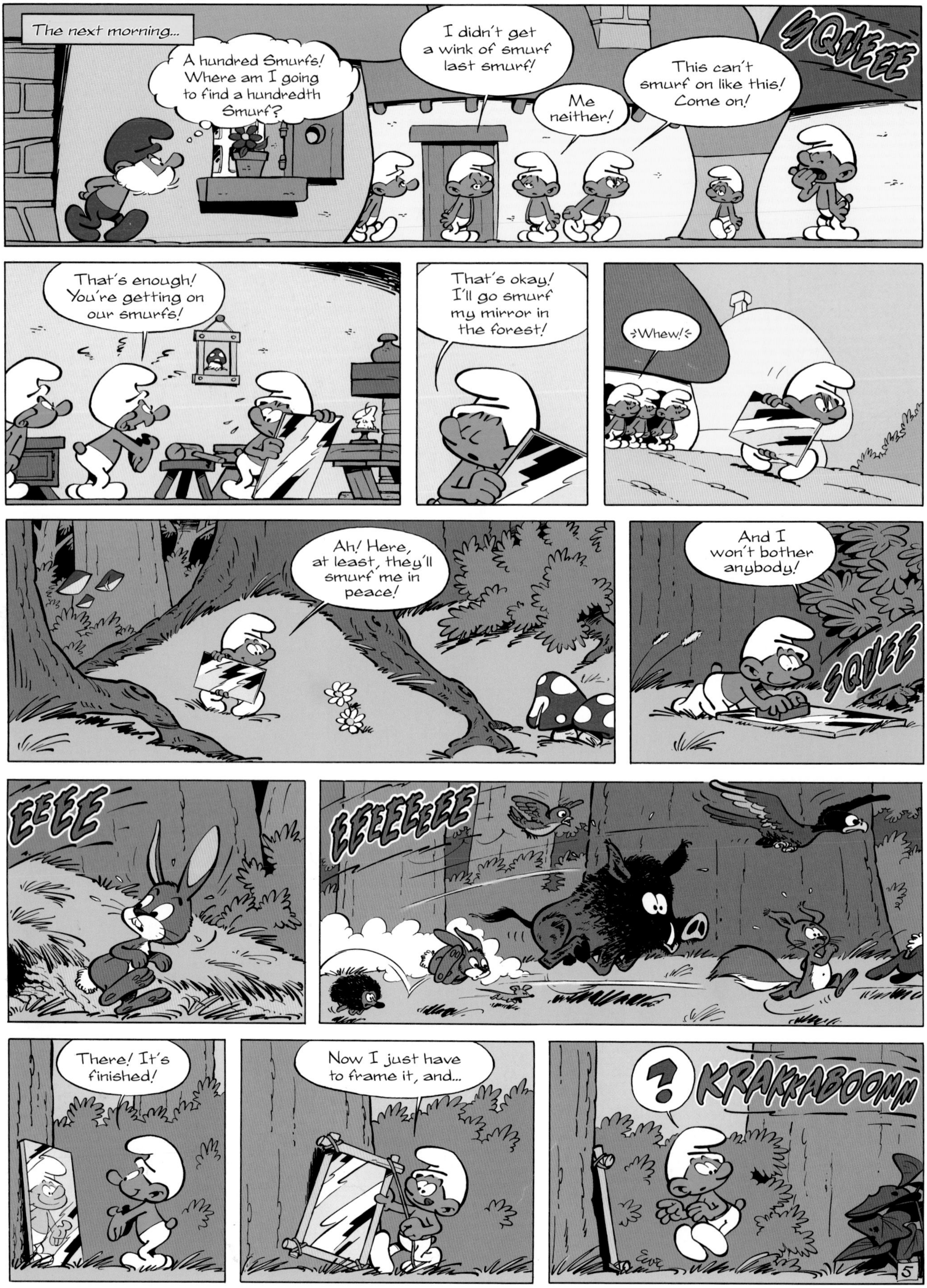
The next morning...
A hundred Smurfs! Where am I going to find a hundredth Smurf?
I didn't get a wink of smurf last smurf!
Me neither!
This can't smurf on like this! Come on!
SQUEEEE
That's enough! You're getting on our smurfs!
That's okay! I'll go smurf my mirror in the forest!
Whew!
Ah! Here, at least, they'll smurf me in peace!
And I won't bother anybody!
SQUEE
EEEE
EEEEEEEE
There! It's finished!
Now I just have to frame it, and...
?
KRAKKABOOMM
5

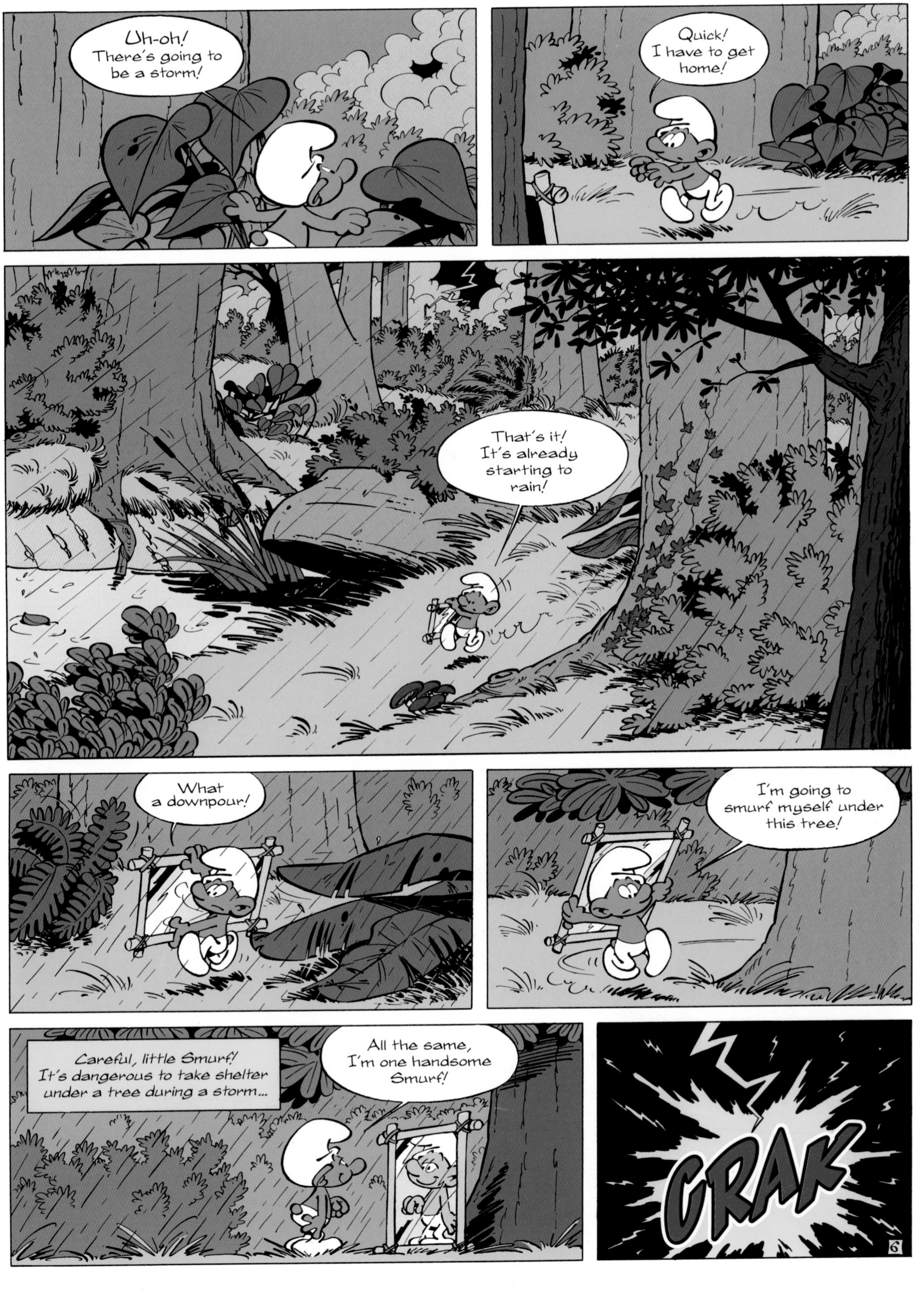
Uh-oh! There's going to be a storm!
Quick! I have to get home!
That's it! It's already starting to rain!
What a downpour!
I'm going to smurf myself under this tree!
Careful, little Smurf! It's dangerous to take shelter under a tree during a storm...
All the same, I'm one handsome Smurf!
CRAK
6

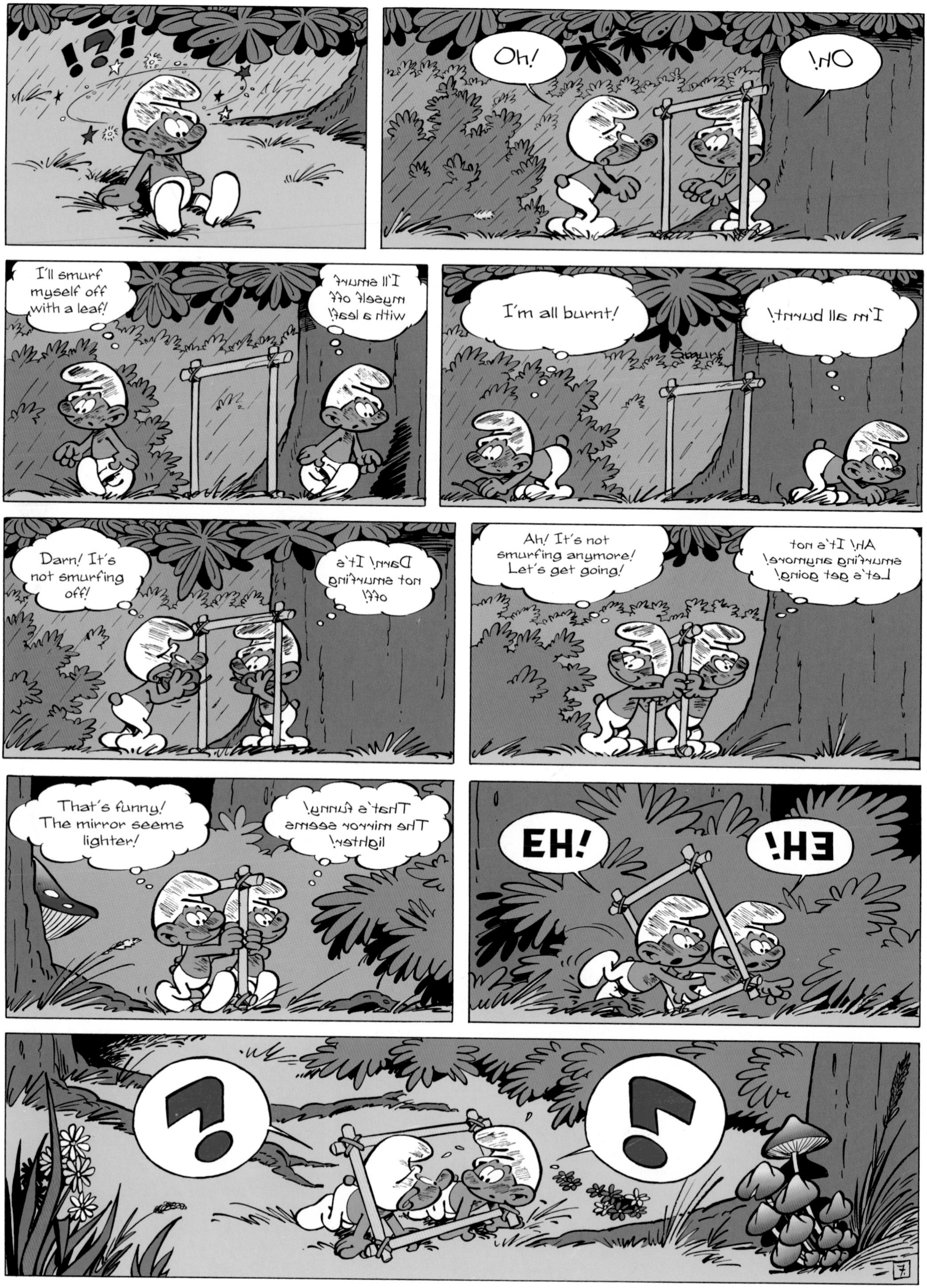
!?!!
Oh!
Oh!
I'll smurf myself off with a leaf!
I'll smurf myself off with a leaf!
I'm all burnt!
I'm all burnt!
Darn! It's not smurfing off!
Darn! It's not smurfing off!
Ah! It's not smurfing anymore! Let's get going!
Ah! It's not smurfing anymore! Let's get going!
That's funny! The mirror seems lighter!
That's funny! The mirror seems lighter!
EH!
EH!
?
?

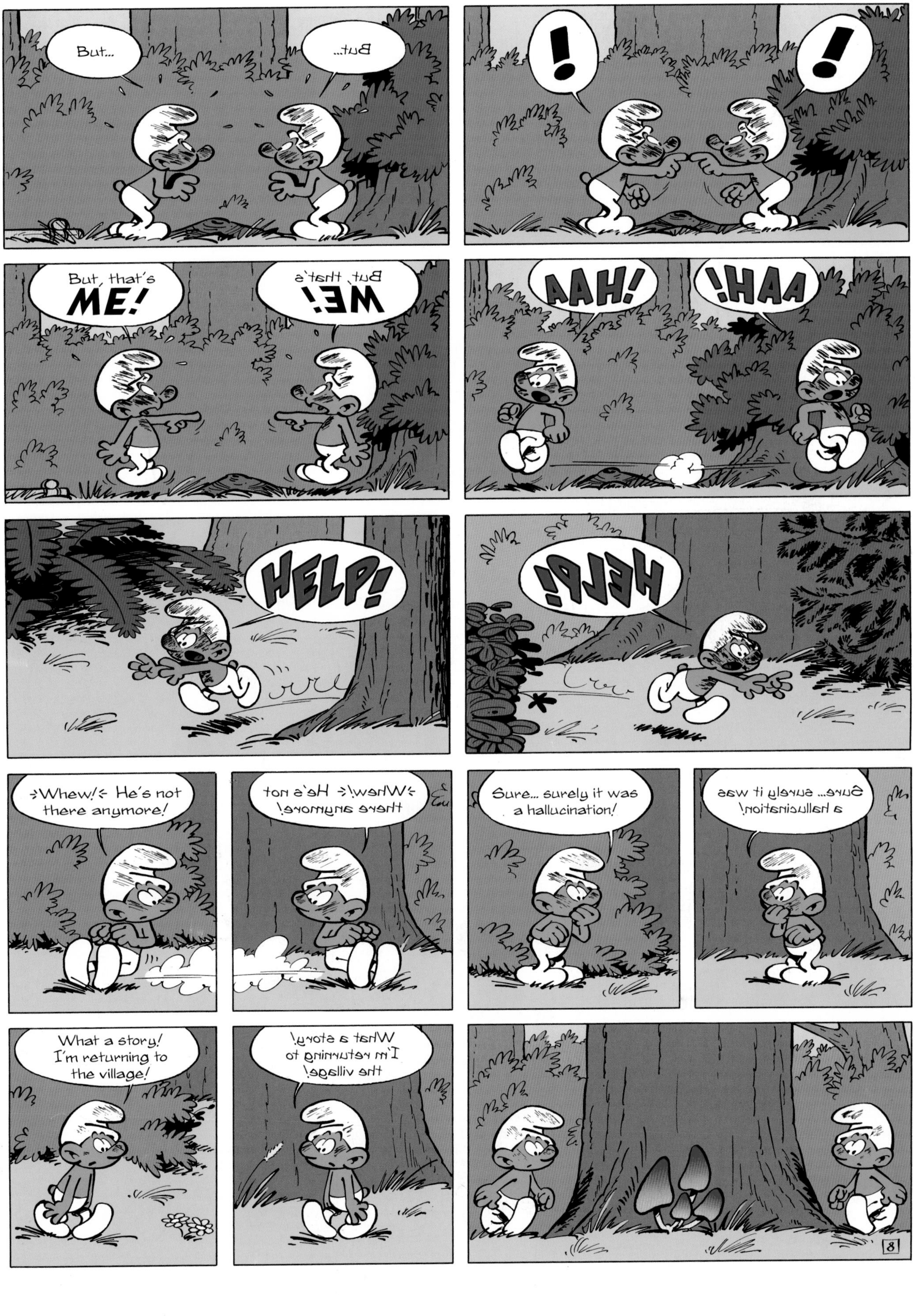
But...
But...
!
!
But, that's ME!
But, that's ME!
AAH!
AAH!
HELP!
HELP!
Whew! He's not there anymore!
Whew! He's not there anymore!
Sure... surely it was a hallucination!
Sure... surely it was a hallucination!
What a story! I'm returning to the village!
What a story! I'm returning to the village!
8

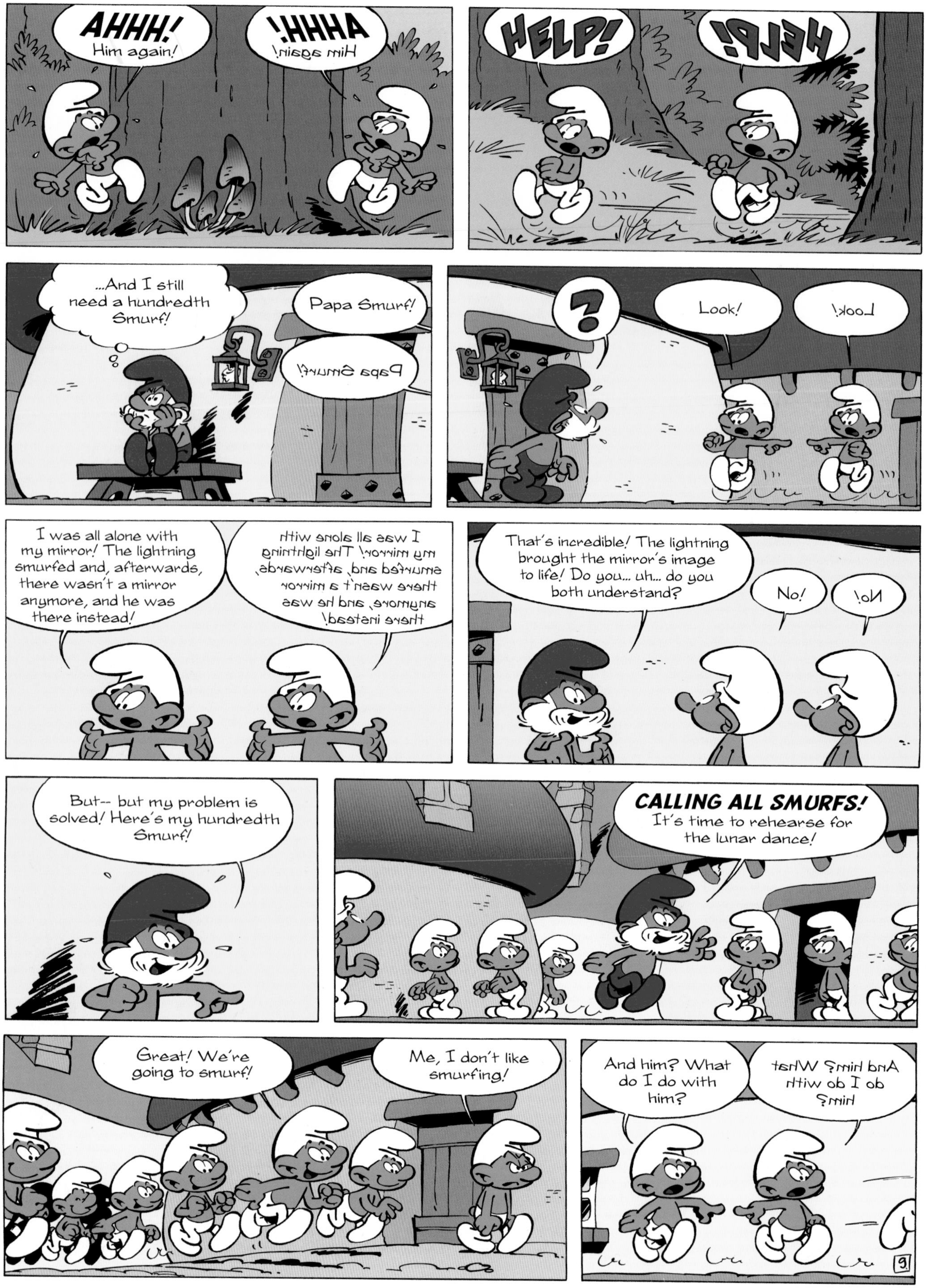
AHHH! Him again!
AHHH! Him again!
HELP!
HELP!
...And I still need a hundredth Smurf!
Papa Smurf!
Papa Smurf!
?
Look!
Look!
I was all alone with my mirror! The lightning smurfed and, afterwards, there wasn't a mirror anymore, and he was there instead!
I was all alone with my mirror! The lightning smurfed and, afterwards, there wasn't a mirror anymore, and he was there instead!
That's incredible! The lightning brought the mirror's image to life! Do you... uh... do you both understand?
No!
No!
But-- but my problem is solved! Here's my hundredth Smurf!
CALLING ALL SMURFS! It's time to rehearse for the lunar dance!
Great! We're going to smurf!
Me, I don't like smurfing!
And him? What do I do with him?
And him? What do I do with him?
9

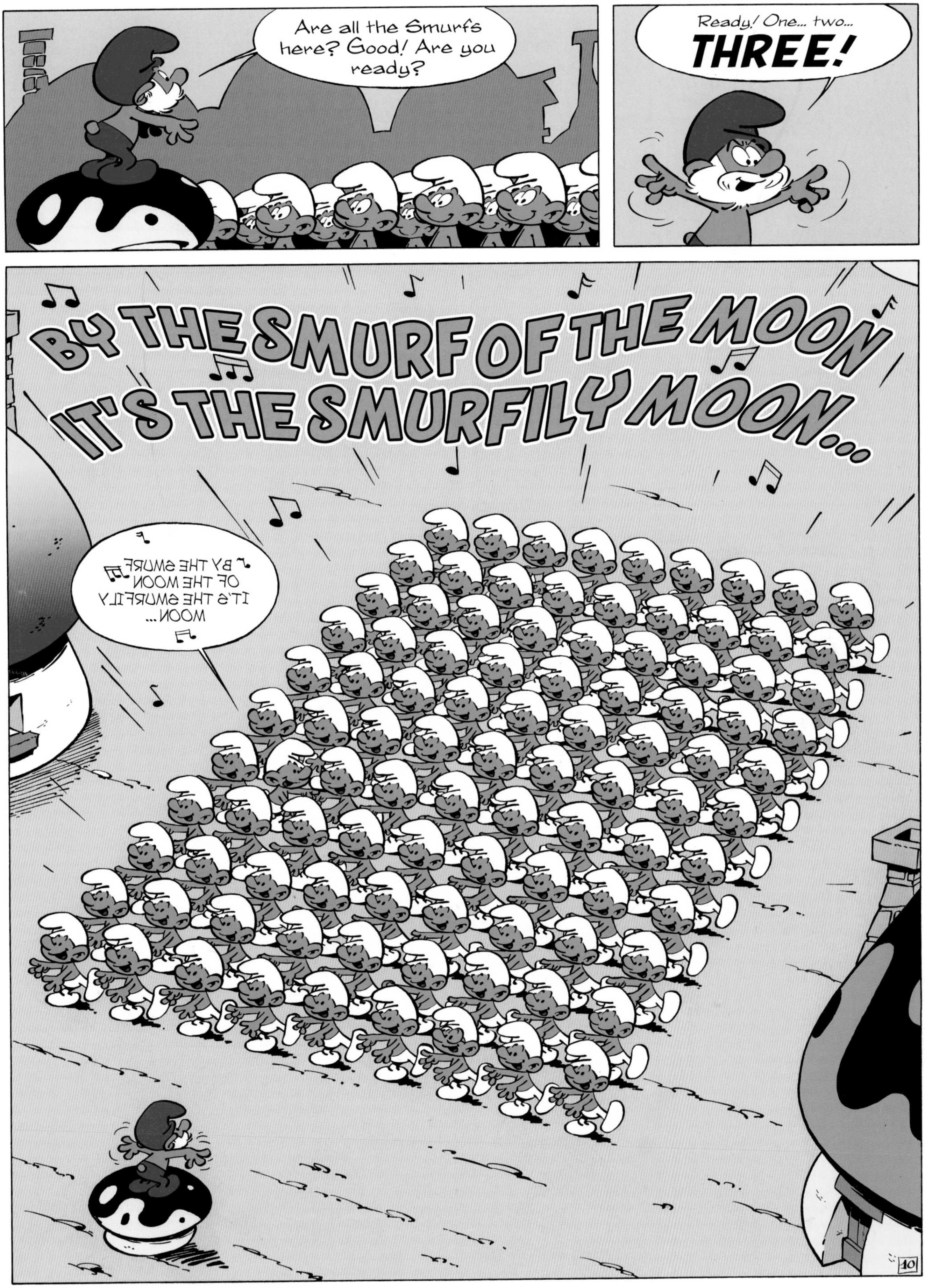
Are all the Smurfs here? Good! Are you ready?
Ready! One... two... THREE!
BY THE SMURF OF THE MOON IT'S THE SMURFILY MOON...
BY THE SMURF OF THE MOON IT'S THE SMURFILY MOON...

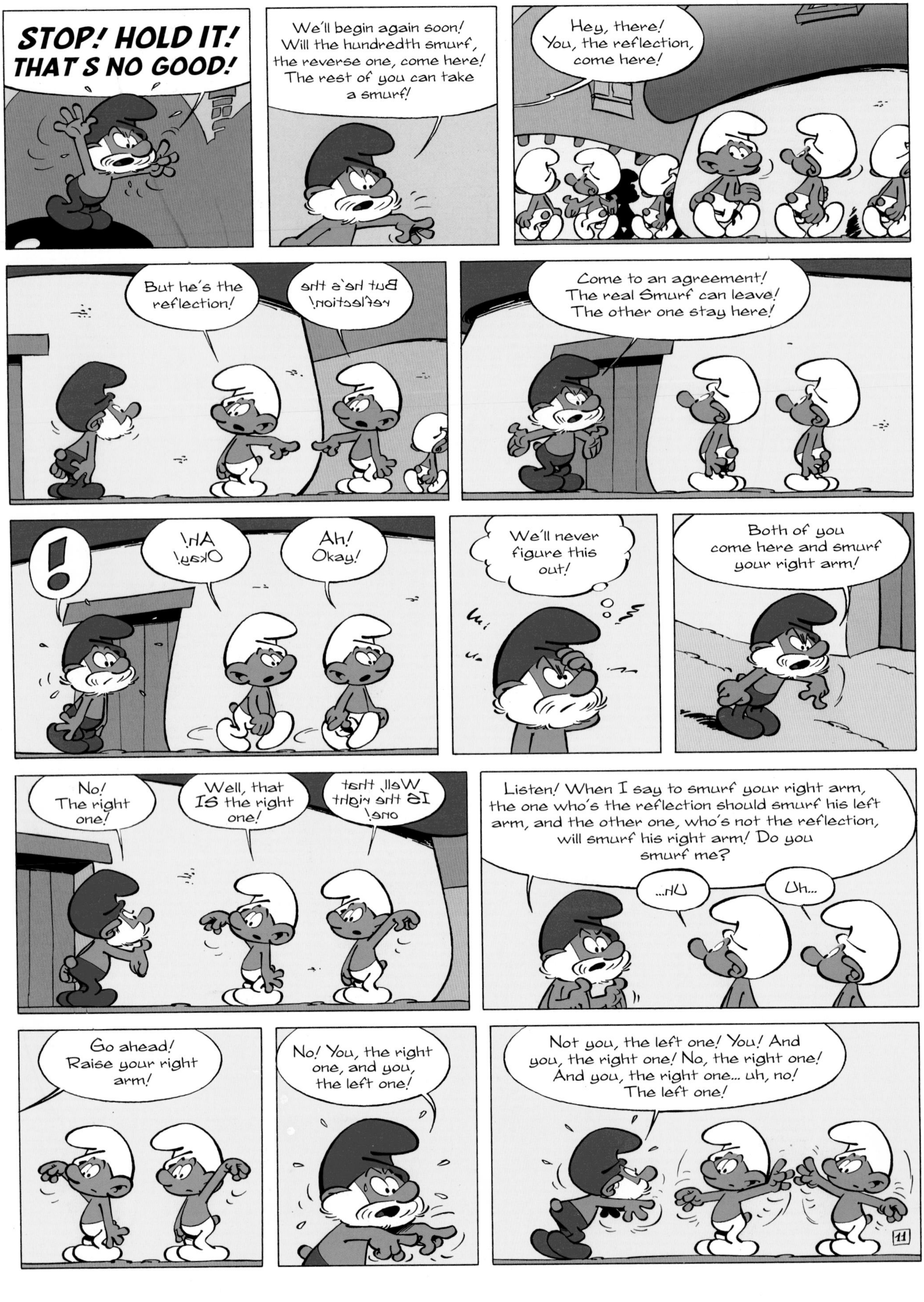

STOP! HOLD IT! THAT S NO GOOD!
We'll begin again soon! Will the hundredth smurf, the reverse one, come here! The rest of you can take a smurf!
Hey, there! You, the reflection, come here!
But he's the reflection!
But he's the reflection!
Come to an agreement! The real Smurf can leave! The other one stay here!
!
Ah! Okay!
Ah! Okay!
We'll never figure this out!
Both of you come here and smurf your right arm!
No! The right one!
Well, that IS the right one!
Well, that IS the right one!
Listen! When I say to smurf your right arm, the one who's the reflection should smurf his left arm, and the other one, who's not the reflection, will smurf his right arm! Do you smurf me?
Uh...
Uh...
Go ahead! Raise your right arm!
No! You, the right one, and you, the left one!
Not you, the left one! You! And you, the right one! No, the right one! And you, the right one... uh, no! The left one!
11

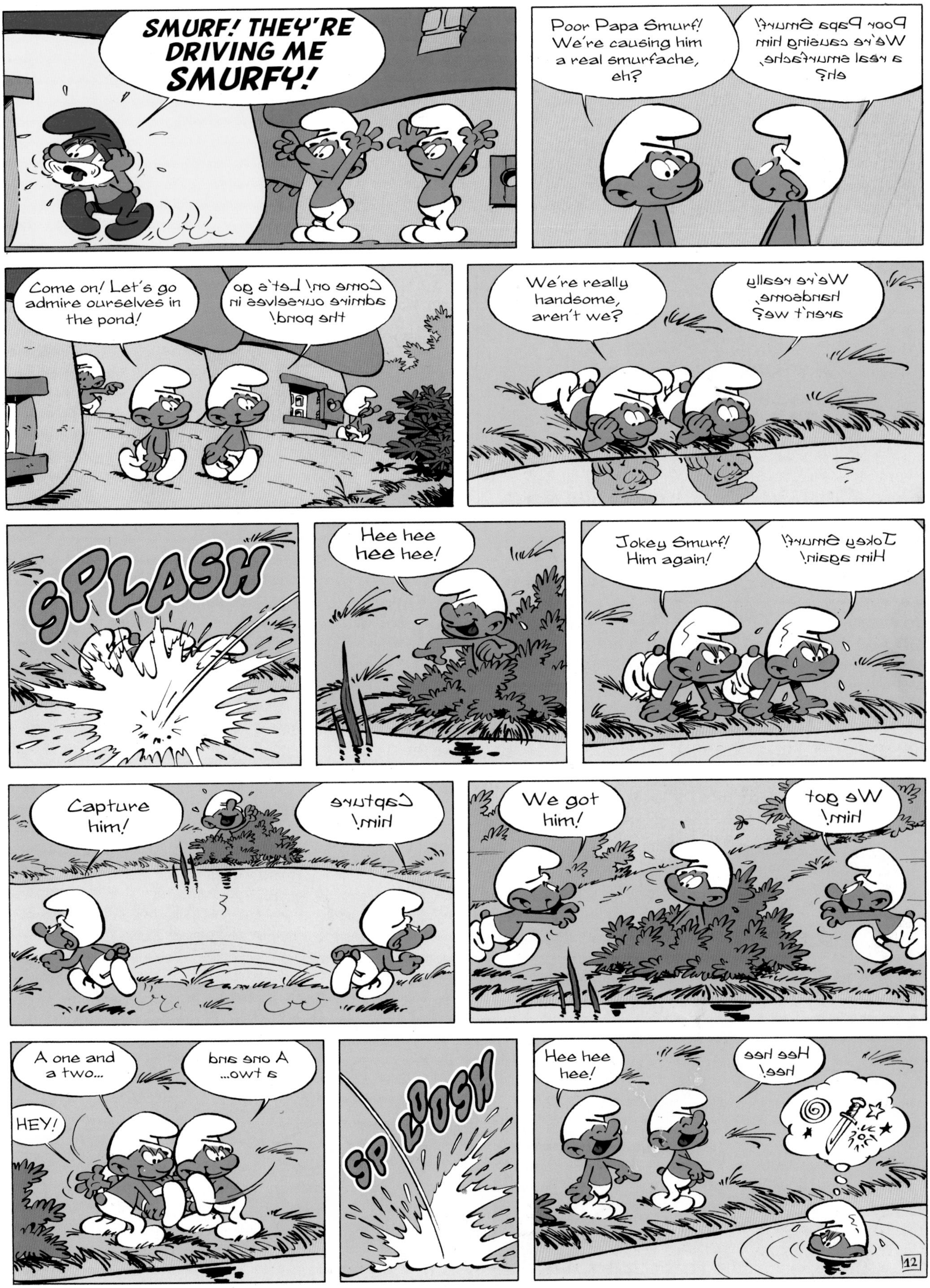

SMURF! THEY'RE DRIVING ME SMURFY!
Poor Papa Smurf! We're causing him a real smurfache, eh?
Poor Papa Smurf! We're causing him a real smurfache, eh?
Come on! Let's go admire ourselves in the pond!
Come on! Let's go admire ourselves in the pond!
We're really handsome, aren't we?
We're really handsome, aren't we?
SPLASH
Hee hee hee hee!
Jokey Smurf! Him again!
Jokey Smurf! Him again!
Capture him!
Capture him!
We got him!
We got him!
A one and a two...
A one and a two...
HEY!
SPLOOSH
Hee hee hee!
Hee hee hee!
12

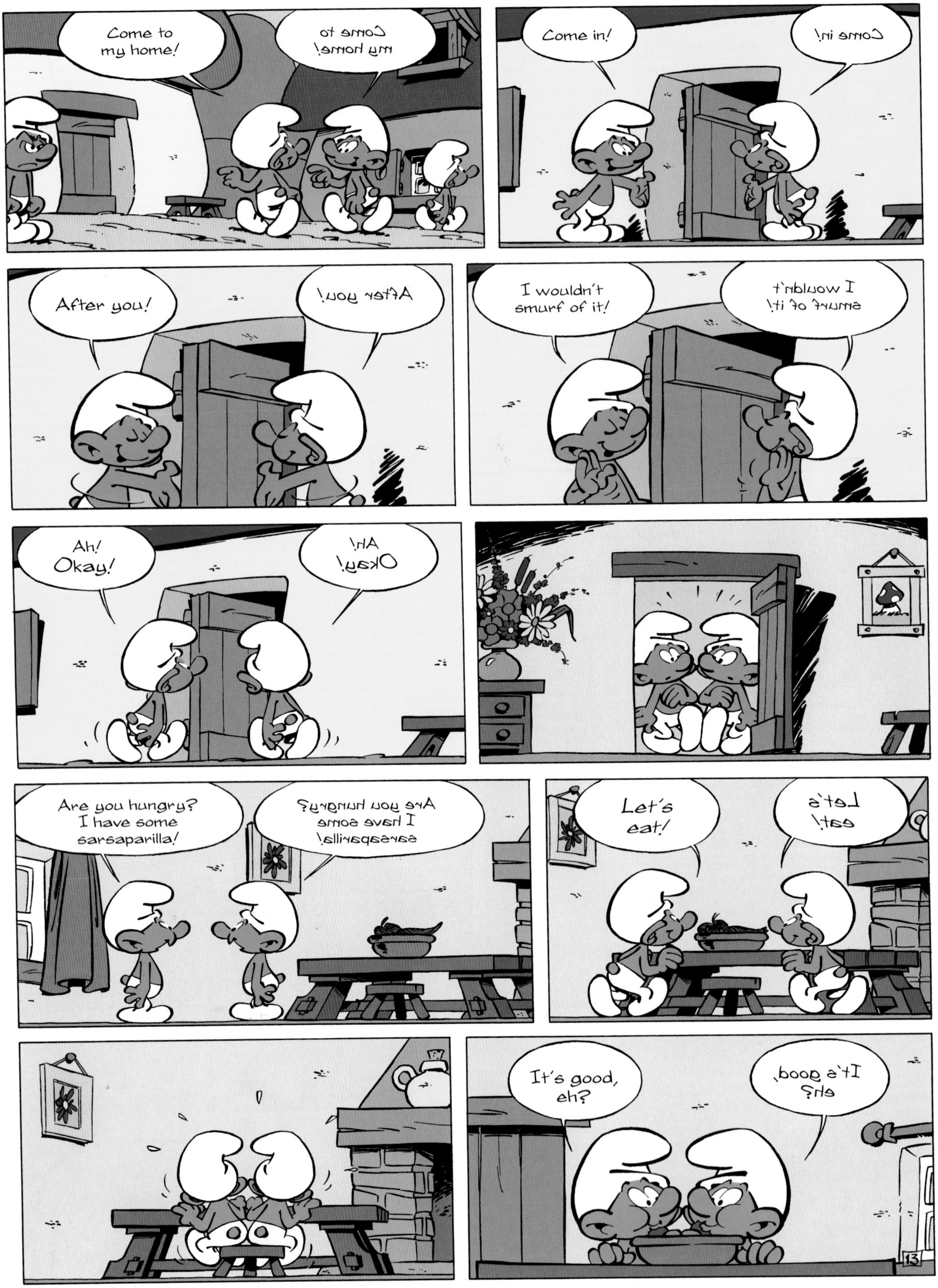
Come to my home!
Come to my home!
Come in!
Come in!
After you!
After you!
I wouldn't smurf of it!
I wouldn't smurf of it!
Ah! Okay!
Ah! Okay!
Are you hungry? I have some sarsaparilla!
Are you hungry? I have some sarsaparilla!
Let's eat!
Let's eat!
It's good, eh?
It's good, eh?
13

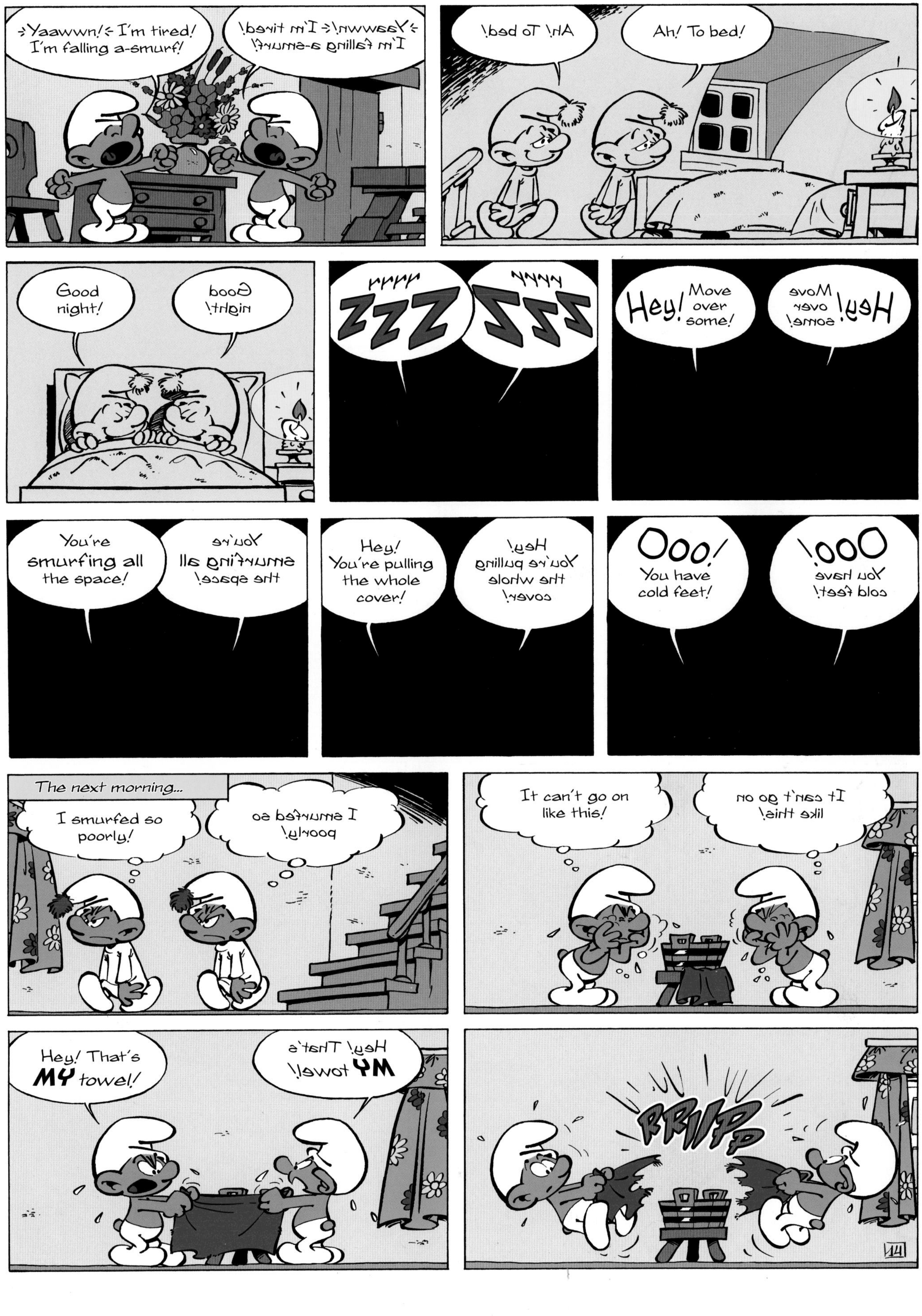

Yaawwn! I'm tired! I'm falling a-smurf!
Yaawwn! I'm tired! I'm falling a-smurf!
Ah! To bed!
Ah! To bed!
Good night!
Good night!
ZZZ rrrr
ZZZ rrrr
Hey! Move over some!
Hey! Move over some!
You're smurfing all the space!
You're smurfing all the space!
Hey! You're pulling the whole cover!
Hey! You're pulling the whole cover!
Ooo! You have cold feet!
Ooo! You have cold feet!
The next morning...
I smurfed so poorly!
I smurfed so poorly!
It can't go on like this!
It can't go on like this!
Hey! That's MY towel!
Hey! That's MY towel!
RRIPP

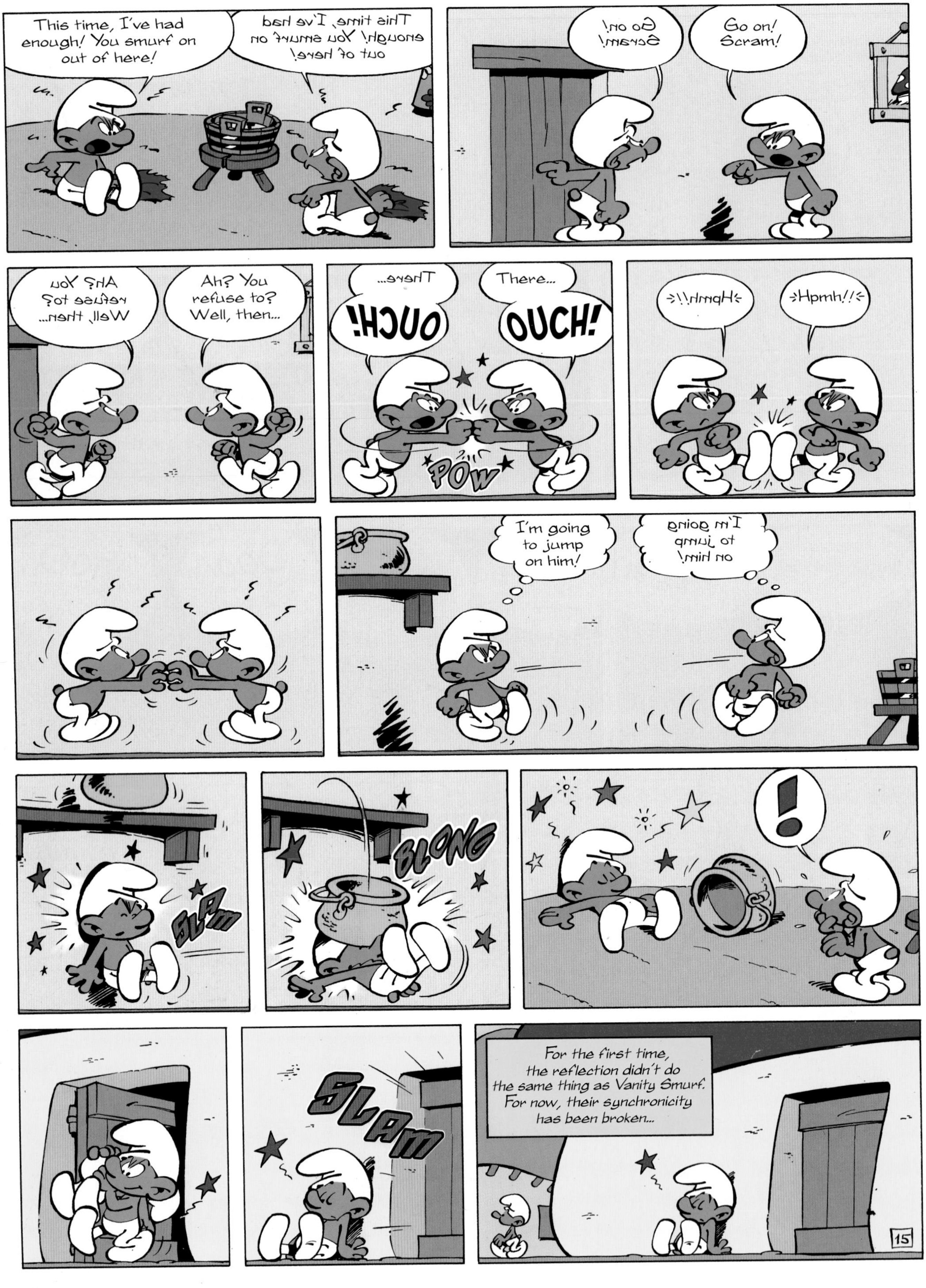
This time, I've had enough! You smurf on out of here!
This time, I've had enough! You smurf on out of here!
Go on! Scram!
Go on! Scram!
Ah? You refuse to? Well, then...
Ah? You refuse to? Well, then...
There...
There...
OUCH!
OUCH!
POW
Hpmh!!
Hpmh!!
I'm going to jump on him!
I'm going to jump on him!
SLAM
BLONG
!
SLAM
For the first time, the reflection didn't do the same thing as Vanity Smurf. For now, their synchronicity has been broken...
15

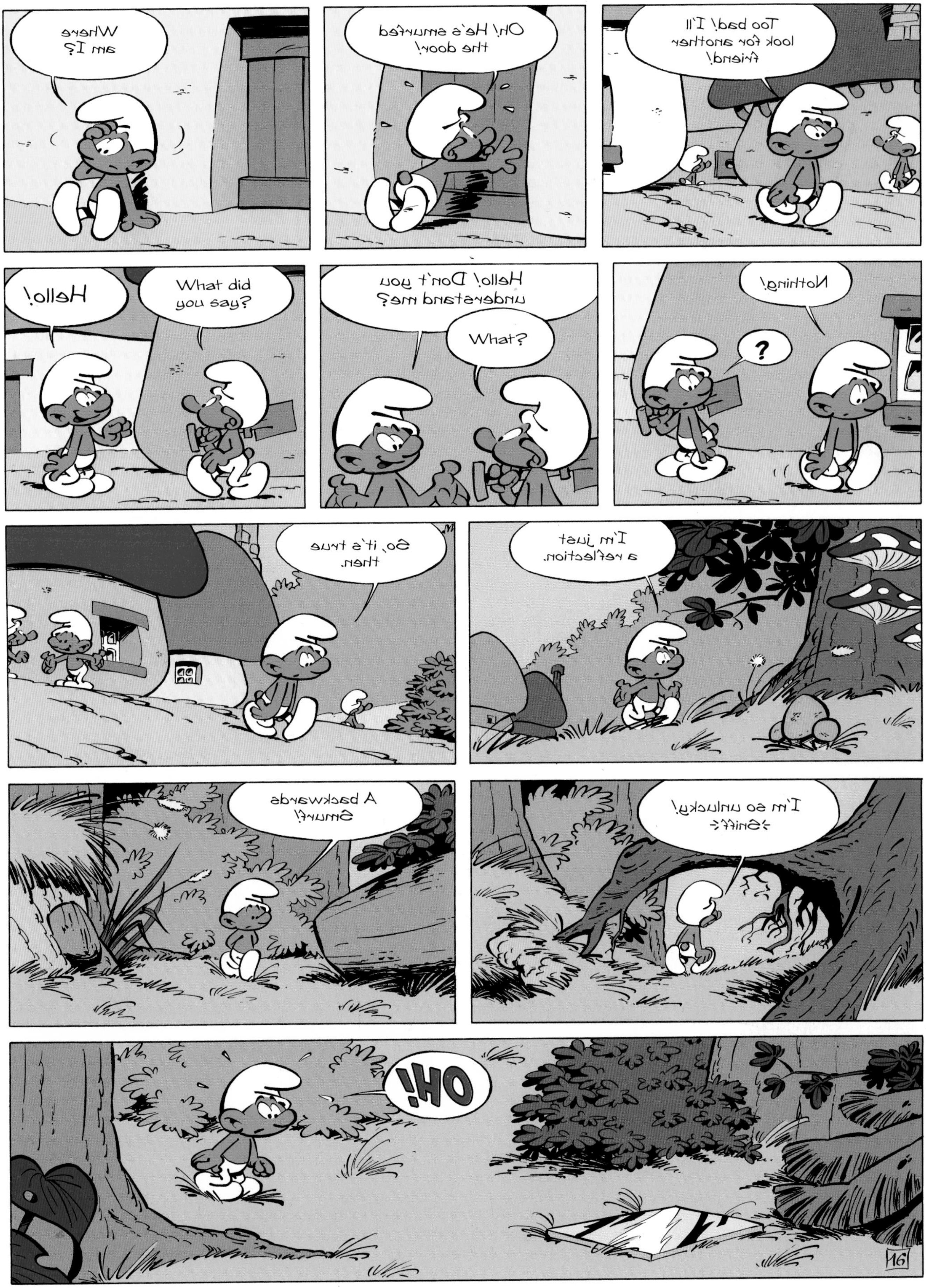
Where am I?
Oh! He's smurfed the door!
Too bad! I'll look for another friend!
Hello!
What did you say?
Hello! Don't you understand me?
What?
?
Nothing!
So, it's true then.
I'm just a reflection.
A backwards Smurf!
I'm so unlucky! <Sniff>
OH!
16

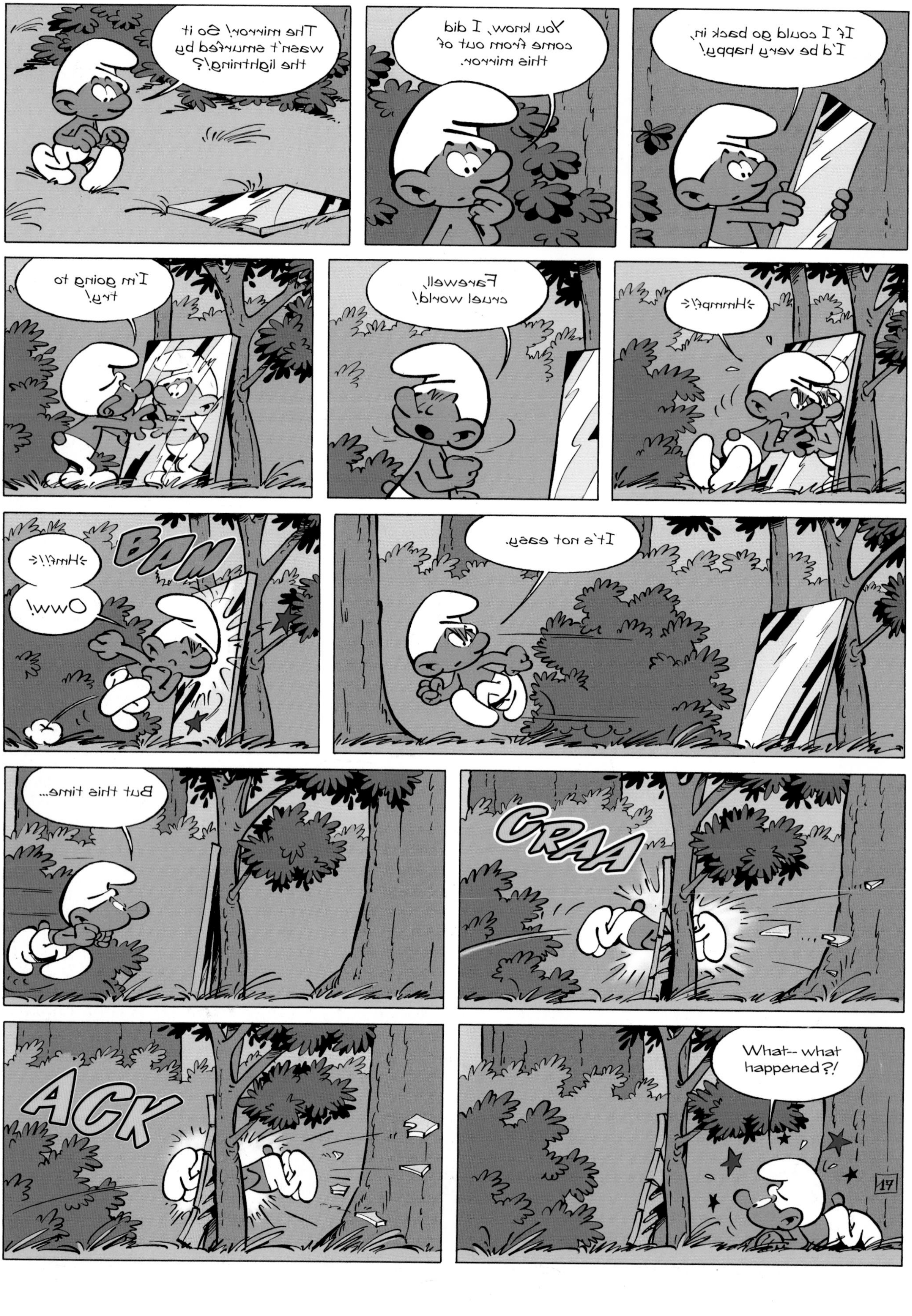

The mirror! So it wasn't smurfed by the lightning!?
You know, I did come from out of this mirror.
If I could go back in, I'd be very happy!
I'm going to try!
Farewell, cruel world!
>Hmmpf!<
BAM
>Hmf!!<
Oww!
It's not easy.
But this time...
CRAA
ACK
What-- what happened?!
17

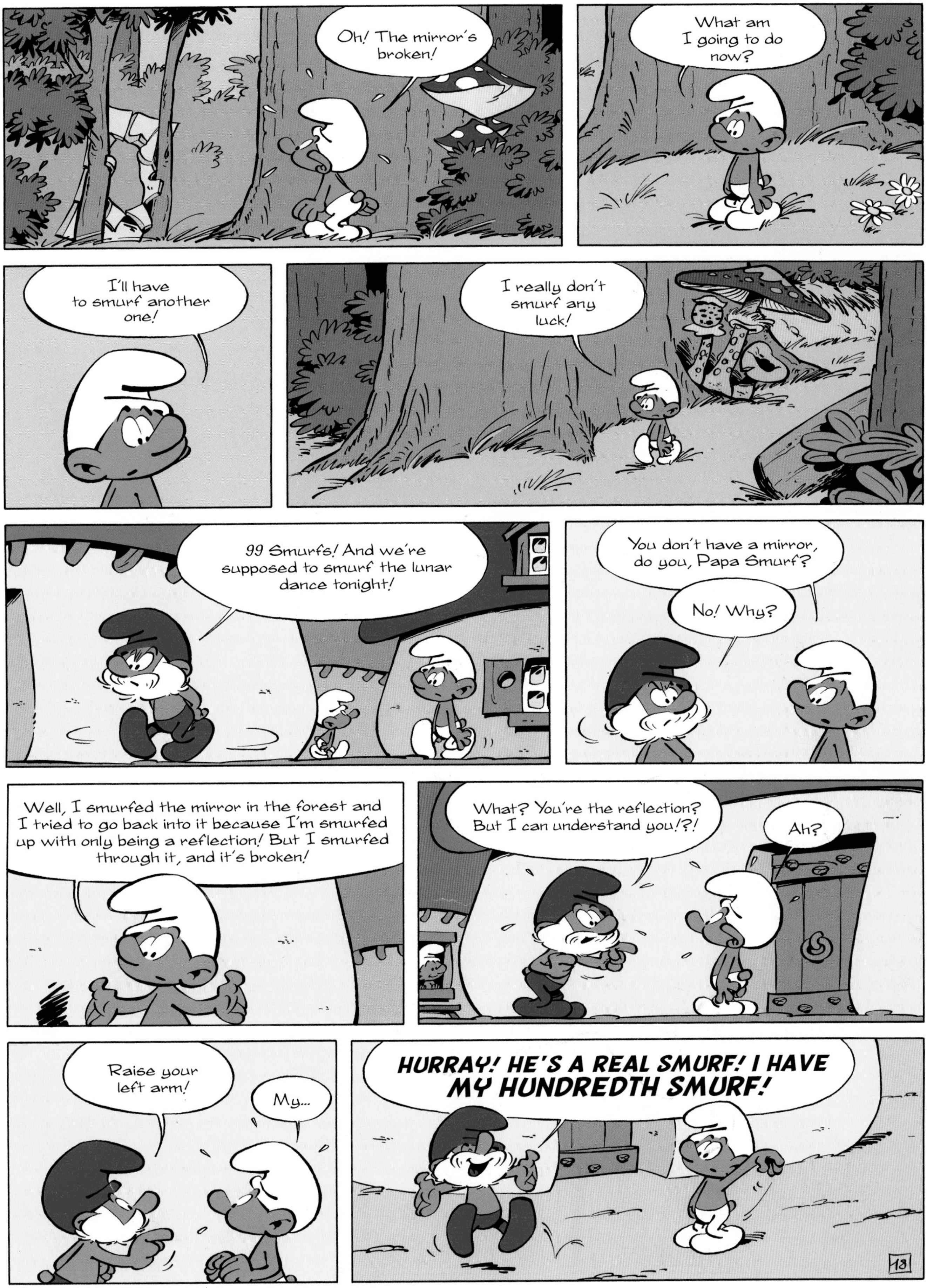
Oh! The mirror's broken!
What am I going to do now?
I'll have to smurf another one!
I really don't smurf any luck!
99 Smurfs! And we're supposed to smurf the lunar dance tonight!
You don't have a mirror, do you, Papa Smurf?
No! Why?
Well, I smurfed the mirror in the forest and I tried to go back into it because I'm smurfed up with only being a reflection! But I smurfed through it, and it's broken!
What? You're the reflection? But I can understand you!?!
Ah?
Raise your left arm!
My...
HURRAY! HE'S A REAL SMURF! I HAVE MY HUNDREDTH SMURF!
13

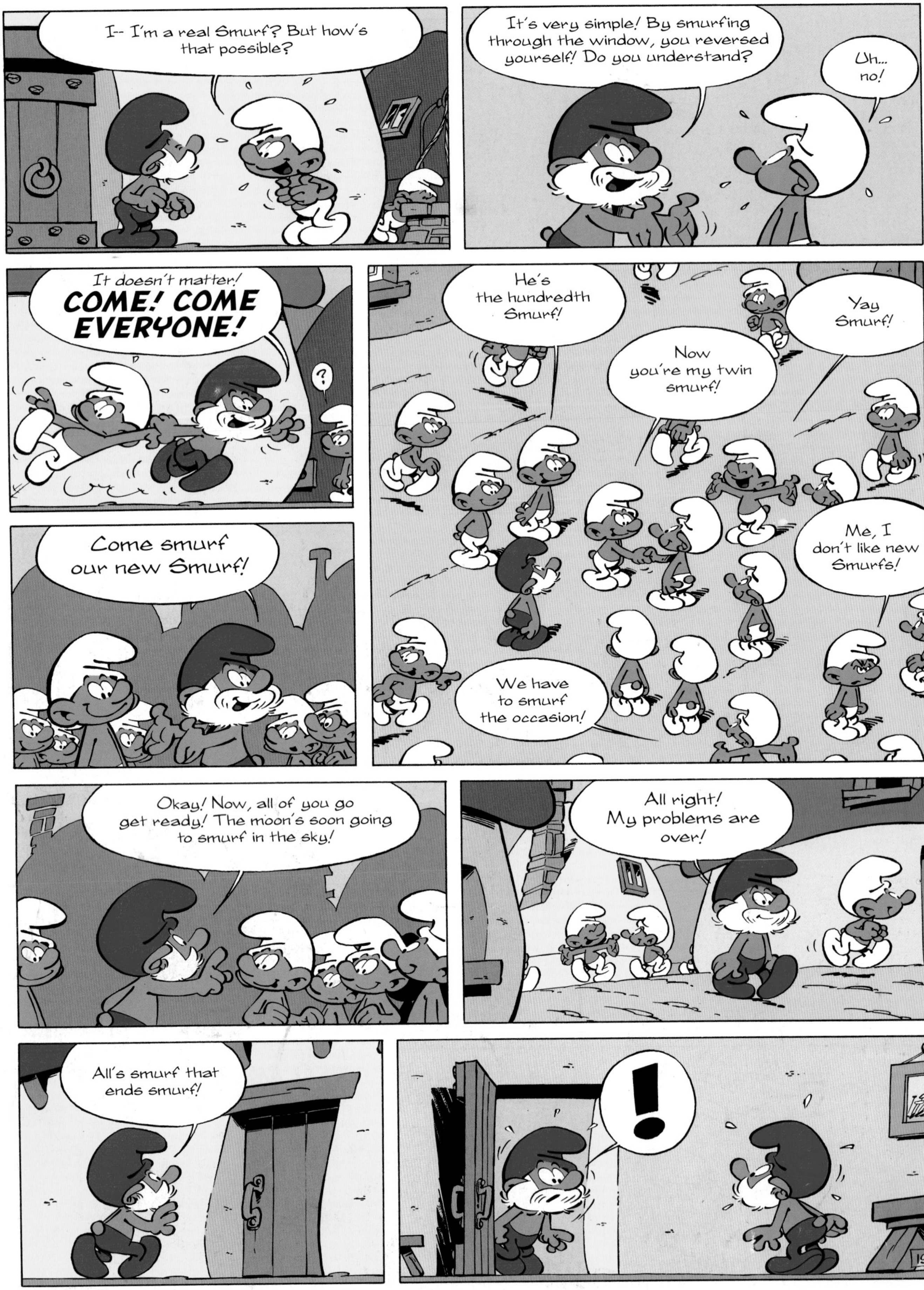

I-- I'm a real Smurf? But how's that possible?
It's very simple! By smurfing through the window, you reversed yourself! Do you understand?
Uh... no!
It doesn't matter! COME! COME EVERYONE!
?
Come smurf our new Smurf!
He's the hundredth Smurf!
Now you're my twin smurf!
Yay Smurf!
Me, I don't like new Smurfs!
We have to smurf the occasion!
Okay! Now, all of you go get ready! The moon's soon going to smurf in the sky!
All right! My problems are over!
All's smurf that ends smurf!
!
19

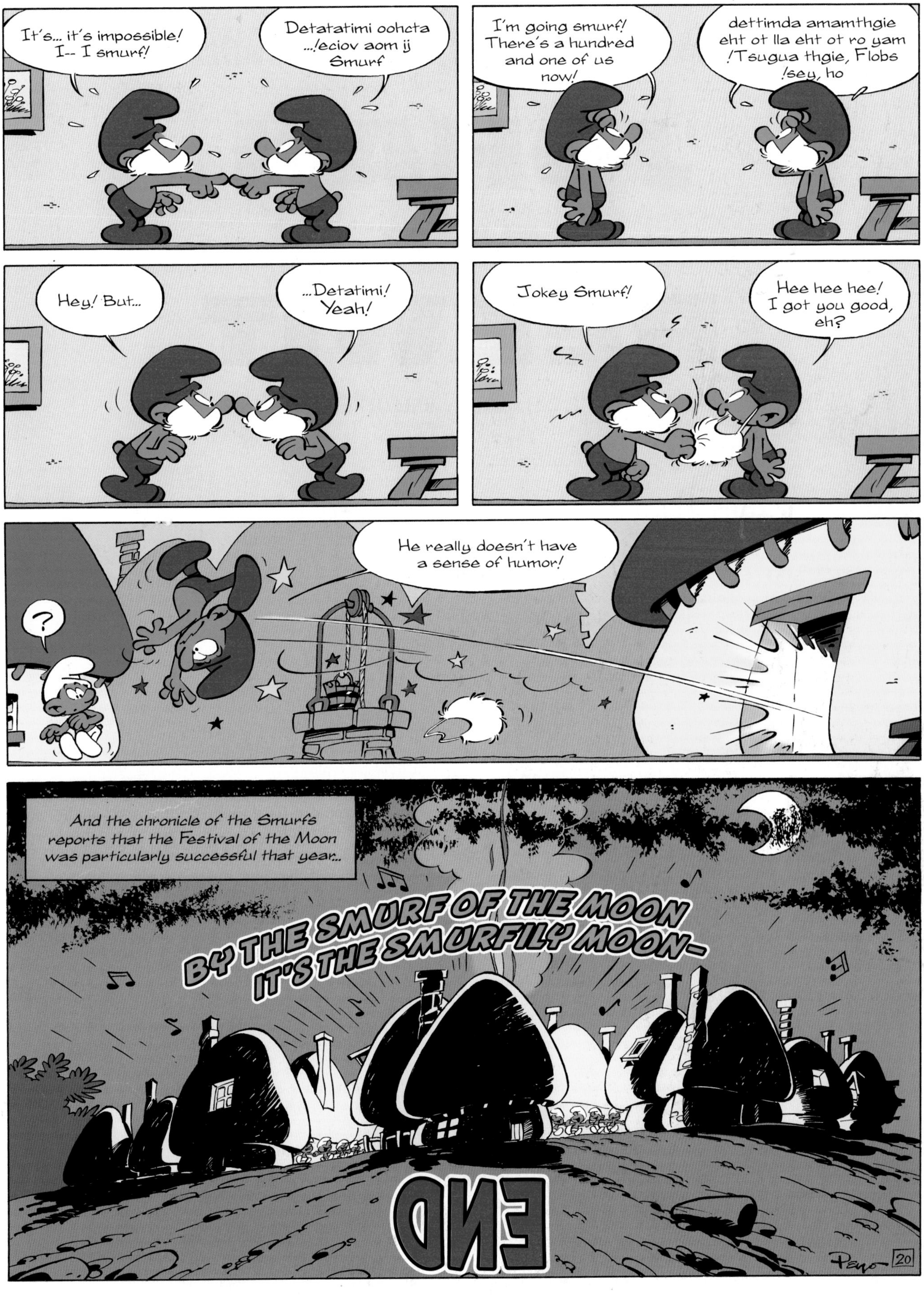

It's... it's impossible! I-- I smurf!
Detatatimi oohcta ...!eciov aom ij Smurf
I'm going smurf! There's a hundred and one of us now!
dettimda amamthgie eht ot lla eht ot ro yam !Tsugua thgie, Flobs !sey, ho
Hey! But...
...Detatimi! Yeah!
Jokey Smurf!
Hee hee hee! I got you good, eh?
?
He really doesn't have a sense of humor!
And the chronicle of the Smurfs reports that the Festival of the Moon was particularly successful that year...
BY THE SMURF OF THE MOON IT'S THE SMURFILY MOON-
END
20

INTRODUCTION TO "THE WAR OF THE 7 SPRINGS"

JOHAN AND PEEWIT

BY MATT. MURRAY, SMURFOLOGIST

Nineteen-fifty-nine was a rather Smurfy year, indeed.

The Smurfs were given their first solo story with the "Les Schtroumpfs noirs" mini-comic, which, that same year, was adapted into an animated short film for Belgian television; the first Smurfs figurines were fabricated and sold to fans of *Le Journal de Spirou*, the anthology magazine the Smurfs comics appeared in; but before all that they were trotted out again in the pages of *Johan et Pirlouit*, for a brief cameo in that duo's tenth full-length adventure "Les sept fontaines."

Collected and published in 1961 as the album "*La guerre des sept fontaines,*" the story is considered to be one of Peyo's better comics, although few non-French speakers have actually had the opportunity to experience it in its original form.

Although Johan and Peewit (the English translation of *Pirlouit*) were Peyo's favorite characters, their popularity never reached that of the Smurfs, or even that of *Benoit Brisefer* (also known as Steven Strong, and currently being published by Papercutz as BENNY BREAKIRON), and therefore only two of their comic strip adventures have ever been translated into English: "*La flute a six trous*" (aka "The Smurfs and the Magic Flute") and "*La fleche noir*" (which was published in 1995 as "The Black Arrow.")

A number of their stories, however, were adapted into animated cartoons during the second season of Hanna-Barbera's ground-breaking Saturday morning cartoon series based on the Smurfs' adventures. It's from there that seasoned Smurfologists may recognize parts of "*La guerre des sept fontaines*" as they were adapted into "The Haunted Castle," which debuted October 23rd, 1982. I say "parts" as there were numerous omissions and two notable changes made in translating the story to the small screen for American audiences.

Warning: there are *SPOILERS* ahead, so you may want to go read the comic now, and then come back here when you're done. It's all right... This introduction isn't going anywhere... I promise...

...la la la-la la la... la la-la la la...

Okay. The first major change was the inclusion of the Smurfs throughout the story. Rather than just serve as a three-page plot device that moves along the magical elements, the Smurfs (a team consisting of Papa, Brainy, and Smurfette) accompany Johan and Peewit on their journey and even help defeat some of the armies vying for control of the castle. This is somewhat understandable, as it was their show, after all, and they were the reason why millions of children (and even adults) tuned in on Saturday mornings. (Although, it's interesting to note that in European markets the Johan and Peewit episodes of *The Smurfs* were marketed as their own animated series.)

The second major adjustment was the exclusion of why there's a drought that drives all of the residents off of Lord Aldebert De Baufort's land. Classified as a serious illness by the American Medical Association in 1956, alcoholism was perceived differently in the States circa 1982 than it was in Belgium during the creation of the strip, and therefore the cause of the drought and ensuing comic scenes of drunken buffoonery amongst human and bovines alike (did you not read the comic when I told you to? I warned you about spoilers.) had to be dropped, even though serious consequences for Aldelbert's choices and the people's (and cow's) actions are explicit and contribute to the overall moral of Peyo's story. Sometimes, though, in the face of television standards and practices of children's television, it's easier to just avoid the issue altogether, than explain or even debate ethical complexities of a rather adult problem.

Over five decades later, the only adjustment found here is a translation from one language to another, French to English, and while alcoholism remains a serious disease that affects millions of people and a specific subset of cows (it's said that Kobe cows are fed up to 700 ml of beer daily)* the ability to appreciate the history of how the illness and those

it affects has been depicted has allowed Papercutz to take a step forward and publish "The War of Seven Springs."

We hope you enjoy it, or if you took my advice and read ahead before, we encourage you to read it again. Just remember to enjoy it in moderation. ●

* CHAVEZ, AMY. "KOBE BEEF'S SECRET: NICE ALCOHOLIC COWS." THE JAPAN TIMES. THE JAPAN TIMES LTD., 20 MAY 2002. WEB. 29 JUL 2013. <HTTP://WWW.JAPANTIMES.CO.JP/COMMUNITY/2002/05/20/OUR-LIVES/KOBE-BEEFS-SECRET-NICE-ALCOHOLIC-COWS/

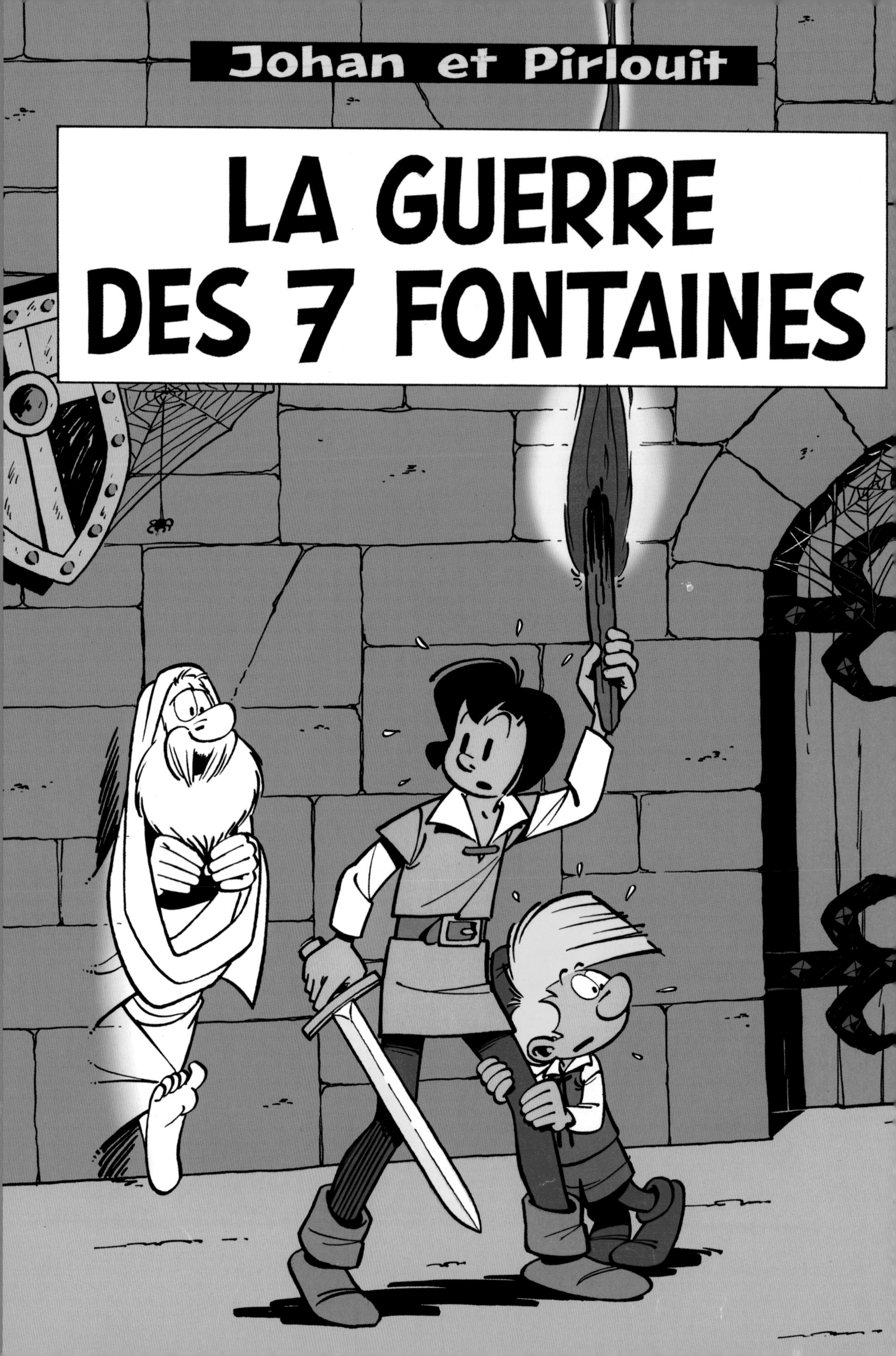
Johan et Pirlouit
LA GUERRE DES 7 FONTAINES

THE WAR OF THE 7 SPRINGS

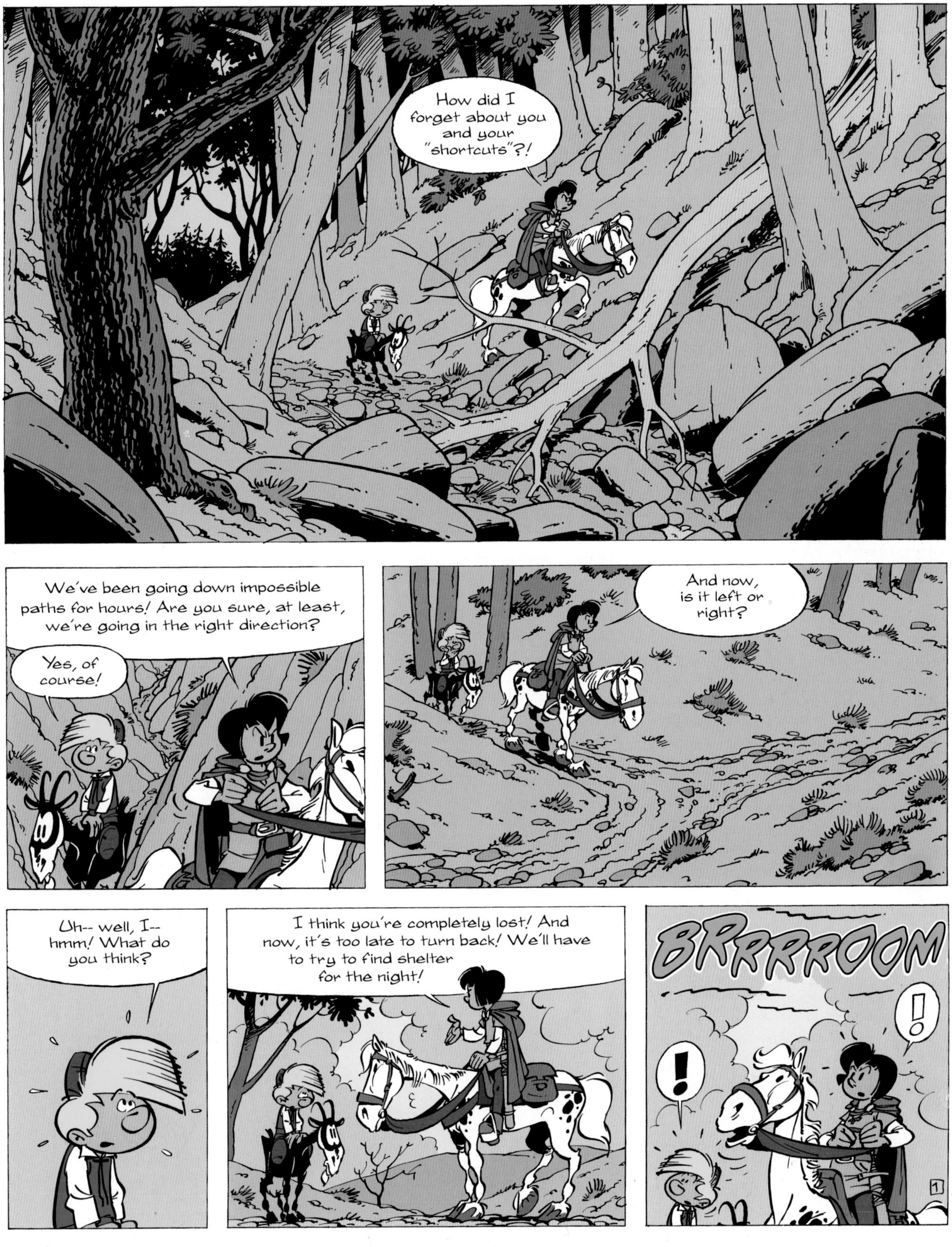
How did I forget about you and your "shortcuts"?!
We've been going down impossible paths for hours! Are you sure, at least, we're going in the right direction?
Yes, of course!
And now, is it left or right?
Uh-- well, I-- hmm! What do you think?
I think you're completely lost! And now, it's too late to turn back! We'll have to try to find shelter for the night!
BRRRROOM
!
!
1

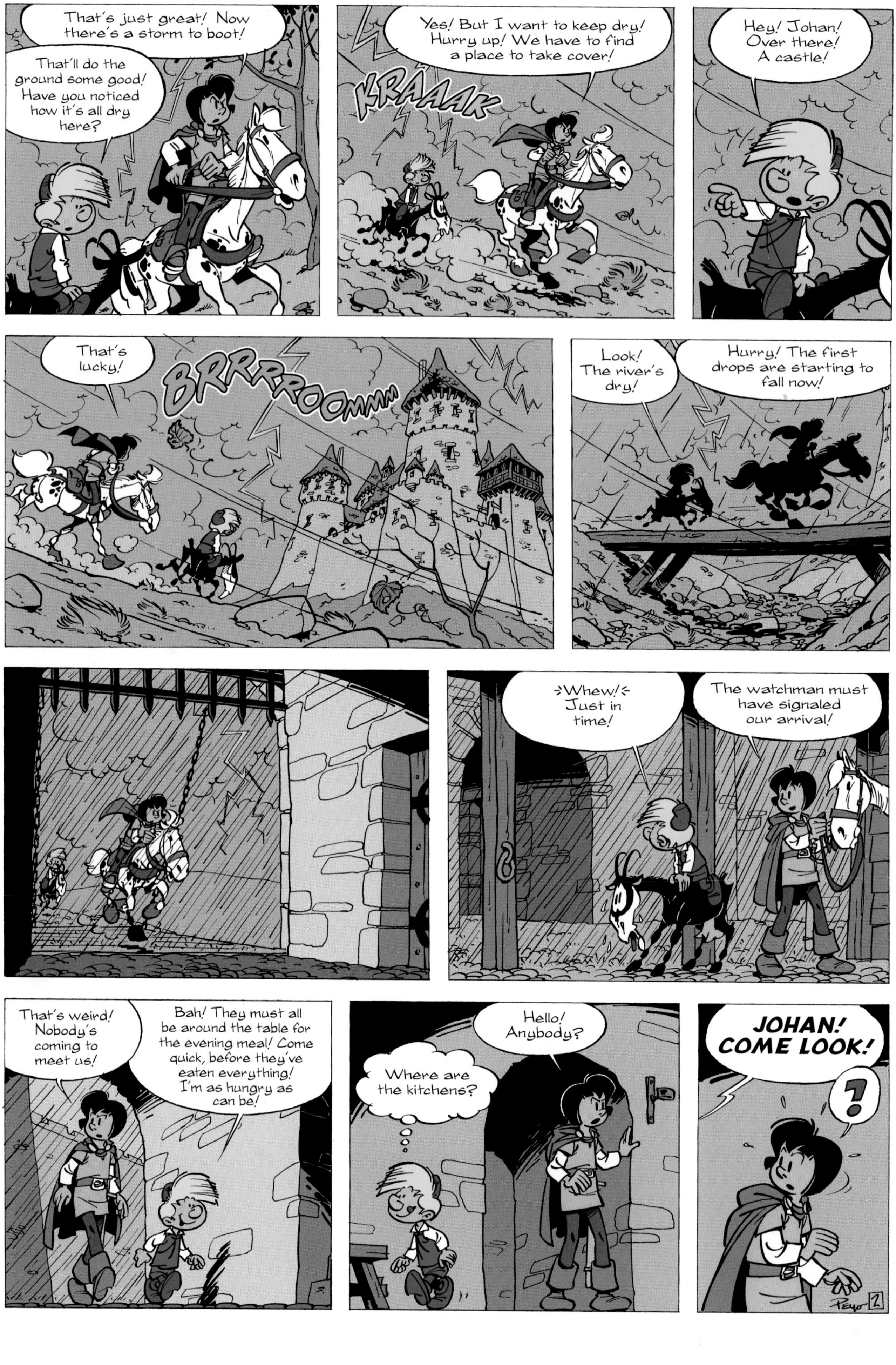

That's just great! Now there's a storm to boot!
That'll do the ground some good! Have you noticed how it's all dry here?
Yes! But I want to keep dry! Hurry up! We have to find a place to take cover!
KRAAAK
Hey! Johan! Over there! A castle!
That's lucky!
BRRRROOMMM
Look! The river's dry!
Hurry! The first drops are starting to fall now!
Whew! Just in time!
The watchman must have signaled our arrival!
That's weird! Nobody's coming to meet us!
Bah! They must all be around the table for the evening meal! Come quick, before they've eaten everything! I'm as hungry as can be!
Hello! Anybody?
Where are the kitchens?
JOHAN! COME LOOK!
?

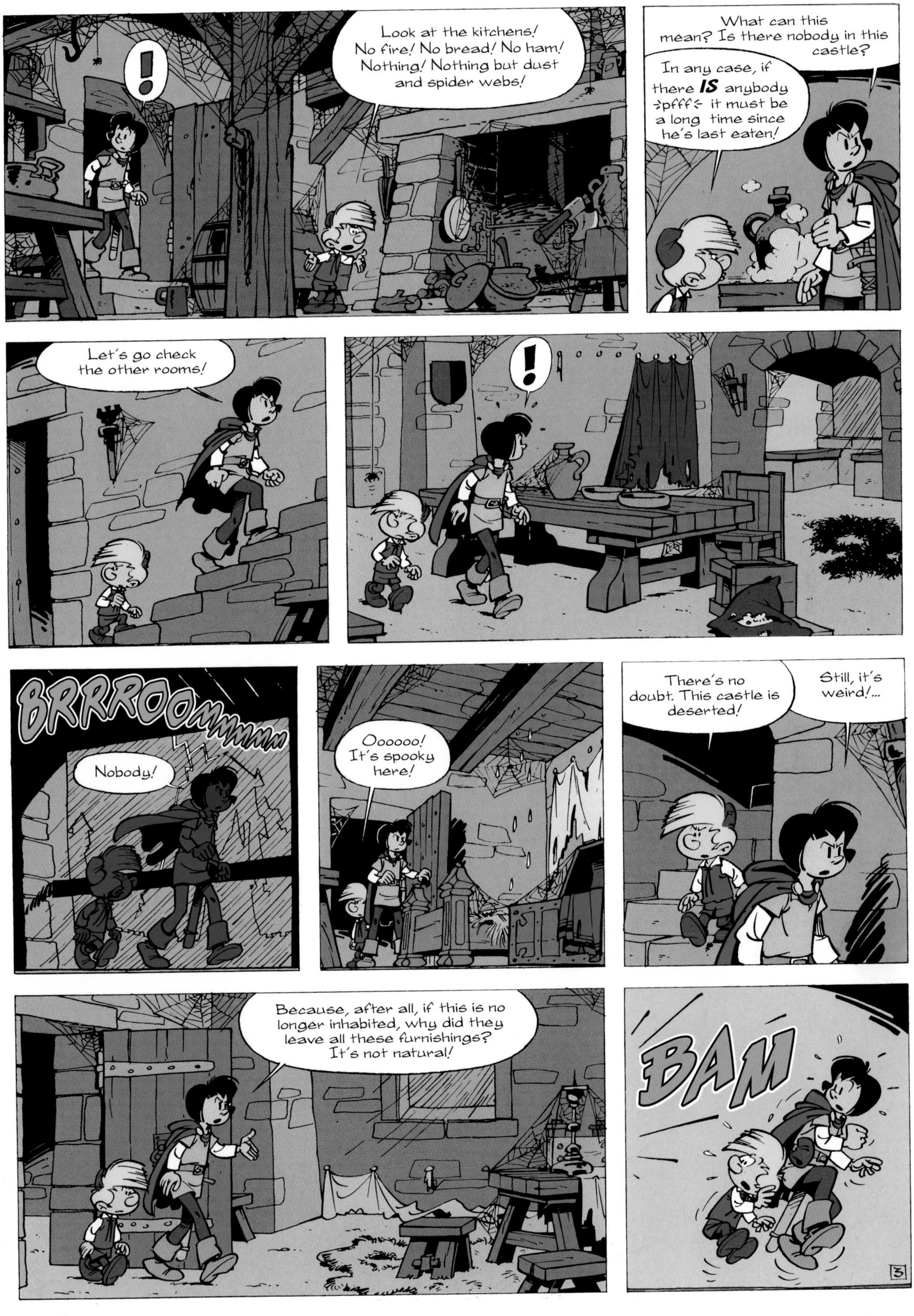
!
Look at the kitchens! No fire! No bread! No ham! Nothing! Nothing but dust and spider webs!
What can this mean? Is there nobody in this castle?
In any case, if there IS anybody >pfff< it must be a long time since he's last eaten!
Let's go check the other rooms!
!
BRRROOMMMMM
Nobody!
Oooooo! It's spooky here!
There's no doubt. This castle is deserted!
Still, it's weird!...
Because, after all, if this is no longer inhabited, why did they leave all these furnishings? It's not natural!
BAM
3

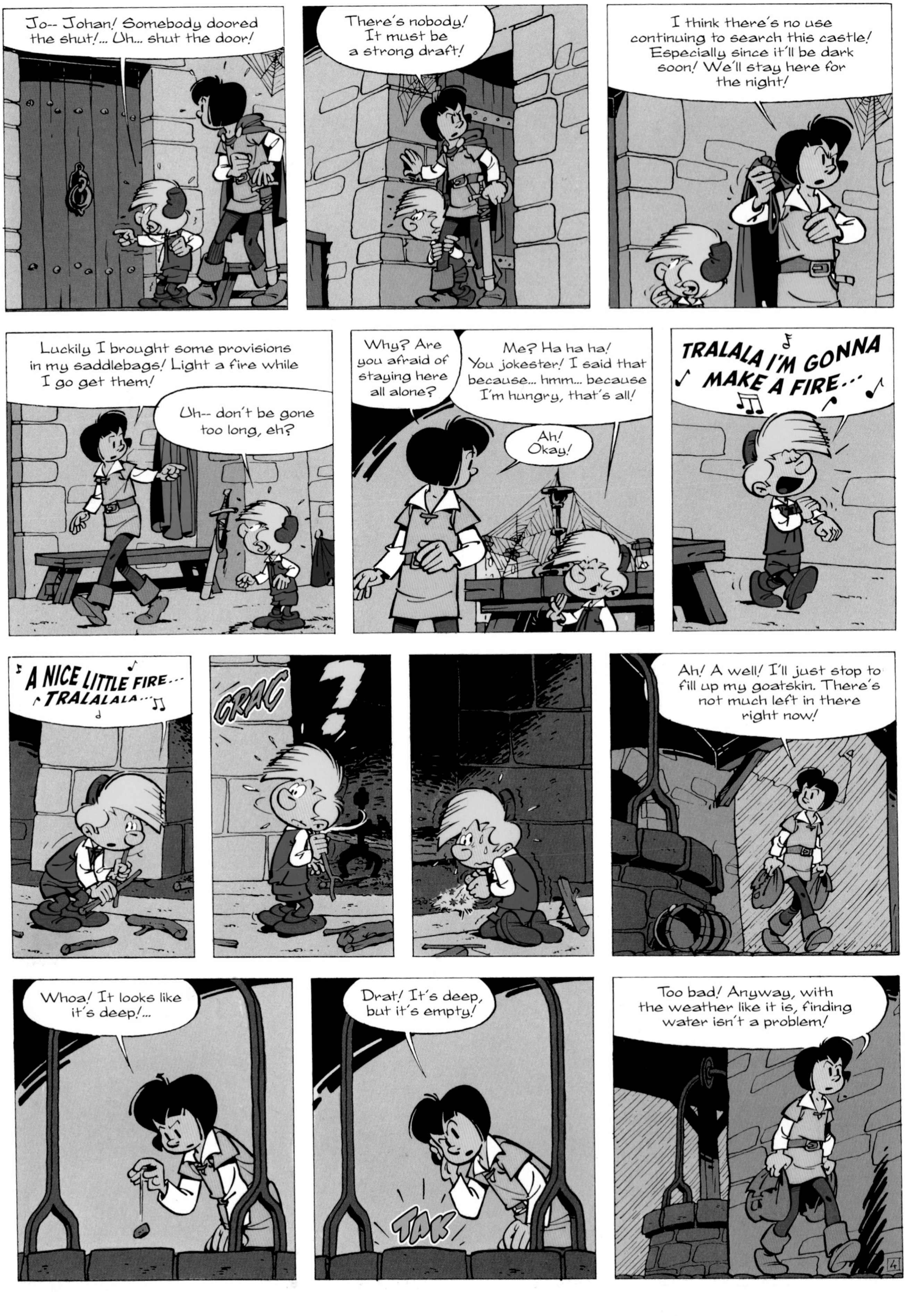
Jo-- Johan! Somebody doored the shut!... Uh... shut the door!
There's nobody! It must be a strong draft!
I think there's no use continuing to search this castle! Especially since it'll be dark soon! We'll stay here for the night!
Luckily I brought some provisions in my saddlebags! Light a fire while I go get them!
Uh-- don't be gone too long, eh?
Why? Are you afraid of staying here all alone?
Me? Ha ha ha! You jokester! I said that because... hmm... because I'm hungry, that's all!
Ah! Okay!
TRALALA I'M GONNA MAKE A FIRE...
A NICE LITTLE FIRE... TRALALALA...
CRAC
?
Ah! A well! I'll just stop to fill up my goatskin. There's not much left in there right now!
Whoa! It looks like it's deep!...
Drat! It's deep, but it's empty!
TAK
Too bad! Anyway, with the weather like it is, finding water isn't a problem!
4

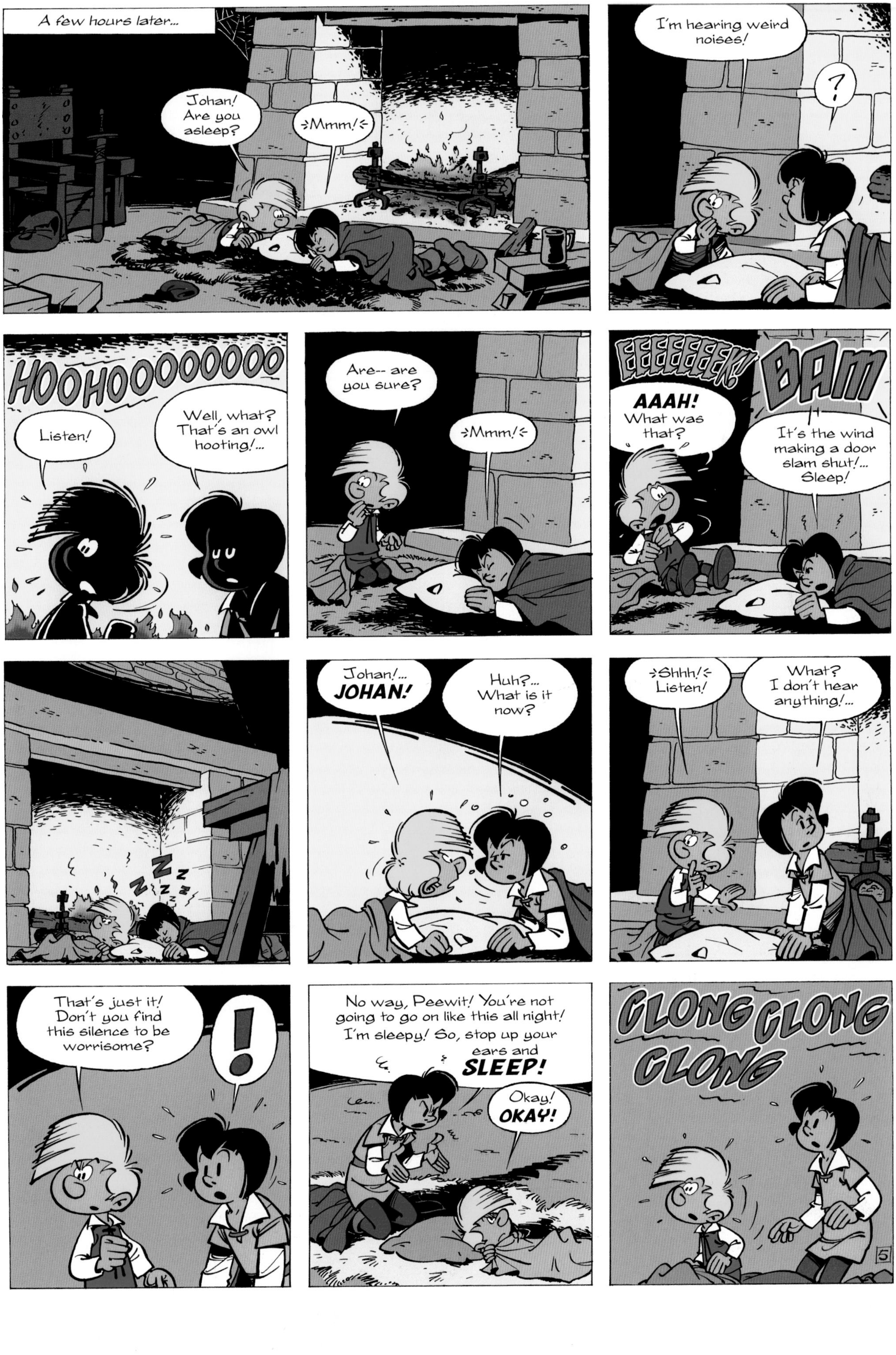
A few hours later...
Johan! Are you asleep?
Mmm!
I'm hearing weird noises!
?
HOOHOOOOOOOO
Listen!
Well, what? That's an owl hooting!...
Are-- are you sure?
Mmm!
EEEEEEEK!
BAM
AAAH! What was that?
It's the wind making a door slam shut!... Sleep!
Z Z Z Z
Johan!... JOHAN!
Huh?... What is it now?
Shhh! Listen!
What? I don't hear anything!...
That's just it! Don't you find this silence to be worrisome?
!
No way, Peewit! You're not going to go on like this all night! I'm sleepy! So, stop up your ears and SLEEP!
Okay! OKAY!
CLONG CLONG CLONG
5

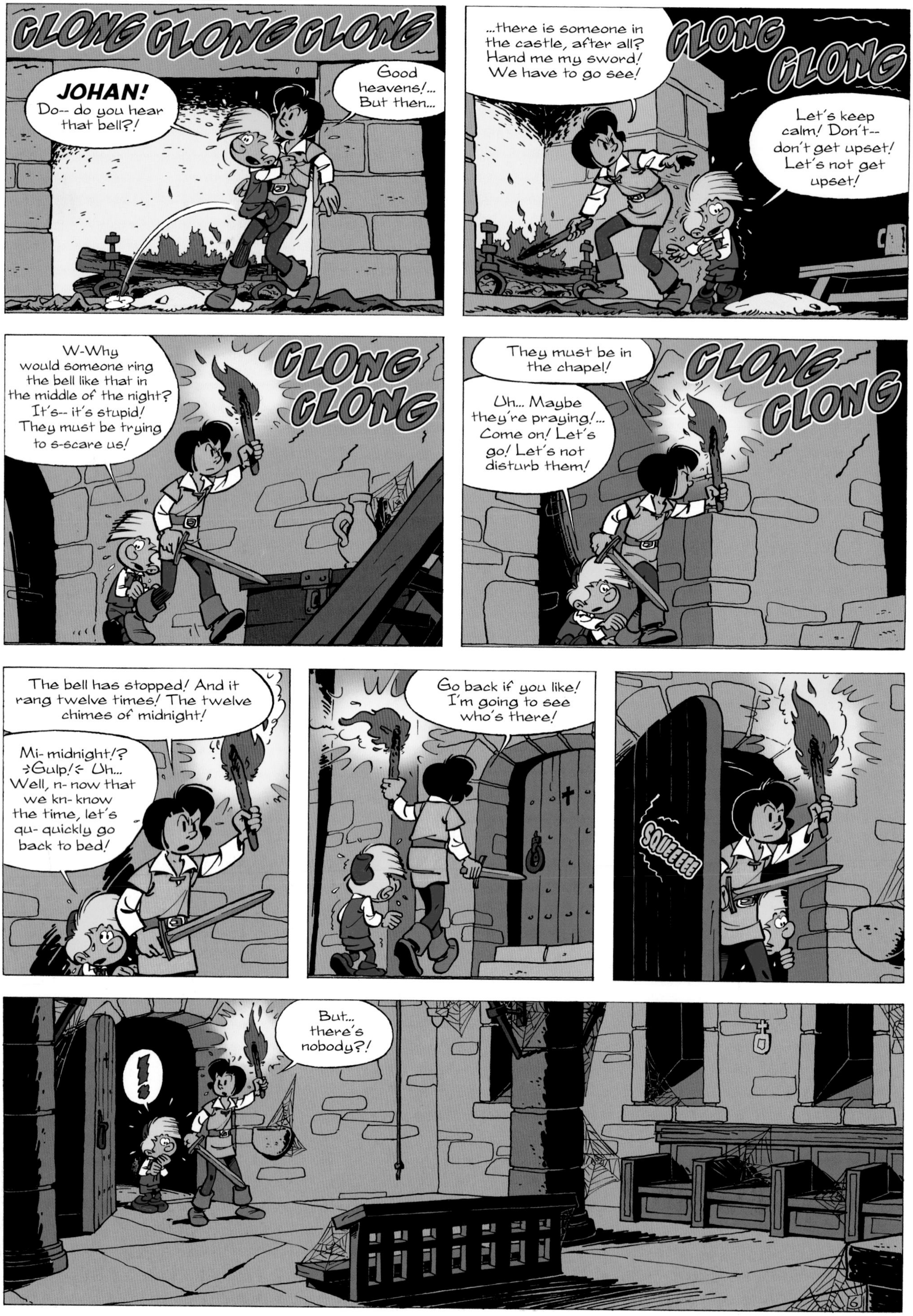
CLONG CLONG CLONG
JOHAN! Do-- do you hear that bell?!
Good heavens!... But then...
...there is someone in the castle, after all? Hand me my sword! We have to go see!
CLONG CLONG
Let's keep calm! Don't-- don't get upset! Let's not get upset!
W-Why would someone ring the bell like that in the middle of the night? It's-- it's stupid! They must be trying to s-scare us!
CLONG CLONG
They must be in the chapel!
Uh... Maybe they're praying!... Come on! Let's go! Let's not disturb them!
CLONG CLONG
The bell has stopped! And it rang twelve times! The twelve chimes of midnight!
Mi- midnight!? →Gulp!← Uh... Well, n- now that we kn- know the time, let's qu- quickly go back to bed!
Go back if you like! I'm going to see who's there!
SQUEEEEE
!!
But... there's nobody?!

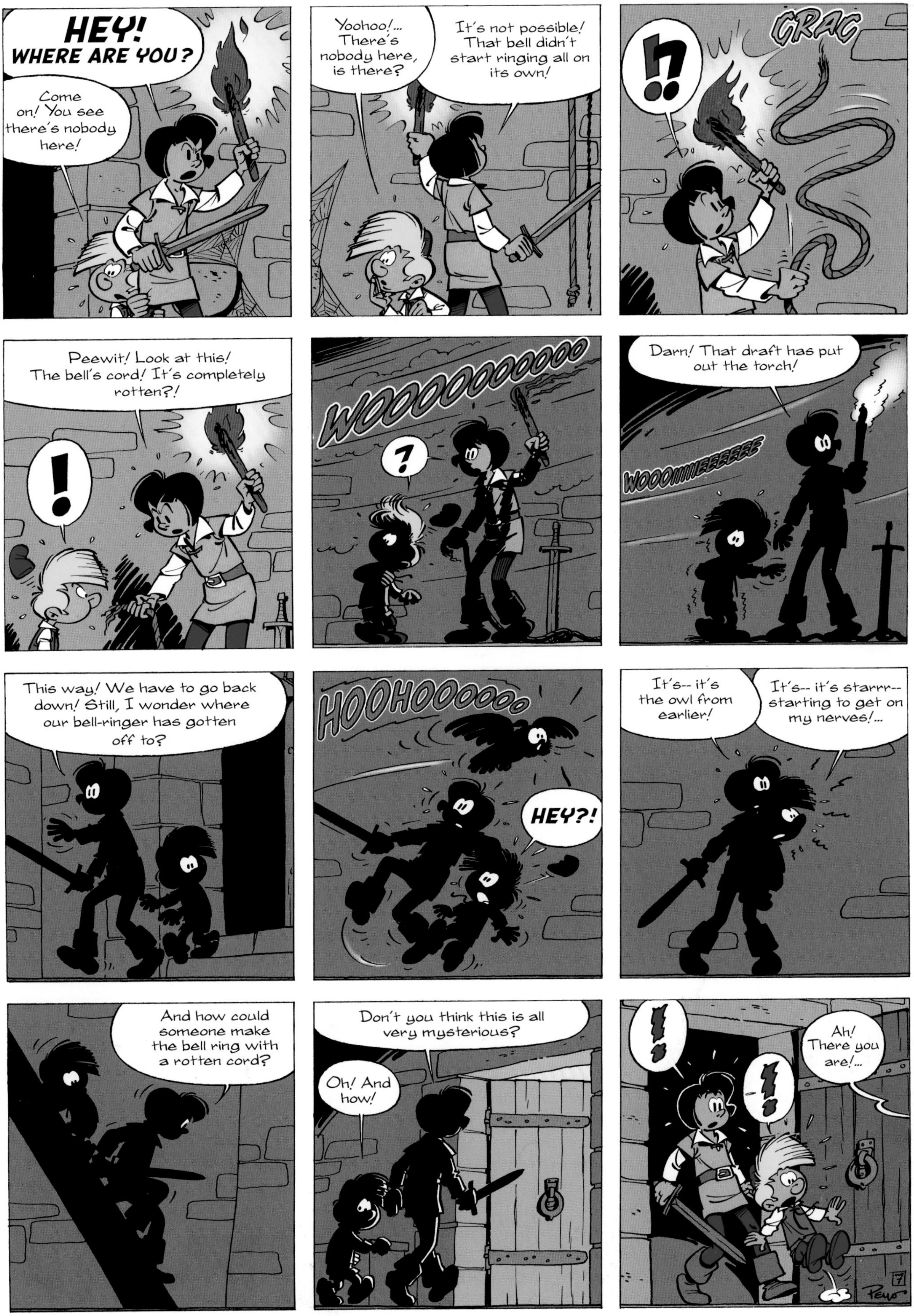
HEY! WHERE ARE YOU?
Come on! You see there's nobody here!
Yoohoo!... There's nobody here, is there?
It's not possible! That bell didn't start ringing all on its own!
!?
CRAC
Peewit! Look at this! The bell's cord! It's completely rotten?!
!
WOOOOOOOOOOOO
?
Darn! That draft has put out the torch!
WOOIIIIIIEEEEEE
This way! We have to go back down! Still, I wonder where our bell-ringer has gotten off to?
HOOHOOOOOO
HEY?!
It's-- it's the owl from earlier!
It's-- it's starrr-- starting to get on my nerves!...
And how could someone make the bell ring with a rotten cord?
Don't you think this is all very mysterious?
Oh! And how!
!
!
Ah! There you are!...
7

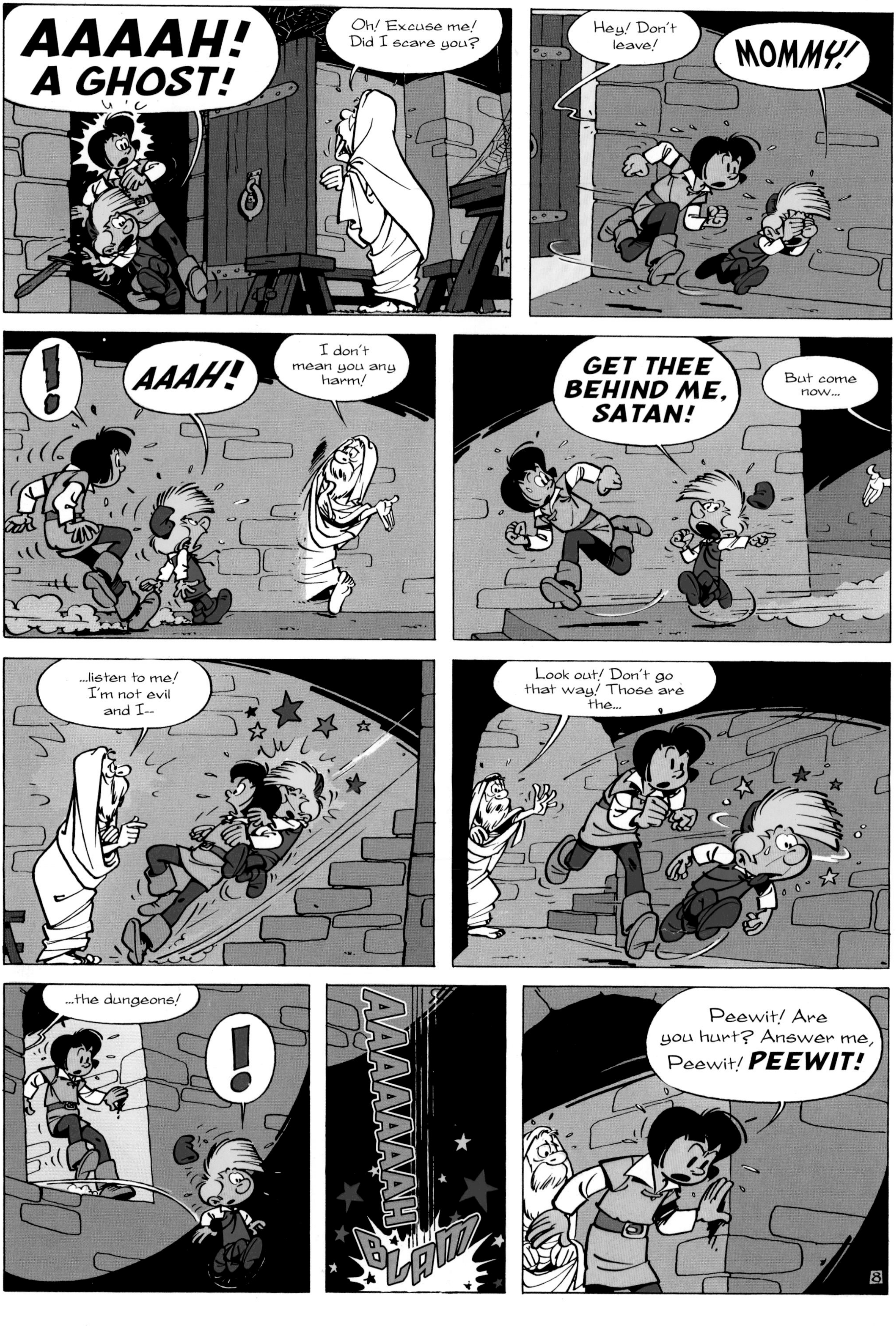
AAAAH! A GHOST!
Oh! Excuse me! Did I scare you?
Hey! Don't leave!
MOMMY!
!
AAAH!
I don't mean you any harm!
GET THEE BEHIND ME, SATAN!
But come now...
...listen to me! I'm not evil and I--
Look out! Don't go that way! Those are the...
...the dungeons!
!
AAAAAAAAH
BLAM
Peewit! Are you hurt? Answer me, Peewit! PEEWIT!
8

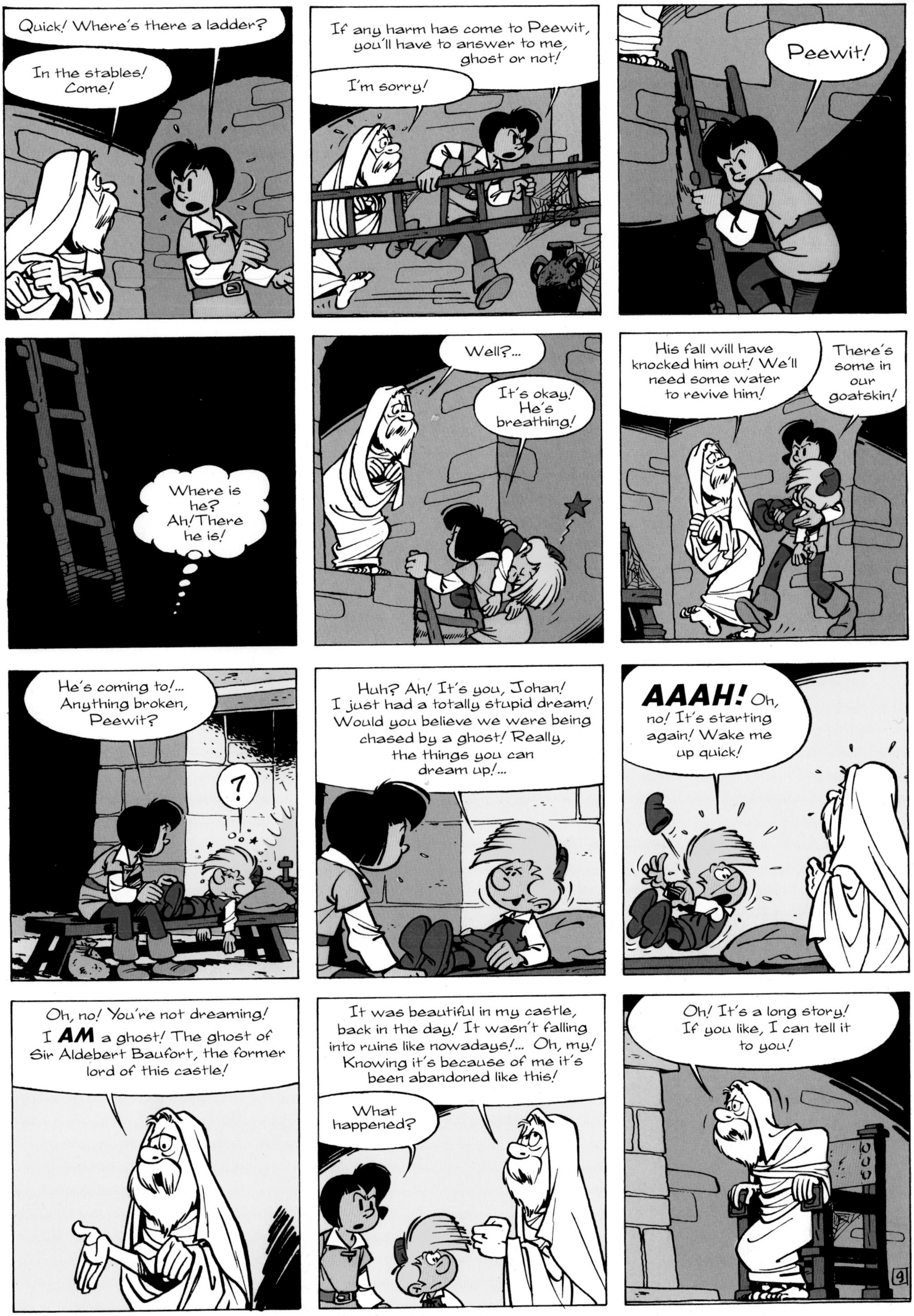
Quick! Where's there a ladder?
In the stables! Come!
If any harm has come to Peewit, you'll have to answer to me, ghost or not!
I'm sorry!
Peewit!
Where is he? Ah! There he is!
Well?...
It's okay! He's breathing!
His fall will have knocked him out! We'll need some water to revive him!
There's some in our goatskin!
He's coming to!... Anything broken, Peewit?
?
Huh? Ah! It's you, Johan! I just had a totally stupid dream! Would you believe we were being chased by a ghost! Really, the things you can dream up!...
AAAH! Oh, no! It's starting again! Wake me up quick!
Oh, no! You're not dreaming! I AM a ghost! The ghost of Sir Aldebert Baufort, the former lord of this castle!
It was beautiful in my castle, back in the day! It wasn't falling into ruins like nowadays!... Oh, my! Knowing it's because of me it's been abandoned like this!
What happened?
Oh! It's a long story! If you like, I can tell it to you!
9

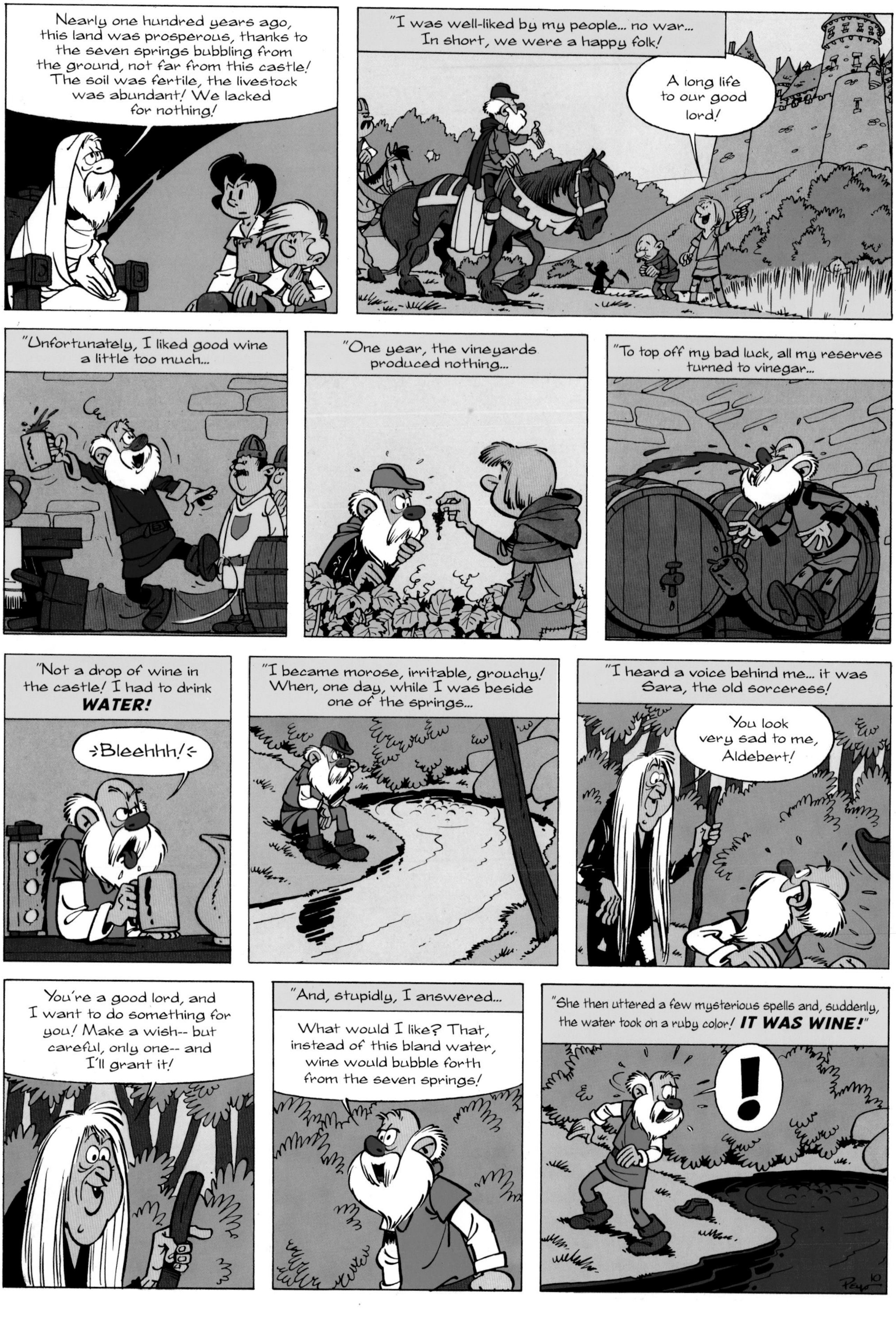
Nearly one hundred years ago, this land was prosperous, thanks to the seven springs bubbling from the ground, not far from this castle! The soil was fertile, the livestock was abundant! We lacked for nothing!
"I was well-liked by my people... no war... In short, we were a happy folk!
A long life to our good lord!
"Unfortunately, I liked good wine a little too much...
"One year, the vineyards produced nothing...
"To top off my bad luck, all my reserves turned to vinegar...
"Not a drop of wine in the castle! I had to drink WATER!
Bleehhh!
"I became morose, irritable, grouchy! When, one day, while I was beside one of the springs...
"I heard a voice behind me... it was Sara, the old sorceress!
You look very sad to me, Aldebert!
You're a good lord, and I want to do something for you! Make a wish-- but careful, only one-- and I'll grant it!
"And, stupidly, I answered...
What would I like? That, instead of this bland water, wine would bubble forth from the seven springs!
"She then uttered a few mysterious spells and, suddenly, the water took on a ruby color! IT WAS WINE!"
!

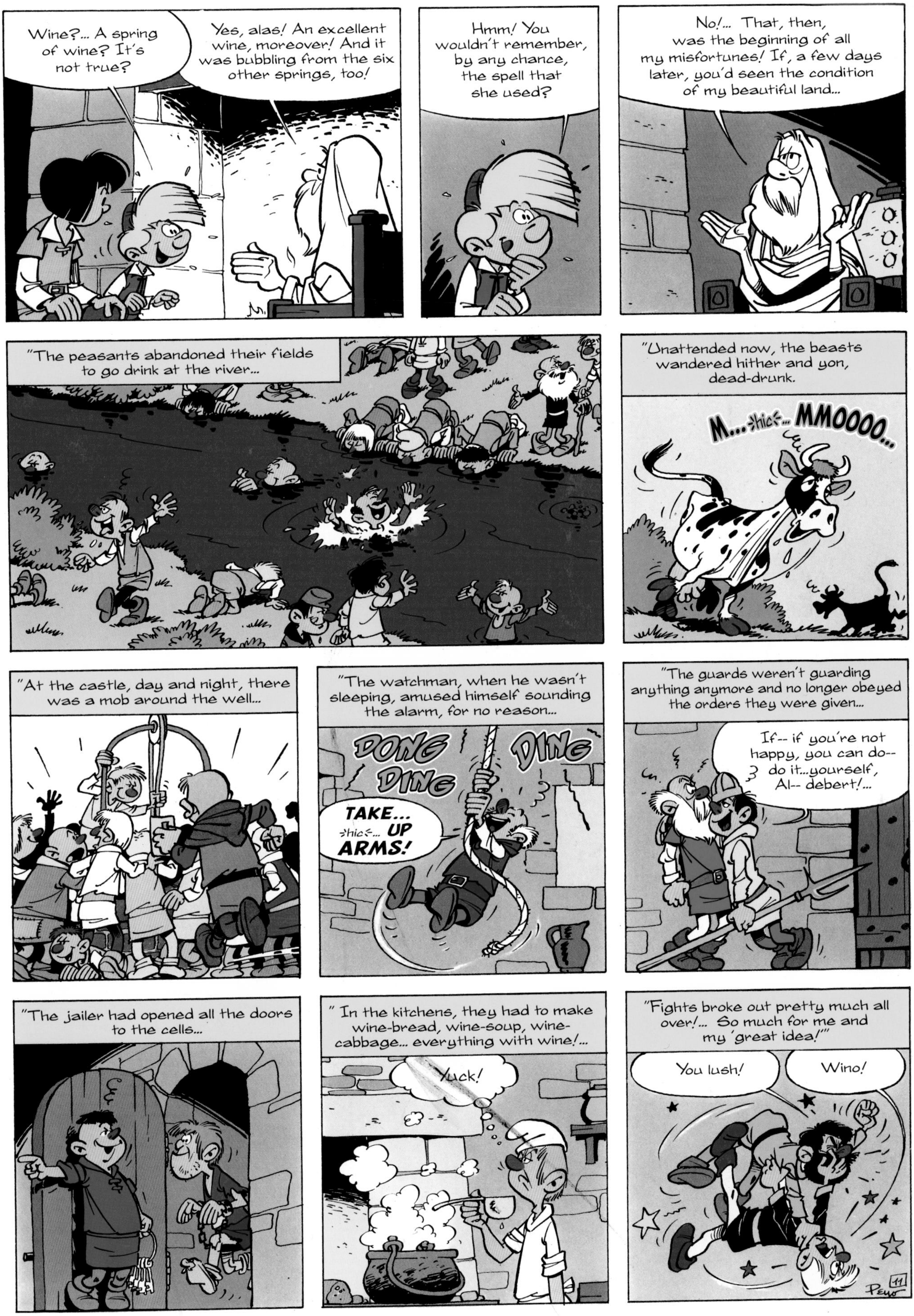
Wine?... A spring of wine? It's not true?
Yes, alas! An excellent wine, moreover! And it was bubbling from the six other springs, too!
Hmm! You wouldn't remember, by any chance, the spell that she used?
No!... That, then, was the beginning of all my misfortunes! If, a few days later, you'd seen the condition of my beautiful land...
"The peasants abandoned their fields to go drink at the river...
"Unattended now, the beasts wandered hither and yon, dead-drunk.
M... hic... MMOOOO...
"At the castle, day and night, there was a mob around the well...
"The watchman, when he wasn't sleeping, amused himself sounding the alarm, for no reason...
DONG DING DING
TAKE... hic... UP ARMS!
"The guards weren't guarding anything anymore and no longer obeyed the orders they were given...
If-- if you're not happy, you can do-- do it...yourself, Al-- debert!...
"The jailer had opened all the doors to the cells...
" In the kitchens, they had to make wine-bread, wine-soup, wine-cabbage... everything with wine!...
Yuck!
"Fights broke out pretty much all over!... So much for me and my 'great idea!'"
You lush!
Wino!
11

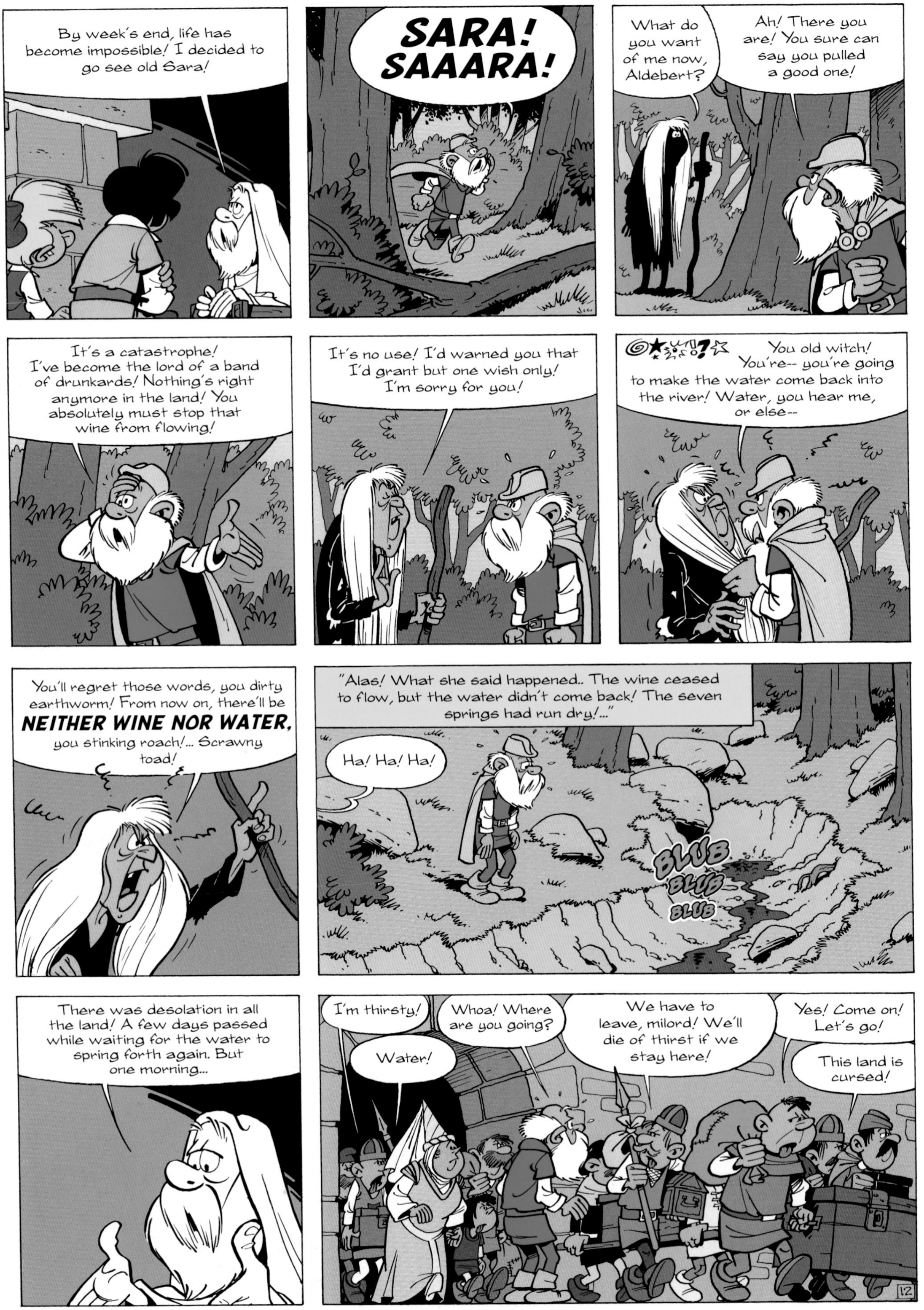

By week's end, life has become impossible! I decided to go see old Sara!
SARA! SAAARA!
What do you want of me now, Aldebert?
Ah! There you are! You sure can say you pulled a good one!
It's a catastrophe! I've become the lord of a band of drunkards! Nothing's right anymore in the land! You absolutely must stop that wine from flowing!
It's no use! I'd warned you that I'd grant but one wish only! I'm sorry for you!
You old witch! You're-- you're going to make the water come back into the river! Water, you hear me, or else--
You'll regret those words, you dirty earthworm! From now on, there'll be NEITHER WINE NOR WATER, you stinking roach!... Scrawny toad!
"Alas! What she said happened.. The wine ceased to flow, but the water didn't come back! The seven springs had run dry!..."
Ha! Ha! Ha!
BLUB
BLUB
BLUB
There was desolation in all the land! A few days passed while waiting for the water to spring forth again. But one morning...
I'm thirsty!
Water!
Whoa! Where are you going?
We have to leave, milord! We'll die of thirst if we stay here!
Yes! Come on! Let's go!
This land is cursed!
12

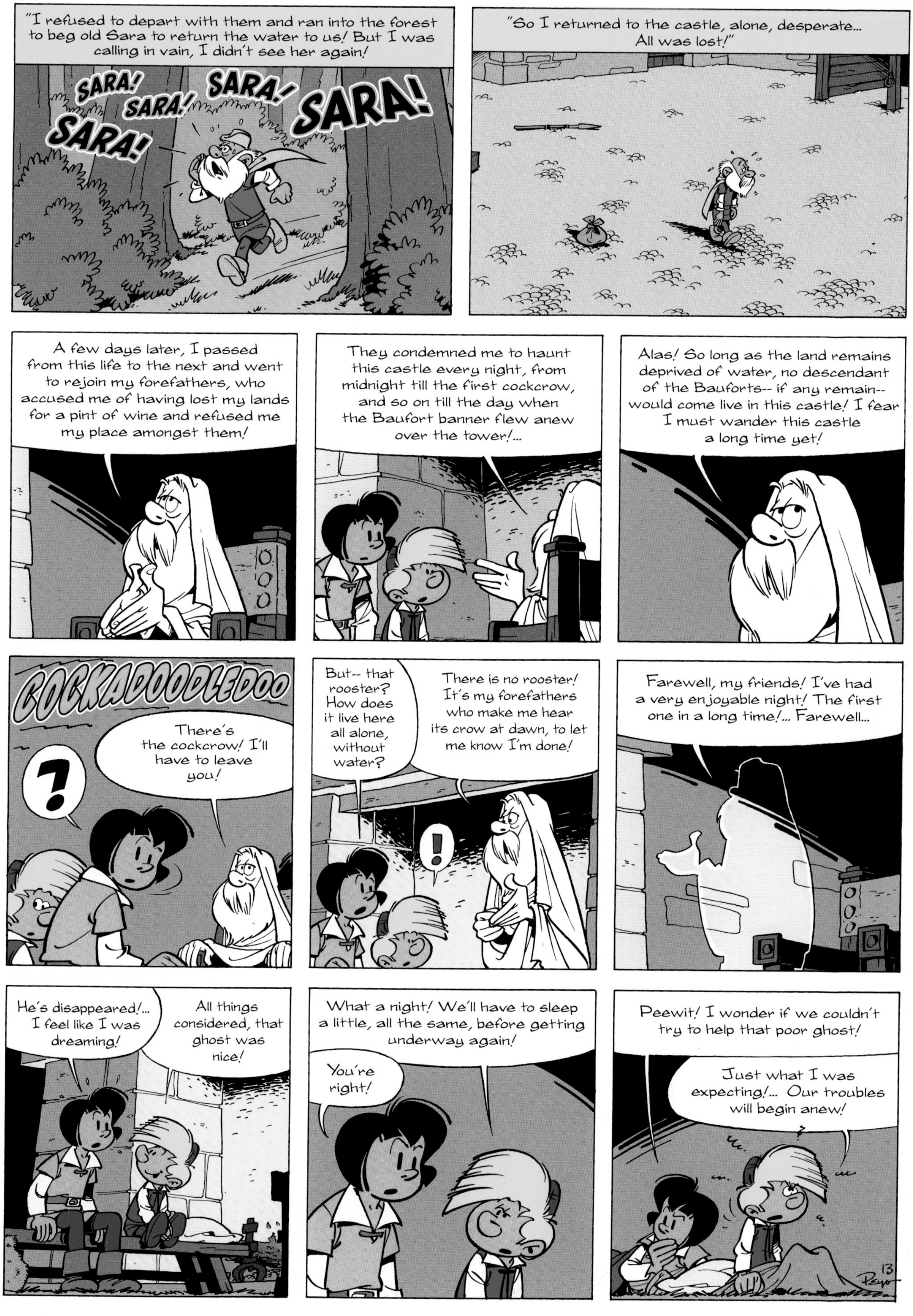
"I refused to depart with them and ran into the forest to beg old Sara to return the water to us! But I was calling in vain, I didn't see her again!
SARA! SARA! SARA! SARA! SARA!
"So I returned to the castle, alone, desperate... All was lost!"
A few days later, I passed from this life to the next and went to rejoin my forefathers, who accused me of having lost my lands for a pint of wine and refused me my place amongst them!
They condemned me to haunt this castle every night, from midnight till the first cockcrow, and so on till the day when the Baufort banner flew anew over the tower!...
Alas! So long as the land remains deprived of water, no descendant of the Bauforts-- if any remain-- would come live in this castle! I fear I must wander this castle a long time yet!
COCKADOODLEDOO
There's the cockcrow! I'll have to leave you!
?
But-- that rooster? How does it live here all alone, without water?
There is no rooster! It's my forefathers who make me hear its crow at dawn, to let me know I'm done!
!
Farewell, my friends! I've had a very enjoyable night! The first one in a long time!... Farewell...
He's disappeared!... I feel like I was dreaming!
All things considered, that ghost was nice!
What a night! We'll have to sleep a little, all the same, before getting underway again!
You're right!
Peewit! I wonder if we couldn't try to help that poor ghost!
Just what I was expecting!... Our troubles will begin anew!
13
Peyo

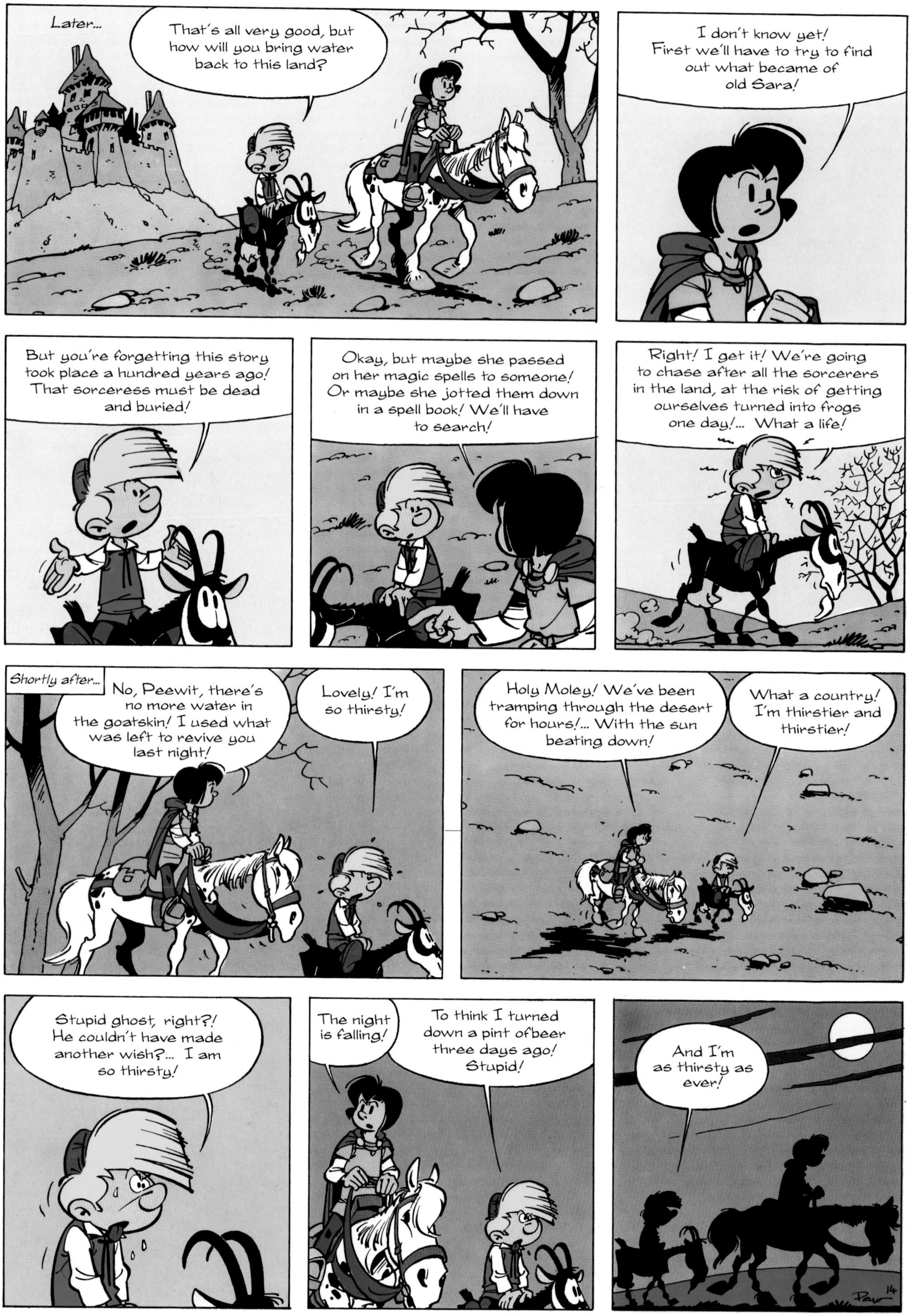
Later...
That's all very good, but how will you bring water back to this land?
I don't know yet! First we'll have to try to find out what became of old Sara!
But you're forgetting this story took place a hundred years ago! That sorceress must be dead and buried!
Okay, but maybe she passed on her magic spells to someone! Or maybe she jotted them down in a spell book! We'll have to search!
Right! I get it! We're going to chase after all the sorcerers in the land, at the risk of getting ourselves turned into frogs one day!... What a life!
Shortly after...
No, Peewit, there's no more water in the goatskin! I used what was left to revive you last night!
Lovely! I'm so thirsty!
Holy Moley! We've been tramping through the desert for hours!... With the sun beating down!
What a country! I'm thirstier and thirstier!
Stupid ghost, right?! He couldn't have made another wish?... I am so thirsty!
The night is falling!
To think I turned down a pint of beer three days ago! Stupid!
And I'm as thirsty as ever!
Peyo 14

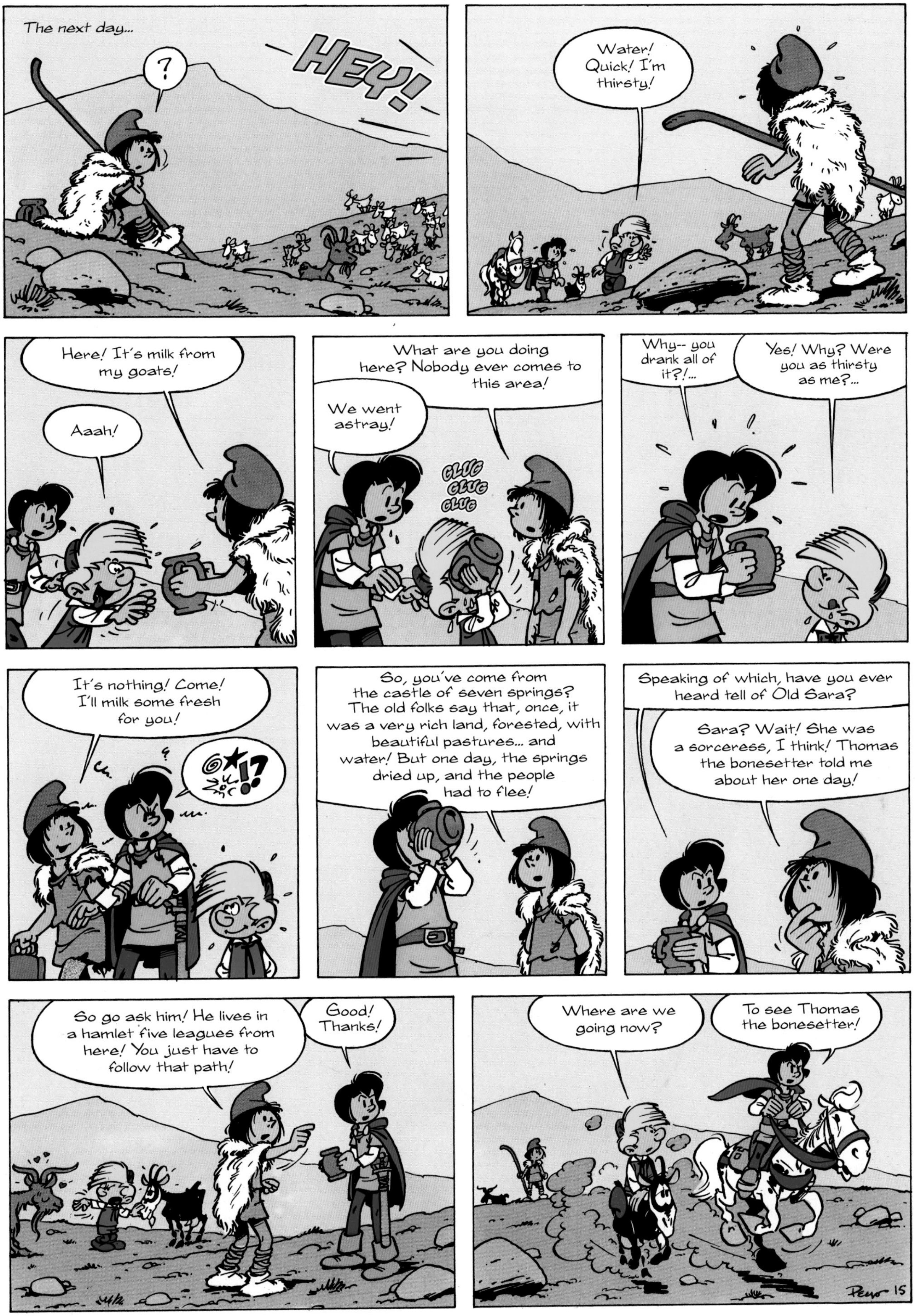

The next day...
?
HEY!
Water! Quick! I'm thirsty!
Here! It's milk from my goats!
Aaah!
What are you doing here? Nobody ever comes to this area!
We went astray!
GLUG GLUG GLUG
Why-- you drank all of it?!...
Yes! Why? Were you as thirsty as me?...
It's nothing! Come! I'll milk some fresh for you!
So, you've come from the castle of seven springs? The old folks say that, once, it was a very rich land, forested, with beautiful pastures... and water! But one day, the springs dried up, and the people had to flee!
Speaking of which, have you ever heard tell of Old Sara?
Sara? Wait! She was a sorceress, I think! Thomas the bonesetter told me about her one day!
So go ask him! He lives in a hamlet five leagues from here! You just have to follow that path!
Good! Thanks!
Where are we going now?
To see Thomas the bonesetter!
Peyo 15

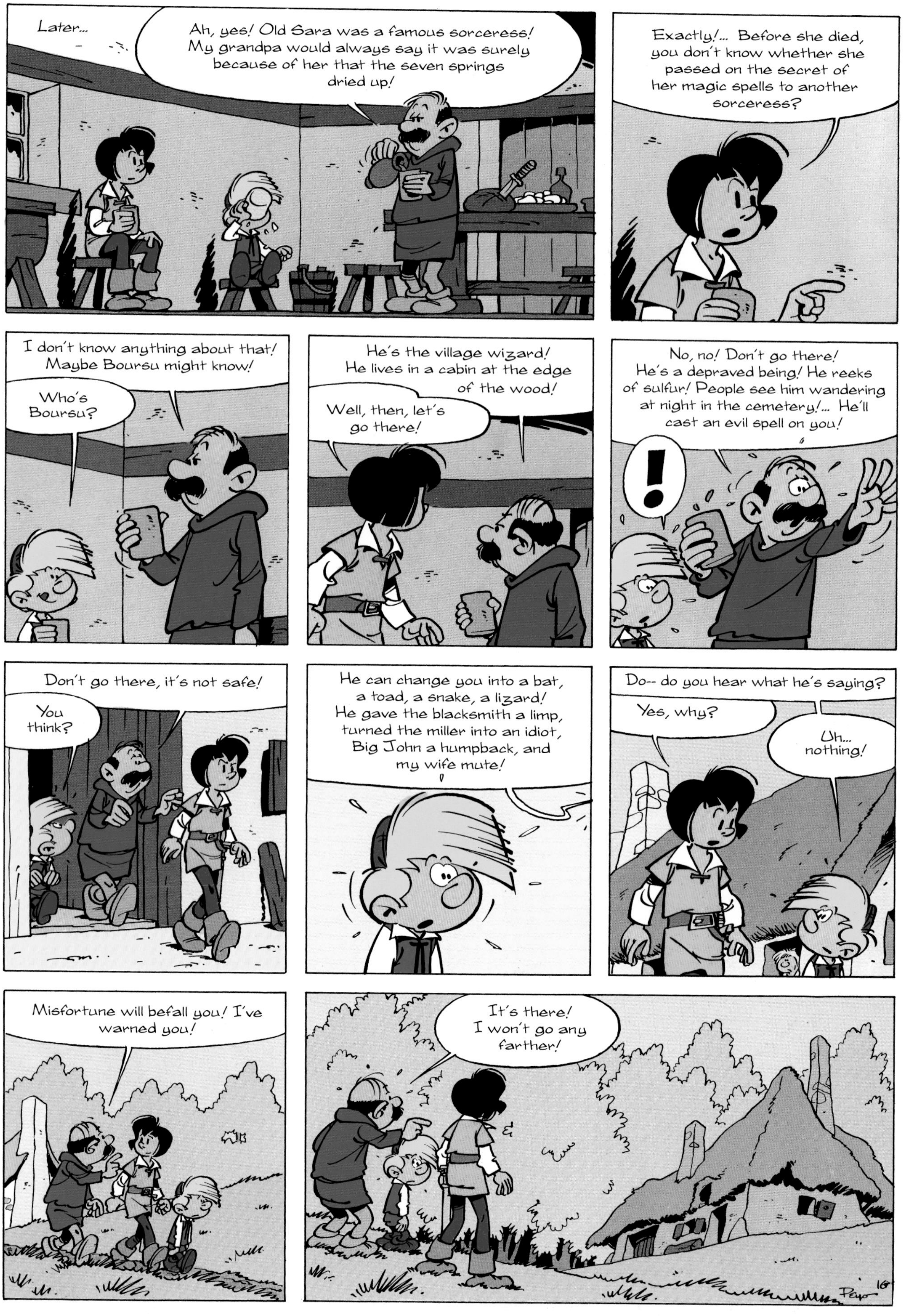
Later...
Ah, yes! Old Sara was a famous sorceress! My grandpa would always say it was surely because of her that the seven springs dried up!
Exactly!... Before she died, you don't know whether she passed on the secret of her magic spells to another sorceress?
I don't know anything about that! Maybe Boursu might know!
Who's Boursu?
He's the village wizard! He lives in a cabin at the edge of the wood!
Well, then, let's go there!
No, no! Don't go there! He's a depraved being! He reeks of sulfur! People see him wandering at night in the cemetery!... He'll cast an evil spell on you!
!
Don't go there, it's not safe!
You think?
He can change you into a bat, a toad, a snake, a lizard! He gave the blacksmith a limp, turned the miller into an idiot, Big John a humpback, and my wife mute!
Do-- do you hear what he's saying?
Yes, why?
Uh... nothing!
Misfortune will befall you! I've warned you!
It's there! I won't go any farther!

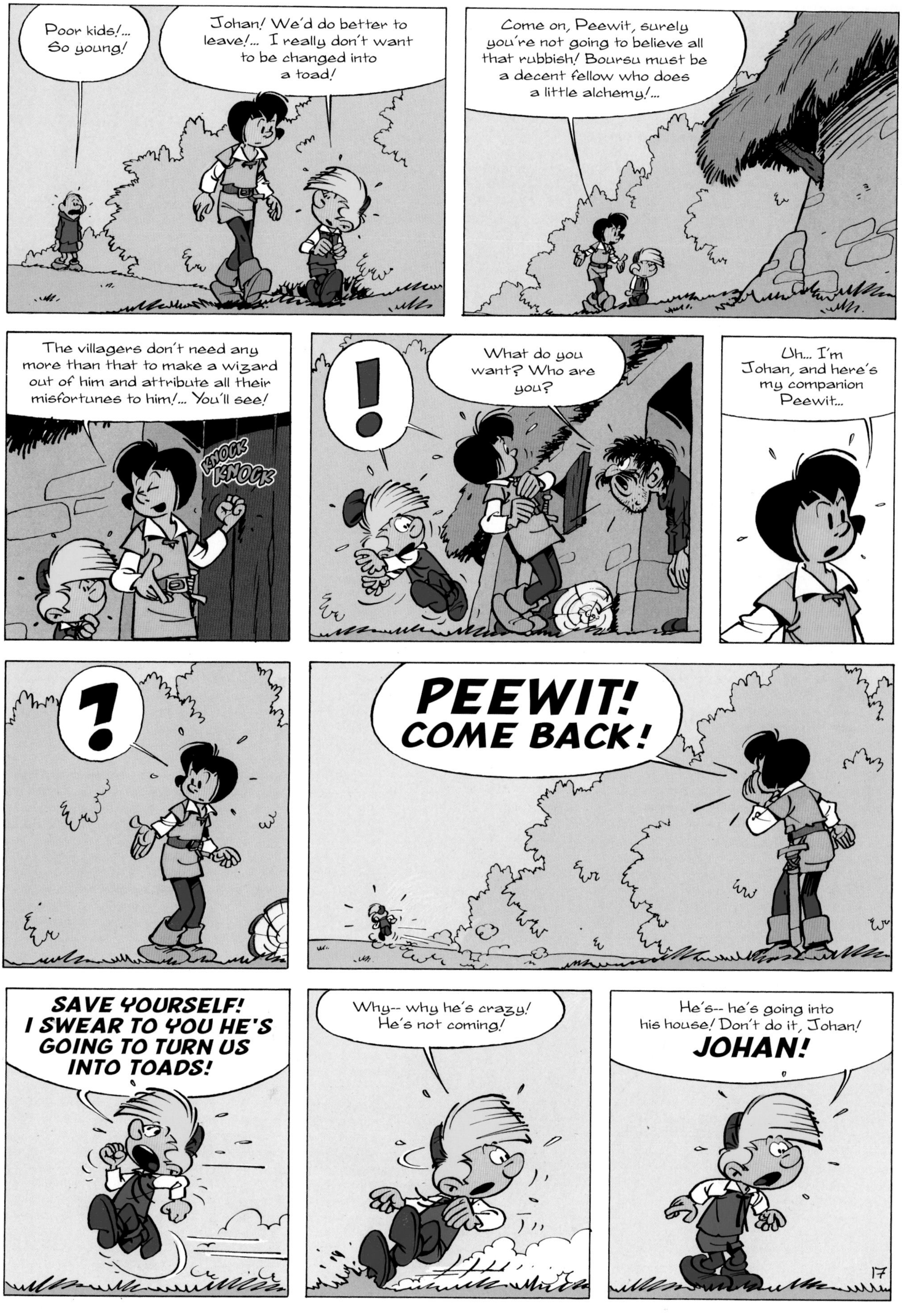
Poor kids!... So young!
Johan! We'd do better to leave!... I really don't want to be changed into a toad!
Come on, Peewit, surely you're not going to believe all that rubbish! Boursu must be a decent fellow who does a little alchemy!...
The villagers don't need any more than that to make a wizard out of him and attribute all their misfortunes to him!... You'll see!
KNOCK KNOCK
!
What do you want? Who are you?
Uh... I'm Johan, and here's my companion Peewit...
?
PEEWIT! COME BACK!
SAVE YOURSELF! I SWEAR TO YOU HE'S GOING TO TURN US INTO TOADS!
Why-- why he's crazy! He's not coming!
He's-- he's going into his house! Don't do it, Johan! JOHAN!
17

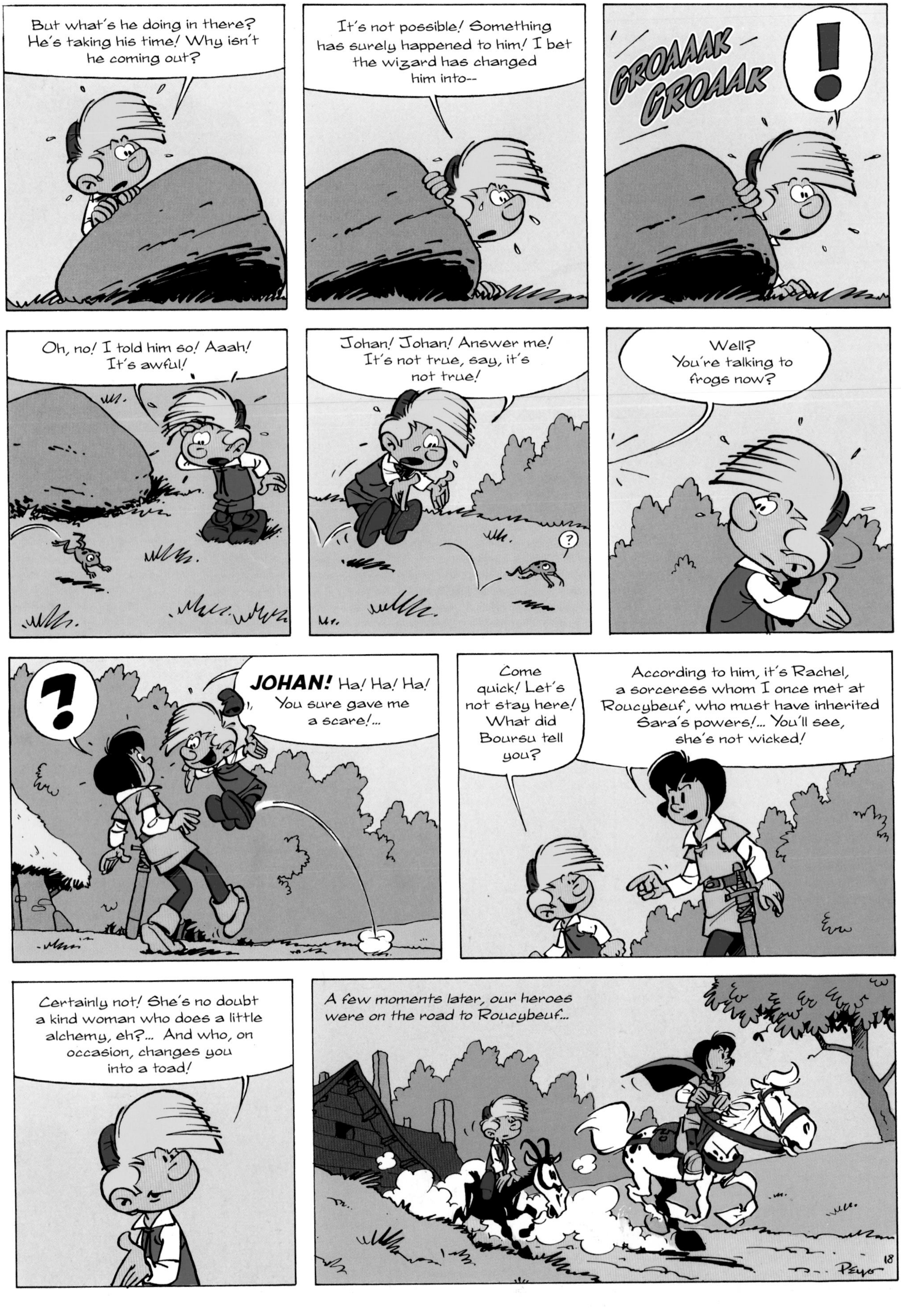

But what's he doing in there? He's taking his time! Why isn't he coming out?
It's not possible! Something has surely happened to him! I bet the wizard has changed him into--
GROAAAK GROAAK
!
Oh, no! I told him so! Aaah! It's awful!
Johan! Johan! Answer me! It's not true, say, it's not true!
?
Well? You're talking to frogs now?
?
JOHAN! Ha! Ha! Ha! You sure gave me a scare!...
Come quick! Let's not stay here! What did Boursu tell you?
According to him, it's Rachel, a sorceress whom I once met at Roucybeuf, who must have inherited Sara's powers!... You'll see, she's not wicked!
Certainly not! She's no doubt a kind woman who does a little alchemy, eh?... And who, on occasion, changes you into a toad!
A few moments later, our heroes were on the road to Roucybeuf...
18
PEYO

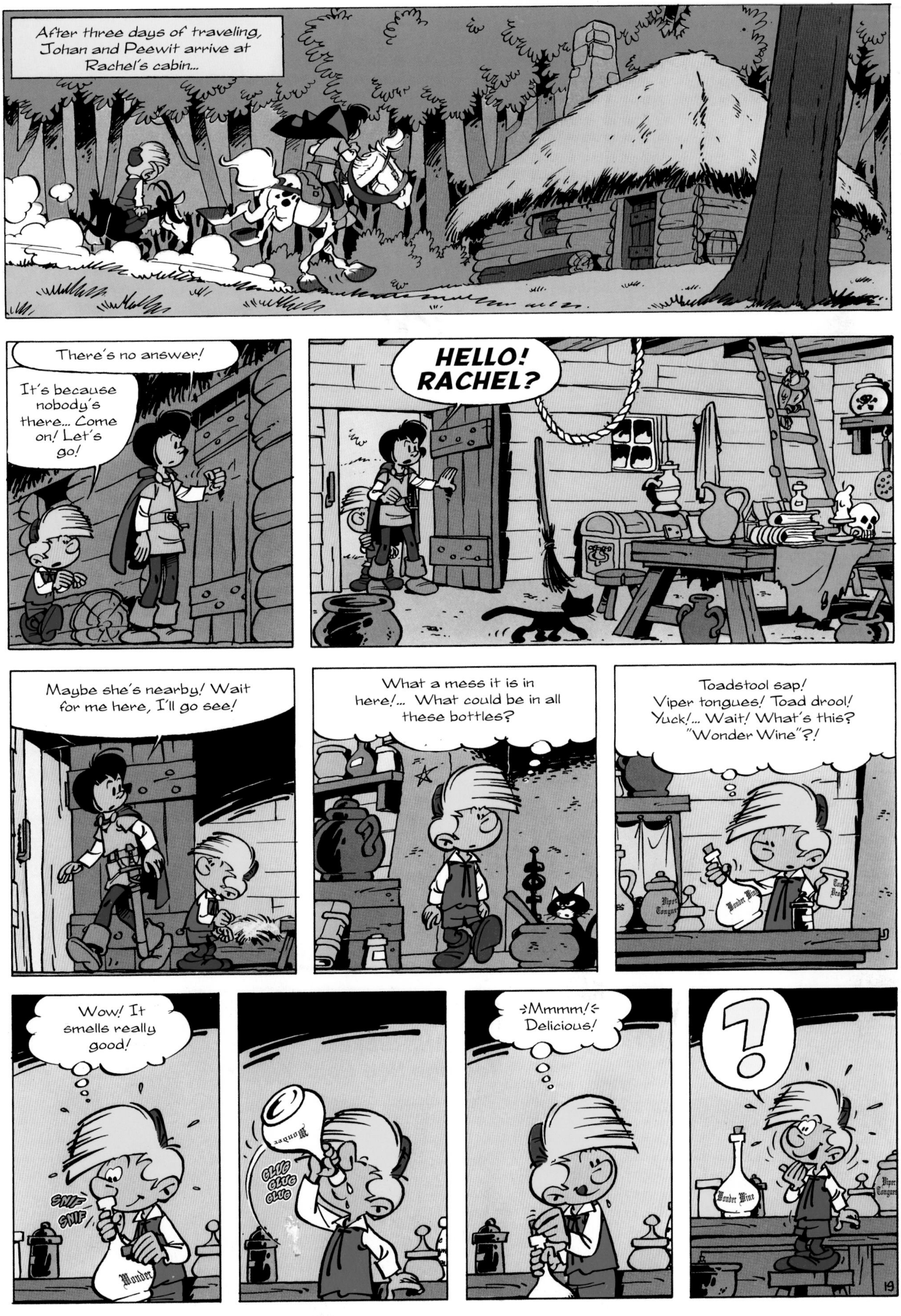

After three days of traveling, Johan and Peewit arrive at Rachel's cabin...
There's no answer!
It's because nobody's there... Come on! Let's go!
HELLO! RACHEL?
Maybe she's nearby! Wait for me here, I'll go see!
What a mess it is in here!... What could be in all these bottles?
Toadstool sap! Viper tongues! Toad drool! Yuck!... Wait! What's this? "Wonder Wine"?!
Wow! It smells really good!
SNIF SNIF
GLUG GLUG GLUG
Mmmm! Delicious!
?
Wonder Wine
Viper Tongues

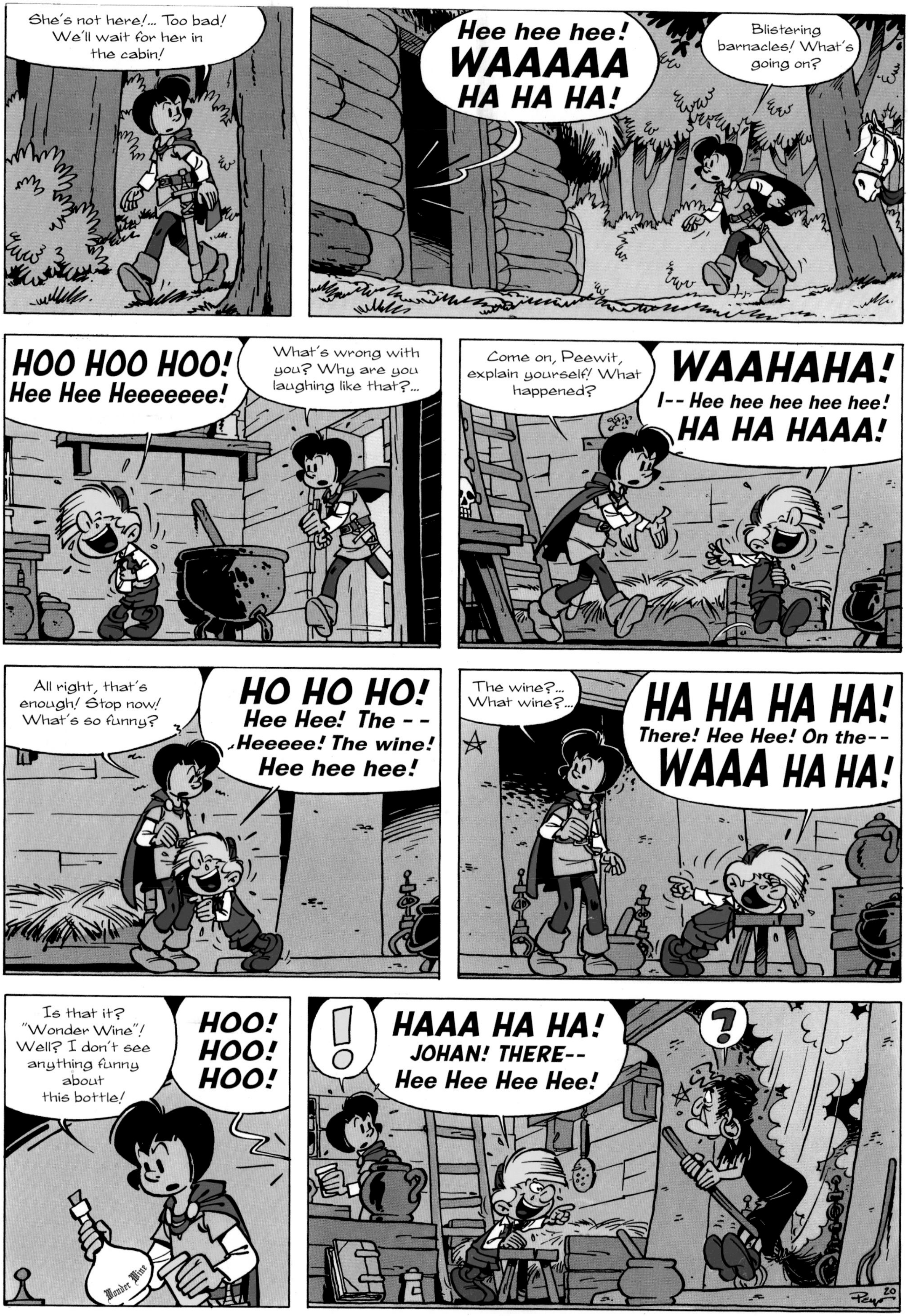
She's not here!... Too bad! We'll wait for her in the cabin!
Hee hee hee! WAAAAA HA HA HA!
Blistering barnacles! What's going on?
HOO HOO HOO! Hee Hee Heeeeeee!
What's wrong with you? Why are you laughing like that?...
Come on, Peewit, explain yourself! What happened?
WAAHAHA! I-- Hee hee hee hee hee! HA HA HAAA!
All right, that's enough! Stop now! What's so funny?
HO HO HO! Hee Hee! The -- Heeeee! The wine! Hee hee hee!
The wine?... What wine?...
HA HA HA HA! There! Hee Hee! On the-- WAAA HA HA!
Is that it? "Wonder Wine"! Well? I don't see anything funny about this bottle!
HOO! HOO! HOO!
Wonder Wine
!
HAAA HA HA! JOHAN! THERE-- Hee Hee Hee Hee!
?
20

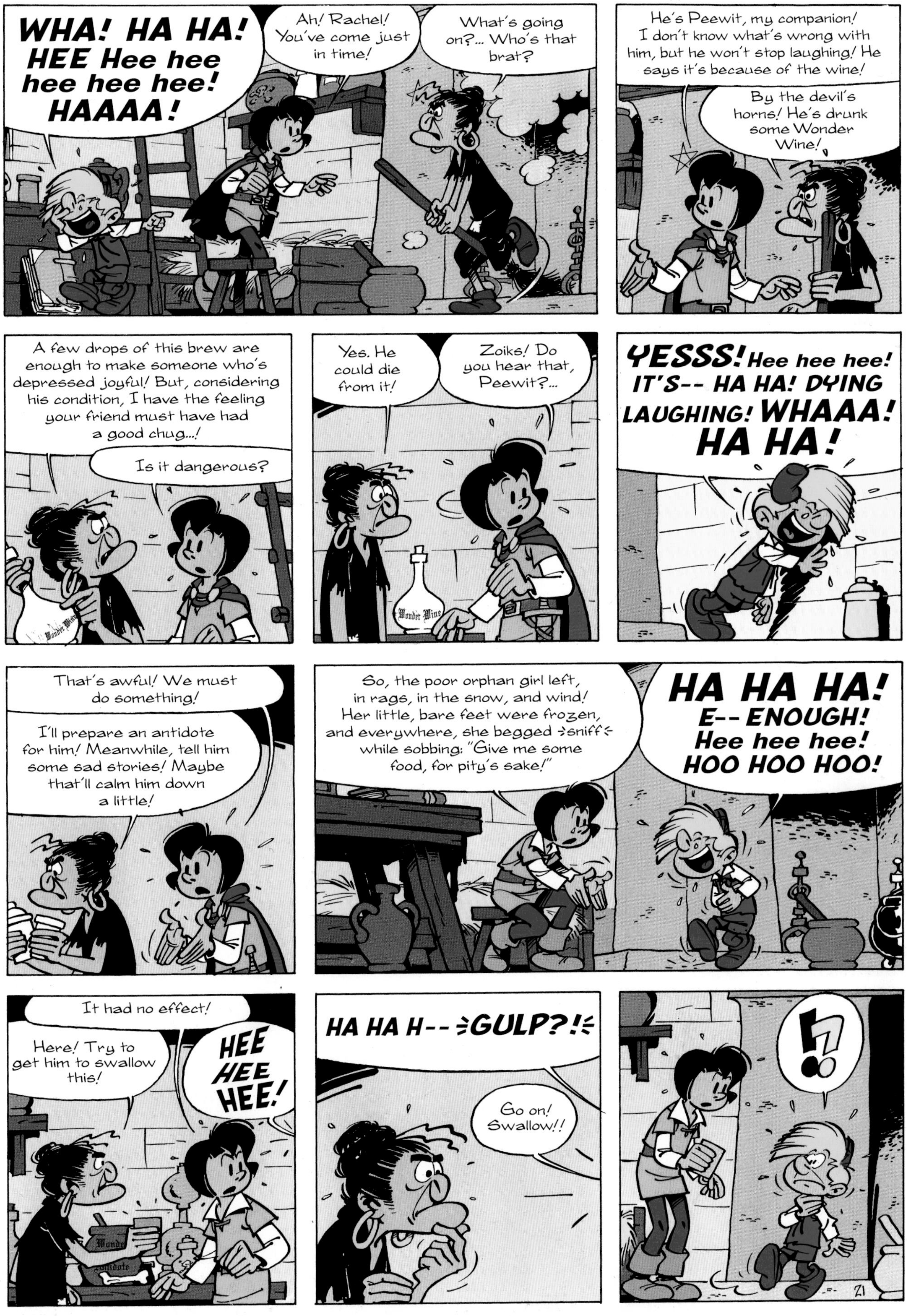
WHA! HA HA! HEE Hee hee hee hee hee! HAAAA!
Ah! Rachel! You've come just in time!
What's going on?... Who's that brat?
He's Peewit, my companion! I don't know what's wrong with him, but he won't stop laughing! He says it's because of the wine!
By the devil's horns! He's drunk some Wonder Wine!
A few drops of this brew are enough to make someone who's depressed joyful! But, considering his condition, I have the feeling your friend must have had a good chug...!
Is it dangerous?
Yes. He could die from it!
Zoiks! Do you hear that, Peewit?...
Wonder Wine
YESSS! Hee hee hee! IT'S-- HA HA! DYING LAUGHING! WHAAA! HA HA!
That's awful! We must do something!
I'll prepare an antidote for him! Meanwhile, tell him some sad stories! Maybe that'll calm him down a little!
So, the poor orphan girl left, in rags, in the snow, and wind! Her little, bare feet were frozen, and everywhere, she begged >sniff< while sobbing: "Give me some food, for pity's sake!"
HA HA HA! E-- ENOUGH! Hee hee hee! HOO HOO HOO!
It had no effect!
Here! Try to get him to swallow this!
HEE HEE HEE!
HA HA H-- >GULP?!<
Go on! Swallow!!
!?

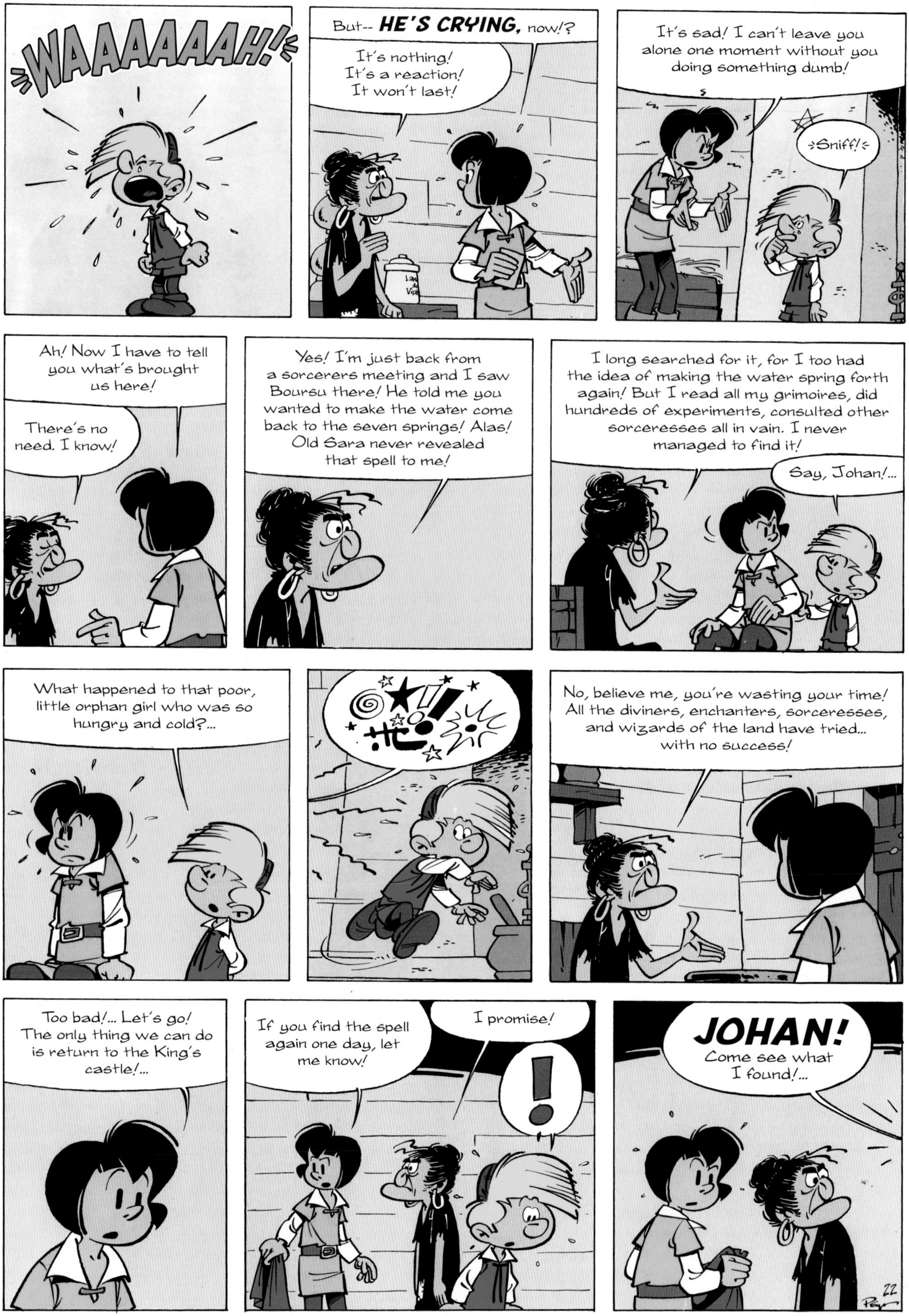
WAAAAAAH!
But-- HE'S CRYING, now!?
It's nothing! It's a reaction! It won't last!
It's sad! I can't leave you alone one moment without you doing something dumb!
Sniff!
Ah! Now I have to tell you what's brought us here!
There's no need. I know!
Yes! I'm just back from a sorcerers meeting and I saw Boursu there! He told me you wanted to make the water come back to the seven springs! Alas! Old Sara never revealed that spell to me!
I long searched for it, for I too had the idea of making the water spring forth again! But I read all my grimoires, did hundreds of experiments, consulted other sorceresses all in vain. I never managed to find it!
Say, Johan!...
What happened to that poor, little orphan girl who was so hungry and cold?...
No, believe me, you're wasting your time! All the diviners, enchanters, sorceresses, and wizards of the land have tried... with no success!
Too bad!... Let's go! The only thing we can do is return to the King's castle!...
If you find the spell again one day, let me know!
I promise!
!
JOHAN! Come see what I found!...
22

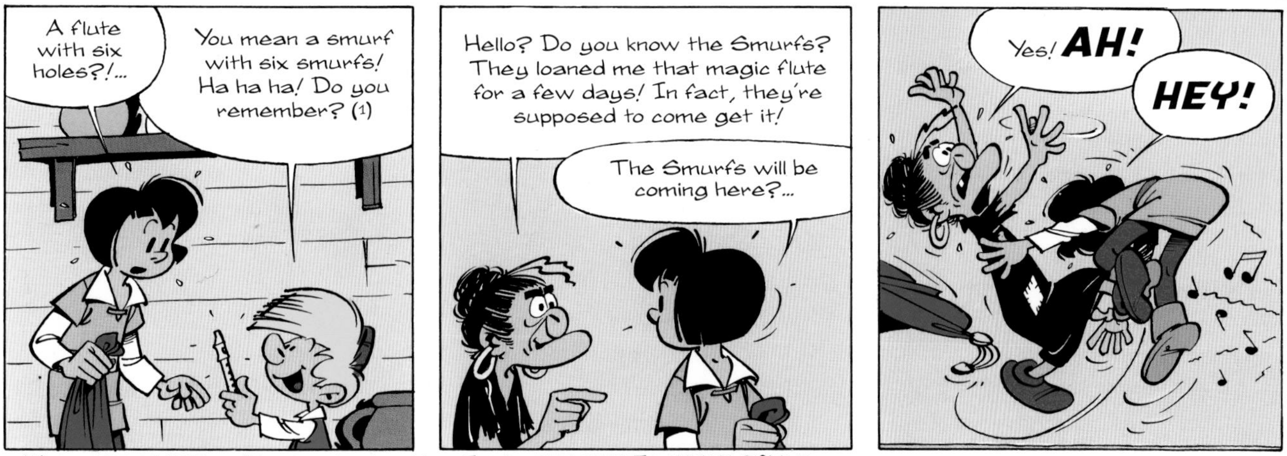
A flute with six holes?!...
You mean a smurf with six smurfs! Ha ha ha! Do you remember? (1)
Hello? Do you know the Smurfs? They loaned me that magic flute for a few days! In fact, they're supposed to come get it!
The Smurfs will be coming here?...
Yes! AH!
HEY!

(1) See: THE SMURFS #2 "The Smurfs and the Magic Flute" or THE SMURFS ANTHOLOGY Vol. 1.

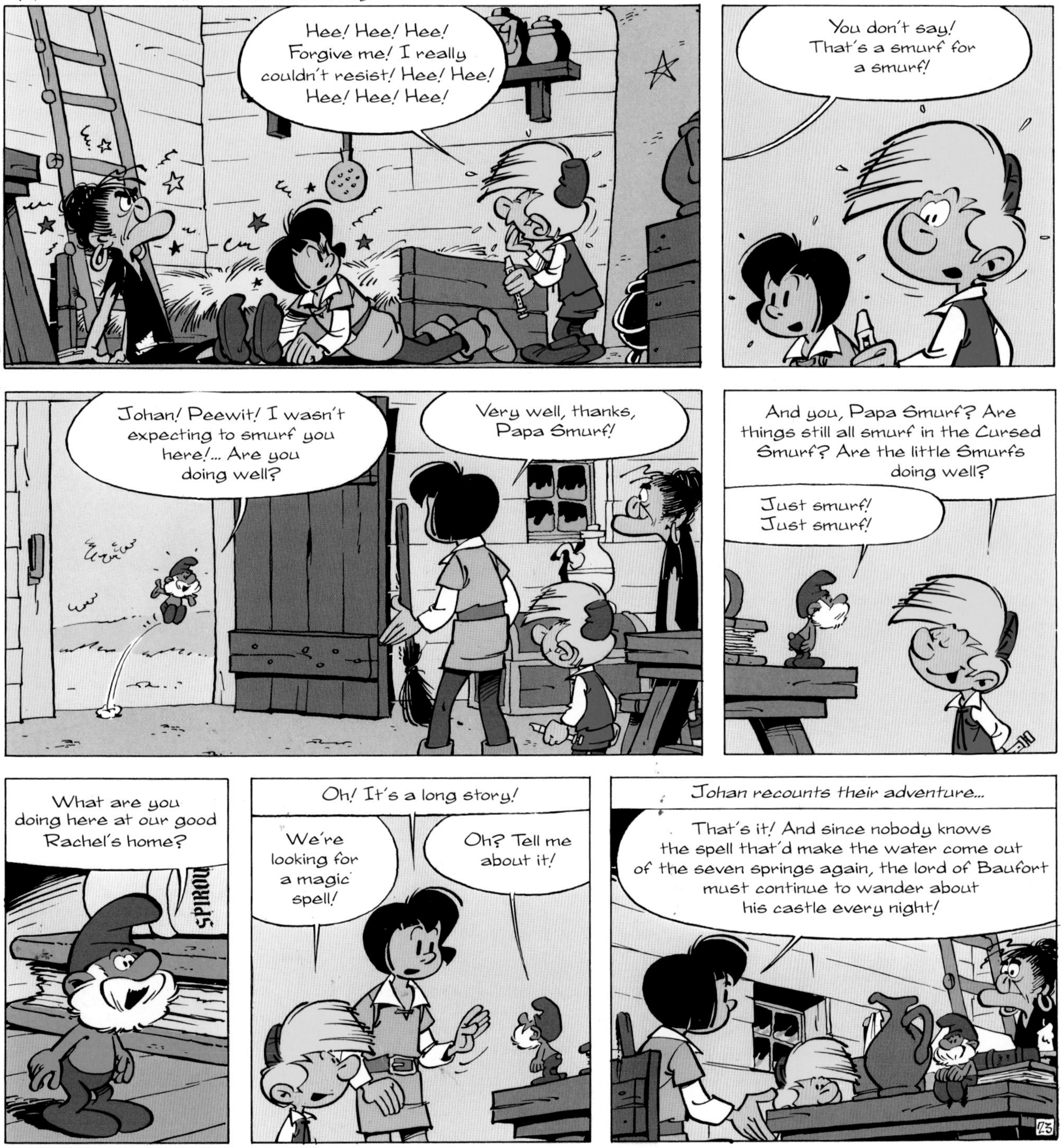
Hee! Hee! Hee! Forgive me! I really couldn't resist! Hee! Hee! Hee! Hee! Hee!
You don't say! That's a smurf for a smurf!
Johan! Peewit! I wasn't expecting to smurf you here!... Are you doing well?
Very well, thanks, Papa Smurf!
And you, Papa Smurf? Are things still all smurf in the Cursed Smurf? Are the little Smurfs doing well?
Just smurf! Just smurf!
What are you doing here at our good Rachel's home?
SPIROU
Oh! It's a long story!
We're looking for a magic spell!
Oh? Tell me about it!
Johan recounts their adventure...
That's it! And since nobody knows the spell that'd make the water come out of the seven springs again, the lord of Baufort must continue to wander about his castle every night!
23

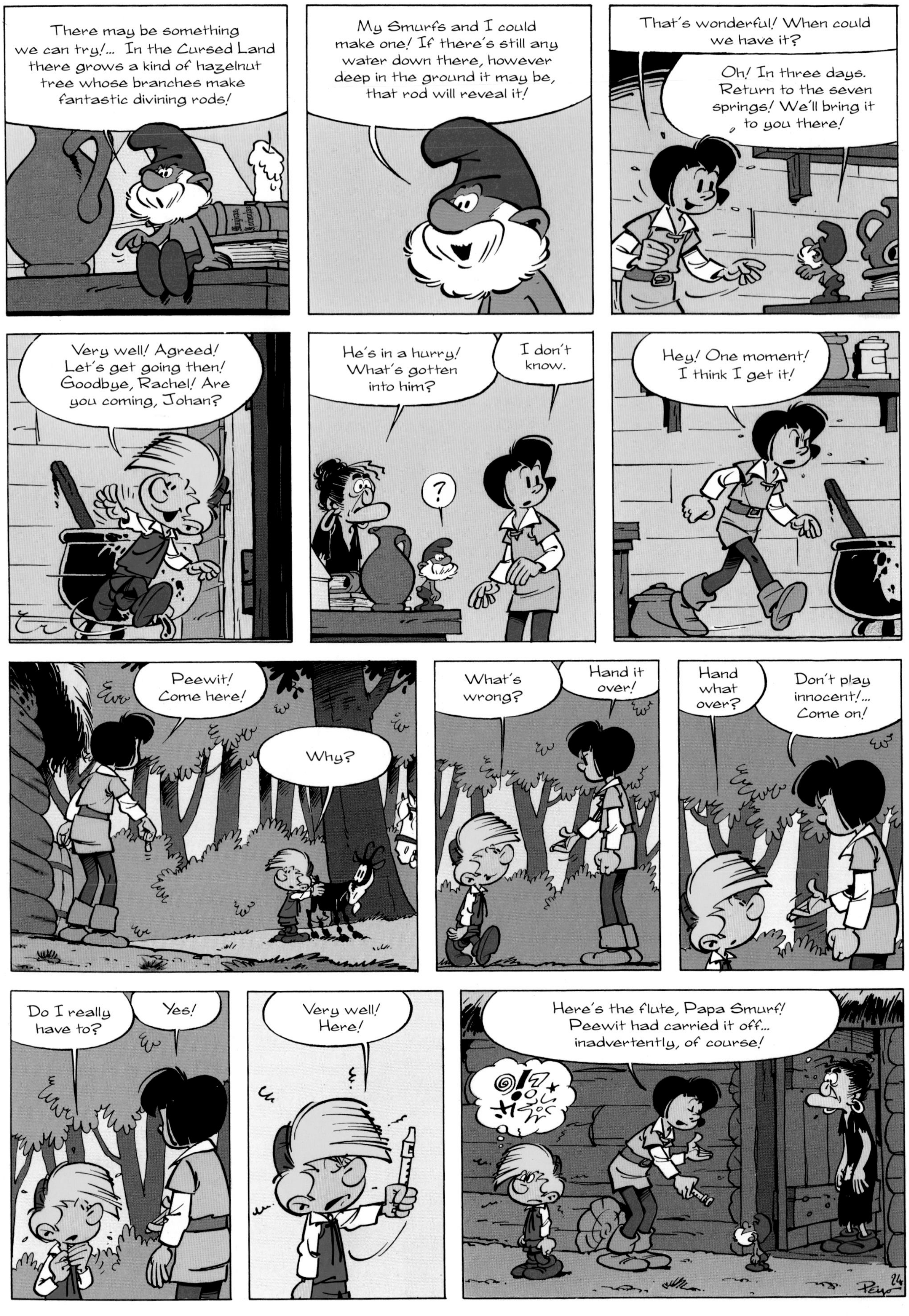
There may be something we can try!... In the Cursed Land there grows a kind of hazelnut tree whose branches make fantastic divining rods!
My Smurfs and I could make one! If there's still any water down there, however deep in the ground it may be, that rod will reveal it!
That's wonderful! When could we have it?
Oh! In three days. Return to the seven springs! We'll bring it to you there!
Very well! Agreed! Let's get going then! Goodbye, Rachel! Are you coming, Johan?
He's in a hurry! What's gotten into him?
I don't know.
?
Hey! One moment! I think I get it!
Peewit! Come here!
Why?
What's wrong?
Hand it over!
Hand what over?
Don't play innocent!... Come on!
Do I really have to?
Yes!
Very well! Here!
Here's the flute, Papa Smurf! Peewit had carried it off... inadvertently, of course!
Peyo 24

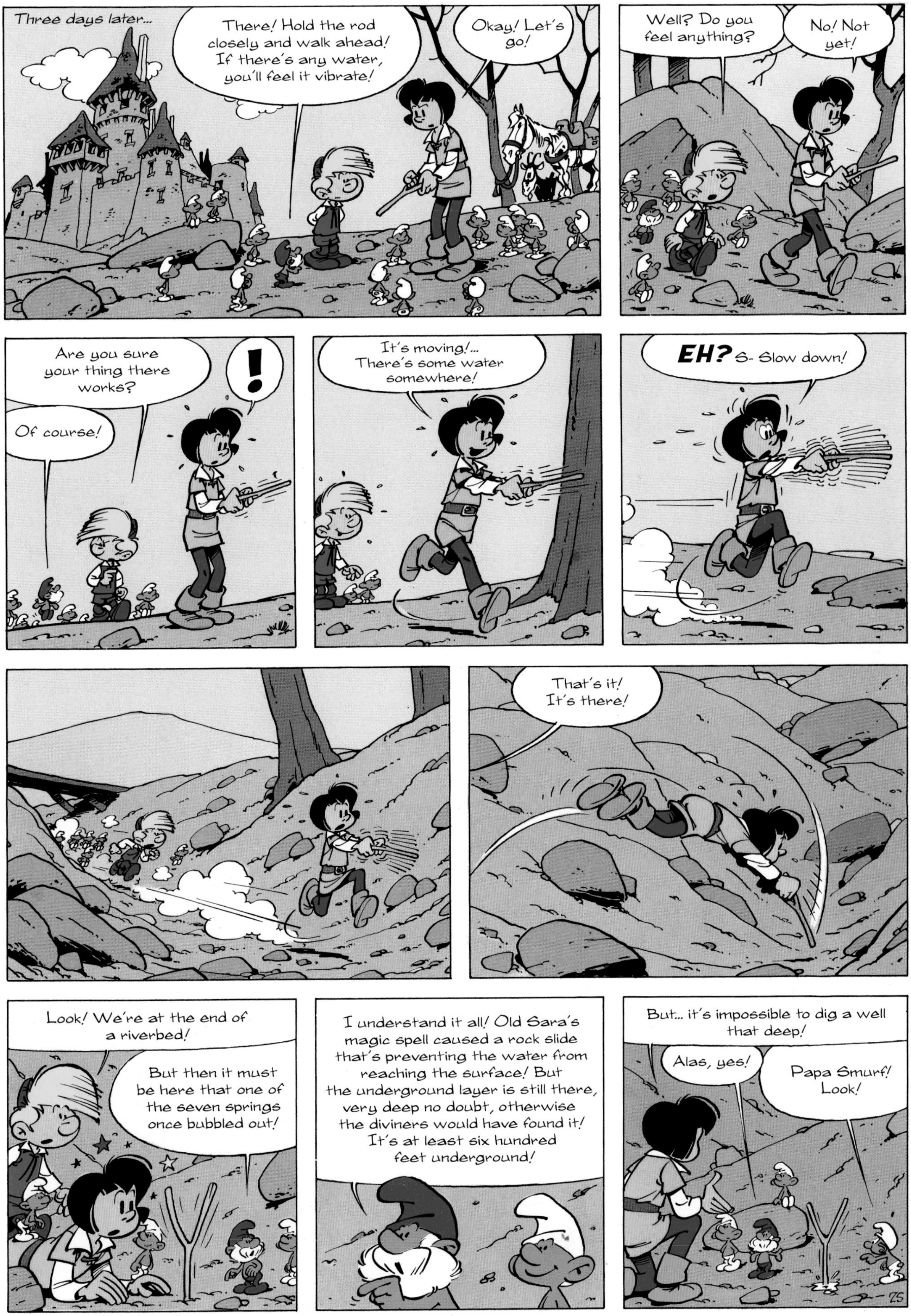

Three days later...
There! Hold the rod closely and walk ahead! If there's any water, you'll feel it vibrate!
Okay! Let's go!
Well? Do you feel anything?
No! Not yet!
Are you sure your thing there works?
Of course!
!
It's moving!... There's some water somewhere!
EH? S- Slow down!
That's it! It's there!
Look! We're at the end of a riverbed!
But then it must be here that one of the seven springs once bubbled out!
I understand it all! Old Sara's magic spell caused a rock slide that's preventing the water from reaching the surface! But the underground layer is still there, very deep no doubt, otherwise the diviners would have found it! It's at least six hundred feet underground!
But... it's impossible to dig a well that deep!
Alas, yes!
Papa Smurf! Look!

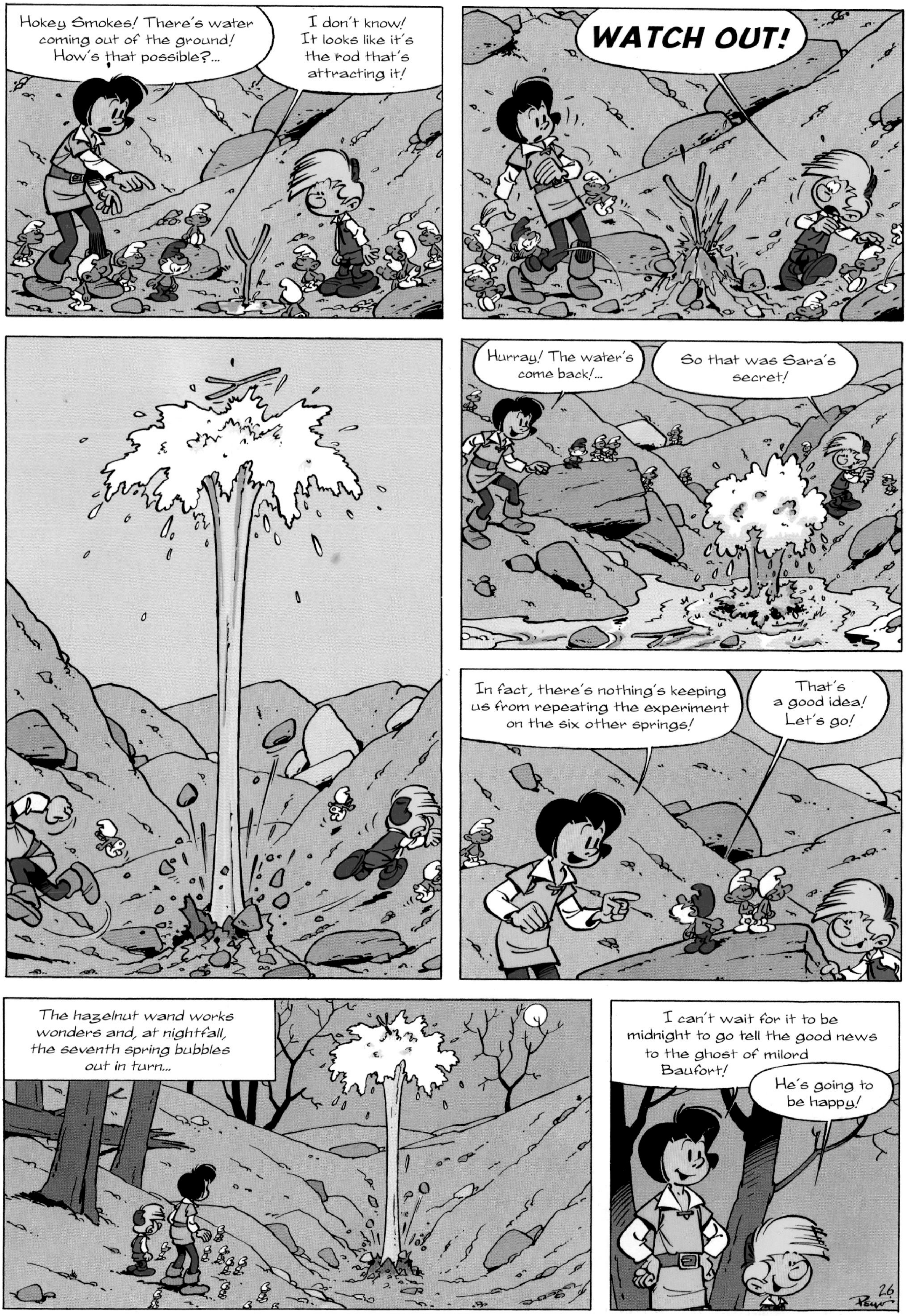

Hokey Smokes! There's water coming out of the ground! How's that possible?...
I don't know! It looks like it's the rod that's attracting it!
WATCH OUT!
Hurray! The water's come back!...
So that was Sara's secret!
In fact, there's nothing's keeping us from repeating the experiment on the six other springs!
That's a good idea! Let's go!
The hazelnut wand works wonders and, at nightfall, the seventh spring bubbles out in turn...
I can't wait for it to be midnight to go tell the good news to the ghost of milord Baufort!
He's going to be happy!
26

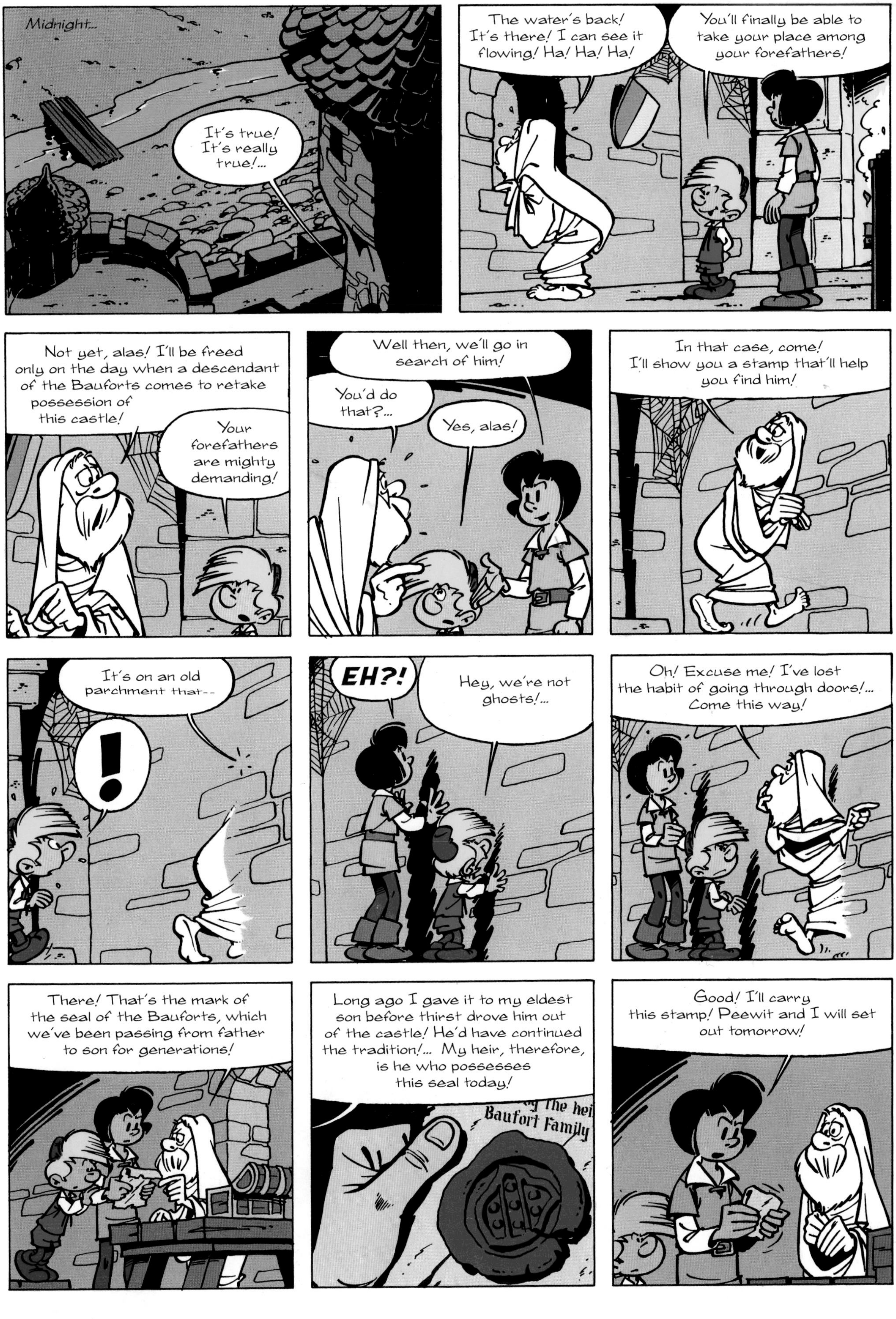
Midnight...
It's true! It's really true!...
The water's back! It's there! I can see it flowing! Ha! Ha! Ha!
You'll finally be able to take your place among your forefathers!
Not yet, alas! I'll be freed only on the day when a descendant of the Bauforts comes to retake possession of this castle!
Your forefathers are mighty demanding!
Well then, we'll go in search of him!
You'd do that?...
Yes, alas!
In that case, come! I'll show you a stamp that'll help you find him!
It's on an old parchment that--
!
EH?!
Hey, we're not ghosts!...
Oh! Excuse me! I've lost the habit of going through doors!... Come this way!
There! That's the mark of the seal of the Bauforts, which we've been passing from father to son for generations!
Long ago I gave it to my eldest son before thirst drove him out of the castle! He'd have continued the tradition!... My heir, therefore, is he who possesses this seal today!
Baufort Family
Good! I'll carry this stamp! Peewit and I will set out tomorrow!

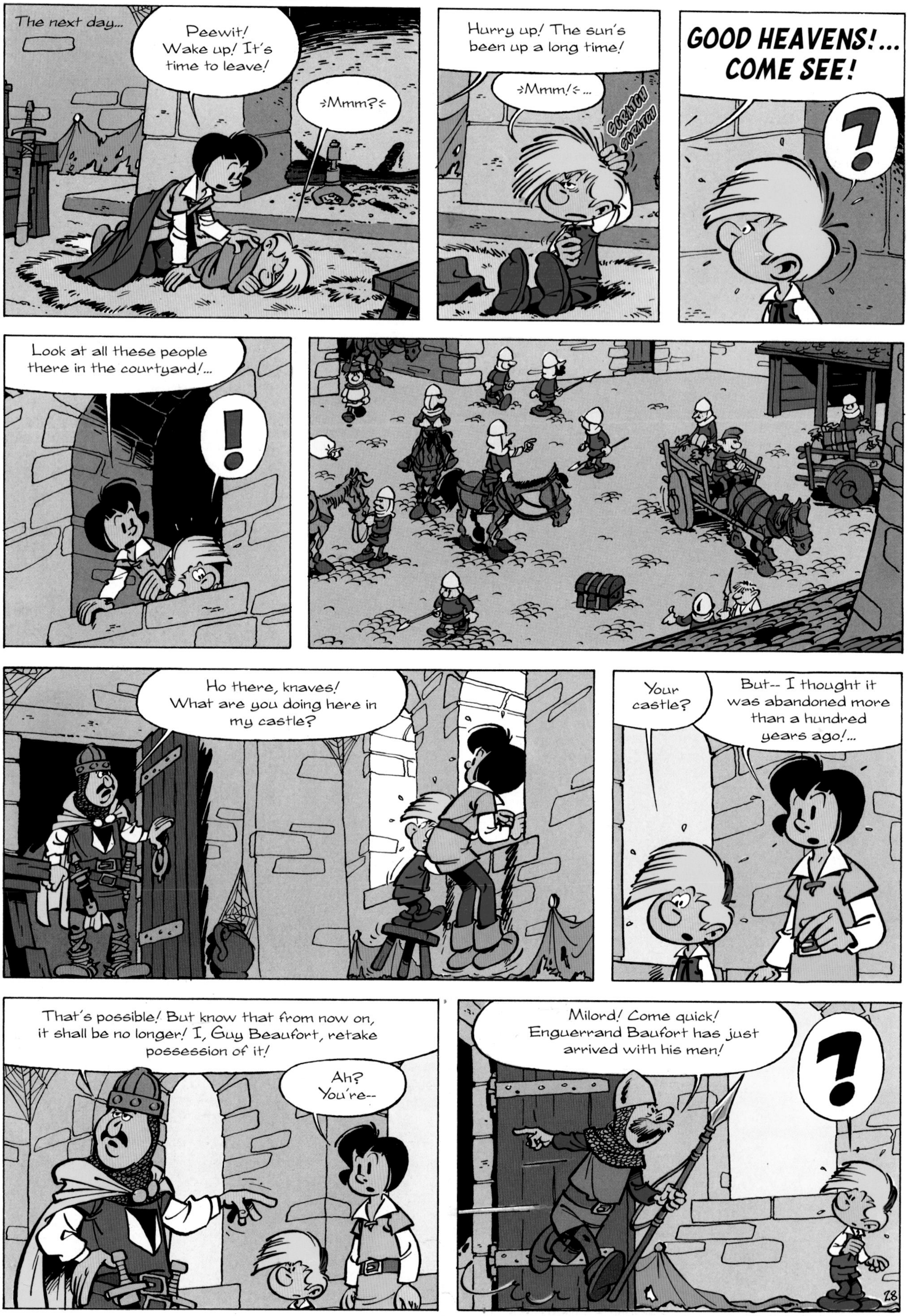
The next day...
Peewit! Wake up! It's time to leave!
Mmm?
Hurry up! The sun's been up a long time!
Mmm! ...
SCRATCH SCRATCH
GOOD HEAVENS!... COME SEE!
?
Look at all these people there in the courtyard!...
!
Ho there, knaves! What are you doing here in my castle?
Your castle?
But-- I thought it was abandoned more than a hundred years ago!...
That's possible! But know that from now on, it shall be no longer! I, Guy Beaufort, retake possession of it!
Ah? You're--
Milord! Come quick! Enguerrand Baufort has just arrived with his men!
?
28

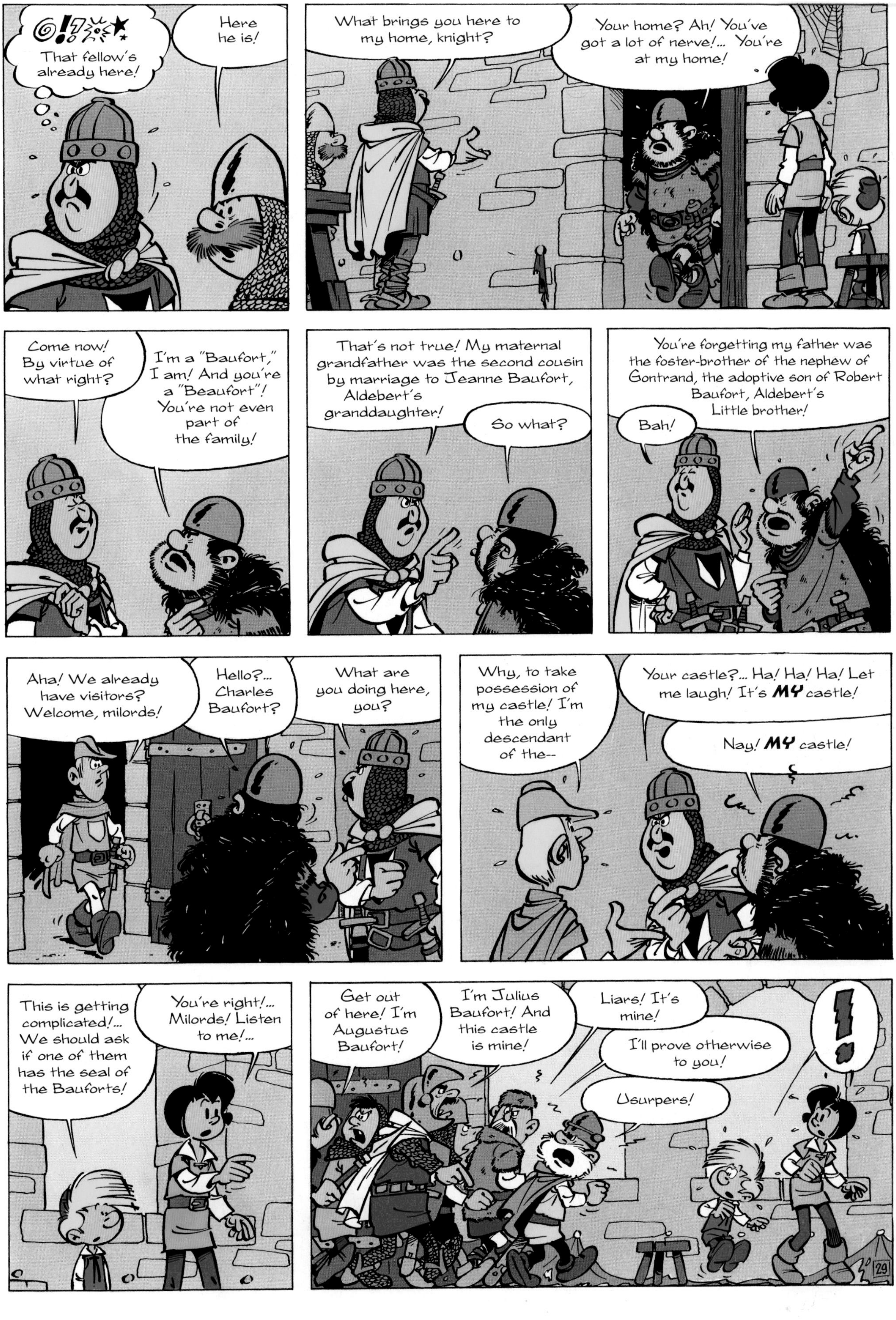
That fellow's already here!
Here he is!
What brings you here to my home, knight?
Your home? Ah! You've got a lot of nerve!... You're at my home!
Come now! By virtue of what right?
I'm a "Baufort," I am! And you're a "Beaufort"! You're not even part of the family!
That's not true! My maternal grandfather was the second cousin by marriage to Jeanne Baufort, Aldebert's granddaughter!
So what?
You're forgetting my father was the foster-brother of the nephew of Gontrand, the adoptive son of Robert Baufort, Aldebert's Little brother!
Bah!
Aha! We already have visitors? Welcome, milords!
Hello?... Charles Baufort?
What are you doing here, you?
Why, to take possession of my castle! I'm the only descendant of the--
Your castle?... Ha! Ha! Ha! Let me laugh! It's MY castle!
Nay! MY castle!
This is getting complicated!... We should ask if one of them has the seal of the Bauforts!
You're right!... Milords! Listen to me!...
Get out of here! I'm Augustus Baufort!
I'm Julius Baufort! And this castle is mine!
Liars! It's mine!
I'll prove otherwise to you!
Usurpers!
!
29

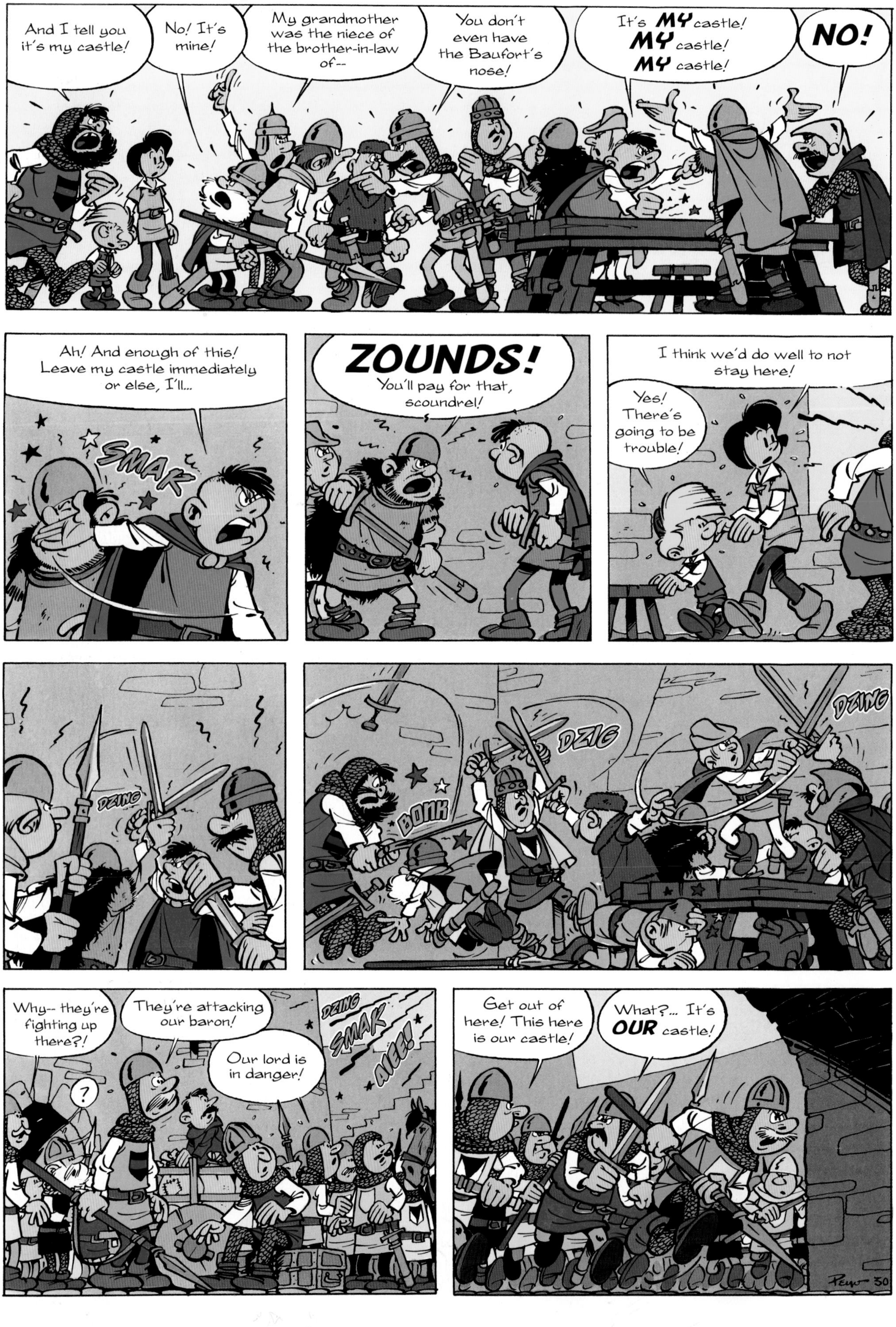
And I tell you it's my castle!
No! It's mine!
My grandmother was the niece of the brother-in-law of--
You don't even have the Baufort's nose!
It's MY castle! MY castle! MY castle!
NO!
Ah! And enough of this! Leave my castle immediately or else, I'll...
SMAK
ZOUNDS!
You'll pay for that, scoundrel!
I think we'd do well to not stay here!
Yes! There's going to be trouble!
DZING
DZIG
DZING
BONK
Why-- they're fighting up there?!
?
They're attacking our baron!
Our lord is in danger!
DZING
SMAK
AIEE!
Get out of here! This here is our castle!
What?... It's OUR castle!
Peyo 30

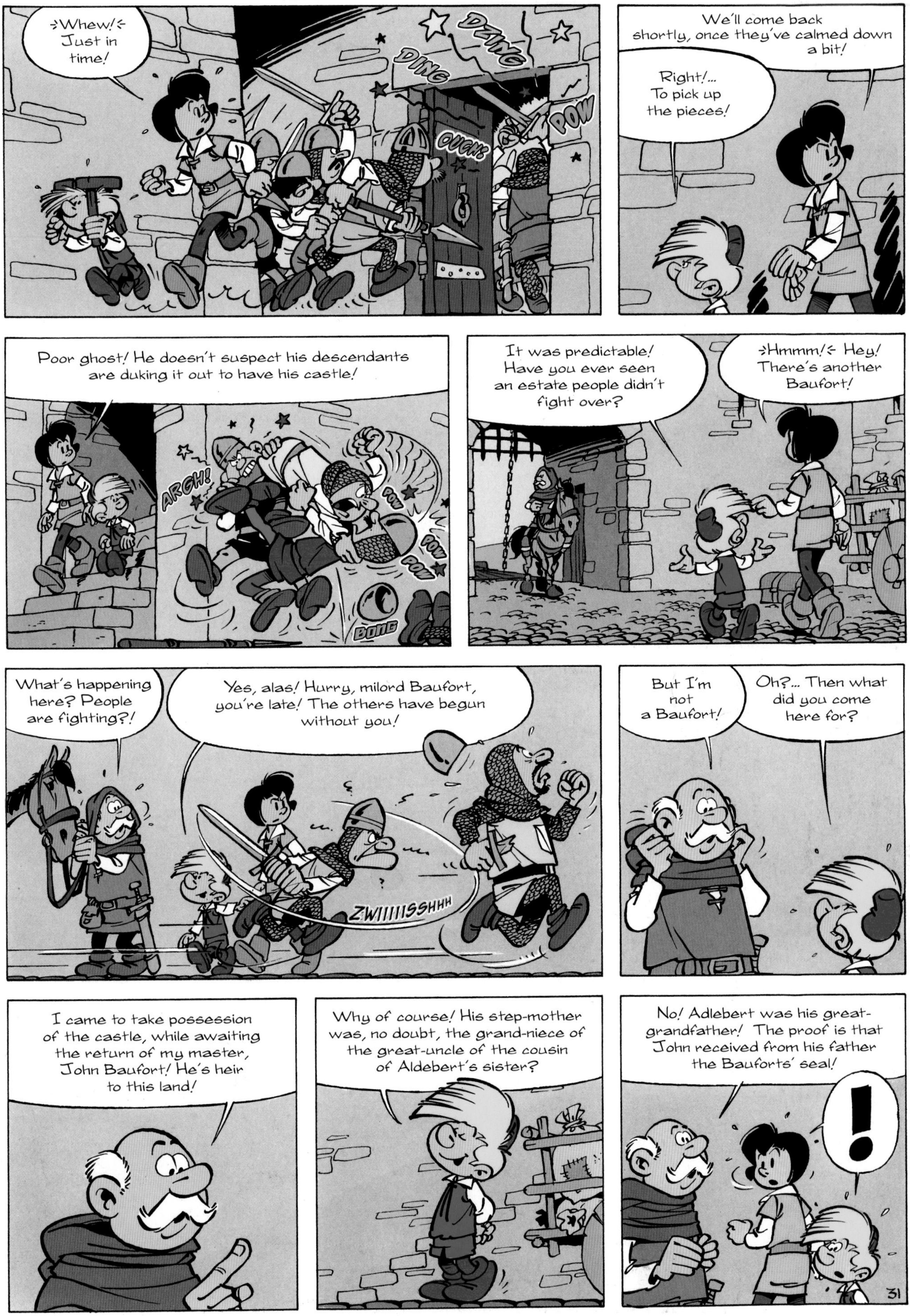

Whew! Just in time!
DING
DZING
OUCH!
POW
We'll come back shortly, once they've calmed down a bit!
Right!... To pick up the pieces!
Poor ghost! He doesn't suspect his descendants are duking it out to have his castle!
ARGH!
POW
POW
POW
BONG
It was predictable! Have you ever seen an estate people didn't fight over?
Hmmm! Hey! There's another Baufort!
What's happening here? People are fighting?!
Yes, alas! Hurry, milord Baufort, you're late! The others have begun without you!
ZWIIIIISSHHH
But I'm not a Baufort!
Oh?... Then what did you come here for?
I came to take possession of the castle, while awaiting the return of my master, John Baufort! He's heir to this land!
Why of course! His step-mother was, no doubt, the grand-niece of the great-uncle of the cousin of Aldebert's sister?
No! Adlebert was his great-grandfather! The proof is that John received from his father the Bauforts' seal!
!
31

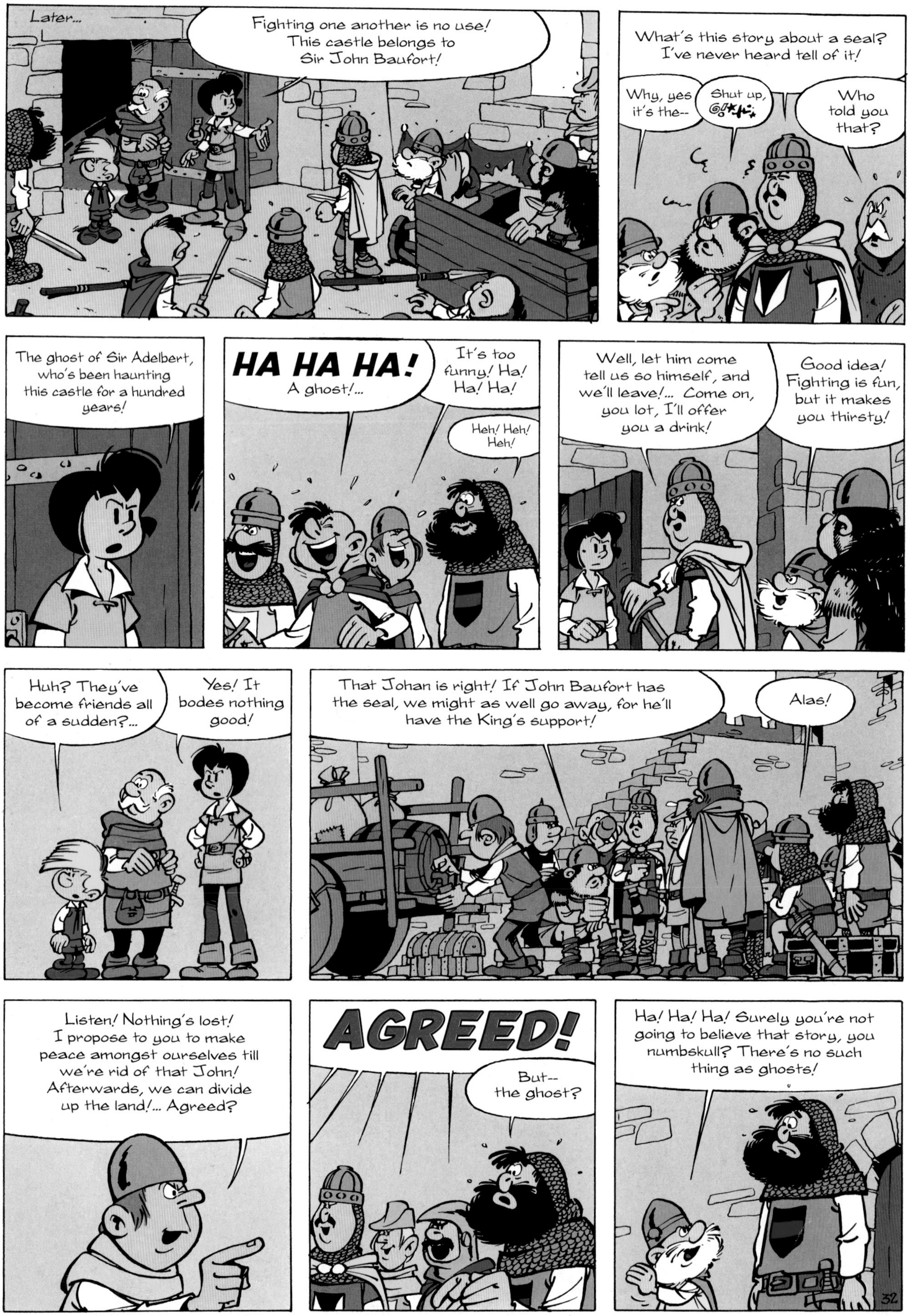
Later...
Fighting one another is no use! This castle belongs to Sir John Baufort!
What's this story about a seal? I've never heard tell of it!
Why, yes it's the--
Shut up,
Who told you that?
The ghost of Sir Adelbert, who's been haunting this castle for a hundred years!
HA HA HA! A ghost!...
It's too funny! Ha! Ha! Ha!
Heh! Heh! Heh!
Well, let him come tell us so himself, and we'll leave!... Come on, you lot, I'll offer you a drink!
Good idea! Fighting is fun, but it makes you thirsty!
Huh? They've become friends all of a sudden?...
Yes! It bodes nothing good!
That Johan is right! If John Baufort has the seal, we might as well go away, for he'll have the King's support!
Alas!
Listen! Nothing's lost! I propose to you to make peace amongst ourselves till we're rid of that John! Afterwards, we can divide up the land!... Agreed?
AGREED!
But-- the ghost?
Ha! Ha! Ha! Surely you're not going to believe that story, you numbskull? There's no such thing as ghosts!
32

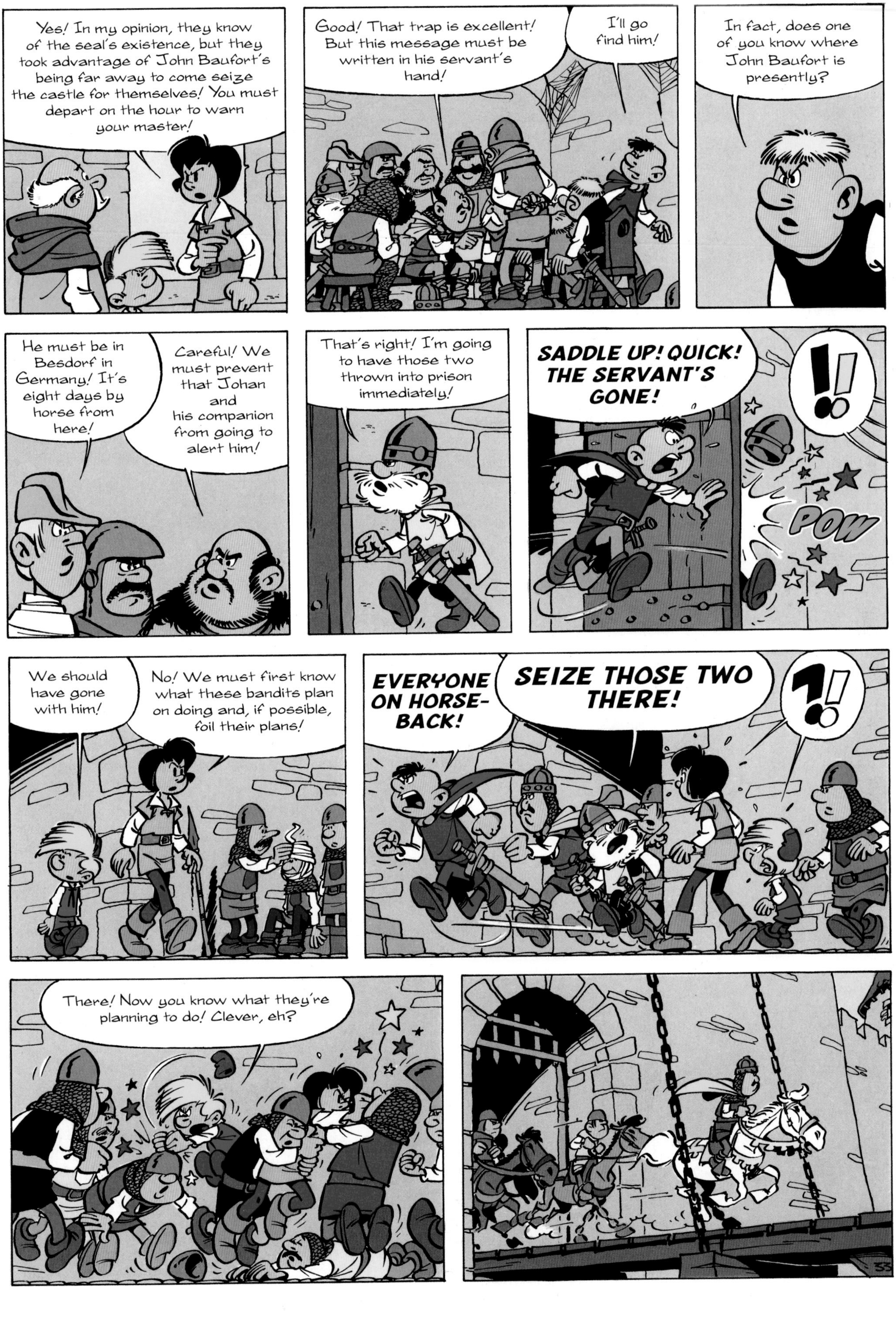
Yes! In my opinion, they know of the seal's existence, but they took advantage of John Baufort's being far away to come seize the castle for themselves! You must depart on the hour to warn your master!
Good! That trap is excellent! But this message must be written in his servant's hand!
I'll go find him!
In fact, does one of you know where John Baufort is presently?
He must be in Besdorf in Germany! It's eight days by horse from here!
Careful! We must prevent that Johan and his companion from going to alert him!
That's right! I'm going to have those two thrown into prison immediately!
SADDLE UP! QUICK! THE SERVANT'S GONE!
!!
POW
We should have gone with him!
No! We must first know what these bandits plan on doing and, if possible, foil their plans!
EVERYONE ON HORSE-BACK!
SEIZE THOSE TWO THERE!
?!
There! Now you know what they're planning to do! Clever, eh?

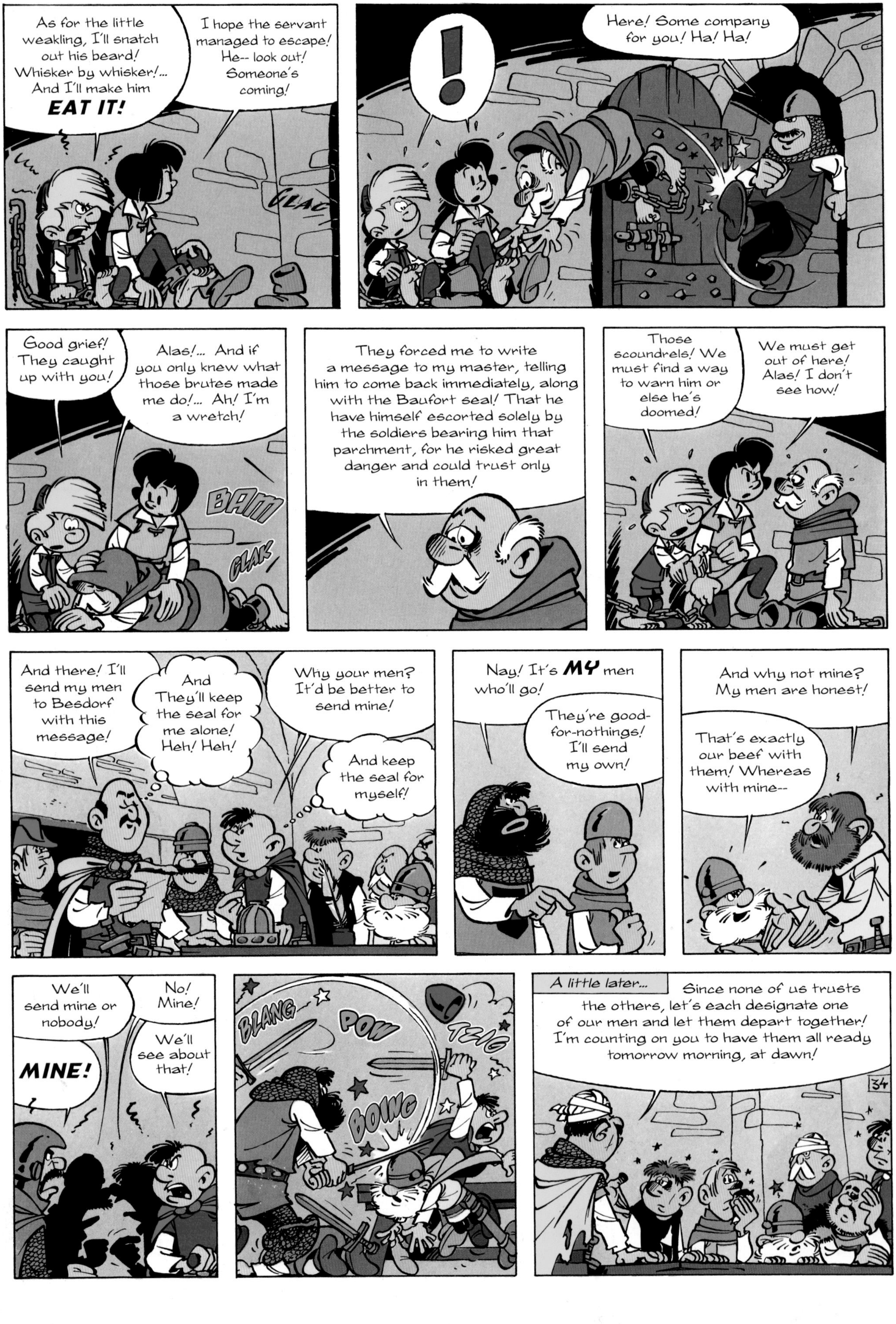
As for the little weakling, I'll snatch out his beard! Whisker by whisker!... And I'll make him EAT IT!
I hope the servant managed to escape! He-- look out! Someone's coming!
CLAC
!
Here! Some company for you! Ha! Ha!
Good grief! They caught up with you!
Alas!... And if you only knew what those brutes made me do!... Ah! I'm a wretch!
BAM
CLAK
They forced me to write a message to my master, telling him to come back immediately, along with the Baufort seal! That he have himself escorted solely by the soldiers bearing him that parchment, for he risked great danger and could trust only in them!
Those scoundrels! We must find a way to warn him or else he's doomed!
We must get out of here! Alas! I don't see how!
And there! I'll send my men to Besdorf with this message!
And They'll keep the seal for me alone! Heh! Heh!
Why your men? It'd be better to send mine!
And keep the seal for myself!
Nay! It's MY men who'll go!
They're good-for-nothings! I'll send my own!
And why not mine? My men are honest!
That's exactly our beef with them! Whereas with mine--
We'll send mine or nobody!
No! Mine!
MINE!
We'll see about that!
BLANG
POW
TZIG
BOING
A little later...
Since none of us trusts the others, let's each designate one of our men and let them depart together! I'm counting on you to have them all ready tomorrow morning, at dawn!
34

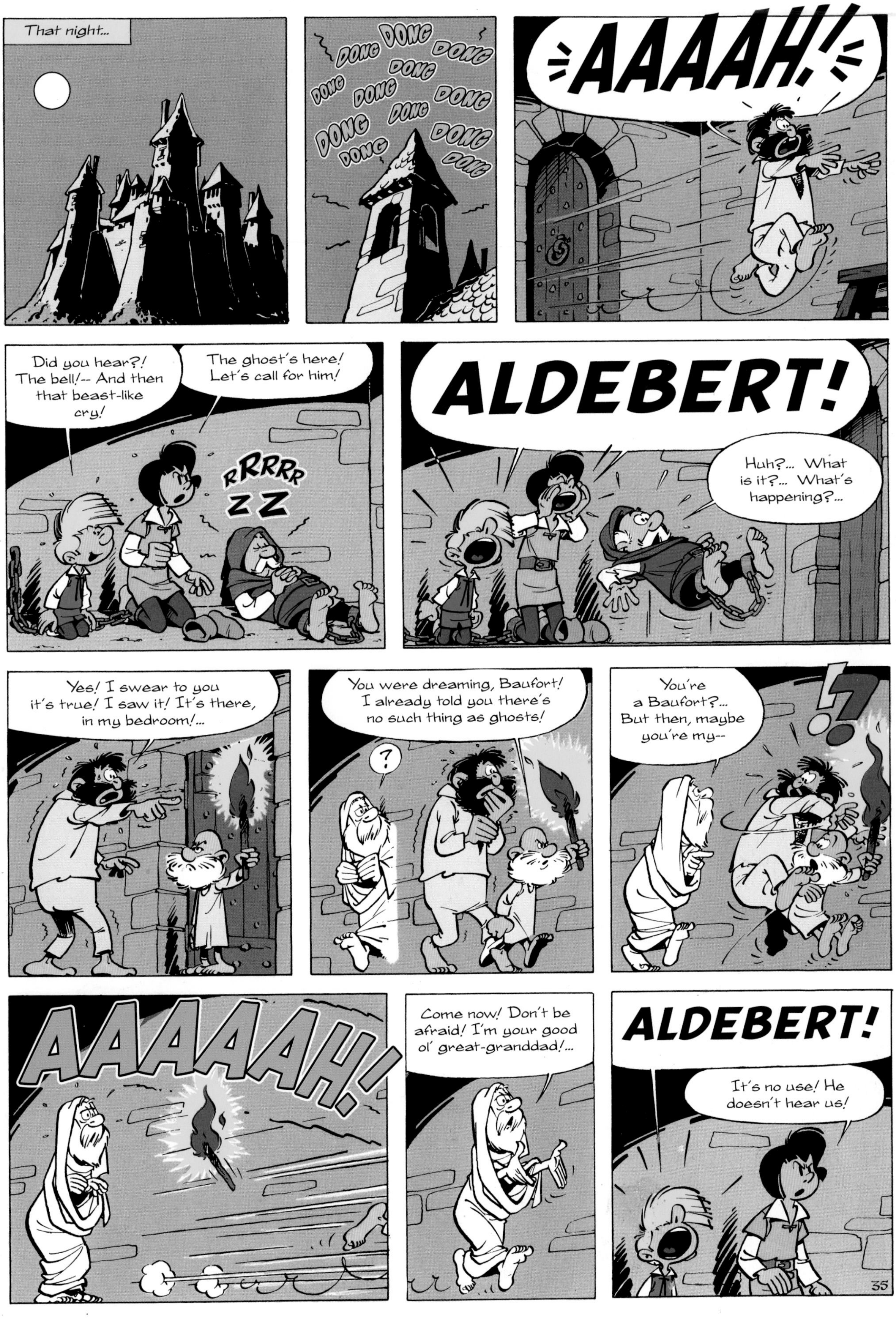
That night...
DONG DONG DONG DONG DONG DONG DONG DONG DONG DONG DONG DONG DONG
AAAAH!
Did you hear?! The bell!-- And then that beast-like cry!
The ghost's here! Let's call for him!
RRRRR
Z Z
ALDEBERT!
Huh?... What is it?... What's happening?...
Yes! I swear to you it's true! I saw it! It's there, in my bedroom!...
You were dreaming, Baufort! I already told you there's no such thing as ghosts!
?
You're a Baufort?... But then, maybe you're my--
!?
AAAAAH!
Come now! Don't be afraid! I'm your good ol' great-granddad!...
ALDEBERT!
It's no use! He doesn't hear us!
35

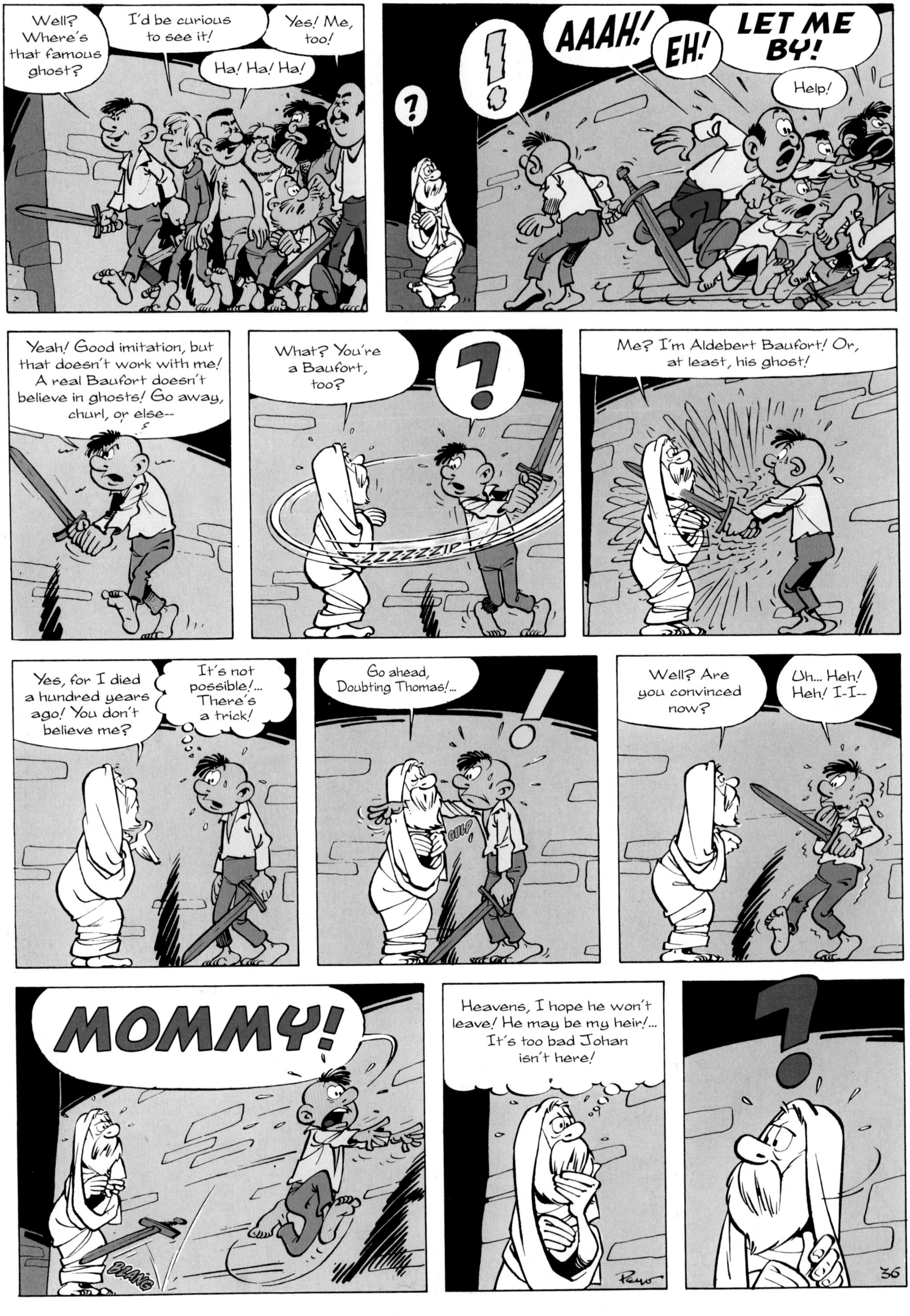

Well? Where's that famous ghost?
I'd be curious to see it!
Yes! Me, too!
Ha! Ha! Ha!
?
!
AAAH!
EH!
LET ME BY!
Help!
Yeah! Good imitation, but that doesn't work with me! A real Baufort doesn't believe in ghosts! Go away, churl, or else--
What? You're a Baufort, too?
?
ZZZZZZZIP
Me? I'm Aldebert Baufort! Or, at least, his ghost!
Yes, for I died a hundred years ago! You don't believe me?
It's not possible!... There's a trick!
Go ahead, Doubting Thomas!...
!
GULP
Well? Are you convinced now?
Uh... Heh! Heh! I-I--
MOMMY!
BLANG
Heavens, I hope he won't leave! He may be my heir!... It's too bad Johan isn't here!
?
36

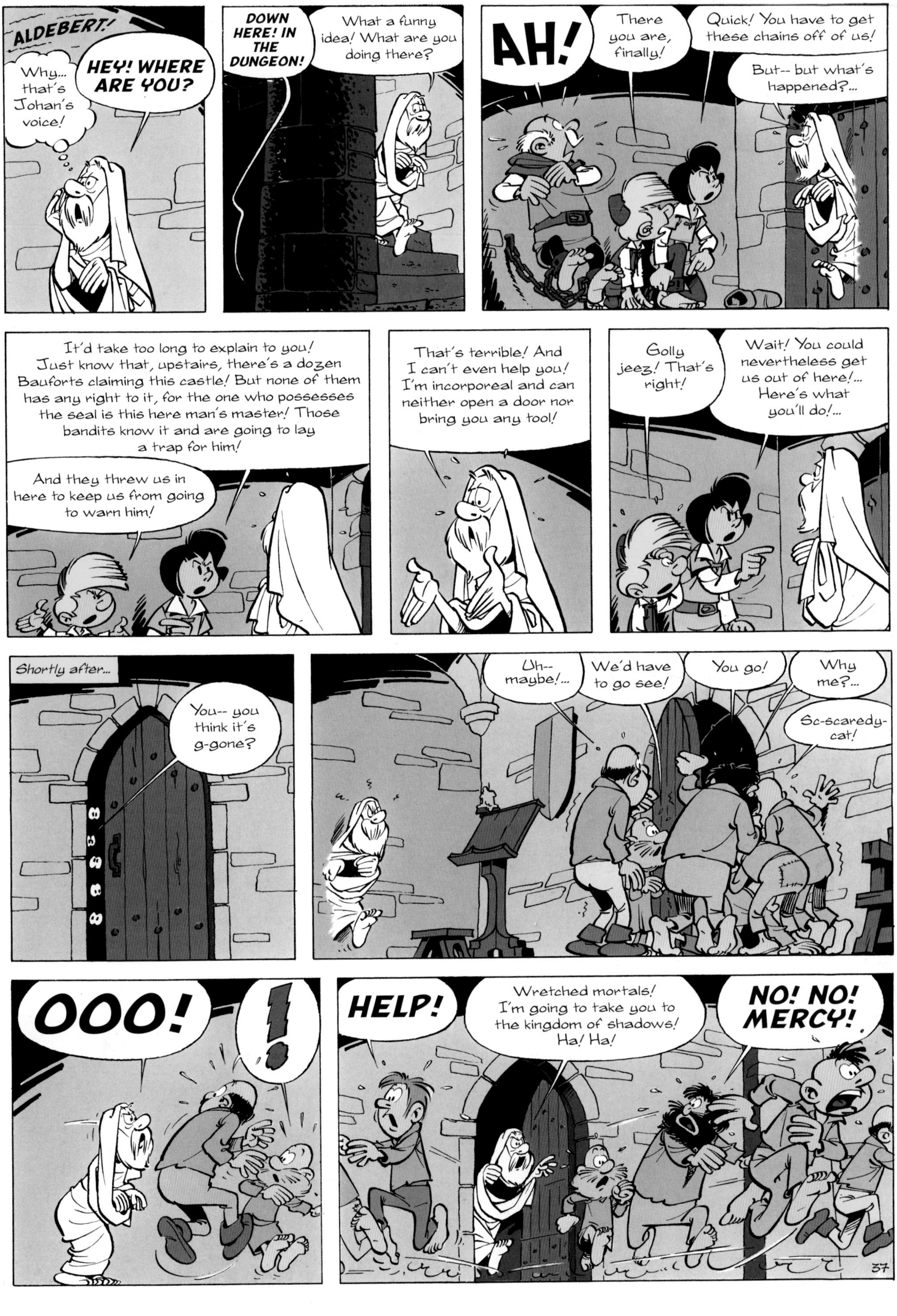
ALDEBERT!
Why... that's Johan's voice!
HEY! WHERE ARE YOU?
DOWN HERE! IN THE DUNGEON!
What a funny idea! What are you doing there?
AH!
There you are, finally!
Quick! You have to get these chains off of us!
But-- but what's happened?...
It'd take too long to explain to you! Just know that, upstairs, there's a dozen Bauforts claiming this castle! But none of them has any right to it, for the one who possesses the seal is this here man's master! Those bandits know it and are going to lay a trap for him!
And they threw us in here to keep us from going to warn him!
That's terrible! And I can't even help you! I'm incorporeal and can neither open a door nor bring you any tool!
Golly jeez! That's right!
Wait! You could nevertheless get us out of here!... Here's what you'll do!...
Shortly after...
You-- you think it's g-gone?
Uh-- maybe!...
We'd have to go see!
You go!
Why me?...
Sc-scaredy-cat!
OOO!
!
HELP!
Wretched mortals! I'm going to take you to the kingdom of shadows! Ha! Ha!
NO! NO! MERCY!
37

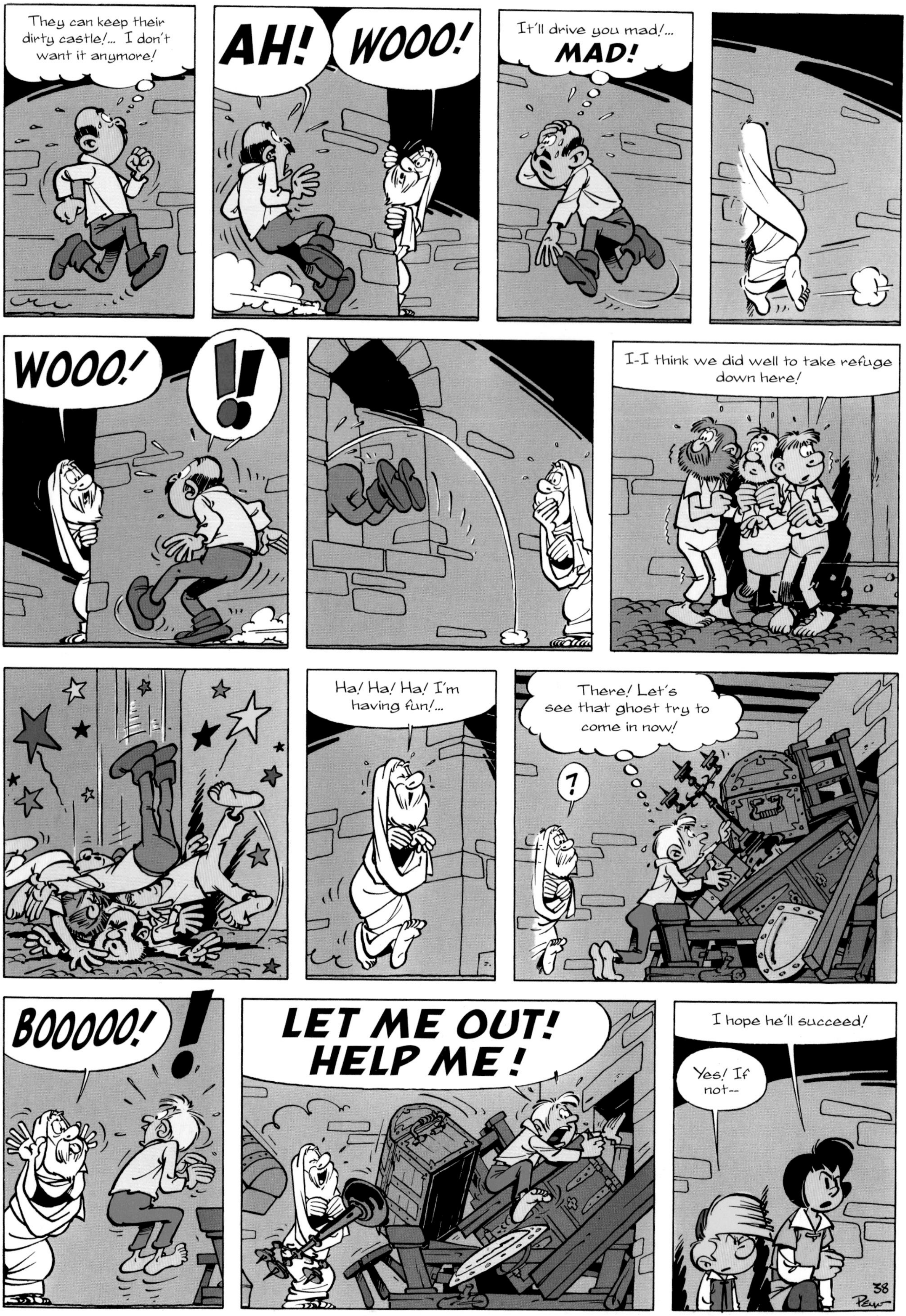

They can keep their dirty castle!... I don't want it anymore!
AH!
WOOO!
It'll drive you mad!... MAD!
WOOO!
!!
I-I think we did well to take refuge down here!
Ha! Ha! Ha! I'm having fun!...
There! Let's see that ghost try to come in now!
?
BOOOOO!
!
LET ME OUT! HELP ME!
I hope he'll succeed!
Yes! If not--
38

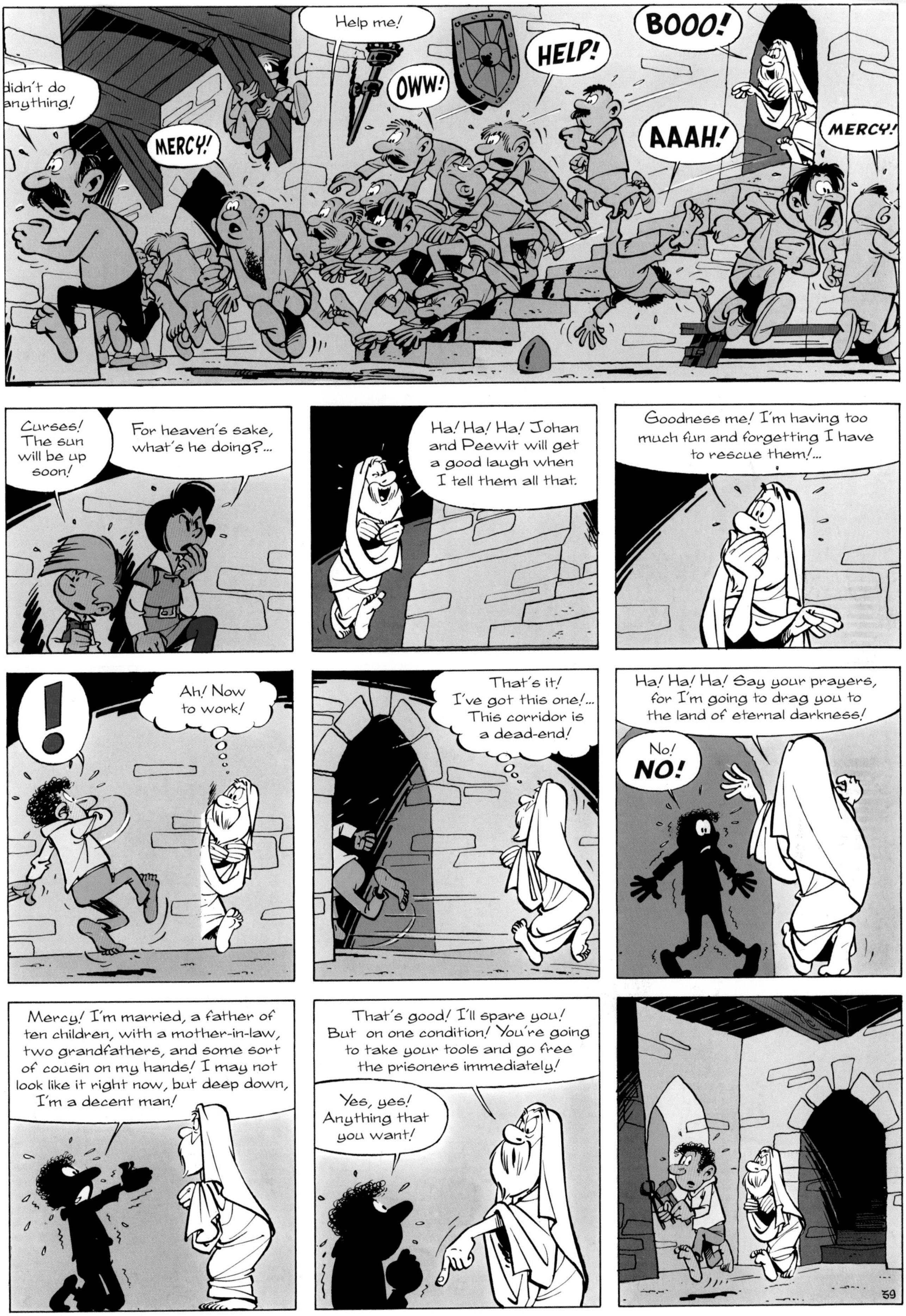

didn't do anything!
MERCY!
Help me!
OWW!
HELP!
BOOO!
AAAH!
MERCY!
Curses! The sun will be up soon!
For heaven's sake, what's he doing?...
Ha! Ha! Ha! Johan and Peewit will get a good laugh when I tell them all that.
Goodness me! I'm having too much fun and forgetting I have to rescue them!...
!
Ah! Now to work!
That's it! I've got this one!... This corridor is a dead-end!
Ha! Ha! Ha! Say your prayers, for I'm going to drag you to the land of eternal darkness!
No! NO!
Mercy! I'm married, a father of ten children, with a mother-in-law, two grandfathers, and some sort of cousin on my hands! I may not look like it right now, but deep down, I'm a decent man!
That's good! I'll spare you! But on one condition! You're going to take your tools and go free the prisoners immediately!
Yes, yes! Anything that you want!
39

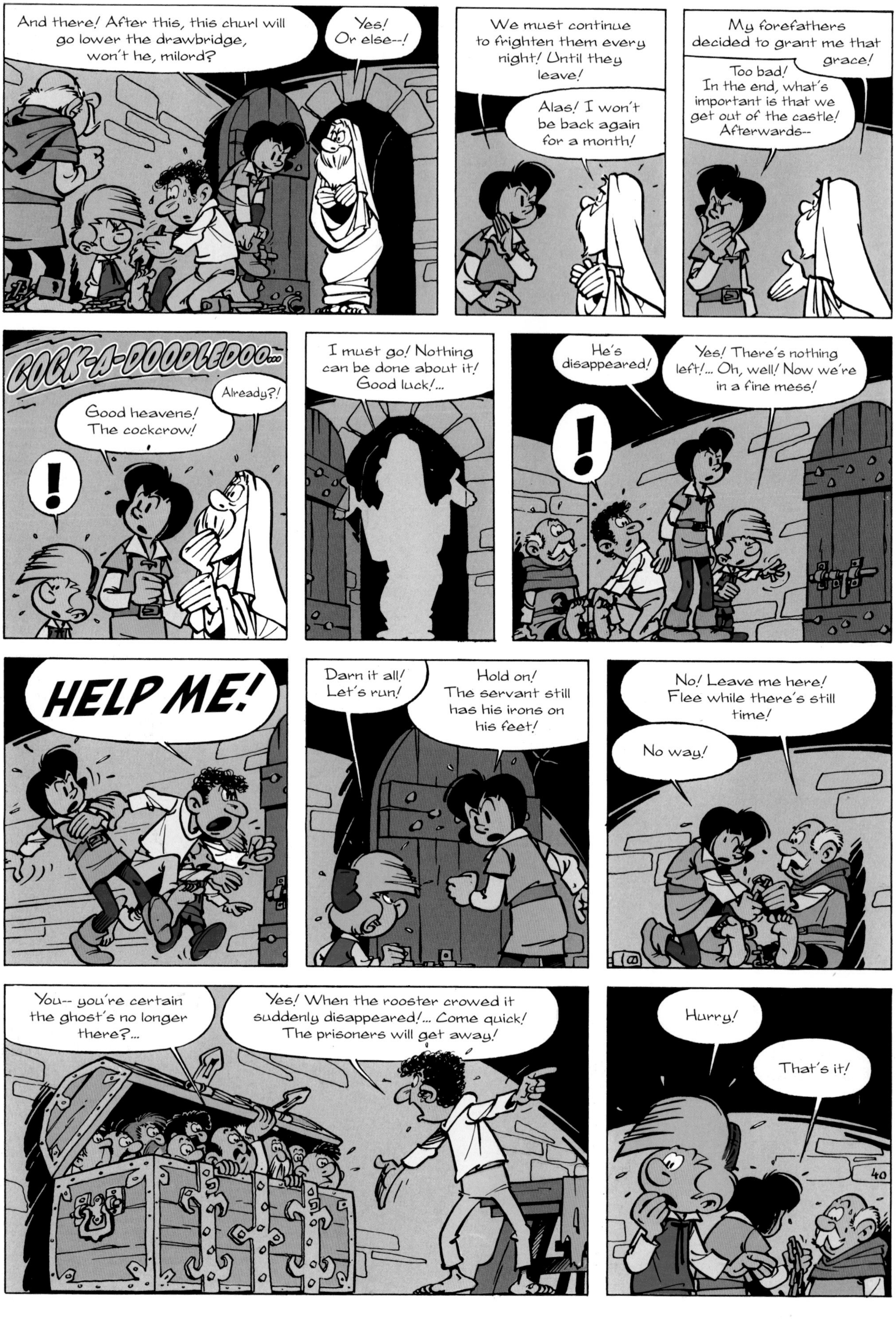
And there! After this, this churl will go lower the drawbridge, won't he, milord?
Yes! Or else--!
We must continue to frighten them every night! Until they leave!
Alas! I won't be back again for a month!
My forefathers decided to grant me that grace!
Too bad! In the end, what's important is that we get out of the castle! Afterwards--
COCK-A-DOODLEDOO...
Good heavens! The cockcrow!
Already?!
!
I must go! Nothing can be done about it! Good luck!...
He's disappeared!
Yes! There's nothing left!... Oh, well! Now we're in a fine mess!
!
HELP ME!
Darn it all! Let's run!
Hold on! The servant still has his irons on his feet!
No! Leave me here! Flee while there's still time!
No way!
You-- you're certain the ghost's no longer there?...
Yes! When the rooster crowed it suddenly disappeared!... Come quick! The prisoners will get away!
Hurry!
That's it!
40

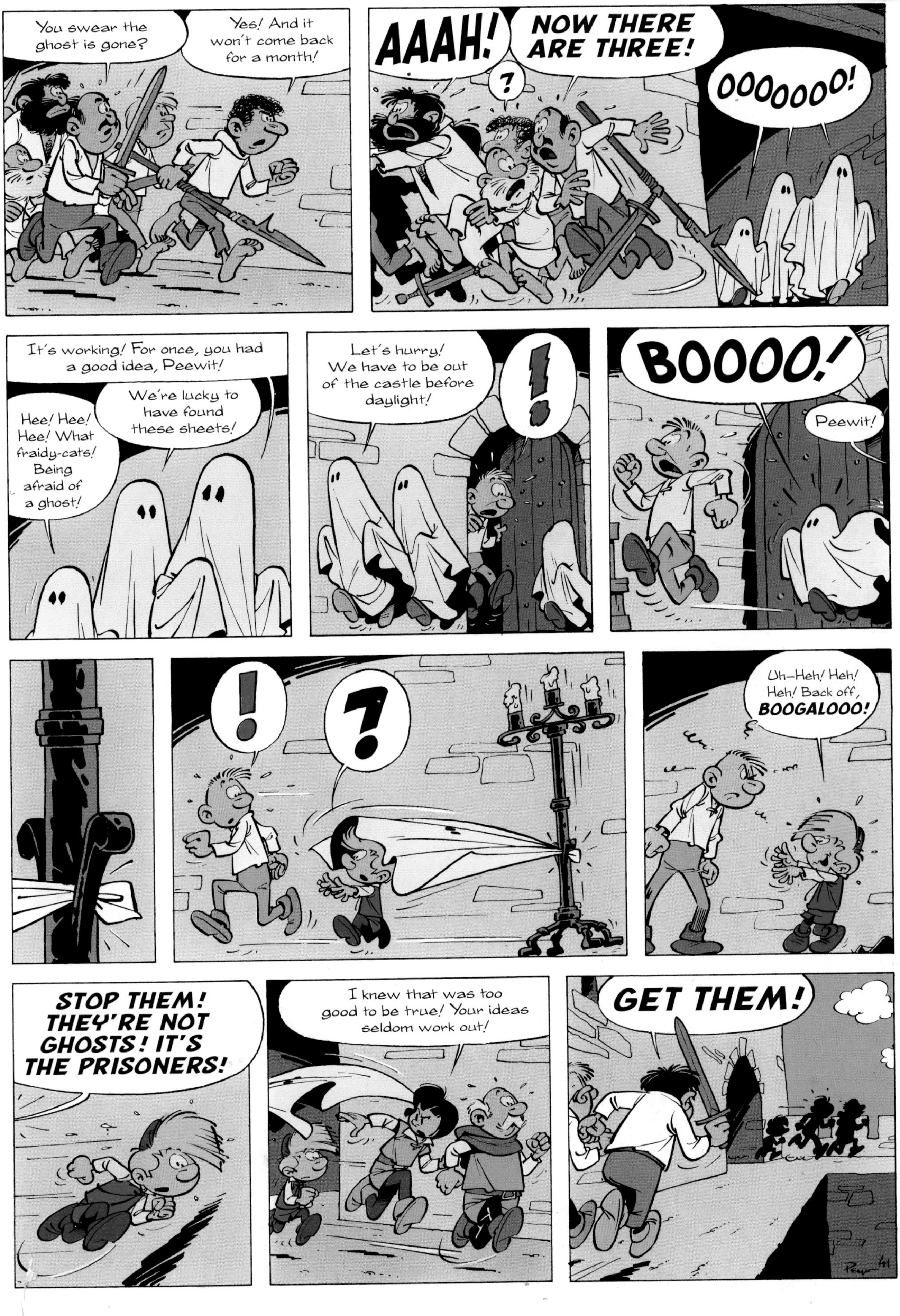
You swear the ghost is gone?
Yes! And it won't come back for a month!
AAAH!
?
NOW THERE ARE THREE!
OOOOOOO!
It's working! For once, you had a good idea, Peewit!
Hee! Hee! Hee! What fraidy-cats! Being afraid of a ghost!
We're lucky to have found these sheets!
Let's hurry! We have to be out of the castle before daylight!
!
BOOOO!
Peewit!
!
?
Uh-Heh! Heh! Heh! Back off, BOOGALOOO!
STOP THEM! THEY'RE NOT GHOSTS! IT'S THE PRISONERS!
I knew that was too good to be true! Your ideas seldom work out!
GET THEM!

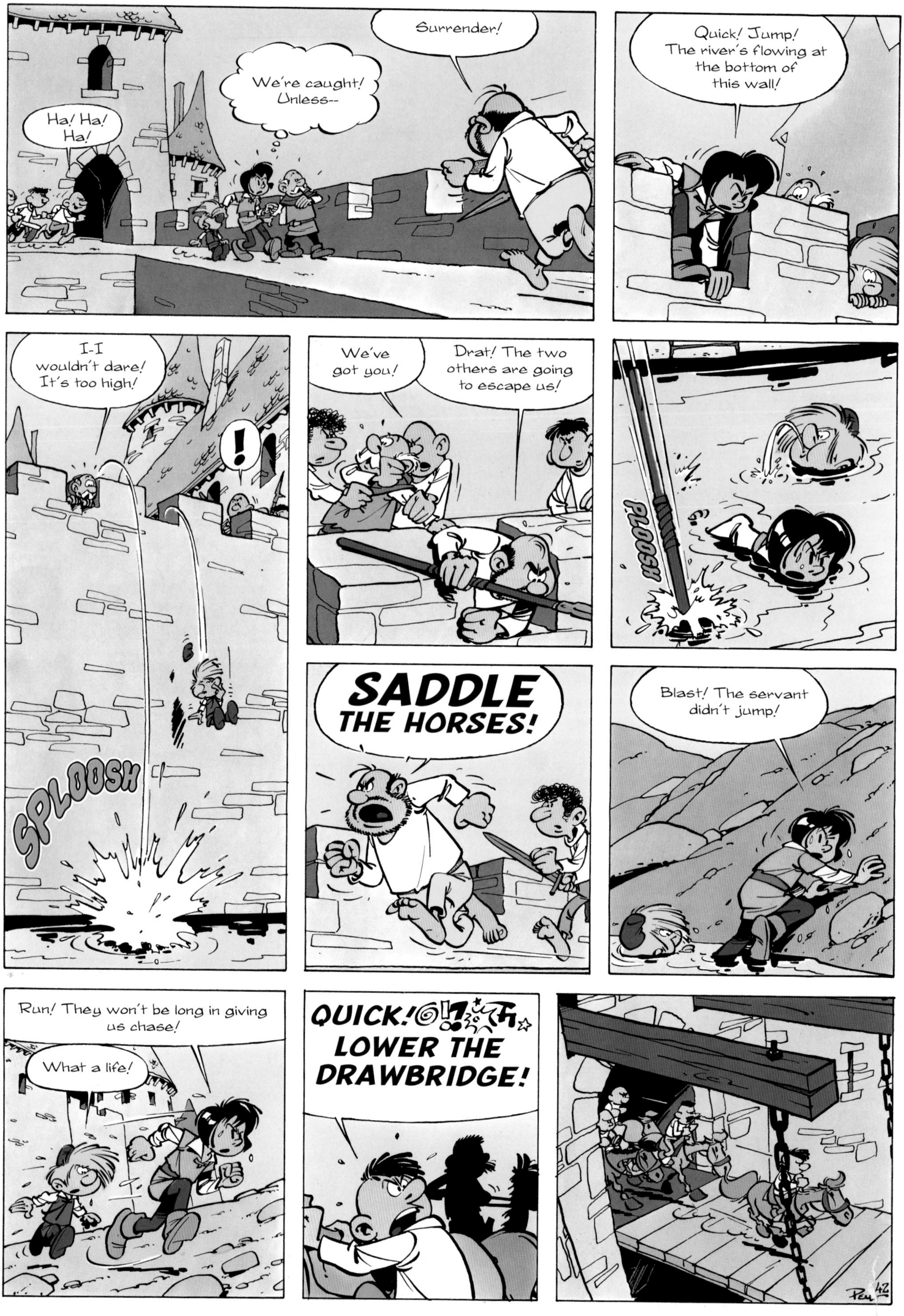
Ha! Ha! Ha!
We're caught! Unless--
Surrender!
Quick! Jump! The river's flowing at the bottom of this wall!
I-I wouldn't dare! It's too high!
!
SPLOOSH
We've got you!
Drat! The two others are going to escape us!
PLOOSH
SADDLE THE HORSES!
Blast! The servant didn't jump!
Run! They won't be long in giving us chase!
What a life!
QUICK! LOWER THE DRAWBRIDGE!

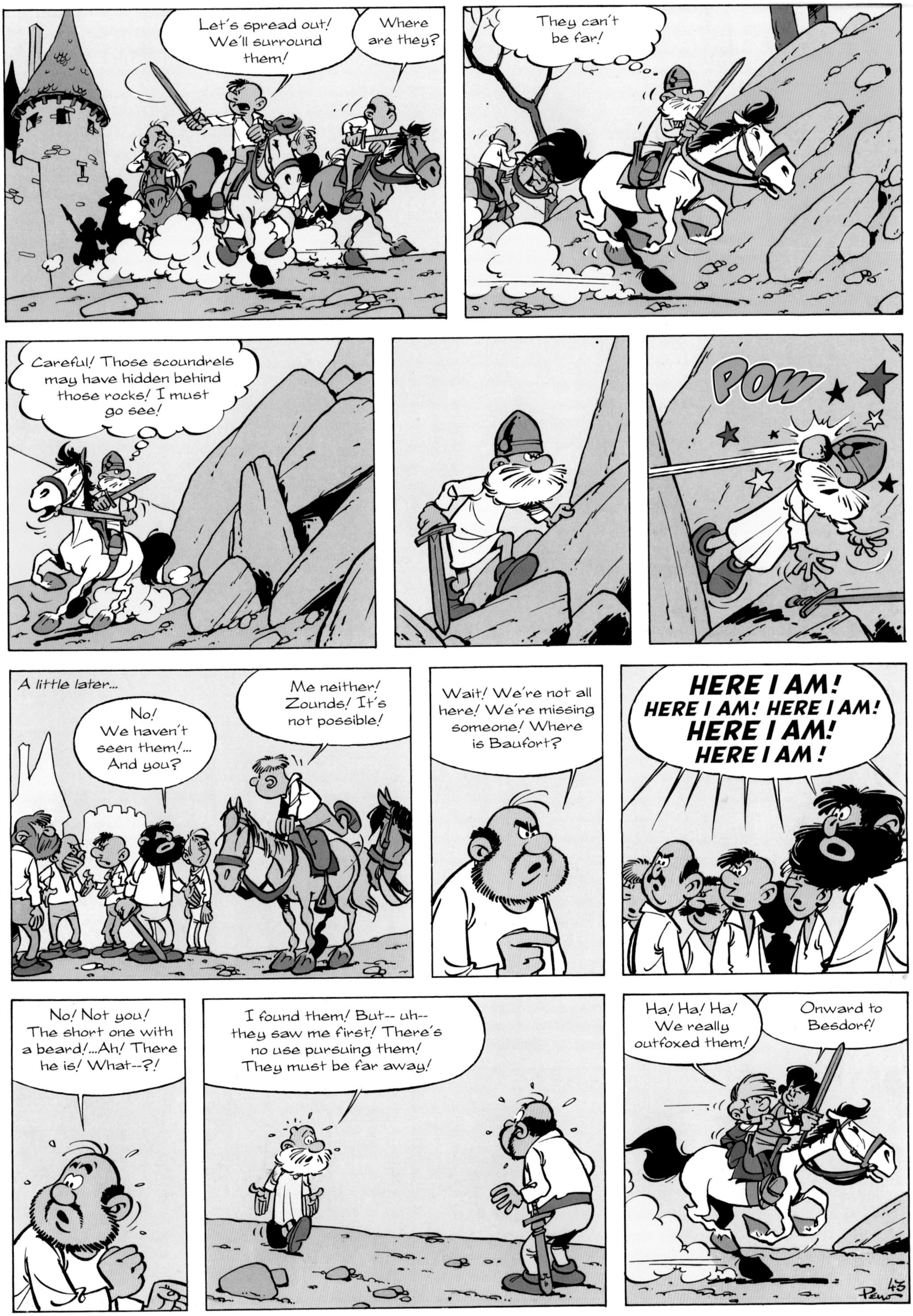
Let's spread out! We'll surround them!
Where are they?
They can't be far!
Careful! Those scoundrels may have hidden behind those rocks! I must go see!
POW
A little later...
No! We haven't seen them!... And you?
Me neither! Zounds! It's not possible!
Wait! We're not all here! We're missing someone! Where is Baufort?
HERE I AM!
HERE I AM! HERE I AM!
HERE I AM!
HERE I AM!
No! Not you! The short one with a beard!...Ah! There he is! What--?!
I found them! But-- uh-- they saw me first! There's no use pursuing them! They must be far away!
Ha! Ha! Ha! We really outfoxed them!
Onward to Besdorf!

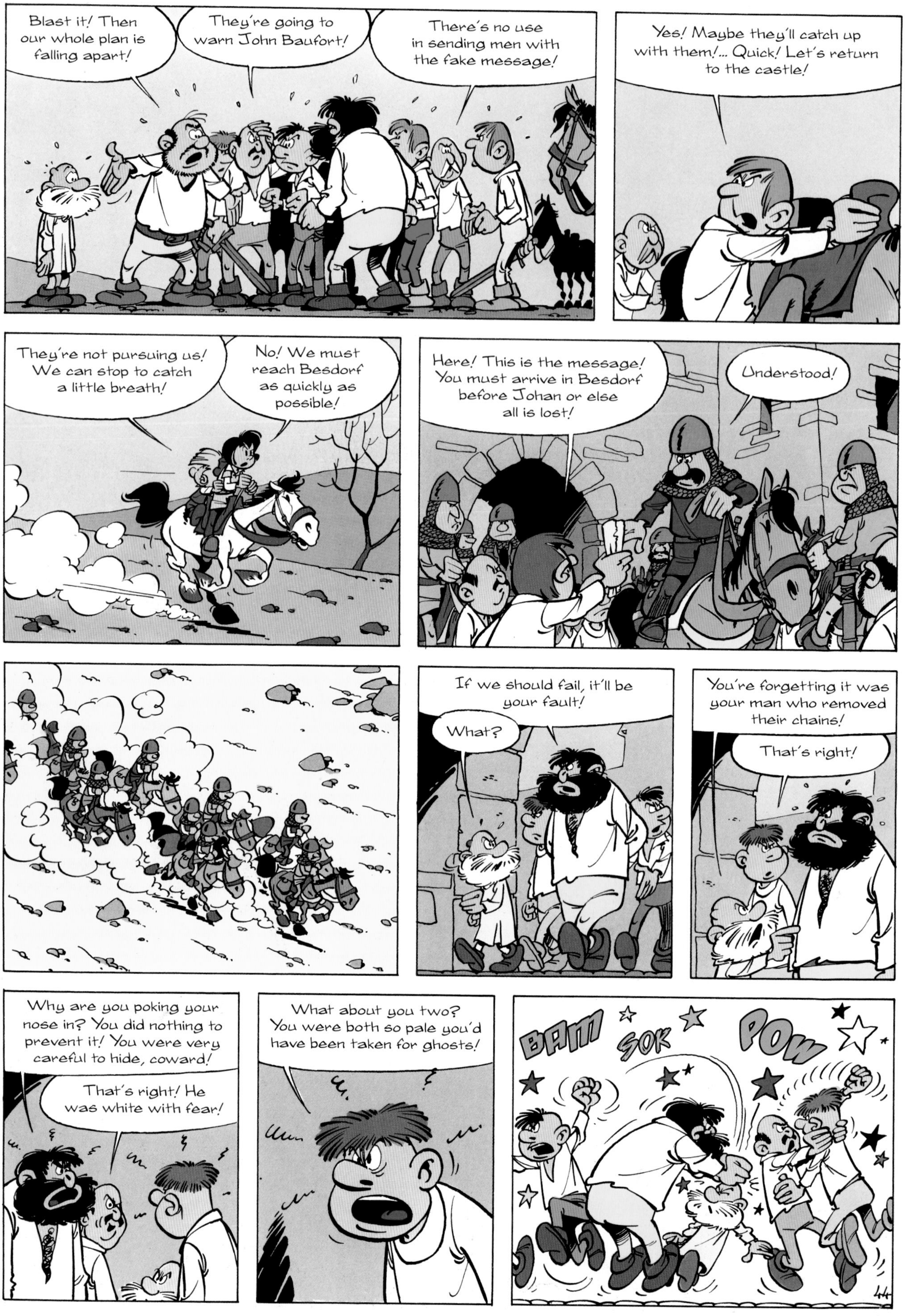
Blast it! Then our whole plan is falling apart!
They're going to warn John Baufort!
There's no use in sending men with the fake message!
Yes! Maybe they'll catch up with them!... Quick! Let's return to the castle!
They're not pursuing us! We can stop to catch a little breath!
No! We must reach Besdorf as quickly as possible!
Here! This is the message! You must arrive in Besdorf before Johan or else all is lost!
Understood!
If we should fail, it'll be your fault!
What?
You're forgetting it was your man who removed their chains!
That's right!
Why are you poking your nose in? You did nothing to prevent it! You were very careful to hide, coward!
That's right! He was white with fear!
What about you two? You were both so pale you'd have been taken for ghosts!
BAM
SOK
POW

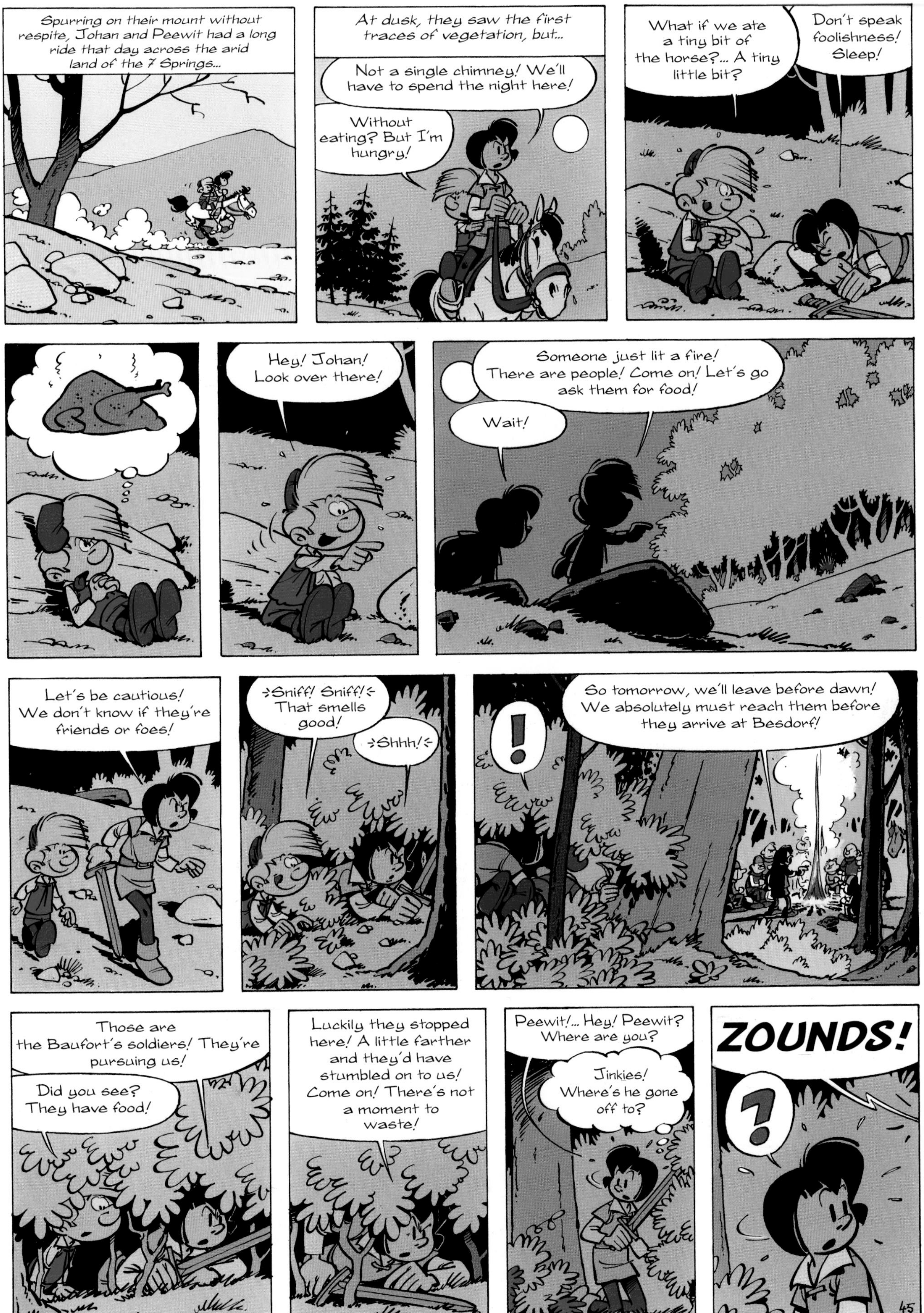
Spurring on their mount without respite, Johan and Peewit had a long ride that day across the arid land of the 7 Springs...
At dusk, they saw the first traces of vegetation, but...
Not a single chimney! We'll have to spend the night here!
Without eating? But I'm hungry!
What if we ate a tiny bit of the horse?... A tiny little bit?
Don't speak foolishness! Sleep!
Hey! Johan! Look over there!
Someone just lit a fire! There are people! Come on! Let's go ask them for food!
Wait!
Let's be cautious! We don't know if they're friends or foes!
Sniff! Sniff! That smells good!
Shhh!
!
So tomorrow, we'll leave before dawn! We absolutely must reach them before they arrive at Besdorf!
Those are the Baufort's soldiers! They're pursuing us!
Did you see? They have food!
Luckily they stopped here! A little farther and they'd have stumbled on to us! Come on! There's not a moment to waste!
Peewit!... Hey! Peewit? Where are you?
Jinkies! Where's he gone off to?
ZOUNDS!
?
45

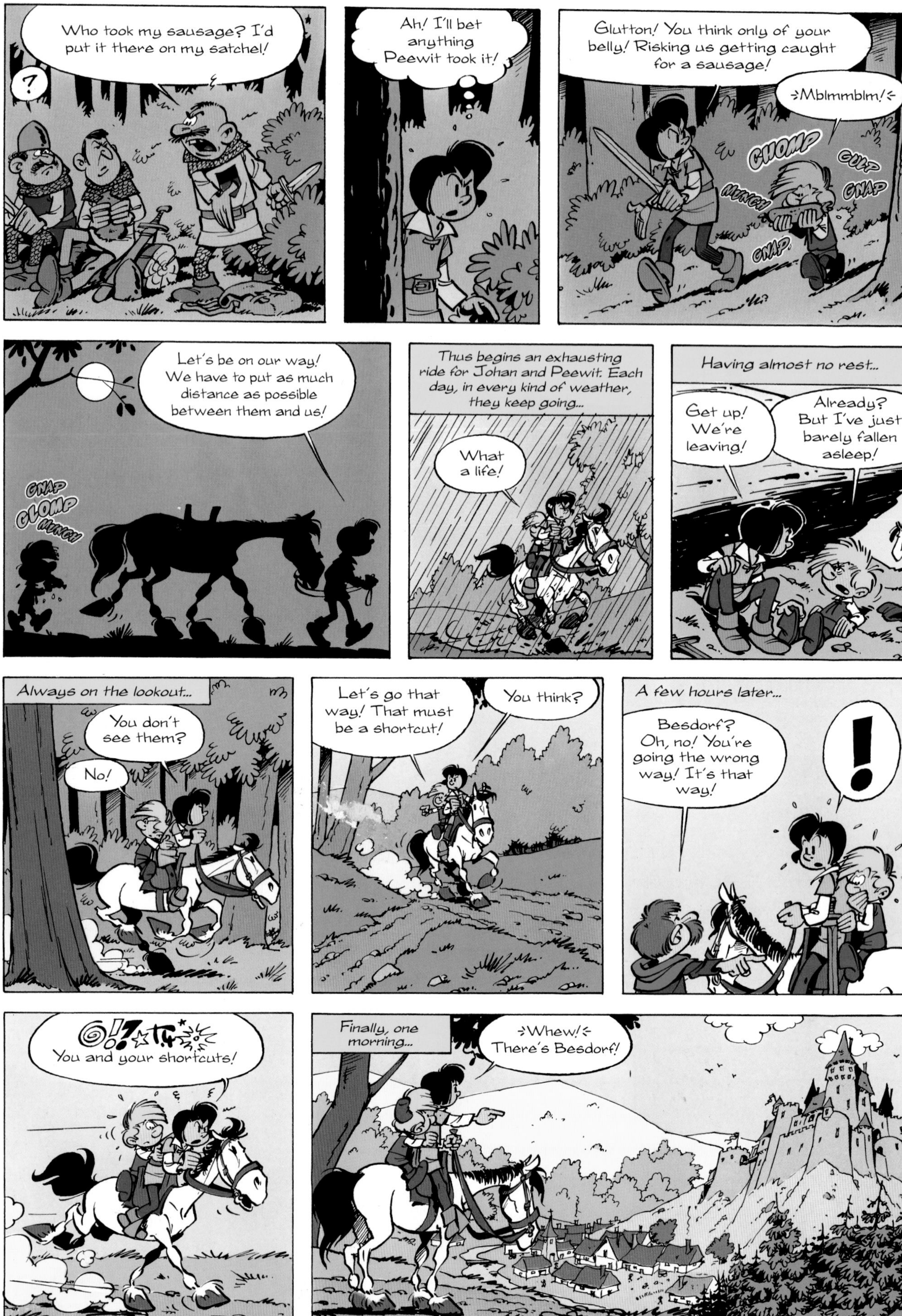
Who took my sausage? I'd put it there on my satchel!
?
Ah! I'll bet anything Peewit took it!
Glutton! You think only of your belly! Risking us getting caught for a sausage!
Mblmmblm!
CHOMP
GULP
MUNCH
GNAP
GNAP
Let's be on our way! We have to put as much distance as possible between them and us!
GNAP
GLOMP
MUNCH
Thus begins an exhausting ride for Johan and Peewit. Each day, in every kind of weather, they keep going...
What a life!
Having almost no rest...
Get up! We're leaving!
Already? But I've just barely fallen asleep!
Always on the lookout...
You don't see them?
No!
Let's go that way! That must be a shortcut!
You think?
A few hours later...
Besdorf? Oh, no! You're going the wrong way! It's that way!
!
You and your shortcuts!
Finally, one morning...
Whew! There's Besdorf!

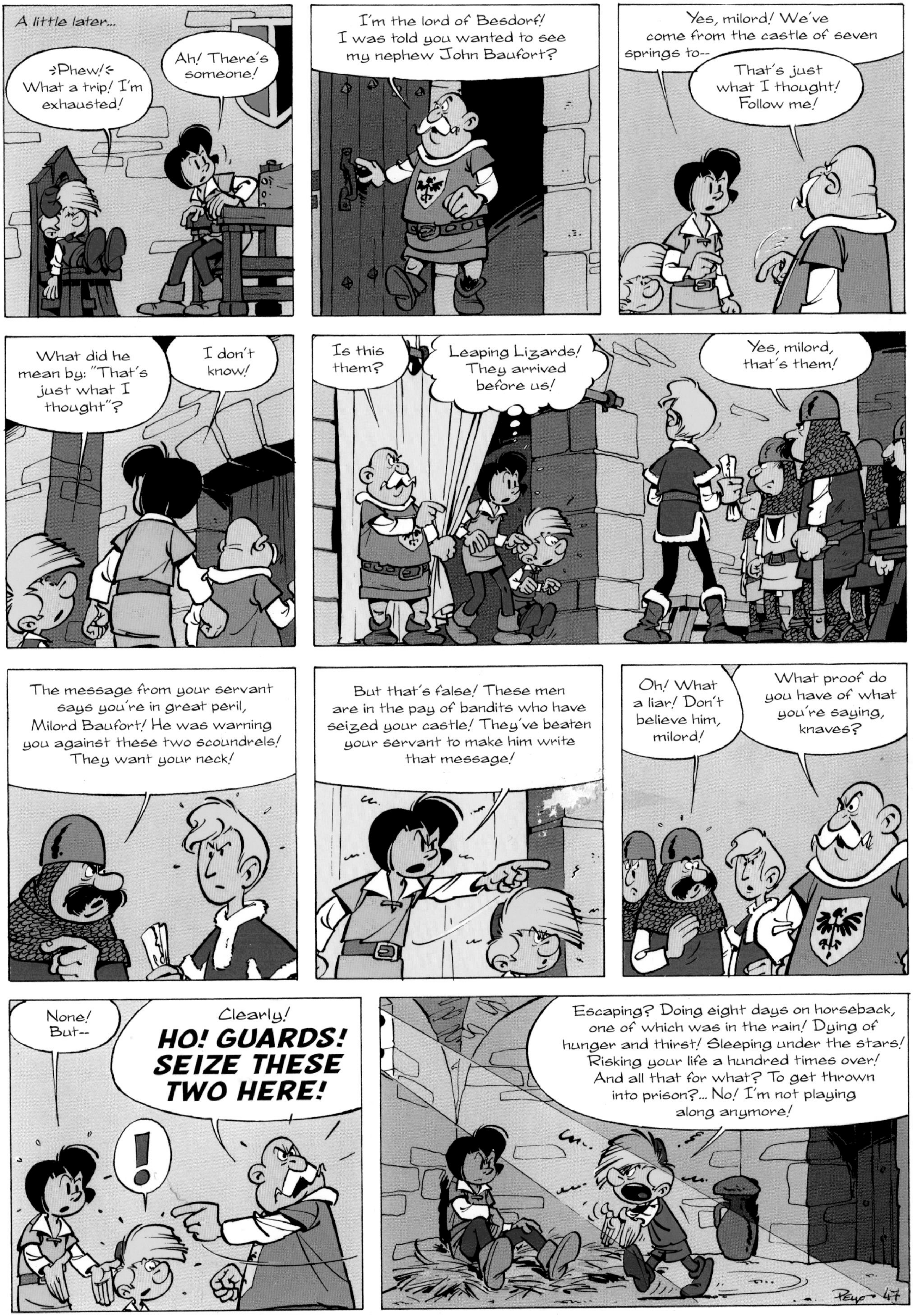
A little later...
Phew! What a trip! I'm exhausted!
Ah! There's someone!
I'm the lord of Besdorf! I was told you wanted to see my nephew John Baufort?
Yes, milord! We've come from the castle of seven springs to--
That's just what I thought! Follow me!
What did he mean by: "That's just what I thought"?
I don't know!
Is this them?
Leaping Lizards! They arrived before us!
Yes, milord, that's them!
The message from your servant says you're in great peril, Milord Baufort! He was warning you against these two scoundrels! They want your neck!
But that's false! These men are in the pay of bandits who have seized your castle! They've beaten your servant to make him write that message!
Oh! What a liar! Don't believe him, milord!
What proof do you have of what you're saying, knaves?
None! But--
Clearly! HO! GUARDS! SEIZE THESE TWO HERE!
!
Escaping? Doing eight days on horseback, one of which was in the rain! Dying of hunger and thirst! Sleeping under the stars! Risking your life a hundred times over! And all that for what? To get thrown into prison?... No! I'm not playing along anymore!
Peyo 47

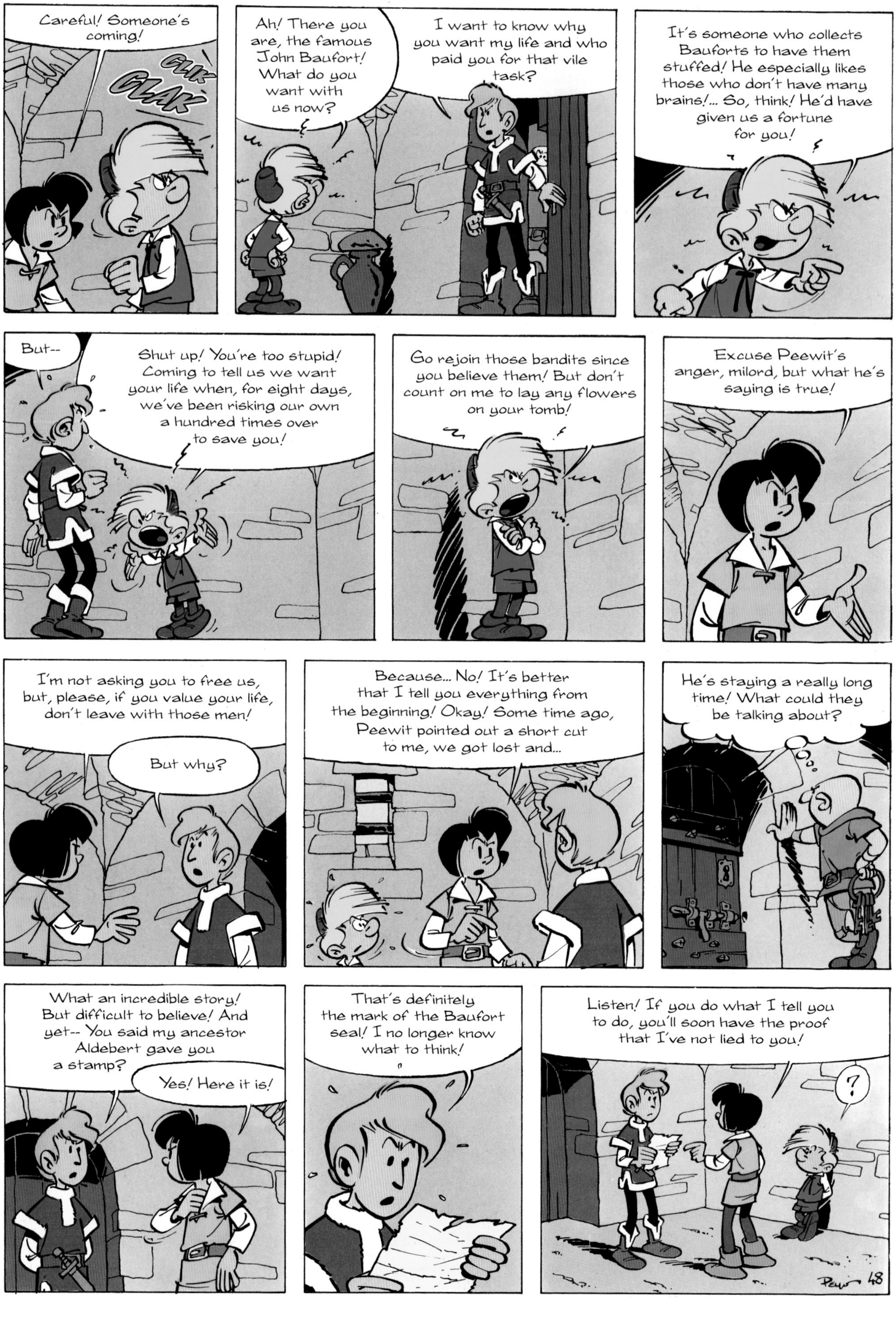
Careful! Someone's coming!
CLIK CLAK
Ah! There you are, the famous John Baufort! What do you want with us now?
I want to know why you want my life and who paid you for that vile task?
It's someone who collects Bauforts to have them stuffed! He especially likes those who don't have many brains!... So, think! He'd have given us a fortune for you!
But--
Shut up! You're too stupid! Coming to tell us we want your life when, for eight days, we've been risking our own a hundred times over to save you!
Go rejoin those bandits since you believe them! But don't count on me to lay any flowers on your tomb!
Excuse Peewit's anger, milord, but what he's saying is true!
I'm not asking you to free us, but, please, if you value your life, don't leave with those men!
But why?
Because... No! It's better that I tell you everything from the beginning! Okay! Some time ago, Peewit pointed out a short cut to me, we got lost and...
He's staying a really long time! What could they be talking about?
What an incredible story! But difficult to believe! And yet-- You said my ancestor Aldebert gave you a stamp?
Yes! Here it is!
That's definitely the mark of the Baufort seal! I no longer know what to think!
Listen! If you do what I tell you to do, you'll soon have the proof that I've not lied to you!
?
48

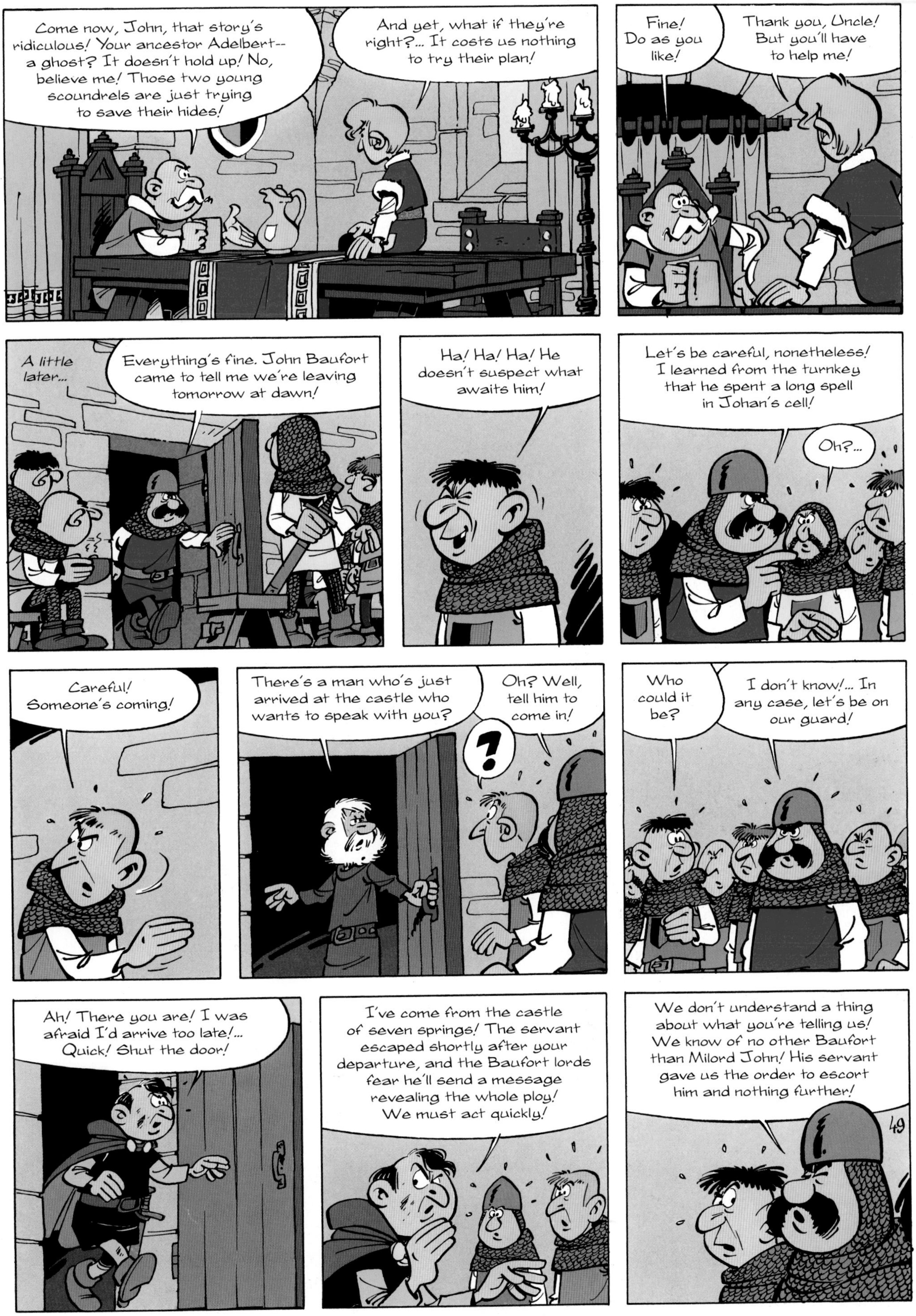

Come now, John, that story's ridiculous! Your ancestor Adelbert-- a ghost? It doesn't hold up! No, believe me! Those two young scoundrels are just trying to save their hides!
And yet, what if they're right?... It costs us nothing to try their plan!
Fine! Do as you like!
Thank you, Uncle! But you'll have to help me!
A little later...
Everything's fine. John Baufort came to tell me we're leaving tomorrow at dawn!
Ha! Ha! Ha! He doesn't suspect what awaits him!
Let's be careful, nonetheless! I learned from the turnkey that he spent a long spell in Johan's cell!
Oh?...
Careful! Someone's coming!
There's a man who's just arrived at the castle who wants to speak with you?
Oh? Well, tell him to come in!
?
Who could it be?
I don't know!... In any case, let's be on our guard!
Ah! There you are! I was afraid I'd arrive too late!... Quick! Shut the door!
I've come from the castle of seven springs! The servant escaped shortly after your departure, and the Baufort lords fear he'll send a message revealing the whole ploy! We must act quickly!
We don't understand a thing about what you're telling us! We know of no other Baufort than Milord John! His servant gave us the order to escort him and nothing further!
49

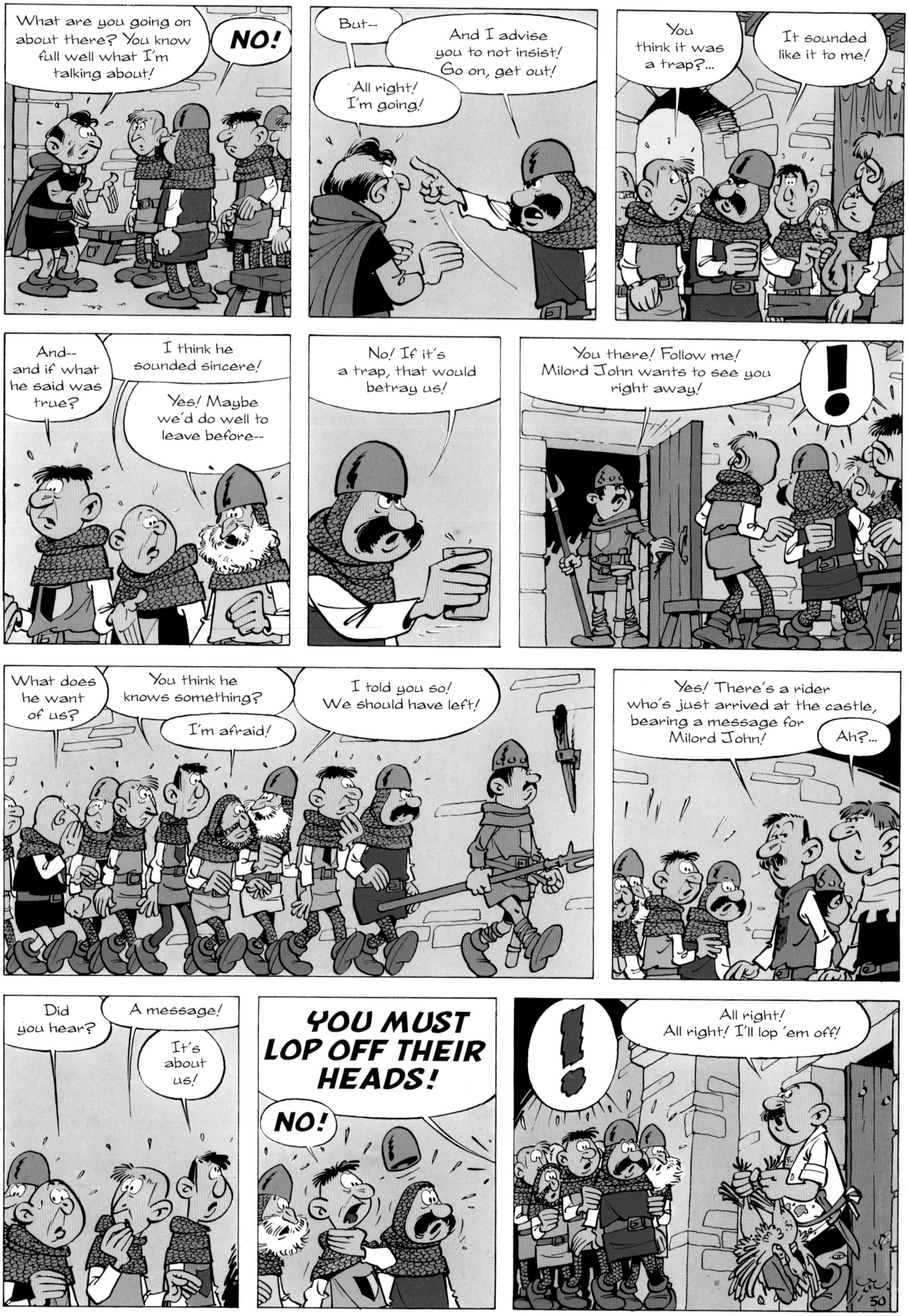
What are you going on about there? You know full well what I'm talking about!
NO!
But--
And I advise you to not insist! Go on, get out!
All right! I'm going!
You think it was a trap?...
It sounded like it to me!
And-- and if what he said was true?
I think he sounded sincere!
Yes! Maybe we'd do well to leave before--
No! If it's a trap, that would betray us!
You there! Follow me! Milord John wants to see you right away!
!
What does he want of us?
You think he knows something?
I'm afraid!
I told you so! We should have left!
Yes! There's a rider who's just arrived at the castle, bearing a message for Milord John!
Ah?...
Did you hear?
A message!
It's about us!
YOU MUST LOP OFF THEIR HEADS!
NO!
!
All right! All right! I'll lop 'em off!
50

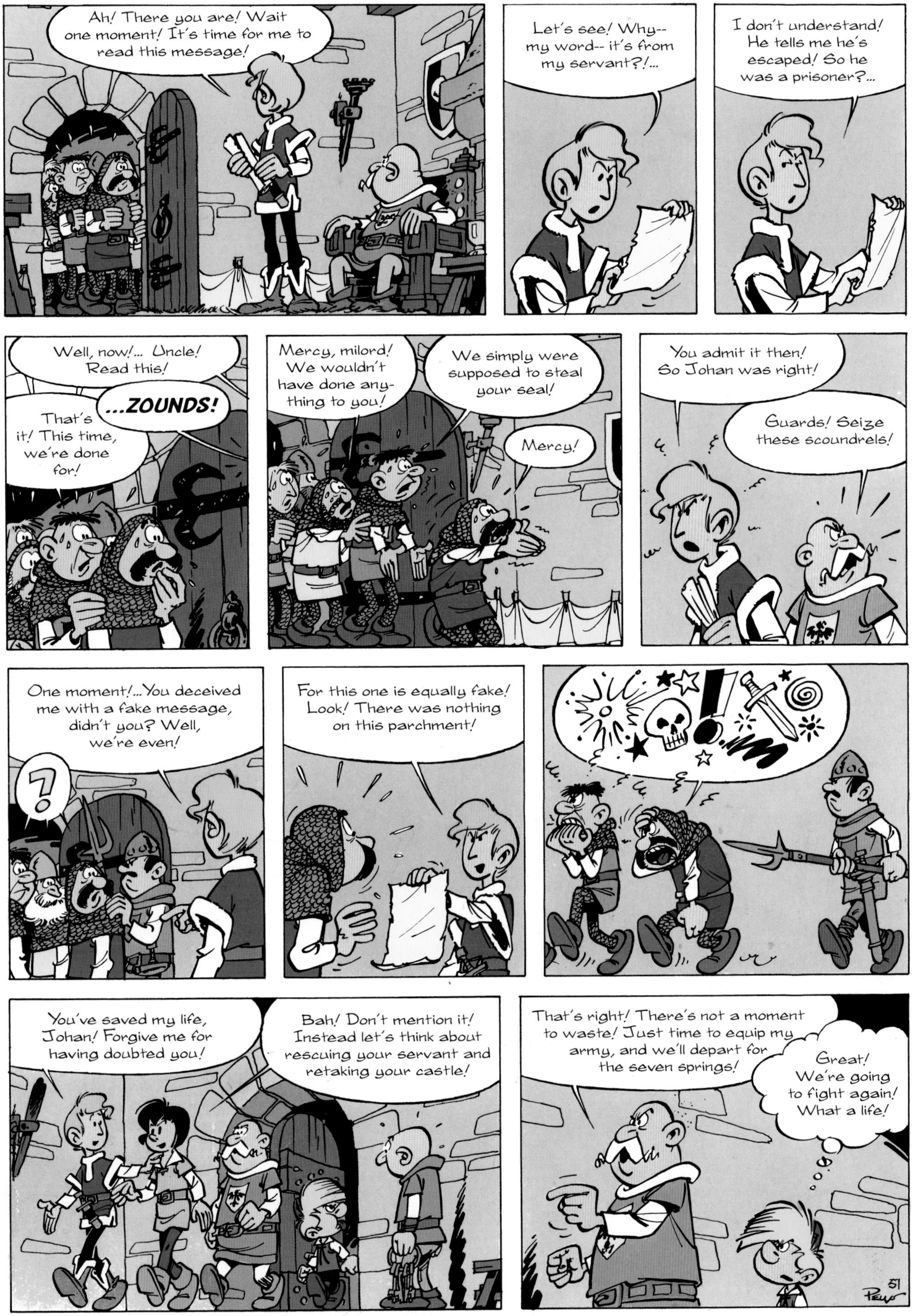

Ah! There you are! Wait one moment! It's time for me to read this message!
Let's see! Why-- my word-- it's from my servant?!...
I don't understand! He tells me he's escaped! So he was a prisoner?...
Well, now!... Uncle! Read this!
...ZOUNDS!
That's it! This time, we're done for!
Mercy, milord! We wouldn't have done anything to you!
We simply were supposed to steal your seal!
Mercy!
You admit it then! So Johan was right!
Guards! Seize these scoundrels!
One moment!...You deceived me with a fake message, didn't you? Well, we're even!
?
For this one is equally fake! Look! There was nothing on this parchment!
You've saved my life, Johan! Forgive me for having doubted you!
Bah! Don't mention it! Instead let's think about rescuing your servant and retaking your castle!
That's right! There's not a moment to waste! Just time to equip my army, and we'll depart for the seven springs!
Great! We're going to fight again! What a life!
51
Peyo

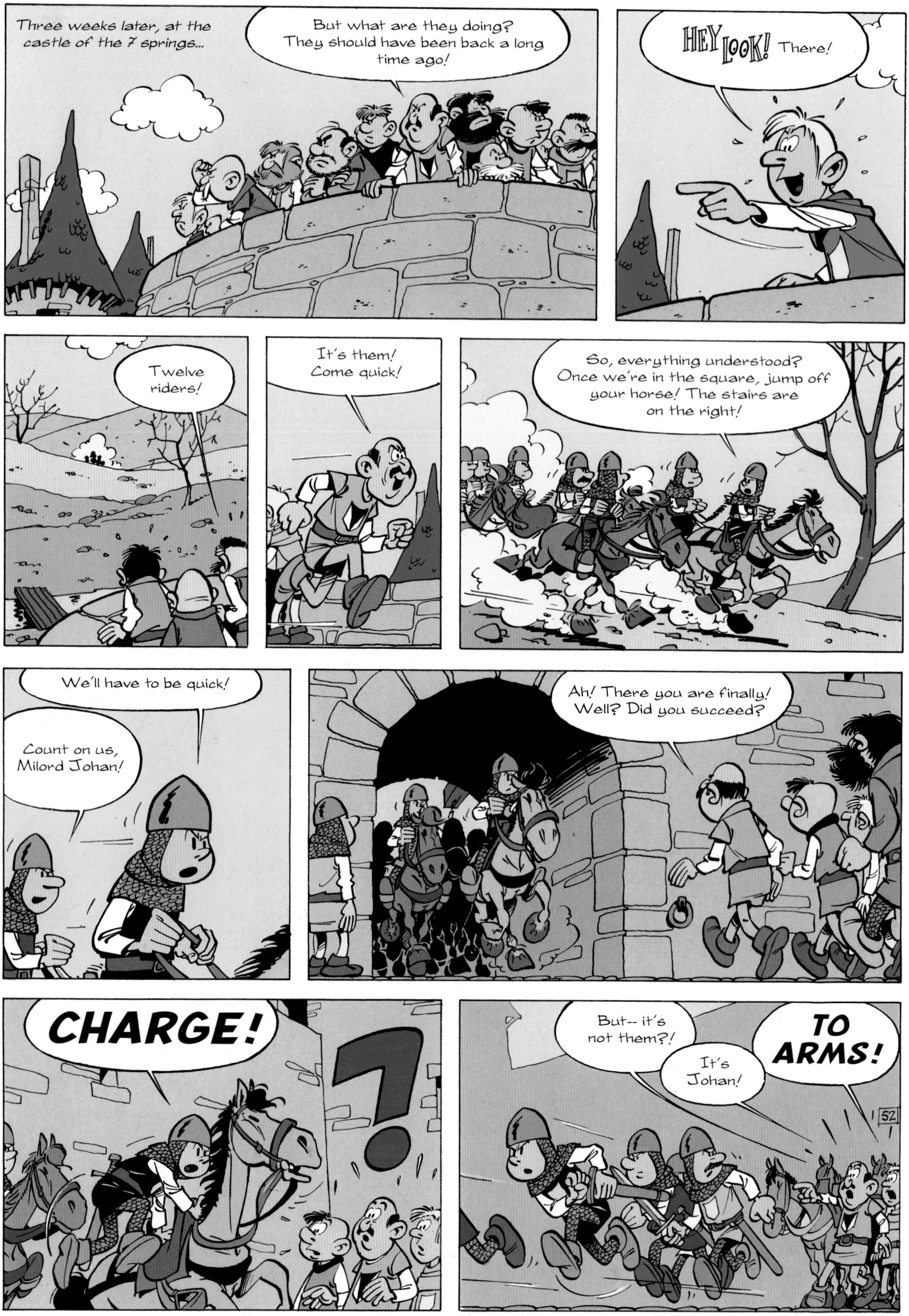
Three weeks later, at the castle of the 7 springs...
But what are they doing? They should have been back a long time ago!
HEY LOOK! There!
Twelve riders!
It's them! Come quick!
So, everything understood? Once we're in the square, jump off your horse! The stairs are on the right!
We'll have to be quick!
Count on us, Milord Johan!
Ah! There you are finally! Well? Did you succeed?
CHARGE!
?
But-- it's not them?!
It's Johan!
TO ARMS!
52

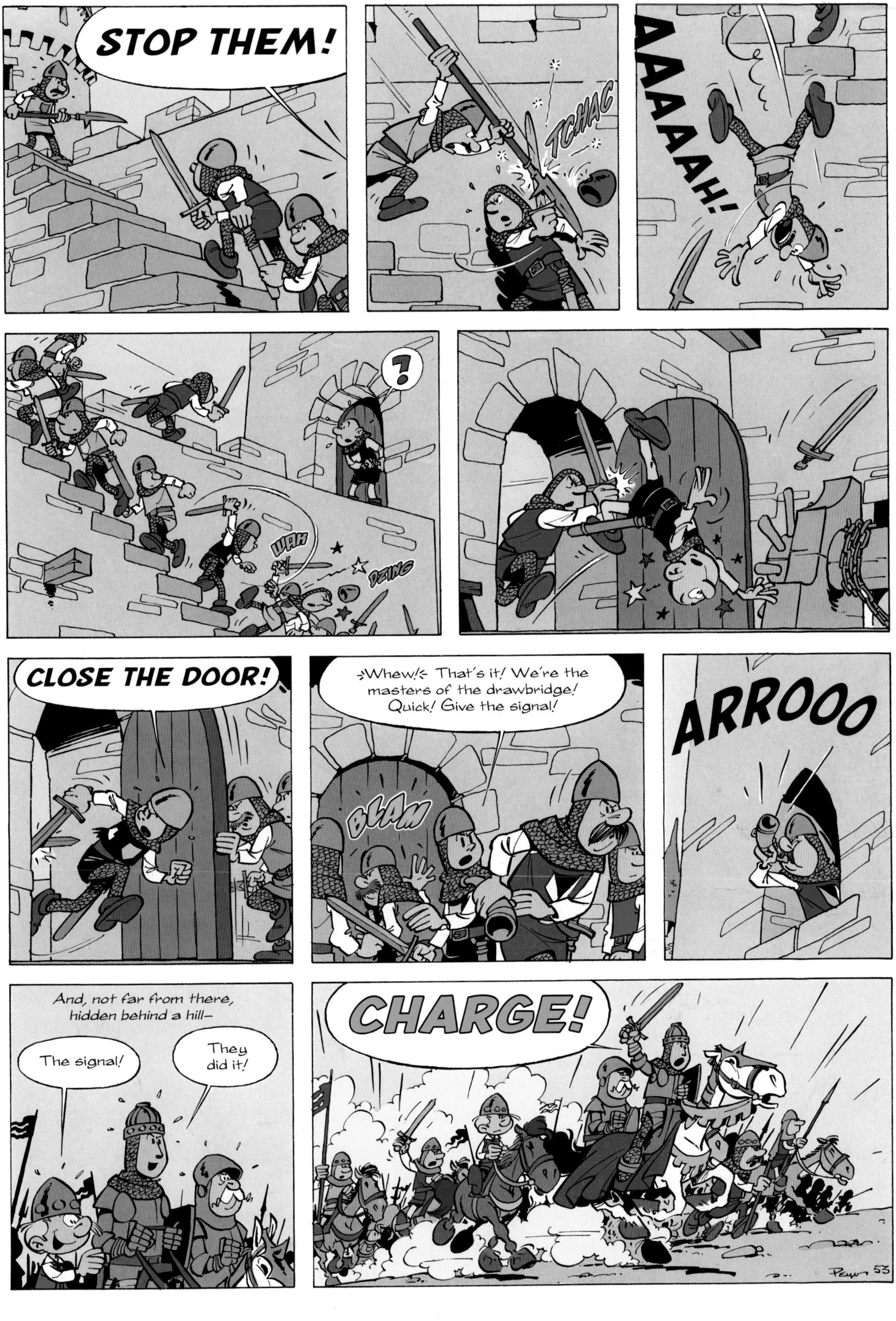
STOP THEM!
TCHAC
AAAAAH!
?
WAH
DZING
CLOSE THE DOOR!
Whew! That's it! We're the masters of the drawbridge! Quick! Give the signal!
BLAM
ARROOO
And, not far from there, hidden behind a hill–
The signal!
They did it!
CHARGE!
53

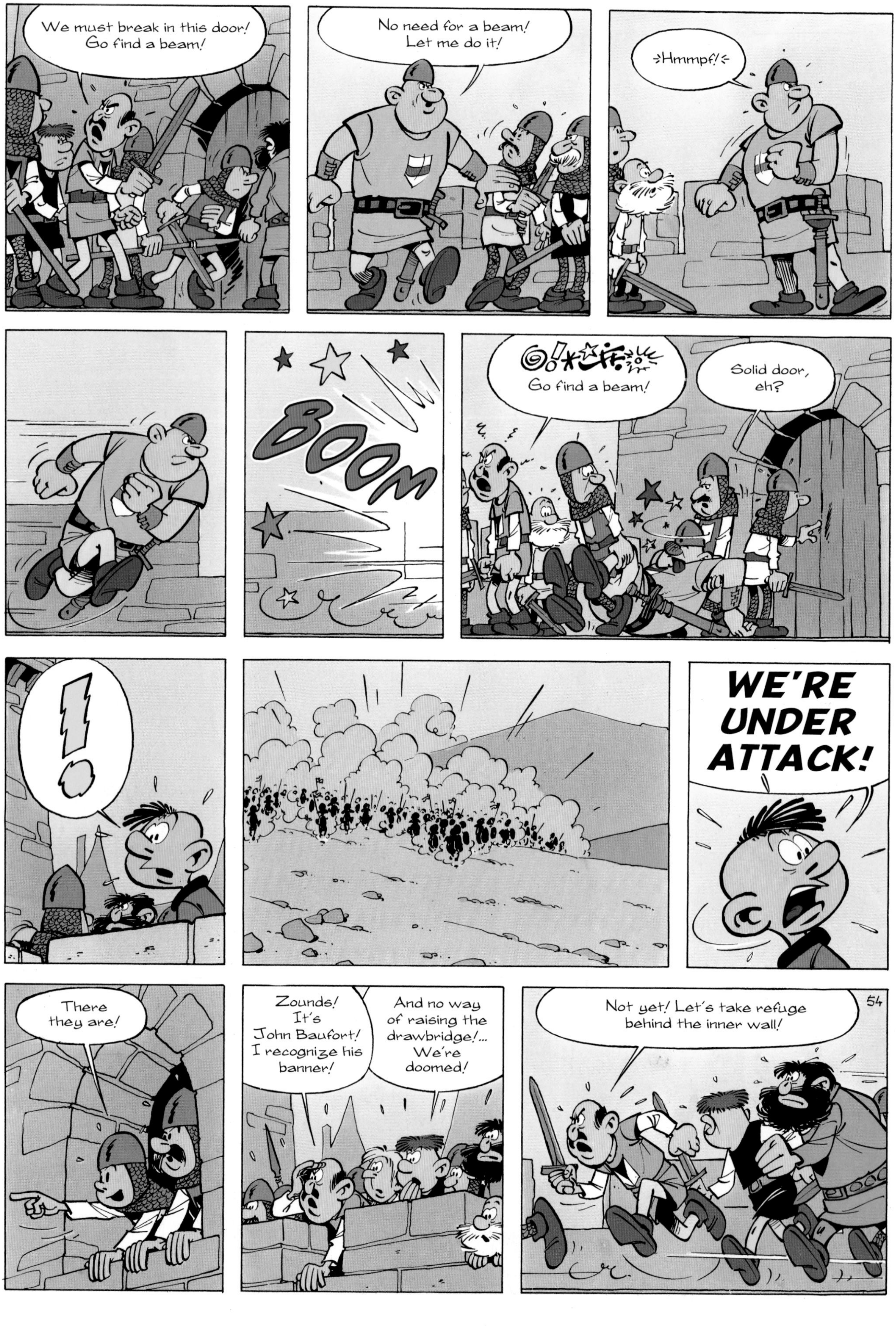
We must break in this door! Go find a beam!
No need for a beam! Let me do it!
Hmmpf!
BOOM
Go find a beam!
Solid door, eh?
WE'RE UNDER ATTACK!
There they are!
Zounds! It's John Baufort! I recognize his banner!
And no way of raising the drawbridge!... We're doomed!
Not yet! Let's take refuge behind the inner wall!
54

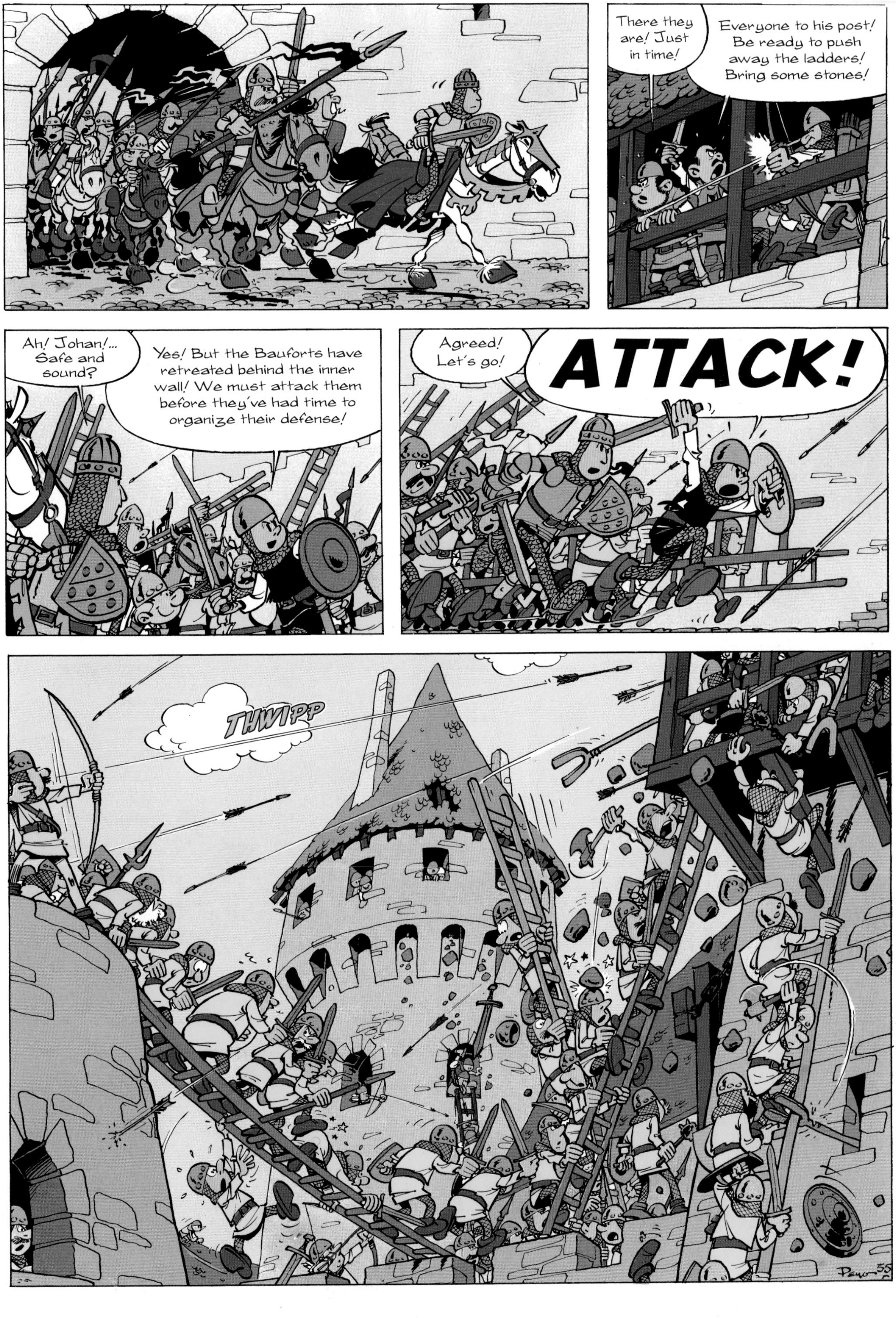

There they are! Just in time!
Everyone to his post! Be ready to push away the ladders! Bring some stones!
Ah! Johan!... Safe and sound?
Yes! But the Bauforts have retreated behind the inner wall! We must attack them before they've had time to organize their defense!
Agreed! Let's go!
ATTACK!
THWIPP

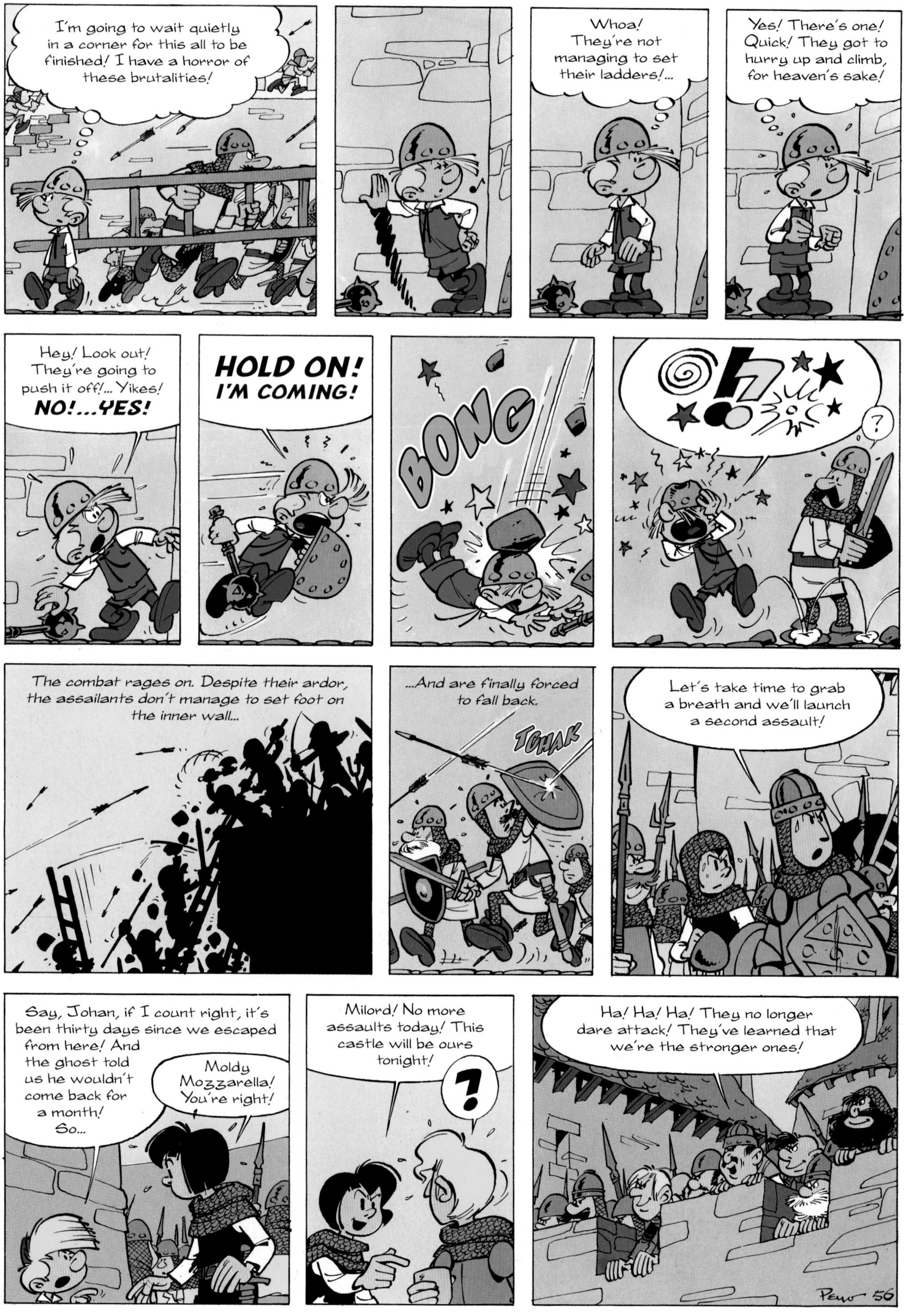
I'm going to wait quietly in a corner for this all to be finished! I have a horror of these brutalities!
Whoa! They're not managing to set their ladders!...
Yes! There's one! Quick! They got to hurry up and climb, for heaven's sake!
Hey! Look out! They're going to push it off!... Yikes! NO!...YES!
HOLD ON! I'M COMING!
BONG
?
The combat rages on. Despite their ardor, the assailants don't manage to set foot on the inner wall...
...And are finally forced to fall back.
TCHAK
Let's take time to grab a breath and we'll launch a second assault!
Say, Johan, if I count right, it's been thirty days since we escaped from here! And the ghost told us he wouldn't come back for a month! So...
Moldy Mozzarella! You're right!
Milord! No more assaults today! This castle will be ours tonight!
?
Ha! Ha! Ha! They no longer dare attack! They've learned that we're the stronger ones!
Peyo 56

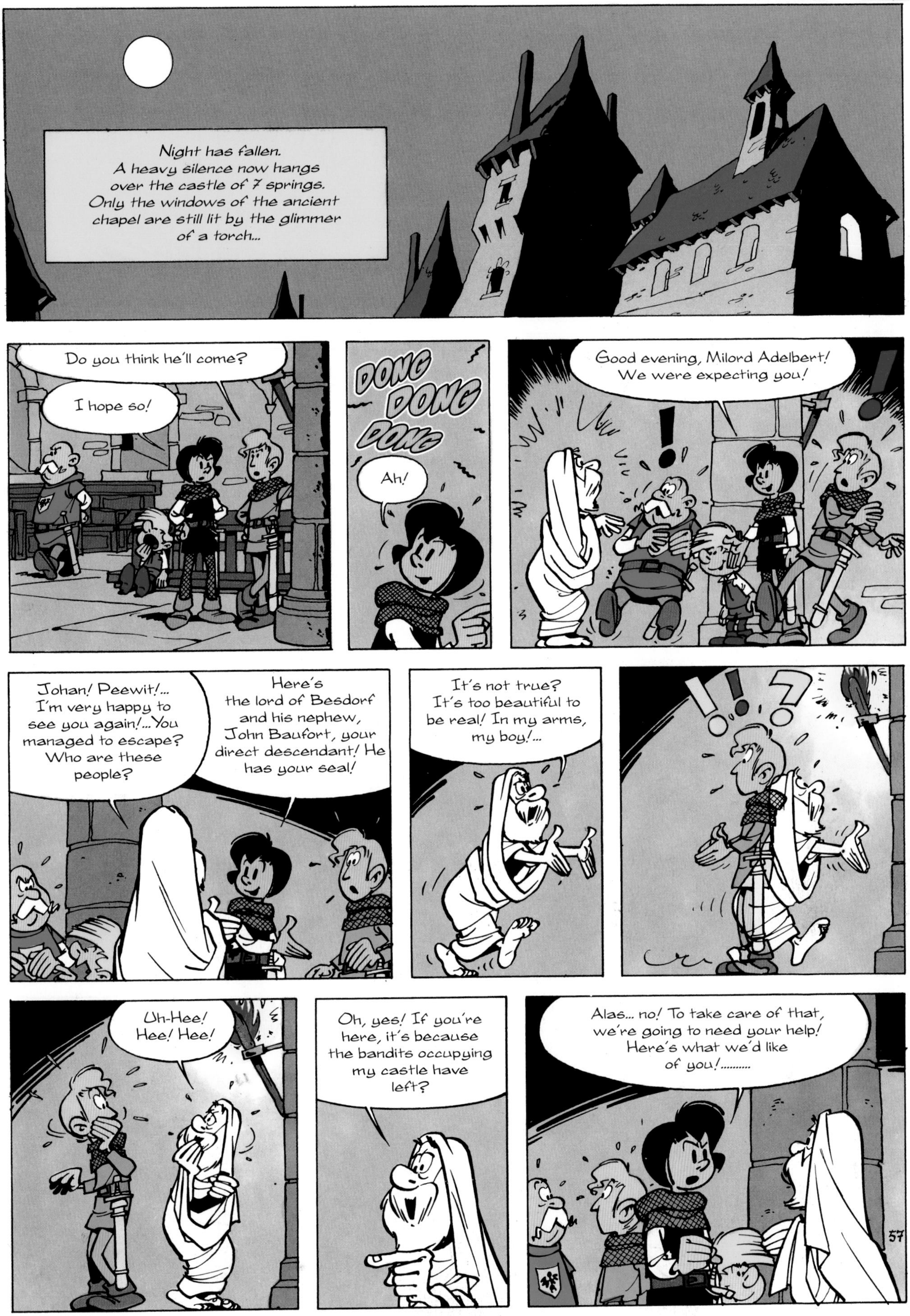
Night has fallen. A heavy silence now hangs over the castle of 7 springs. Only the windows of the ancient chapel are still lit by the glimmer of a torch...
Do you think he'll come?
I hope so!
DONG DONG DONG
Ah!
Good evening, Milord Adelbert! We were expecting you!
Johan! Peewit!... I'm very happy to see you again!...You managed to escape? Who are these people?
Here's the lord of Besdorf and his nephew, John Baufort, your direct descendant! He has your seal!
It's not true? It's too beautiful to be real! In my arms, my boy!...
Uh-Hee! Hee! Hee!
Oh, yes! If you're here, it's because the bandits occupying my castle have left?
Alas... no! To take care of that, we're going to need your help! Here's what we'd like of you!..........
57

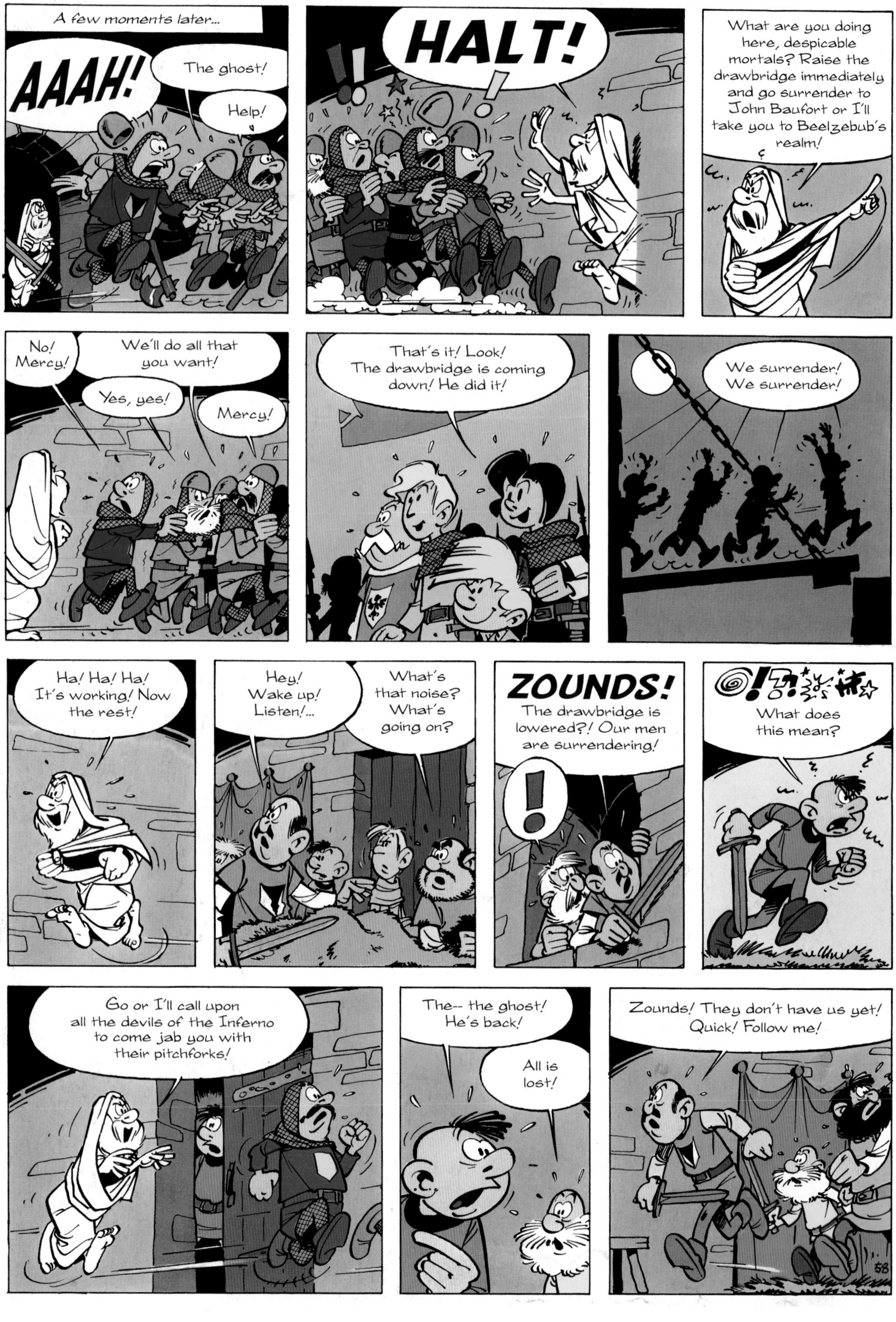
A few moments later...
AAAH!
The ghost!
Help!
HALT!
What are you doing here, despicable mortals? Raise the drawbridge immediately and go surrender to John Baufort or I'll take you to Beelzebub's realm!
No! Mercy!
We'll do all that you want!
Yes, yes!
Mercy!
That's it! Look! The drawbridge is coming down! He did it!
We surrender! We surrender!
Ha! Ha! Ha! It's working! Now the rest!
Hey! Wake up! Listen!...
What's that noise? What's going on?
ZOUNDS!
The drawbridge is lowered?! Our men are surrendering!
What does this mean?
Go or I'll call upon all the devils of the Inferno to come jab you with their pitchforks!
The-- the ghost! He's back!
All is lost!
Zounds! They don't have us yet! Quick! Follow me!
58

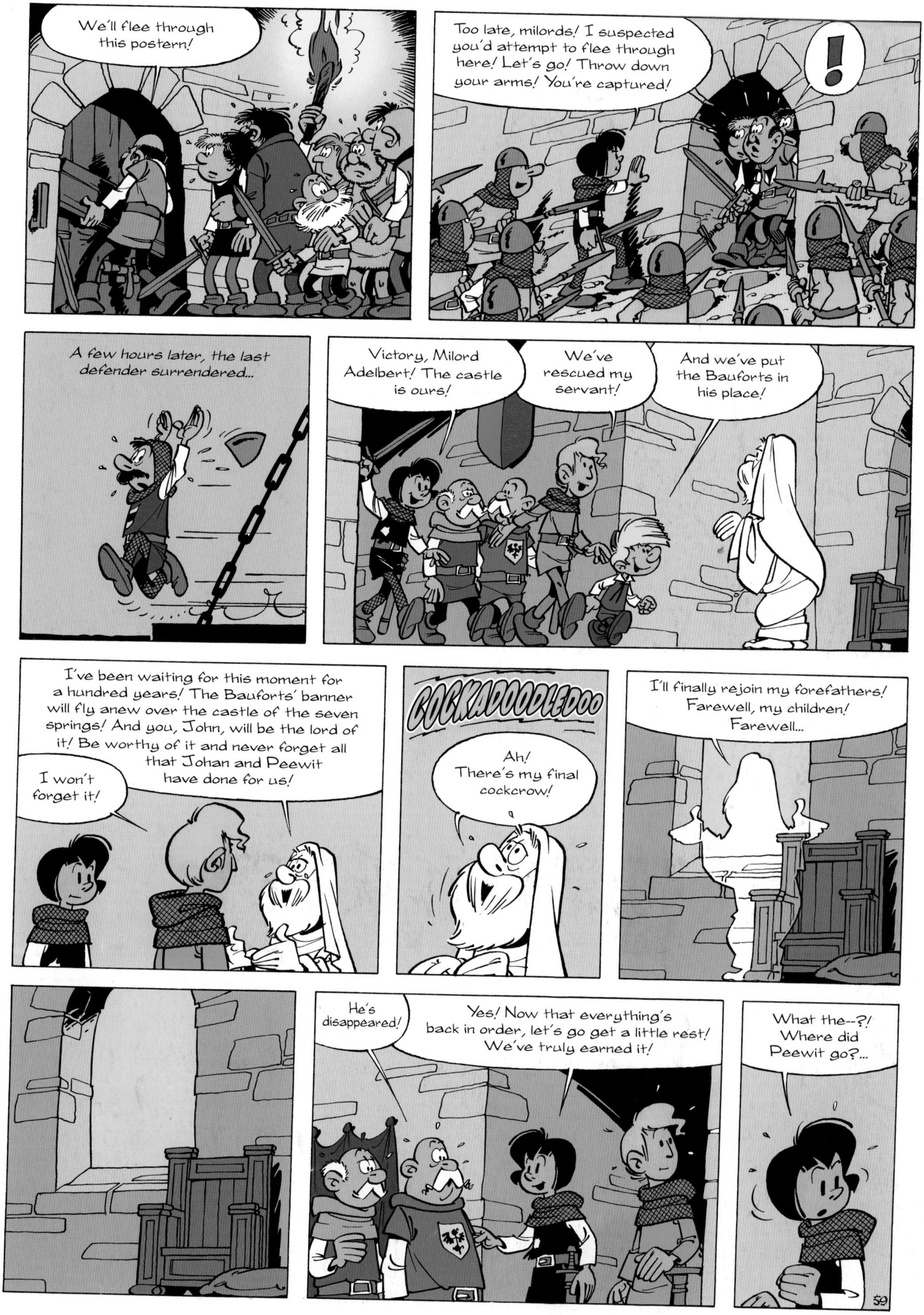
We'll flee through this postern!
Too late, milords! I suspected you'd attempt to flee through here! Let's go! Throw down your arms! You're captured!
!
A few hours later, the last defender surrendered...
Victory, Milord Adelbert! The castle is ours!
We've rescued my servant!
And we've put the Bauforts in his place!
I've been waiting for this moment for a hundred years! The Bauforts' banner will fly anew over the castle of the seven springs! And you, John, will be the lord of it! Be worthy of it and never forget all that Johan and Peewit have done for us!
I won't forget it!
COCKADOODLEDOO
Ah! There's my final cockcrow!
I'll finally rejoin my forefathers! Farewell, my children! Farewell...
He's disappeared!
Yes! Now that everything's back in order, let's go get a little rest! We've truly earned it!
What the--?! Where did Peewit go?...
59

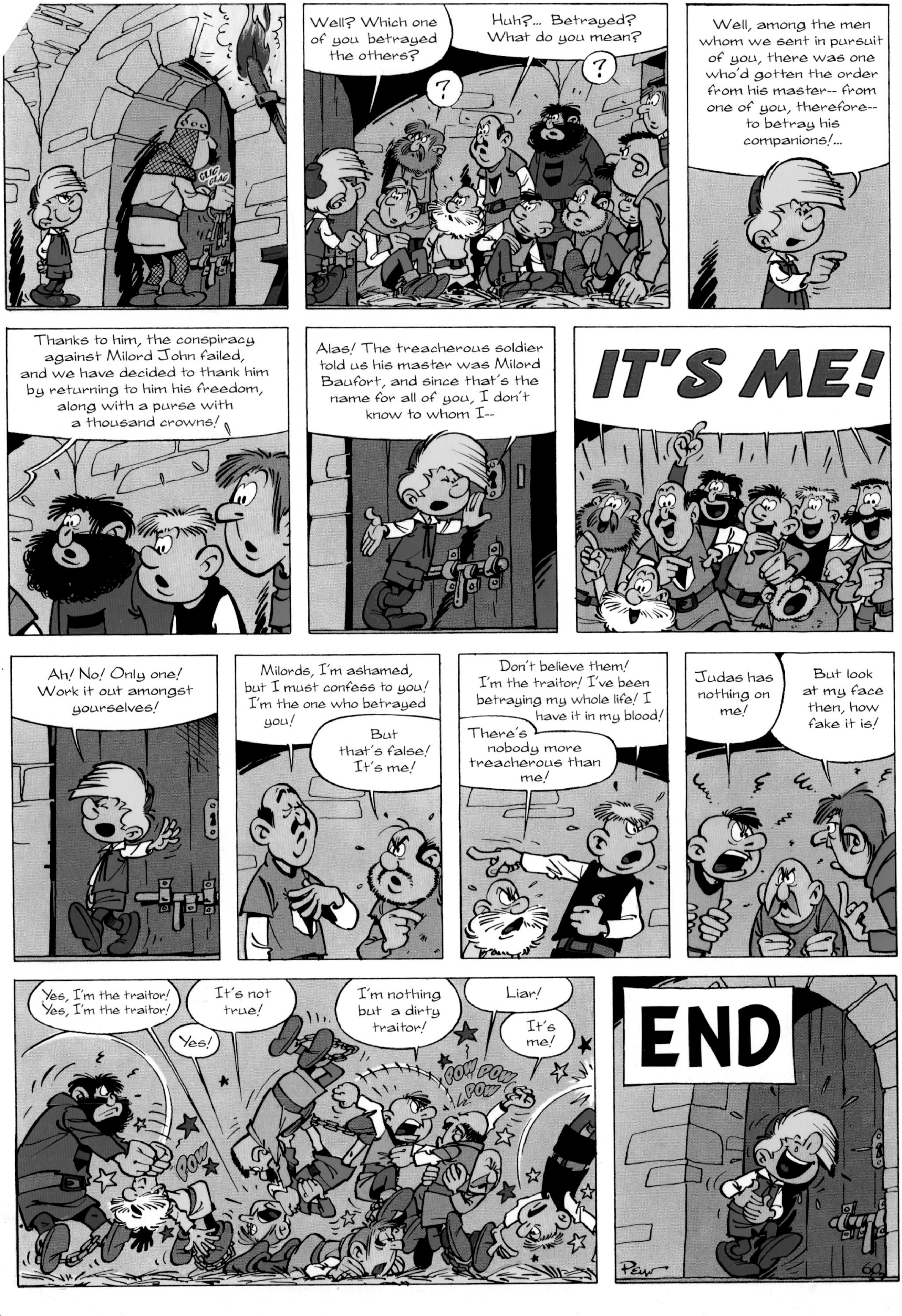
CLIC CLAC
Well? Which one of you betrayed the others?
Huh?... Betrayed? What do you mean?
?
?
Well, among the men whom we sent in pursuit of you, there was one who'd gotten the order from his master-- from one of you, therefore-- to betray his companions!...
Thanks to him, the conspiracy against Milord John failed, and we have decided to thank him by returning to him his freedom, along with a purse with a thousand crowns!
Alas! The treacherous soldier told us his master was Milord Baufort, and since that's the name for all of you, I don't know to whom I--
IT'S ME!
Ah! No! Only one! Work it out amongst yourselves!
Milords, I'm ashamed, but I must confess to you! I'm the one who betrayed you!
But that's false! It's me!
Don't believe them! I'm the traitor! I've been betraying my whole life! I have it in my blood!
There's nobody more treacherous than me!
Judas has nothing on me!
But look at my face then, how fake it is!
Yes, I'm the traitor! Yes, I'm the traitor!
It's not true!
Yes!
I'm nothing but a dirty traitor!
Liar!
It's me!
POW POW POW
POW
END
PEYO